AFTERBURN

A NOVEL

MICHAEL BODHI GREEN

Copyright © 2025 by Michael Bodhi Green

All rights reserved. No portion of this book may be reproduced, copied, distributed or adapted in any way, with the exception of certain activities permitted by applicable copyright laws, such as brief quotations in the context of a review or academic work. For permission to publish, distribute or otherwise reproduce this work, please contact the author at professormichaelgreen@gmail.com.

Cover and book design by Christian Storm.

For Allyson
who always believed in me,
and who will always
be remembered and missed.

"Consider Icarus, pasting those sticky wings on, testing that strange little tug at his shoulder blade, and think of that first flawless moment over the lawn of the labyrinth. Think of the difference it made!"

—ANNE SEXTON, "TO A FRIEND WHOSE WORK HAS COME TO TRIUMPH"

"Men go crazy in congregations / They only get better one by one."

—STING, "ALL THIS TIME"

PREFACE

AND THOUGHTS ON SELF-PUBLISHING

I WROTE, REVISED (and revised and revised), and attempted to "legitimately" publish this novel during 2018 - 2024, the most difficult period of my life. During that time I lost my truest love and the home we built together, my father, my beloved Australian Shepherd, my career and retirement, my pride and — throughout the longest and hardest of the nights — a not insignificant portion of my sanity.

The pandemic played a role, as I struggled to find work and well-being in Los Angeles, one of the most-locked down places in the country. But the more urgent issue was that I had not sufficiently healed the wounds of my past. Doing so might have stopped me from sabotaging myself anytime I got close to the kind of success I've always dreamed of.

Not that I wasn't trying to achieve that success. After teaching full time at a university for a decade, I moved to LA to be with the aforementioned love of my life and pursue our shared ambitions to get into the entertainment industry. Like a lot of teachers, I had never planned to teach. I earned my MFA in Creative Writing, had some background in journalism, and planned to make my living as a professional writer. But teaching had other plans for me and that decade went by in a blink. Ironically, leaving to write this novel helped me realize that teaching had become a vital part of my identity. Indeed, the hero of this story is a teacher.

Another vital part of my identity is "writer" and hopefully even "novelist," though I'm not sure, even as I write this introduction to my novel, if I can claim it. My first novel was my unpublished MFA thesis. Surely that doesn't count, right? Can I count this one if it doesn't have the legitimization of a traditional publisher? I pitched the manuscript to many agents and got no bites, after which I hired an editor to help me with the query letter, synopsis and opening pages, then sent the revised materials to many more agents. Only about half of all the agents I queried even bothered to send me a rejection letter. After a while, I stopped keeping track.

Legacy publishing and book selling are tough gigs, even tougher in these digital times. Only a few genres sell well and Romantasy has been queen for a while now. This novel is sci-fi, action, adventure, war, family drama, prison drama, coming of age. It doesn't really fit into a prescribed genre, or even a typical mashup of genres.

Failing to nail down a marketable genre, I tried to pitch the story — about a future American society splintering around issues of racial identity — as contemporary and relevant in these fraught times. After all, good science fiction is allegory. In the end, I'm not shocked that nobody thought they could sell a politically charged, tough-to-classify book that might alienate great swaths of its potential readership.

Of course, its possible the agents just didn't think the story was compelling or the writing good enough, which is hard to face. We crave legitimization because legitimization tells us we belong to the good-enough club. Self-publishing is like bellowing into the void or casting a line into the murky depths. You have no idea what, if anything, will come back to you. It's a leap of faith.

Another reason I've decided to self-publish—and to spend several thousand dollars on art and layout and editing and proofreading—is because our work, especially in the Humanities, is increasingly no longer our own. AI is vacuuming up content, copyrighted or not, and using it as grist for its virtual mill. I'm worried that six months from now I'll discover some AI-generated version of my unpublished manuscript floating through the cyber-ether.

Anyway, it's time to move on, time to put this difficult chapter behind me (pun intended) and write the next book, whatever it will be. I'm disappointed to not have a traditional publisher, but I'm pleased with the work. I told a story I wanted to tell.

Like the hero of this story, I'm not always convinced of my worth, not always good at giving myself credit. But I give myself credit for never giving up on this novel, even through those years of agony. I started it. I finished it. Here it is.

MICHAEL BODHI GREEN

AUGUST 2025

AFTERBURN:

A psychological term coined by Eric Berne, who defined it as "the period of time before a past event is assimilated."

The cool-looking shit that trails a thrusting rocket engine.

PART I

PROLOGUE

OCTOBER 2070

ALTON WEPT AS he dragged his punctured leg, throbbing under the weight of the enormous railgun, through the freezing mud outside the internment camp.

It had been a long time since he had cried—not since he had cried himself to sleep that first night, when he lay in his narrow prison bed fearing that his life was over.

After a few months, he had grown numb to it all, even coming to believe that he deserved his fate. But now the desire to live and the desire to be free—jolted awake by the rage of the waterboarding—had reanimated other emotions as well.

He knew now what he had to do, even if it meant he would hurt a lot more before it was over.

Behind him, flashes lit up the sky, and men screamed and shouted as the battle rolled through the camp. He felt confident that darkness, distance, and rain kept him beyond the scopes of the drones.

But the "Slim Reapers," as they were called, would come after him soon enough, and he had seen what they could do. He set his teeth against the pain and forced himself to pick up the pace.

He reached his boulder within a minute and dropped the railgun into the muck, patting the big rock like an old dog while he caught his breath. As he uncoiled the rope and tied on the grappling hook, he thought of the friends he was leaving behind and felt the urge to turn back.

But that would be pointless. He couldn't help them now—especially not Simon—so he searched for a place to attach the hook, futilely wiping the rain from his face shield as he did. He didn't want to use more light, but he couldn't see, and so he tapped it one lumen brighter, which helped nothing. He knew he was taking a big chance, but he held his breath and tapped it once more.

When he felt satisfied no drone had detected him, he secured the hook quickly in the improved visibility, then tugged the rope as hard as he could. Satisfied, he slipped the rope around his waist and tiptoed as close to the cliff's edge as he dared in the dark. Then he set the beam to max and shined it into the abyss.

Even through the deluge, he could see the canyon floor, hundreds of feet below. Would the dropship be waiting out there as promised? Even if it was, he had foolishly thrown the beacon to signal the ship over the cliff several days earlier. It would certainly be smashed to bits.

But that worry could wait. As he turned to make his final rope adjustments, he realized that he had forgotten to lower the lamp setting and a Reaper was up and over the camp's east wall immediately.

It sped silently toward him, its roving blue eye fixed in the direction of the beam. He killed the light, grabbed the railgun, and fired just as it bore down on him. The immense recoil knocked him onto his ass, but the drone angled up and away, narrowly avoiding the blast.

He crawled behind the boulder as it turned to make another pass, this time jamming the butt of the railgun against the rock before he fired. He missed again but at least the rock absorbed the massive kick. As the Reaper zipped past, it fired a slender blue bolt that scorched the nearby earth.

You missed, bastard, he thought, and fired again while it was still in an evasive maneuver.

Direct hit. The eye flashed orange-blue as the body whirled down like a skewered raven and rammed into the earth, splattering him with mud from twenty yards away.

He sprang up and almost whooped in triumph before remembering himself. More drones would follow, and it was now or never. He tightened the rope around his waist, slid the railgun under his arm, then seized the rope and yanked to make sure it was secure.

But to his shock, there was no tension at all, and he went fumbling backward, dropping the gun and just grabbing the cliff's edge before toppling over. His legs dangled in space as he scrambled to hoist himself back up.

The muddy cliff disintegrated as his frantic clawing sent rocks and roots flying over the ledge. Just as he was about to go over, his left hand grasped onto a rock lodged firmly enough into the earth to stop his fall.

Even in the icy rain, he could feel the warm blood coursing from his gashed palm as he squeezed the jagged stone with what remained of his fading strength.

His only chance was to grab the heavy gun and use its weight to pull himself up, but it lay just out of reach. He flung his free arm up and grasped for it, straining his fingers until he felt the tendons would snap and his arm would tear from its socket.

Again and again, he flung his right arm toward the gun, howling with each attempt. He finally got a fingerhold just as the stone in his left hand wiggled free from the earth. Hauling himself against the gun's weight gave him the extra few inches he needed to heave himself onto flat ground. Unfortunately, the gun went flying into the chasm with the force of his pull.

He rolled onto his mangled thigh and pounded his fists in the mud. When the pain stopped blinding him, what he saw almost made him laugh. The energy bolt hadn't missed at all. The drone, recognizing his intentions, had scissored his rope. He was left with a hook tied to maybe eight feet of it.

For the first time, he considered giving up, slinking back to the camp and begging for mercy. But then he remembered the men who had leaped onto the drone from the barracks roof during the initial attack, wrestling it to the ground. And that gave him a very stupid and desperate idea.

He struggled to his feet, pain hammering his leg, and shined his light toward the camp at top setting. "Come on, motherfucker," he snarled. His teeth chattered even beneath his face shield. He had never felt so cold in his life.

Finally, another Reaper elevated above the camp walls and approached with lethal swiftness. Was it a malevolent intelligence? They still maintained that AI could never be sentient, but thinking of it as an enemy psyched him up for what he was about to do.

At fifty feet, it opened up on him, and he dove behind the rock, the bolts turning the clay sludge behind him to steam. The drone whirled about, its black face scowling down, the neon blue eye smoldering through the downpour. Alton scrambled to the opposite side of the rock.

As the drone began to descend, he doubled-knotted the shorn rope through his belt loops, then crouched, squeezing the base of the hook until his good hand turned white.

When it was close enough that he could see into the shallow depths of its artificial soul, he leapt out from behind the rock and snared the hook onto the face, then wheeled around so that he was opposite the eye.

The drone rocketed straight up, jerking him into the air, legs flailing wildly. His good knee smashed into the rock, and he almost let go, but rage gave him the strength to hold on. He hoisted one fist on top of the other—the rope tearing so deep into the wound in his left hand he thought it would scrape bone—until he had tugged his foe down enough so that toes touched the ground.

Then he ran straight off the cliff.

They hung for a moment, and he felt exhilarated by the weightlessness—the sensation pleasurably reminding him of floating high above Earth with Bernardo all those years before—until the bastard drone sprayed burning aspirates straight through his nostalgia.

They coated the mask, blinding him, a few drops penetrating and searing his throat and lungs, spreading white pain far worse than any ghost pepper he had ever eaten on a dare. But still he hung on through his hacking and coughing while the drone wriggled and jerked under his weight, his fear of falling more compelling than any pain.

He had no plan for when they landed. Maybe the railgun would be intact and within reach? He kept hoisting one hand over the other, one hand over the other, tugging them down, closer and closer, until he noticed a fuzzy light blinking through his smeared visor.

Another drone? No, it was surging toward them from far out in the canyon.

But there was no mistaking the eye of the second Reaper now streaking down the canyon wall. *Just need a few more seconds,* he thought, as the blue flash enveloped him and his body went numb. He lost feeling in his fingers, and the rope slipped away.

He must have passed out because hitting the ground awakened him with a jolt that he could feel in his teeth. His stun-numbed body didn't register pain, so it wasn't until he tried to move that he recognized something was wrong.

A splintered tree branch had pierced him just above the knee, protruding at a strange angle. The branch was clean and shone white where the rain washed away the blood. He gaped at it until his groggy mind realized he wasn't looking at a branch, but a bone.

There was nothing to do but lie back and welcome unconsciousness.

But the light that flooded the area was not cobalt, but white and blinding, and he had the impression of the drones settling to the ground like tamed animals. Then he was floating inside the light, a comforting and gentle levitation, and settling into a pearl and silver bay. A hatch sealed behind him. There was a soft hum, and the last thing he saw was the canyon floor gliding by, silent and dark...

CHAPTER 1

ALTON STEPPED TO the front, clutching the two disintegrating paperbacks, and the class fell silent, leaving only the sound of the unrelenting wind battering the school's molded polymer shell. As it always did, his pulse quickened the moment before beginning a lesson. Part of it was performance anxiety, but part of it was excitement. Even in this hellhole, he still loved to teach.

"Even though they are set in the future, these two novels are pretty old," he said. "With some outdated ideas about space travel. Not to mention society. So, why are we reading them now?"

The mostly young men stared at their tablet screens, pretending to study the text—all but his fellow "Civvie" Simon, who gave Alton a patient smile from in between his graying mutton chops. It was not unusual for a full minute to pass before one of the *Nibelungs* mustered the courage to volunteer a thought—and even then, they usually needed to be prodded.

Having been recruited as teens or even small children to fight for Hagen, the "Neebs" had little formal education. They might roam around camp with their chests puffed out, but they shrank considerably in the classroom.

Alton said, "Think about recent events."

Finally, Lars, a hulking Neeb, tentatively raised his ham hock of a hand and grunted, "The launch?"

"Yes! The US sends its first colony to Mars in, what . . . three weeks now?" He pretended that he didn't know the exact day, the exact *minute*, of the launch. But of course, he had always dreamed of interplanetary travel, of being part of such an expedition.

"Years late, some would say," Simon lamented. "The United States was first to the moon, after all." The Neebs nodded with enthusiasm. American exceptionalism was something they could get behind.

"But why have I asked you to read these *particular* novels instead of something that reflects a more realistic depiction of what interplanetary travel is like now?" Alton asked. "Think beyond technology to the ideas about society and scientific progress. Like we did with *Frankenstein*."

As always, Alton couldn't help but stare at their crudely de-augmented faces. When they were but fresh-faced recruits—some still children—Hagen insisted his people implant biosynthetic nanochips that equipped them with VR/AR, AI, GPS, comms, weapons control, multi-spectrum vision, and who knew what the hell else. Their augmentation allowed Hagen to track and control them, and—Alton supposed—to destroy them if necessary.

Careful extraction of the chips might have left little evidence of their existence. But the med-techs at Gypsum couldn't thin-slice roast beef at a deli counter, let alone perform the meticulous procedure required to remove them without tearing.

Alton also suspected that permanent disfigurement was the Neebs's punishment for insurrection. Even if the camps closed and society reconciled—as fanciful a notion as Alton moving to Mars—the rebels would toil in the subbasement of the new caste system for the rest of their lives.

Their faces now featured rough scars running down their cheeks like permanent tear tracks. Some bore thicker scars on the undersides of their limbs as well, where electric veins had been carved out. EVs were created from biomaterial that melded with bone, muscle, and tendon to forge arms and legs as strong as titanium—Alton had heard their removal was particularly agonizing.

When no one seemed likely to follow Lars's brave example, Simon came to his usual rescue. "It's about getting into the mindset of the writers," he said, turning to face the class like the co-teacher he basically was. "Seeing how they saw. Then, identifying problematic thinking on their parts."

"What do you mean by 'problematic thinking'?" Alton asked.

"Bradbury was very imaginative," said Simon, brushing away his overgrown forelock. "But when it came to how a Martian civilization might behave, he couldn't escape his 1950s values."

"Right! As we've discussed, novels are more than just stories. They're also windows into the thinking of another time."

As he spoke, Alton gestured to a library of maybe five hundred ratty paperbacks at the rear of their structure. To have them on hand thrilled him. New copies of physical books had been rare even when he was a kid—saving every tree possible had become a mandate, especially in the age of digital ubiquity when even the poorest could access free material.

But as a teen, he would snatch up tattered volumes down at the North Hollywood Stalls, initially for his own collection, then later, carefully considering what Kiara might like to read as well.

"Reading them now allows us to see how we've changed," Simon finished.

"Or how we *haven't*," huffed Oliver, another Civvie, through ruddy, middle-aged cheeks.

Damien, a gnarled and intense Nibelung in his early twenties, stabbed a double-jointed finger in the air and said, "My grandda' told me the 1950s was the last great time for this country. The last time 'eybody knew their place."

The Neebs murmured their agreement, while Oliver rolled his eyes as though to say that his point had been made. Alton spent a few minutes explaining how social resistance actually did exist back then but was largely repressed.

As he spoke, he found himself glancing at the tall and bony man sitting in the back. His name was Crow, and he was older than most of the Nibelungs in camp, maybe in his mid-thirties, though his sallow cheeks, hooded eyes, and chafed face made it hard to tell.

The rumor was that he had been one of Hagen's top digital infiltrators on the outside, so he was probably a more advanced thinker than his classmates. But he wasn't there for the intellectual engagement. He was there to spy for Lance, Hagen's lieutenant, who ran the Nibelungs in Gypsum.

Watching him take notes, Alton nervously wondered what he found subversive enough from today's lecture to report back. Alton constantly worried that Lance would forbid the Neebs to return, and without them, there weren't enough pupils to fill a class.

He shook it off. "So, this was Bradbury's idea of Mars 120 years ago. How might we imagine an alien society today?"

"Chinese are Martians now," said Zane.

Alton forced himself to not wince whenever he looked at Zane's savage facial scars.

"What do you mean *now*?" Lars said, pulling his eyes into a squint with his beefy fingers and sticking his front teeth out.

Alton waited while the class guffawed. If he tried to police every racist comment, they'd never get through a session.

"And we'll be fightin' 'em when we get up there," said Lars. More murmurs of agreement.

"Nobody's sending the dregs of humanity to the frontier of human discovery," Oliver said, shifting his bulk toward them. How he stayed overweight with the food they were given remained a mystery to Alton.

"Then we get our own ship, our own colony," Damien said. "The Leader will make this happen. Then we start over, keep things pure this time."

Oliver laughed. "Sure, kid."

"I'm not a kid," Damien growled.

Alton interjected quickly. "You don't see a scenario where you could live alongside the Chinese? They've been colonizing and terraforming Mars for five years now. Perhaps we should tread lightly on territory they've already established? Why should we automatically be entitled to it?"

Zane jumped in again. "Hell no. They'll zap us. Or try to chain us. You know how they do. Best zap them first."

"Historically, it's impossible for one group to maintain indefinite control over another," Simon said. "You're better off trying to live in harmony. We may as well if we're starting over anyway."

"Others failed because they weren't as strong as Nibelungs," Lars boomed, and a buzz swelled through the room like the birth of a tsunami.

Oliver's voice went an octave higher in disbelief. "The Nazis weren't committed? The Soviets? Al Qaeda? The North Koreans? Liang? They all went into the ash bin of history. And Hagen will join them . . . if he hasn't already."

The room went deadly quiet, and Alton shot Oliver a *watch-it* look.

"He's not in the *assben*," Damien growled. "He'll liberate us soon."

"How long have you been waiting?" Oliver asked. "Two years?"

"He's been preparing for the final battle," Zane said. "And he'll have lost all tolerance for nonbelievers like you."

"All right," Alton said, trying not to sound firm and failing. "Let's get back on track."

"They come to this class every week," Oliver said. "Maybe they should make an effort to actually learn something."

"You're the one that needs a lesson," Damien said, leaning forward.

Alton looked to Crow for help. He thought Lance's lieutenant might intervene if push literally came to shove. But his expression remained unreadable.

"Enough," said Alton. "Or I'm ending class for the night. And canceling next week's too." He was about to move on, then added, "Everybody learns in their own way, in their own time. Let's all respect the process."

But he wondered if these Nibelungs ever would learn. If they *could* learn given their programming. He felt a twinge of shame. He knew a good teacher should never believe a student was beyond reaching.

They relaxed a little, as much of an admission as he would ever get that they enjoyed being here. There was little else in camp to keep them engaged.

As they switched texts on their pads, Alton was grateful that Simon didn't wait to chime in. "Seems like Verne had a little figured out ahead of his time. With rocket technology. We're still using rockets more than two hundred years later, although of course they've changed a lot."

"He was famous for that," said Alton. "He had lots of ideas about technology that later came true: giant balloons, submarines, inner-planetary expeditions." Alton listed some of the novels.

"What about *War of the Worlds*?" said Zane.

"That was H. G. Wells."

"What's that about?" said someone in the back.

"It's about destroying an alien race that tries to conquer us," Damien said, grinning. "We should read *that* next!"

"You can read that on your own," Alton said. "Next week's book *is* about war, though. I hope you see how the author criticizes the arrogance of men who try to impose their way of life on others." He paused, then added, "Of course I would never tell you what you should take from your reading."

There was a strange nasally sound, and Alton was surprised to see that Crow had laughed. Although he rarely reacted to anything, Lance's man couldn't help but find this funny. Alton wondered if he should be relieved or more worried than ever.

CHAPTER 2

AFTER CLASS, ALTON huddled with Simon and Oliver in the protective alcove molded over the Ed-Shell's entrance. They waited as the other students strapped on their masks and disappeared into the grinding dust. Some nodded to Alton as they passed, while Damien lifted his mask and tried to spit on the ground near Oliver's feet. Oliver laughed when the rough wind carried the spit back into Damien's face.

"You had better be careful," Simon said once they had gone.

"He's not going to do anything," Oliver said. "Not unless my skin changes color. Otherwise, my big mouth would've been shanked in the shower ages ago." He grinned.

Whites stood with whites, whether they were down for the cause or not. That had been the rule as long Alton could remember. Even as a teen in North Hollywood, he remembered the white priders insisting that their numbers were too small and had to be preserved, especially against the flood of "racial contamination," as they put it.

They could sort out the nonbelievers once ultimate victory had been achieved, designate them for a lower status then.

"Maybe," Simon said, frowning. "But something feels different lately." He reached into his jacket for an e-pen filled with a solution of synthetic nicotine and mild THC—a perk from the camp administration in exchange for providing medical treatment to the prisoners in the Med-Shell. He took a few puffs and handed it to Alton.

Alton took a drag and passed it to Oliver. "How so?"

Simon shrugged. "Things have just been too quiet for too long. You said it in class, Oliver. It's been two years since Hagen disappeared. The threat appears quelled, at least for now, and a democracy can only tolerate internment on its own shores for so long. Of course, we'd never get news of it here, but there's got to be a movement against the camps. Pressure against Guerrero. Especially with a presidential election next year. I think there's reason to be hopeful."

"And if there is no movement?" Oliver asked. "And we're here indefinitely?"

"The tension has to be released somehow. I suggest not giving these hotheads an excuse."

Simon and Oliver returned to the barracks, and Alton slipped back inside the school. Six months earlier, he had hauled a bookshelf forward to retrieve a fallen volume and noticed that a small hole just big enough for a man to crawl through had been cut into the shell. Someone had covered it with a panel, then dragged the shelves in front of the panel to hold it in place.

Alton was stunned to discover that the opening led to a second ragged gap cut into the eastern fence and straight outside of camp. Because the structure edged up against the fence, the gap was invisible except from inside. Alton had guessed someone hoped to escape that way.

Still, he liked to get out of camp, treat himself to an occasional measure of freedom and solitude away from the other men. He pulled the shelf back now and slipped out into the wind, huddling into his thin jacket as he crunched over the mounds of Gypsum that led away from the fence.

The camp was supposedly named for the abundant mineral, although Simon—seemingly possessed of boundless general knowledge—had proposed that some ironic fucker had christened it *Gypsum* to allude to Topaz, as in the Topaz War Relocation Center, where Franklin Roosevelt had detained Japanese Americans not too far from their general location.

Alton advanced slowly in the dark, being careful not to take a wrong step. Because the horizons were so uniform in all directions, it was impossible to tell from inside the camp that it had been built on a high plateau. Until he was near the edge the first time, Alton hadn't discovered that a cliff stretched for miles in either direction, dropping straight down over a jagged face to a valley hundreds of feet below.

It had taken his breath away. Whoever had taken the risk to carve that hatch must have been very disappointed to discover that he wouldn't find his freedom this way. Unless, of course, he had just jumped.

When he was near the edge, he settled onto his usual seat—a flat-topped boulder about waist high—and gazed out onto the darkness. Its inky depths terminated in the spires of distant mountains that stabbed upward into a violet firmament finely speckled with light. From behind them, the celestial highway of the Milky Way ribboned upward in a blazing arc.

Having grown up in the light sewer of Los Angeles, he occasionally wondered if the civil war, his arrest, torture, internment, crippling depression, PTSD, and abject loneliness, was all worth it for this astonishment, even if it couldn't rival his own eleven minutes up there, that momentous day he had burst the seams of his old reality.

He thought of it every time he sat here, remembering the surge in his loins as the rocket erupted, the effervescence not just of body, but of spirit, when they reached space. Floating weightless through the capsule, trying to high-five his friend Bernardo, the two of them cracking up as they kept missing each other's hands.

He had never stopped dreaming about another flight, one that wouldn't hurtle him back to Earth this time, dump him back on the disappointing ground. And he had promised himself, God, the cosmos—whoever might exist or be listening—that if the opportunity came to escape for good, he would do whatever it took to seize it.

Most of the men were in the dayroom when he returned, zoned out as usual in the cracked vinyl sofas around the 3Dia, their shaved heads and pasty faces in rows like posed mannequins. Alton came in, shaking off the cold, and walked by his students, who ignored him. They might pay him heed in the classroom, but elsewhere in camp, he was just one more Civvie.

Alton paused to see what was playing. The feed projected five 3D shows simultaneously in a digital hexagon without bleed-through. The interns wore foam earbits tuned to the show they wanted.

He saw *Third Rock Band from the Sun*, about an AsiaPop band searching the galaxy for a long-lost member while winning over alien populations with their killer sets; *Warming Warning*, a popular reality series about a grizzled tracker who located missing persons in climate-ravaged areas; and a special about the upcoming Mars Colony Mission that had been on repeat for weeks.

As he did whenever it was on, Alton paused to marvel at the rocket ship on its pad, floodlights illuminating its gleaming contours against the night. This would be the final mission departure. Unmanned ships had been dropping materials and supplies for the last year and a half, while bots built the infrastructure. All the crew had to do now was show up—and survive, of course.

Even when Alton had been a teenager, the prevailing thought had been that Europa, or perhaps even Titan, would be better suited for long-term human settlements. But the big AI brains were still working out the logistics for getting humans to those places and keeping them there long term. Or, perhaps, the AI were planning on getting themselves there and leaving humans behind, Alton thought.

He watched until the image changed to the familiar publicity shot of the command crew in their dark navy patch-adorned Cosmost jackets—an Indian American, a Filipino American, an African American, a Mexican American, an Iraqi American, a Native American of the Lakota tribe, and an Anglo American of Dutch descent.

Alton knew their backgrounds because Cosmost and the United States government, who were partnering on the mission, had heavily emphasized the crew's multicultural makeup. The other twenty-three members of the colony were of similarly varied heritage.

As always, Alton's eyes went not to their faces but to their beautiful jackets and the effortless cool they bestowed. He had briefly owned one when he was a kid, and for a few heady hours, it had been his most treasured possession.

Whenever he admired them now, a dull pain spread underneath his rib cage. It was hard to look at them and think that under different circumstances, he could have been one of the crew. He doubted anyone could have wanted it more than he had.

The dorm lights flashed on and off, and the images sizzled and died as Central Command powered down the feed to the usual grumbling and boos. Lights out in fifteen.

Alton went through the dayroom into the sleeping area, where rows of single beds were interspersed between metal lockers. Between the dayroom and the bunk room, two guards kept watch overnight on a platform cage. Violence between the interns was unlikely, but if a melee did kick off, the guards could lock themselves in and send for backup from Central Command.

Alton glanced at Simon as he passed his bed, but the older man was writing with pen and pad and didn't look up. Oliver was in the bed next to him, a pillowcase wrapped around his eyes, trying to push another day from his consciousness.

He stuffed his jacket and boots inside his locker and grabbed his toothbrush, letting his glance linger on the fading pic taped inside the door. Kiara stared out at him with her insouciant smile, her brunette hair streaming over his shoulders, the ends glowing with the neon tips that had been in fashion a few years back. He didn't feel much these days, but looking at her at least made him *remember* feeling.

After brushing his teeth, he got into bed and pulled the blanket up to his neck while his barrack mates settled in around him. He was in possession of a tattered copy of Graham Greene's *The Quiet American*, next week's novel, but just as he turned to its opening pages, the lights snapped off. He fell asleep quickly and dreamed of silver-jacketed astronauts bounding through red dust.

CHAPTER 3

THE NEXT DAY after breakfast, Alton loaded books from the school shelves onto a wobbly cart. One day a week, he ferried them around camp, checking them in and out for the men, ensuring the precious volumes didn't disappear into the dust under some bunk or get used for kindling on an especially frigid day.

No chance of that at the moment. Not only was it warm for late October in the high country—with the clear, bright morning affording stunning views of the Rockies—but the ceaseless wind had given them a rare reprieve.

Tensions could simmer when they were forced inside for long stretches by the dust or extreme temperatures, but today everybody was outside lifting weights, sunning themselves, or kicking a soccer ball around the dirt.

He wrangled the cart onto a gravel path about 150 yards long that ran through the middle of the camp. At the far end, on the other side of a razor-topped iron enclosure, the Central Compound housed the camp guards and staff. That side also contained admin and storage structures, a weapons depot, and a landing platform, along with the infamous Intake Center, where they had been "interrogated" and de-auged upon arrival.

The prisoner side enclosed ten barracks, a kitchen/chow hall, the Med-Shell, the Ed-Shell, a workout platform cluttered with weights and benches, and a few padlocked storage shells for tools and equipment. Each barrack was shaped like an upside-down Bundt cake mold and housed fifty men, five on each side of the main drag, about ten yards apart.

Guard towers rose into the sky on either end, but they were used only occasionally for fire-spotting. Simon had told him he suspected this wasteland had been chosen for the camp at least partially because there was so little fuel to burn—not that the lack of fuel would stop a full-blown cyclone fire. Once they got going, those vicious bastards could survive for days on dirt and rock alone.

He finished up the book exchange at the first barrack and went out the rear exit toward the adjacent one. Behind it, Lance and a few Neebs were repairing a section of the western fence that had been damaged in a recent storm.

They were struggling to pull a heavy post upright with some rope. Lance's shirtless flesh gleamed in the white sunlight like whittled alabaster. Alton never saw him lifting weights, and yet his body remained permanently sculpted even after the trauma of Intake.

Gypsum was not a work camp, but sometimes work needed to be done, and it was typically given to Lance. Not as punishment per se but to maintain the hierarchy. Commandant Miller knew that every Nibelung in camp would follow Lance's orders without question—to the death if asked—and he took opportunities to remind everyone that he, not Lance, was in charge.

As such, two guards in anti-web vests and armor supervised the operation from folding chairs. Across their laps lay web-guns that could neutralize the crew in an instant.

Lance saw him and let go of the post. Without his superior strength, the others had no hope of keeping it upright. They leapt back, cursing, as it thudded into the dust. Alton pushed the cart faster but not fast enough.

"Hey, Prof!" Lance called.

Alton pretended not to hear.

"Prof!"

Alton sighed and kicked on the wheel brake.

"I heard class yesterday was insurgent!" Lance bellowed as he approached. He wore shorts and shoes only, and Alton eyed the mottled slashes along his calves and forearms where they had torn out the electric veins. Up close, scalp scars showed through his buzz cut.

"You know it," Alton said with a weak smile. "Guerrilla warfare for the mind. Or something."

Lance grinned and slapped him hard on the back. Alton winced.

"Hey!" Lance exclaimed, as though the idea had just occurred to him and not been his plan the moment he had seen Alton walking by. "We could use another man on this."

"I'm kind of busy, Lance."

"Come on, Prof," he scoffed. "A little real work would do you good."

A gaggle of Nibelungs loitered in the immediate vicinity. Lance could have enlisted any of them. But like Miller, Lance had to make a show of strength to remind everybody who ran the men. To keep the peace, Alton had to go along with the charade. He didn't want Lance to get upset and forbid the Neebs to attend his class.

The men had tied a grappling hook to the rope and affixed it to the thick oaken beam, which was about four meters tall. Alton grimaced at how heavy it looked. He had once weighed around 170 pounds with some discernible muscle tone. That was before two years in Gypsum.

Now he could maybe shout in the direction of 140. On bad days, his bones felt like bags of cement. He kept meaning to lift weights, but he just couldn't dredge the energy from beneath his malaise.

"Not too much for you, is it?" Lance asked, with mock concern. He challenged Alton with gleaming black eyes, the ragged gashes underneath, which had healed poorly.

Alton suspected the surgeons had been extra careless with Lance during Intake. The big man had spent a few weeks in his bunk recovering, his face and limbs swaddled in bandages seeping blood and puss. His boys volunteered their personal linens and supplied him with food and water and e-cigs and kept vigil.

Not that there was any need for the men to guard him while he recovered. No prisoner at Gypsum was going to hurt the legend who had fought on the front lines with Hagen. As far as they were concerned, he was right hand to God.

Indeed, the Nibelungs had all but soiled themselves with excitement when Lance had arrived six months earlier. Stories about him charged through the camp. He had been fourteen when he killed his first "cockroach," they said. Walked right up to her on the street and blew her brains out, then sauntered away while her little cockroach baby squalled on the sidewalk.

That level of heartless extermination was a hardcore initiation, and it wasn't long before Hagen had recruited him into the national outfit.

That was the story anyway. But Alton wasn't completely convinced. From what he knew of Hagen, the Nibelung commander ran a tight crew. He didn't seem to be the type to trust important work to a loose cannon psychopath.

When Lance had become aware of Alton's class, he cornered Alton one day and suggested some white-supremacist-themed literature.

Alton had tried to demure tactfully, saying, "It's sort of my job to broaden their horizons."

Lance had seemed amused. "Job? Who gave you that job?"

Of course no one had given it to him. He had just started doing it one day, and no one had yet told him to stop. He guessed Miller felt like it was a good way to keep the Neebs occupied.

"Maybe you want to feel better about yourself?" Lance continued. "Like you're not as bad as Nibelungs."

Alton hadn't known what to say. He hadn't felt quite threatened, but confronted with Lance's physical perfection, he was suddenly self-conscious about his own skinny frame, scraggly dirt-blond hair, and bags like inkblots under his eyes. He certainly didn't feel like he was better than anyone—not even the Nibelungs.

Another time, Lance had asked him what he was doing there.

Alton gave him a quizzical look. "I'm doing time, Lance. Same as you."

"No, I mean, why your soft ass *here*?"

A chill spread through Alton as he realized what Lance was asking. There were lower-security camps, mixed gender camps, camps for families, places better suited for sympathizers and Civvies like him. He was a college professor with no known ties to the movement—about as low risk as anyone.

And yet he was mixed in with the most hardcore of Hagen's men in the most remote and secure of all the camps.

"It's funny," Alton had said. "When they detain you without due process, they don't feel especially obliged to explain why."

Alton knew he didn't buy it, but he wasn't about to reveal that he did actually have a pretty good idea of why they had brought him here. Ironically, if Lance knew the reason, he would probably never harass Alton again.

But harass him he did, and if Alton wanted to maintain any credibility with his students, he couldn't let Lance punk him. So, he found himself lined up with the others behind the fallen pole, Lance in front, the other three behind. He crouched down and grabbed the rope.

"Okay..." Lance said. "Now!"

As they stepped and heaved, the post began to lift. With a half-dozen pulls, they had it upright.

"Hold!" shouted Lance. He let go again, and immediately the post began to waver.

Alton grunted and crouched lower, muscles buckling. He was the only one without gloves, and the rope chafed and seared his hands as it slid through them. Sweat burned his eyes.

Lance, meanwhile, sauntered over to the tool pile. "You got this, Prof!" he cried. The onlookers snickered. Even the guards seemed to be enjoying the show.

Lance was making his way back to them, when he exclaimed, "Damn! Forgot the mallet."

More guffaws from his audience as he searched through the pile with affected deliberation. Alton squeezed his eyes shut and held tight. He wasn't about to give the prick the satisfaction of letting go.

He sucked air, trying to ignore the savage burning of his palms. Then the ground began to shake, and Alton realized that Lance was pounding the spikes around the base of the post. Final stake in hand, he paused and held it up as though inspecting a diamond he had just mined.

The men behind Alton exploded in exasperation, and Lance, chuckling, slammed it into the earth. Everyone let go, and Alton reeled away, gasping. His lungs felt scrubbed by steel wool.

Lance gave Alton another slap on the back, which sent him into a spasm of coughing. "Thanks, Prof," he said. "*They* didn't think you could do it, but I believed in you."

Alton tried to give him a side-eye but just made himself dizzy. Lance chuckled and rubbed his hands together, as though he couldn't believe how well everything had worked out for him. He signaled for a Neeb to bring over some water and handed it to Alton.

Alton managed to stand and sip a little while he recovered. They were facing east toward the snowcapped Wasatch Mountains that loomed over the barren landscape.

"Why they got us fix shit fence anyway?" Lance asked. They were thinking the same thing. Nobody was getting over those mountains on foot.

"Maybe it's psychological," Alton said.

A look came into Lance's eye that chilled Alton. "Doesn't matter," he said. "When Hagen is ready, we'll join him whatever stands in our way. Fences, mountains, or men."

CHAPTER 4

ALTON AWOKE TO an excitement a few mornings later and wandered into the dayroom to discover all five holofeeds tuned to the same news anchor. Lance stood at the front with his hands on his hips. Every Neeb in the camp seemed to be packed in behind him.

Alton saw Oliver lingering in the back. He looked at him groggily for an explanation.

Oliver gave a grim nod toward the feed, where a blonde anchor intoned from a glitzy studio. "Again, we are reporting that Hagen, the terrorist leader whose whereabouts have been unknown for the past several years, has broadcast a message this morning." She paused. "In which he states his intention to continue the armed insurgency that led to his detonation of a dirty bomb in a suburb outside of Washington, DC, more than two years ago.

"The bomb killed scores of people and left many others sick with radiation poisoning, necessitating the temporary relocation of the White House to Los Angeles." She paused. "Hagen has not been seen since its detonation and was presumed by some to have perished in it."

Now, they cut to a shot of Hagen, which elicited a roar from the men that rattled Alton's skull. When the image appeared, he felt cold to his bones. Save for features that had become gaunter and more severe, Hagen looked the same as he remembered: tall, sinewy, sandy-haired, and contemptuous. He was military-auged and sheathed in gray TALOS body armor.

Alton was surprised to see amethyst Electric Veins glowing underneath the suit, surprised because he remembered that they had once been hot pink.

"My dear Nibelungs," Hagen began. Lance gave a signal, and the men sank to their knees and bowed their heads. The men were magnetized toward the object of devotion; Alton was terrified by how palpable the energy felt. Oliver must have been as well because he took a few steps back and eyed the exit.

Hagen continued: "First, let me thank you so much for your sacrifice. You have committed no crime, yet you suffer for resisting Maximillian Guerrero's dictatorship."

Alton swallowed. He felt exposed and vulnerable standing among them. He had a direct eyeline over their bowed heads to the image of their supreme leader, which seemed to skewer Alton with its gaze. He did the math. If this was real—if Hagen was actually alive—he would be thirty-two now, two years older than Alton.

"I know it must have seemed like I abandoned both you and the cause, but nothing could be further from the truth. I have been regrouping, preparing for the final battle, one that will be a historic success in reestablishing the natural hierarchy. Prepare yourselves for glory, and await my signal, which soon will come. This time, we will defeat the Huns. Our greatest moment is upon us!"

The broadcast cut back to the studio, which now had a panel discussion going, while in the dayroom, Lance motioned for the Nibelungs to stand and huddle. They began to chant. Alton couldn't make out the words, but it rose to a peak of fervor, then broke up into a boisterous celebration. Even Crow, who rarely showed emotion, was grinning and bear-hugging.

"I haven't heard him use the term *Huns* before," Oliver said.

Alton shook himself from his stupor. "It's a reference to a German myth," he said. "*The Nibelungenlied*, written around 1200. Hagen was a sixth-century warrior and leader of the Burgundians, who fought the Huns in a last stand. Later, he was celebrated as a German hero during World War II, inspiring the *Wehrmacht* to fight loyally despite overwhelming odds."

"Fits with the Aryan identity," said Oliver. "How do you know so much about it?"

"I . . . took a history course in grad school." But of course, he had known about the myth well before college.

Now, Simon joined them.

"Did you see?" Oliver asked him.

"I saw enough," he said grimly. "And here I thought the tide might be turning."

Alton was worried to see his friend so dismayed. They looked to Simon to maintain a baseline of optimism. If Simon lost hope, Alton didn't think he had a prayer of holding on to it.

"They've supposedly been looking for the bastard for years," Oliver said. "Are you telling me they've had no clues? With the uplink hunters they have now? The DNA tracking?" He snorted. "Somebody's been covering something up."

A young Nibelung moved past them in a daze, tears flowing down the rivulets carved into his cheeks. He seemed not to know where he was.

"Maybe," Simon said. "But why look too hard when he's the thing justifying your security state."

Now, Damien and a few others strutted by, laughing. "Better hope there's a place for you in our world," said Damien and pointed a finger gun at Oliver.

For once, Oliver showed enough wisdom to ignore him. "But if they can track him from the source of that message, maybe doves like Secretary Áquilar will have leverage to close the camps. You said yourself they've got to be under pressure in an election year."

"The alternate possibility is that they double down, insist that things are too dangerous with Hagen still out there," Simon said.

"You think this could be a false flag?" Oliver asked. "A holo-vid like that would be easy to fake."

"Or maybe it's real and they've just been sitting on it for a while. Who knows when it was made?"

"It's real," said Alton. "And it's recent." He stared at the specter of Hagen suspended in the blue tint of the projection behind the yapping panel guests. His piercing eyes stared straight back. They were as alive and calculating as ever.

Simon raised an eyebrow. "You know something we don't?"

But he was saved from answering by Lance strutting toward them.

"What I say, Prof? Nothing can hold us!" He made the crossed forearm sign, and several others mirrored him. They looked like they were doing a synchronized dance.

Stump, a bulldog of a Nibelung missing a hand, fixed Alton with his crazy eyes. "Let's do it now!" he panted, and Alton took a step back.

"Not just yet, loyal one, but keep this fire stoked!" Lance cried. He grabbed Stump by the shoulders. They banged foreheads.

"Ouch," said Simon.

Lance threw his head back and laughed, but it was drowned out by a savage hissing and booing. Alton froze, thinking the boos were for them, but then the five holograms flickered, and President Guerrero appeared at his desk in the Oval Office. Alton assumed it was the one in Los Angeles.

"My fellow Americans," he began. His hair was silver-tipped now, but his mustache was as dark and full as it had been during his days as California's governor a decade earlier. "As you have likely heard by now, the terrorist leader Hagen has emerged after an extended absence. While his specific intentions are vague, we can guess he intends to continue his campaign of intimidation and violence against the citizens and the government of the United States.

"To those currently relocated," he continued, "it is especially important that you make no move to support or join him. As my administration has made clear in the past, the relocation situation is an unfortunate necessity to protect citizens during these troubled times. We are no happier about it than you . . ."

The men exploded at this, and even Lance couldn't bring them under control. Alton strained to hear the rest of the comments.

". . . and every day we discuss the viability of bringing everyone home. Should the violence escalate again, it's unlikely that would happen anytime soon."

"Fuck you, Cockroach!" rang out.

"Rest assured," he continued, "the terrorists will be neutralized soon. In the meantime, we ask that everyone remain vigilant. Thank you and may God bless America."

Alton turned to go, but it still wasn't over. Now the projectors flickered to reveal Commandant Miller, broadcasting from the Central Compound. On the big screens, his attempt at a mustache looked especially feeble. The striped epaulets on his military-style jacket evoked some wannabe dictator.

"I'll keep this brief," he said in his nasally drone. "You heard the president. Any insurrection will be suppressed. Since our last bit of unpleasantness, you men have been model interns. No point in blowing it now."

Miller broadcast from the Central Compound partially because he was lazy but also because he didn't have enough men to suppress five hundred raging Nibelungs should they elect to revolt.

"Keep to your regular routine," Miller continued. "In the meantime, there will be a forty-eight-hour 3Dia blackout to allow tensions to calm." The feed fizzled and died. The men groaned and cursed.

"Let's get the hell out of here," Alton said.

They went to the Meal Shell. With Lance and the Nibelungs occupied elsewhere with the news, the three men were able to linger over their coffee in peace.

"Do you think they'll try something?" Alton asked.

"Without a doubt," Simon said. "This is what they live for. Death to them is just glory for the cause."

"Great," Oliver said. "What are we supposed to do in that event?"

"Hide under your bed," Simon said. "Or I guess you could join them."

"No thanks," he said. "I want my daughters to know what happened to me."

He was referring to the disappearance of the men who had attempted an uprising eighteen months earlier, when outside security had come to restore order. The rioters were taken away and never returned. Since the worst offenders were already at

Gypsum, Alton couldn't imagine where they'd gone. He had wondered if they'd simply been dumped in the mountains.

The only time anyone had left the camp and returned was when a cyclone fire had thrashed into the valley a year earlier. FloaterBarges had appeared and quickly vacuum-loaded all the men, but when the fire turned south, they were shunted back down the tubes.

That night, Alton snuck out to the cliff ledge and watched fire-fighting ships futilely engage the flames as they roared along the horizon. The light pollution obscured the stars, making it seem as though the apocalypse had reached all the way into space. It had seemed to him only a matter of time before the whole universe burned to ash.

CHAPTER 5

ALTON HELPED SIMON in the Med-Shell until midafternoon, unloading and organizing batches of vaccines and supplies that had been delivered the day before. Simon didn't really need assistance, but Alton felt uneasy after the morning's events, and he wanted a distraction. Anyway, he was always happy to help in return for Simon's support in the classroom.

He admired Simon, who had run a triage outfit for wounded guerrilla fighters with his wife, Sarah, a few years earlier, when the fighting had been especially fierce. They had operated deep in the Pacific Northwest, stabilizing fighters until they could make it out of the wilderness to a hospital.

Politically, the outfit was neutral, but helping Nibelungs in any capacity was more than enough to be branded a sympathizer. The only positive was that Simon's wife had been spared internment. Alton knew that Simon missed her desperately.

Finally, when there was nothing left to do, Alton departed for a late lunch. Lance surprised him as he was approaching the Meal Shell.

Alton squinted through the blowing dust. "Were you waiting for me?"

The big man stared at his feet as though he didn't want to admit it.

Alton sighed. "Another fence to mend?"

"One to tear down."

"You know they're expecting you to try something. Maybe let things calm down for a while."

"No choice," he said. "They already send security reinforcements to every camp."

"*Every* camp?" Alton asked. "How do you know that?"

He shrugged. "Just do."

Simon had been right. False flag or not, Guerrero was already using Hagen's transmission as an excuse to clamp down.

"It's now or never, then? Even if you get crushed? What's the point in that?"

"The Leader has called us to him. Nibelungs can't let him down."

"What if what we saw today wasn't real? What if Guerrero is just trying to lure you into trying something stupid?"

Lance was shaking his head before Alton even finished. "This has always been the Leader's plan," he said. "And I know where he will be."

So, he was alive. Alton's blood went cold. "How?"

"I ran raids for him. That's how I come here. They snatch me during raid."

"What kind of raids?"

"We grabbed supplies, weapons, even scientists. Whatever was needed."

Scientists? "Needed for what? Another bomb?"

"Help and you learn more."

The wind gusted, and Alton shivered, but Lance didn't so much as tremble. Alton had noticed he never seemed to get cold. "Can we go inside at least?"

"Too many ears. Come this way."

Lance preening for a crowd was harmless. Alton felt uneasy following him to some place with no witnesses. But he went with him to the tool and equipment pods and squeezed into the narrow space between them. When Lance reached into his pocket, Alton started, ready to bolt.

"Damn, Prof, relax," Lance said and withdrew a vial from his pocket that glowed amber even in the cruddy light. He uncapped it, took a long swallow, and handed it to Alton.

Alton sniffed and his eyes went wide. He took a sip, then another, and his insides fluttered like dancing fireflies. He closed his eyes, reeling a little, then passed it back to Lance, who took another healthy pull and returned it to his pocket.

"How'd you get that?" Alton sputtered, the fumes strong on his breath. There had been a global ban on real whiskey so that peatlands could be preserved as carbon sinks. Alton had tasted synthetic stuff before but never anything this good.

"Nibelungs take care of Hagen's primo man in camp," Lance said. "Take care of you too . . . if you help."

Lance clamped his bear paws on Alton's shoulders. It felt smothering, but Alton allowed it. The man had just given him his first drink in two years.

"Nibelung are fierce committed," he continued. "But you and I both know Civvies have primo brains. And primo access. You, Simon, a few others, open doors we can't. Physically and . . ." He searched for the word.

"Metaphorically?"

Lance smiled. "See? Primo brain."

"I don't need a primo brain to guess that the door you want opened is the one between the camp and the Central Compound so that you can slaughter everybody on the other side. Simon and the others aren't going to help you with that, no matter what you promise them."

"People die in war. They chose their side when they locked up this nation's greatest patriots."

Alton raised his eyebrows at this last bit. "It's not my war," he said. "And it never will be."

They stood in silence for a few moments, staring at the rain-streaked horizon. The sky was the color of cinders.

"That's too bad, Prof," Lance said finally.

"Why, are you going to hurt us?"

"Neebs never purposely hurt their white brothers," Lance said. "You know this. But . . ."

"But what?"

"I can't help if you get sliced in crossfire. And if you live—*if*—your place in the new order not secure."

"Come on, Lance, you said it yourself. There's no place to go. We still don't know what happened to the last guys who tried this."

"Is it not worth it to fight? They took everything from us. I never even seen you angry!"

"I'm angry," he said. Though the truth was, he wasn't sure he felt anything at all anymore. "But not enough to help your kind."

"My *kind*?" Lance snorted and shook his head. "This was a white nation once. We just want it back!"

"It was a red nation. Or, I should say, a collection of them. I realize that's inconvenient to your narrative. But even if you were morally justified in using violence to take it back, has it not occurred to you that you're sabotaging your own cause? You're making white people into worse pariahs than we already are!"

Lance smiled.

"What?" Alton sputtered. He thought he might actually be feeling angry now. Or maybe it was just the booze.

"That's the first time you've ever claimed to be white."

Alton stared into the muddled early twilight. "I don't think of myself in terms of race," he said.

"Bullshit, Prof. Everybody think of themself as race."

Alton stepped out from between the sheds. "Thanks for the drink, Lance. Please don't do anything insane."

As he pushed against the wind through the gathering darkness, he half expected Lance to charge him from behind. Once he was back in the center of camp and felt safe again, he let himself wonder how much Lance really knew about Hagen's plans.

Could he tell Alton what he wanted to know above all else: if this indeed was Hagen's last stand, had the bastard persuaded *her* to stand with him?

CHAPTER 6

HIS MOTHER WAS shaking him by the shoulders. She kept asking him why he didn't have any white friends, and he kept insisting that he only had white friends now, thanks to her, but she wouldn't believe him.

The shaking continued until he opened his eyes to find a guard staring down at him. His first thought was that the revolt had begun, but the stillness around him belied that. The guard indicated for him to get dressed.

Outside, two more guards in lined coats and headlamps led him down the main drag, past the darkened barracks on either side, toward the Central Compound. The wind had died down in the night, and a light snow had begun. The flakes felt exquisite on his face. He leaned into them like a man condemned.

The guards on the other side heaved back two heavy bolts and slid open the razor-topped steel gate. They escorted him through, and his abdomen tightened as they continued toward the Intake Center.

Had Miller already gotten word of Lance's plot? If so, how much should he confess to knowing? Was it better to be tortured by Miller or to become an enemy of Lance? He was being forced into an impossible choice, and he hadn't even agreed to help.

The Intake chamber was an icy crypt, somehow even more

frigid than the high desert outside. As his eyes adjusted, he made out the devices from his ordeal two years earlier—the benches and straps and hoses and buckets and rusty tools and wires and the giant speakers, their mesh screens woolen with cobwebs and dust.

He had long ago shut the experience out of his mind—the haze of pain, fear, and humiliation—but now he tried to remember what might be in store for him.

There had been waterboarding, light electrocution, some blaring noise—enough to convey the serious intent of their captors but nothing crippling. No German chair. No Syrian box. No branding irons. Not even sleep deprivation. They hadn't kept them in there long enough for that.

Mercifully, they had also spared him the VR torture, although he had heard the shrieking of those being subjected to it. Some of his fellow prisoners had been administered psychotropic drugs, had their eyes forced open, and were immersed in virtual reality scenarios.

These included being chucked out of an airplane at twenty thousand feet, or buried alive, or stuffed into a box of black widows, or submerged into a school of thrashing sharks, or forced to cross a live minefield strewn with the body parts of children.

The algorithms sifted through a thousand different scenarios until they elicited the most bloodcurdling screams. Alton remembered thinking that George Orwell would not have been surprised.

During his own intake, Alton's torturers had demanded details about his "radical" work at the college, which had amounted to little more than standing near various student protests. Evidently, it had never occurred to the thugs that he simply had been encouraging his students' free expression.

But for all the political persecution, they never asked what he was expecting, what he could actually answer. *How long have you known him? What was the nature of your friendship? Have you been in recent contact? Why did you help him when you were both younger?*

But torture wasn't on tonight's agenda—at least not yet. Instead of strapping him down, they elbowed him through the frozen chamber into a bright room beyond where three strangers waited. Two young Hispanic officers sat facing him from behind a centrally placed table, an empty chair between them.

The officers were military-auged, EVs glowing softly through their uniforms in hot pink and frosty blue. They were built like athletes and great-looking. Alton tried to catch the eye of the woman—the first he had seen in person in two years—but she wouldn't acknowledge that he had even come into the room.

A balding white man in plain clothes stood behind them, clutching a thermos and valise. The man motioned Alton toward a solitary chair, ten feet or so across from the table, then dismissed the guard and went to stand behind the table again.

They all waited in silence, Alton trying to control his mounting dread, until they heard a woman's voice echoing through the Intake Chamber.

"This is fucked up, Miller," the voice said. "I shouldn't even be seeing this."

"Forgive me, Madame Secretary," said the commandant. "We've rarely used this equipment since the early days."

"It should *never* have been used."

"We had orders from the president—"

"Those orders have been superseded. Permanently," she said. "Do you understand? Get rid of this stuff immediately."

"Yes, Madame Secretary," Miller mewled as he entered the room. In his droopy uniform, he was like a little boy playing commandant.

A fit, middle-aged woman of average height followed him in and took the chair between the two soldiers. She wore a tactical vest over a black suit. Her dark hair was in a bun tucked into the high collar of the vest. She wore sleek leather boots and gloves, the latter of which she removed as she spoke. Her charisma lit up the room, as it had done at all those campaign rallies.

"Hello, Alton," Diana Áquilar said. She put on a smile that seemed to indicate a conscious effort to move past her aggravation with Miller, who stood shame-faced near the door.

Alton nodded, trying to conceal his shock of recognition.

Her aide stepped forward with the thermos and poured a steaming cup of tea. When she noticed Alton breathing in the scent of jasmine, she said, "Give our guest a cup, will you?"

The man poured another and handed it to Alton.

"Do you remember me?" she asked.

Alton nodded, relaxing a little as the mug warmed his hands. "We said hello once, at a campaign event when you were running for Congress the first time."

She nodded. "And you know that President Guerrero appointed me a deputy undersecretary for defense last year?"

"There aren't many perks here in Club Paradise, but they do let us follow current events. I guess so we'll be reminded of who's in charge," he said. He could feel Miller scowling at him.

"I'm glad to hear that because that's what I'm here to discuss." She blew on her tea, then said, "Do you know a woman named Kiara Cunningham?"

He hesitated. "I thought you were here to discuss *current* events. Kiara is old news."

"Answer the question, intern!" Miller barked.

"Of course I know her. We were seeing each other when she worked on your first campaign," Alton said. "That's how I met you."

"Kiara was invaluable to me. We haven't spoken in some time, but I do remember her telling me how close you had been when you were young."

"We weren't that young. It was only, what ... six years ago?"

"I meant when you were youn*ger*."

His stomach dropped. He knew where this was headed now. And it was cold comfort that it had nothing to do with Lance's plans to escape. Or, actually, in a roundabout way, it *did* if you considered who she was talking about.

"You weren't orphans, exactly," she continued. "But the three of you each had been parentless in your own way. So, you formed a kind of surrogate family. To not feel so alone. Is that right?"

He put on his best poker face. "The three of us?"

She gave him a *don't-play-dumb* look. "You, her, and Alex Weber."

It was surreal and unnerving to hear his real name spoken after all this time. He wanted to take a drink of tea, but his trembling hands threatened to spill it. "That's ancient history," he said. He snuck a glance at Miller, but the dolt seemed as clueless as usual.

"Even so, those formative bonds stay with us, often despite our efforts to shed them."

"I stayed as close to Kiara as she would let me," Alton said. "But Alex blew up our little family pretty early on."

"Literally," she said with an innocent smile.

He glared at her. He wanted to punch her in the face for that remark.

"I'm referring to his first major attack," she said. "The one on the governor's campaign fundraiser."

"I know what you're referring to," he snapped.

"And that's why they arrested you, isn't it?" Áquilar said. "Because of your close history with the domestic terrorist leader now known as Hagen?"

In his peripheral vision, Alton saw Miller's mouth drop open.

"I thought so at first, but nobody ever asked me about him." He shrugged. "Maybe they didn't know."

"Well," she said, sitting back. "That certainly doesn't surprise me. Not exactly a robust intelligence-gathering outfit here, is it?"

She sipped her tea innocently while Miller's face went crimson.

"And now Alex—Hagen—has made a dramatic return, pledging to finish what he started," she said. "And President Guerrero, in turn, has pledged to kill him. Sheesh, *men*." She elbowed the female officer, who just shook her head, her dagger eyes stabbing into Alton's.

"I hope he does kill him," Alton said.

"See what I mean?" She sighed. "Miller, could I have some time alone with Alton, please?"

"If this intern represents a security threat based on—"

"I'll take responsibility for any security threats, Commandant. You are dismissed."

He snapped to attention. "Of course, Madame Secretary."

When the sound of his petulant footsteps had faded, she regarded Alton with new urgency.

"Believe it or not, I'm sorry this happened to you," she said. "It's no secret that some of us are at odds with the president. Stripping due process. Rendition. Internment. It's not American."

Alton snorted. "Of course it is."

"Then it's not what America *should* be." She stood up now and paced the room while she spoke. "For five hundred years, Hispanic people fought to get the boots of white men off our necks. We fought for equal rights and equal opportunities and equal justice under the law. Now, we have power, and I . . . *we*"—she gestured toward the others—"won't abide its abuse."

Alton remembered from one of Áquilar's speeches—or perhaps Kiara had told him about it; his memory failed him often these days—that Áquilar's family had got caught up in the ICE massacres of the late 2020s before that depraved outfit was finally dissolved.

"People in power have always behaved the same way, and they always will," Alton said, lapsing into professor mode. "It doesn't matter what color they are or what their background is. You can't change human nature."

"Well, I believe you can," she said. "And now is the time to prove it. The United States is finally colonizing Mars. Why even go if we're just going to pollute a new world with our petty tribalism?"

It occurred to Alton suddenly that perhaps the Mars mission was Hagen's new target. The timing of his reappearance around the launch made too much sense. The mission was a perfect symbol of multiculturalism for the twenty-second century. Destroying it would be a crippling blow to the nation's fragile psyche and a huge victory for his cause.

She stopped pacing. "Guerrero doesn't just want to kill Hagen," she said. "He wants to put his head atop the castle wall. But a contingent of us—a sizable contingent—want him captured and tried publicly so that all of our constitutional mechanisms are in effect and on display."

Alton finally understood. "Guerrero didn't send you. He doesn't even know you're here..."

"Our contingent wants this to be the first step toward closing the camps and restoring civil rights. It still matters what we do, even if the world stopped looking to us for moral guidance a long time ago."

"Soldiers don't face civilian criminal courts. How are you going to try him?"

"Alex was wanted for civilian crimes long before he was branded an enemy combatant. Any number of courts could try him for all the shit he's done in his life."

"Guerrero must have mobilized the entire armed forces since that holo-vid dropped," Alton said. "But you're going to find him first?"

"The president doesn't know where to look. And even if he did, it's hardly his top agenda, despite what he professes publicly."

"Let me guess; you do know where to look," he said. Alton studied the two officers, but their faces betrayed nothing.

"I think Kiara might."

Irritation flared in him. "If that's true, why are you wasting your time here, putting me in hot water with this asshole,"—he jerked a thumb toward where Miller had departed—"and making all my delightfully paranoid fellow prisoners wonder where I got dragged off to in the middle of the night and what kind of rat I might have become."

"Because Kiara has disappeared."

Her words rang in the room.

"Since when?"

"We're not sure," said the aide. "We tried to contact her soon after Hagen's message dropped but got no response. We searched, but she's off the grid."

"She knows shit's about to hit the fan," Alton said. "She's probably sunbathing in Norway by now."

"We're positive she hasn't left the country," said the aide.

"If she's off the grid, and she hasn't left the country, it's pretty obvious where she is." He felt the deep pain of that and realized he hadn't let it go even a little bit.

"Kiara told me she gave up on Alex after he went underground years ago," Áquilar said. "He was too dangerous, and she wanted a legit life. Why go back to him now?"

He shrugged. "Maybe she lied to you. Or maybe he kidnapped her."

"Would he do that, given their history?"

"I'm in no position to speculate on his motives or state of mind. Would *you* put anything past a crazed terrorist?"

"Actually, we believe that you are *uniquely* qualified to speculate on the state of mind of both Alex and Kiara," said the aide. "That's why we're here."

Áquilar nodded. "We want you to help us find them. More precisely, if we can find her, she might lead us to him."

"If we can determine his location and get a small unit into his vicinity—eight or ten specialized soldiers—your presence might... coax him out," the aide said. "Then we capture him."

"*My* presence?"

"Or, who knows, maybe you could talk him into coming in willingly," Áquilar said.

"You must be really desperate. You think he's going to be lured into capture or give himself up because of some childhood friendship?"

She looked at him intently. "Kiara told me he owes you."

Alex *absolutely* owed him, but he didn't think Alex would see it that way.

"You could save a lot of lives if we bring Hagen in quickly and peacefully before this war resumes," she continued. "As well as weaken Guerrero's excuse to keep the camp open for who knows how long. Maybe other people close to you get swept up under those circumstances."

There are no other people close to me, he thought but just said, "Alex's head on a spike sounds pretty good, honestly."

"Could you live with Kiara's head on the spike next to his?"

Some part of him knew that he couldn't. But if she *had* returned to him after everything . . . he felt so hurt and disgusted at that moment, it was hard to say for sure.

"If you help us, I'll make sure you have a nice life somewhere, whether we succeed or not," Áquilar said. "I'll put you in a cabin by a lake in Saskatchewan, whatever you want. You'll never see a camp again."

"*If* I survive."

"Yes. But time is of the essence, Alton."

"Not in here, it's not," he said. "Not even a little bit." His tea was cool enough to drink now, and his hands had stopped shaking. Sensing the interview was coming to an end, he drained it in one long swallow.

"Your government ripped me from my life, tortured me, and buried me in this wasteland," he said. "Now, you want me to help you capture your enemy and end a civil war that Guerrero has made worse at every turn? Even if I believed in your plan, I wouldn't help you just out of spite."

He glared back at the female officer, but she looked unrepentant. Was it his imagination, or did her EVs glow a little hotter?

Áquilar sighed and said, "We can give you a few days to think about it but no more."

The aide produced a smooth black device from his case and dropped it into Alton's palm. It was no bigger than a paper clip and almost as weightless.

"Put it in one ear," said the aide. "It will signal a dropship to retrieve you within fifteen minutes and bring you to the secretary's location. The dropship will be concealed nearby."

"I'll order Miller not to interfere with your pick-up," said Áquilar. "Come to the compound gates when you're ready, ask to be taken to the landing platform, and activate the beacon."

Alton looked at the tiny device in his hand and said, "Don't hold your breath." On the way back, it felt so good to finally have a choice about something, he hardly minded the cold.

CHAPTER 7

THOUGH HE WAS back in his bed a long time before he began to feel warm again. Certainly, it wasn't thoughts of Kiara that finally warmed him.

Still, there was no point in feeling betrayed. Kiara would have done anything for Alex, and if standing by him until the bitter end meant sharing details of their childhood, he was certain she had never hesitated.

But what exactly had she told Áquilar that made her think he would help her doomed cause? That Alton had a guilty conscience? That he was a good guy? Compared to Alex, he supposed he was.

For the thousandth time, he remembered the night of his epic humiliation. The three of them liked to climb the hills behind the Cosmost facilities, get high, and gawk at the fire erupting against the violet sky. As the billowing smoke and surging contrails traced orange and white in their unsteady vision, they made lofty pledges to travel to space together, defying whatever odds they had to. Humans had been visiting Mars for several years by then, and they talked of joining a colony, maybe even leading their own one day.

Of course, Alton had imagined himself and Kiara as lovers in these scenarios, with Alex as some kind of older brother figure. Admittedly, Alex was tall and strapping, more handsome, experienced, charismatic, and confident than Alton. Also, he and Kiara shared a much longer history.

But Alton had been convinced that *he* and Kiara had developed something more crucial: a guarded and ironic way of looking at the world that the arrogant Alex couldn't fathom, along with a secret romanticism that was expressed in their shared passion for reading.

Those Saturday mornings when the two of them combed the Stalls together, snatching up old volumes, then racing back to her house to pore over their new treasures, were among the greatest times in his life. They were especially satisfying because it was just the two of them. Alex didn't care about reading. Alton didn't know *what* he cared about other than his dad's stupid cause.

This made him feel especially assured that night. He imagined them standing hand in hand, gazing out into that great unknown, their eyes following the rocket's burning trajectory until it faded to a pale streak. With unspoken resolve, they would turn and face Alex. He might not like it, but he would have to accept it, because it was what Kiara wanted.

But when he actually turned, he found Alex and Kiara had reclined onto the blanket. He blanched as Alex put his hands on her smooth face and kissed her tenderly, the way that Alton had visualized doing a thousand times.

He didn't think they even noticed when he fled down the hill, eyes stinging, breath coming in ragged gasps. He understood in that instant that, of course, *he* would always be the brother in the scenario, the *little* brother. Given his life thus far, he knew he would be lucky to have even that much.

So, it had astonished him years later when he and Kiara fell into a brief affair of their own, when he had been in Maryland earning his graduate degree in literature, and she had come to DC to work on Áquilar's first campaign.

Many had proposed moving the US Capitol farther inland, but the new seawall and hurricane protections were working, and the politicians and lawyers and lobbyists and journalists and contractors were returning to the swanky suburbs. The government was anxious to show the world that the seat of Western power was still intact despite massive global instability, and it encouraged and even underwrote much of this.

Alton knew Kiara was part of the returning influx, having seen her in local campaign speech vids with Áquilar, and so he contrived to run into her. He hadn't expected her to seem so unreasonably happy to see him.

Over drinks that night, she claimed to have ended things with Alex permanently, though she was vague about the last time she had seen him. He wasn't publicly *Hagen* yet, but he had been doing nasty business with his father's movement for years, and she would never compromise his whereabouts, not even to Alton.

But her emotional state strongly suggested they had been together recently. Her lovemaking felt distracted, and she was hollow-eyed and moody in the predawns before her long days on the campaign.

When Áquilar took her campaign on the road after a few weeks, Kiara promised to consider a future with him. But when she wouldn't let him take her to the airport in the morning, he knew it was over, that he had just been a rebound.

He hadn't seen her since, and he knew that was a good thing. He should have written her off after high school and the attack on Guerrero's gubernatorial fundraiser. She was abetting a murderer, one who had almost killed people Alton cared about.

But the same way that she could never tear himself from Alex, he could never tear himself from her. His love for her had twisted his heart into something unrecognizable. Or maybe it had just exposed it for what it had always been: needy, selfish, and hypocritical.

In the morning, when he opened his locker to dress, he pulled down her picture and stuffed it in his jacket pocket, then left for breakfast.

A bitter downpour had drowned the snow, and even though it was always welcome when the rain tamped down the dust, Alton felt disappointed to see the previous night's ethereality give way to dreary familiarity.

At breakfast, some of the men stared at him, talking in whispers. He was right: they must have seen the guards escorting him from the barracks. He ate in haste, grabbed some fruit for lunch, and departed for the classroom. He needed to spend the day reading *The Quiet American* and prepping for his upcoming class.

When he wandered in for dinner, he was alarmed to find the Nibelungs openly glaring at him. Lance and Crow were absent, and he realized with a jolt that he hadn't seen them at breakfast either. It wasn't like Lance to miss a meal.

Had Miller detained them? If something happened to Lance and the others blamed Alton, it would get ugly for him in a hurry, whether the Nibelungs were supposed to lay off their white brothers or not.

He almost turned and left but knew he would look guilty or afraid, so he sat with Oliver and a few other Civvies, not touching his food. He shuddered a sigh of relief when Lance finally arrived, Crow trailing behind. Nothing seemed amiss, although Lance did shoot Alton a strange, knowing smile.

"Everything okay?" Oliver asked.

He nodded. "Where's Simon?"

"Been giving vaccines all day. He took his meals in the Shell. Oh, I forgot to tell you, he wants you to stop by."

He would, but he had something to do first. Once it was dark enough, he made his way to the Ed-Shell and slipped out of camp, squaring his shoulders against the gusts, which had picked up again now that the rain had passed.

Mars couldn't be much different from this wasteland, he thought, with its extreme winds, suffocating dust, blistering summer heat, and freezing year-round nights. Only an idiot or a madman would dream of leaving paradise for this desolation.

At the cliff's edge, the icy wind pummeled the valley, and the vast cloud-bruised sky stretched over the canyon. As always, he was taken aback by its immensity and by its sheer, raw beauty.

Shivering, he pulled the snapshot of Kiara from his jacket, reached down for a stone, then reached into his pocket for the dropship signaler. He crumpled the photo around the stone and the device and pitched it.

The package was just heavy enough to sink through the gusts. Along with it—if he was lucky—went the fantasies of love and adventure he had clung to like a fool.

The quasi-existence of the camp had given him an excuse to remain stuck. But maybe now he could accept his reality. He was a prisoner. And after what he had let happen to Bernardo, he believed that he deserved to be.

CHAPTER 8

IN THE COZILY lit Med-Shell, Simon was slumped in his chair behind his desk, looking especially glum. Empty vaccine cartons were piled in a corner. Alton never ceased to admire his commitment. Simon didn't have to dispense these vaccines or run the Med-Shell. That was the camp administration's responsibility.

But Simon gave the interns better care, and it was easier for them to get it. If the men had to be processed through Compound security, even something as straightforward as a shot or a checkup could take weeks. Simon was so efficient and trustworthy that Miller had even enlisted him to administer shots to his staff.

Alton shimmied out of his jacket and perched on the edge of the patient table. "Warmest place in camp," he said. "No wonder you never leave."

Simon gave an exhausted smile. "Let me give you this," he said. "Last one."

He pulled on gloves, peeled open the package on his desk, then grabbed a disinfectant swab. Alton wasn't sure what he meant by "last one" since two more unused shots lay next to the one reserved for him. Maybe they were for Simon and Oliver.

Alton rolled up his shirtsleeve. "I could have waited until you got the next shipment in."

Simon swabbed his upper arm with disinfectant and jabbed him. "Can't have our professor getting ill," he said. "Who would enlighten the masses?"

He disposed of the used shot and removed his gloves. "All right," he said. "Done for the day." He rifled around his desk for the e-pen, took a drag, and tossed it to Alton, who did the same.

Alton closed his eyes. "I may pass out on this table," he murmured.

"One more thing before you do."

Alton opened his eyes.

"I saw a lot of Neebs today while I was giving shots. There's some . . . talk about you in camp."

Alton felt his stomach drop. So, he hadn't been imagining it.

"I got dragged down to CC in the middle of the night," he said. "They're all wondering why."

"What did they want?"

Alton debated telling him the truth, but then he would have to explain his connection to Alex. And he wasn't ready to reveal that. Not even to Simon.

"Miller wanted to know if Lance is planning anything now that Hagen has announced his grand return. Someone must have seen us talking yesterday."

"And is he?"

Alton nodded. "And he wants our help. The Civvies, I mean."

Simon snorted. "Of course he does. We're race traitors until he needs something from us."

"Somehow Lance knows that a garrison is coming to beef up security," Alton continued. "He wants to try to steal their transport. He wants us to help him get inside the CC so he can be waiting for them."

"That garrison could show up at any moment."

Alton nodded. "Thus his urgency."

"What did you tell Miller?"

"Nothing. Fuck him."

"Have you considered it?"

"Telling Miller? Of course not."

"No, I mean helping Lance."

He gave his friend a *please-tell-me-you're-joking* look.

Simon picked up a folded letter from his desk, shook it from its envelope. "From my wife," he said. "Breaking the news that she has been considering leaving the country. With Hagen back on the warpath, I'm sure she's all but decided."

Alton grimaced. "We won't get out anytime soon now."

"Probably not," said Simon. "And Sarah has family abroad. She's tired of being alone. I don't blame her. So am I."

"I'm sorry. It's a shitty situation," Alton said. "But I don't think helping Lance escape is your ticket to reuniting with your wife. I can't imagine what could be worse than this hellhole, but if you fail, I'm sure you'd find out."

Simon put the letter back in its envelope. "You're right," he said. "Just desperate thinking on my part."

Alton felt relieved. He reached for the pen and took another drag.

"But your midnight meeting with Miller wasn't the topic of conversation today," Simon said.

Alton raised an eyebrow at his friend.

"There's a rumor going around that you're . . ." Simon paused, seeming to struggle with the words. "That you're of . . . Hispanic descent."

Despite the warmth of the Med-Shell, a chill ran through Alton.

"I'm sure it's just some bullshit," Simon continued. "Made up by—"

"It's true," Alton said. "My father is of Mexican descent, but I only met him once, a long time ago. He could be dead now for all I know. My mother raised me . . . if you could call it that."

"She was white?"

"And proud of it. She would have fit in great here."

"But how did this get out?" Simon asked. "And why now? You've been here almost since the camp opened."

"It's got to be fucking Miller," Alton said. "Pressuring me to tell him what Lance is up to. Put me in danger, then be my lifeline in exchange for information."

But how the hell did he find out? Or has he known all along, just waiting for the right time to use it? Miller was a small man, easily threatened. Maybe he wanted to punish Alton for witnessing Áquilar's humiliation of him. Put him back in his place.

"Just tell Lance that Miller is spreading lies because you won't rat him out," Simon said. "Lance will appreciate you having his back and get the Neebs to heel."

Alton nodded, but he wasn't so sure. Suddenly, it was too warm, and he felt sick. He slid off the table and retrieved his jacket.

"I'm sure this will go away," Simon said. "But be careful. This is not the time to make a wrong move."

That goes for you too, Alton thought, and he went out into the cold night.

Later, he lay awake trying to figure out how his background had suddenly become public knowledge after all this time. It must have been a part of his record that Miller didn't discover until he went looking for dirt after Áquilar's visit.

If Alton had known that was why the Nibelungs had been shooting daggers at him all day, he never would have sat with Oliver and the others at dinner. The last thing he wanted was for them to be in danger because of him. If the Neebs believed he was Hispanic, what a *primo* target he would be.

He hardly breathed, listening for any sound. Two or three testosterone-and-rage-fueled young men could break his ribs before the guards in the cage even looked up from their brandied coffees. He had to piss, but what if they were waiting to ambush him at the urinal, bash his head into the porcelain?

After a while, the rain started to spatter lightly on the barracks shell, relaxing him a bit. Eventually, he slept, but it was the second night in a row that he did so very poorly.

CHAPTER 9

IT WAS EVEN colder the next day as he made his way to breakfast, churning with nerves. The wind snapped at him like a chained Rottweiler. A storm amassing to the east was poised to unleash a heavy downpour later.

He felt fuzzy, and his head ached. He would go to the classroom after breakfast and crash in his safe space for a few hours. He was supposed to teach tonight, but he didn't know if it was a good idea given the circumstances. Anyway, he wasn't remotely prepared.

The chow hall fell silent as he entered, but he pretended not to notice the hush, or the six baleful faces who had obviously not come for the oatmeal (in fairness, few did, he thought). As he made his way down the line, even the servers glared at him, slapping the food onto his tray.

The Civvies, including Simon and Oliver, were at their usual table, but Alton took a seat by himself near the door. He gulped a few bites, filled his coffee mug, and got the hell out.

He didn't make it ten yards before he turned to see the six men from the Chow Hall following. Better to try to talk them down out in the open, with people watching, he thought, but they were already closing fast.

He dropped his mug to shield his face, yelping as coffee scalded him, but the blows never came. Instead, they grabbed him under the arms and steered him toward the equipment shells, shoving him inside the nearest one and slamming him down into a rusty wheelbarrow.

"Take it easy, goddammit!" As he tried to right himself, he scanned the dimly lit space for weapons. The steel grappling hooks and the rubber hammer and stakes they had used to repair the fence post hung from the wall opposite him. The nylon rope was piled in a corner. Then his eyes fell on Lance, be-throned on an overturned bucket. Crow squatted next to him in the darkness like a gnarled jester.

"Thank you, my brothers," said Lance. The minions filed out, disappointed, clearly believing their service had earned a seat to the show.

"What the hell, Lance?" Alton massaged his bruised armpits.

"Let's not play games. We know you know what we know." Lance chuckled, amused at his own wordplay. The jester sniggered in response.

"And it's complete bullshit," Alton said. "Look at me. I'm whiter than you. Somebody is trying to screw me over."

"Who would screw over Prof? Everybody love Prof! Civvies, guards, even Nibelungs! Prof is the great *enlightener*!"

"You tell me," Alton said. "You run this place."

"I don't run Central Compound. And that's where Prof was two nights ago."

"They dragged me up there to ask me about *you*. And I didn't tell them shit. Even when they threatened to torture me!"

"It's true they haven't come for me yet. But maybe you help them set a trap."

"Why would I help them? They're as much my enemy as they are yours."

"Get rid of Lance, and you can teach the men whatever you want," Lance said. "With no one to stand in your way."

"That's the *opposite* of what I'm trying to do! I'm trying to get them to think critically, not to indoctrinate them. That's your tactic."

Lance sighed. "It doesn't matter if it's true. All that matters is that everyone believes it. And now time is up. We need to take Gypsum tonight. You have special privileges. You can get those gates open."

"I don't have the access you think."

"The doc, then."

"You're going to put Simon in danger after everything he's done for your men?"

"I don't want to see him hurt. Or you. But the cause comes first. The cause *always* comes first."

Alton nodded at Crow. "Mr. Hacker can't get the gates open?"

"I'll bypass the transport controls once we get on board," Crow said. "Until then, you know as well as anyone there's nothing here to interface."

It was true. Except for the 3Dias, the prisoners' area was as analog as a thirteenth-century dungeon. No electronic back doors to exploit. Only the literal kind, like the one Alton had discovered.

"Even if we fail, I will make sure everyone knows these rumors are lies," Lance said.

Áquilar had said something similar. *Just try! You're likely to die, but we'll appreciate it!*

"Think of it this way," Crow said. "If the Nibelungs get fired up to fight the cockroaches and don't get a chance, they'll need an outlet. And you'll be the only cockroach left to squash."

"I'll get your gates open," Alton spat. "Clearly, I have no choice. But doesn't it bother you that the rumor about me might be true? How can you trust a half-breed cockroach?" He glared at them both.

Lance grinned. "Help me and you'll have proved that you're as white as you need to be."

Alton just shook his head. He wasn't remotely surprised.

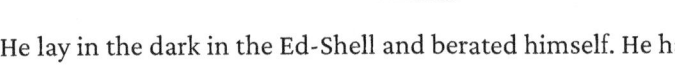

He lay in the dark in the Ed-Shell and berated himself. He had literally thrown his way out of this situation over a cliff. At least if he had left with Áquilar, he could have tried to escape at some point.

Because despite what he had just promised the lunatic, he would never help Lance. He had aided Alex's cause once, and the only reason he didn't give him up to the authorities back then was because he was afraid Kiara would hate him for it.

He would never make that mistake again, but how the hell was he going to get out of this?

Lance had instructed him to hold class that evening so that everything seemed normal. He felt unexpectedly sad, realizing it might be his last time teaching. He had begun offering the class to maintain some kind of normalcy and a connection to his old life, but he had also hoped to open up the men with ideas, depth of feeling, empathy. Maybe he could give them some notion of how to lead better lives should they ever get that chance.

Once he had proven the value of the class as a steadying influence on the Nibelungs, he was able to convince Miller to give them the cheap electronic reader tablets. With more content available, he began to expand the curriculum.

If he gave them a few novels by white men, he could get them to grudgingly accept something by a woman. In place of racial diversity—which they would never tolerate—he had slipped them authors who might criticize or satirize white hegemony. He had assigned *The Quiet American* for that reason, hoping that they might respond to the novel's moral clarity.

But maybe he should never have started teaching in the first place. Doing so had gotten him into the mess he was in now. Maybe he should have kept his head down. Or maybe he should have taken the one choice available to him and hurled himself into the gorge. He could still do it now—rush out the back and take a dive into the abyss.

But a line from the novel intruded into his dark thoughts: *You cannot exist unless you have the power to alter the future.*

If he ceased to exist now, he would never find out if he could keep making a difference, even in his small way. He wasn't dead just yet, even if he felt like he was.

CHAPTER 10

AT THE GATES, he said, "I want to see Miller."

The guards gazed on him with suspicion, then contempt, before one of them trudged off.

As he waited, he watched the advancing storm, praying it wouldn't delay his pickup and flight out of there . . . if he could even still arrange it.

After an eternity, the guard reappeared and led Alton to a warehouse at the edge of the landing platform where Miller was supervising a bustling reorganization—probably making room for the soon-to-arrive troops and equipment.

"Yes, intern?" Miller snapped, without looking up from the virtual manifest floating before him.

"*Áquilar* told me to tell you when I was ready for her."

Alton wondered if the commandant had heard him until he flicked the manifest toward a subordinate and said, "Come with me."

Alton's heart flared as he followed Miller. *Would it really be this easy?*

Outside, gusts blew grit into Alton's eyes, while Miller dropped his protective face shield.

"Let me ask you something, intern. How long do you think she's going to last in this administration?"

Alton's heart sank. So, the bastard wasn't going aid his escape after all.

"You were just in there," Miller said, gesturing toward the Intake Center. "Despite what she instructed, I'm never going to shut it down. Guerrero is going to win reelection on an anti-terror campaign. Your buddy Hagen just made sure of that."

Alton's teeth chattered in the cold. Or was it fear?

"It's true what I said," Miller continued. "We haven't used it in a while. Which means that it could probably stand a test, in case we need it, with all this fresh insurrection in the air. Should we test it on you?"

"That might scare me if I had anything to lose," said Alton. "But you know I'm fucked either way."

"What are you talking about?"

"You made sure the entire camp found out about my background."

"About being childhood butt buddies with Hagen?" A tinny little snort echoed beneath his face shield. "Why would I advertise that and turn you into a celebrity like Lance? The last thing I need in here is another peckerwood folk hero."

"Not that. My *racial* background."

"Your what?"

"That I'm half Mexican?"

It was obvious he had no idea what Alton meant. The creep wasn't clever enough to be a good liar. Then it dawned on him, cold and white, like the morning after an apocalypse.

It had been Áquilar who had spread it to the camp to put Alton in danger with the men.

So that he would have no choice but to use her as his escape hatch. She was taking an awful chance that the Nibelungs wouldn't tear him to pieces first. He had just been lucky that Lance needed his help, which was the last card he had to play.

"I have information about Lance," he said. "Once my transit is arranged, I'll tell you what I know."

"I'm not helping that bitch," Miller said. "Even if it's in my own best interests. What does she know about homeland security? She's not even from the homeland."

Alton stared at him. The racist fuck was no better than the Nibelungs.

"Torture me, then."

"On second thought, I suppose Señora Due Process was right," Miller said. "We can't abide rendition in a democracy, can we?" He signaled two nearby guards. "Put him back in."

"What do you think is going to happen to you if she finds out you didn't help me?" Alton said.

"Nothing," Miller said as the guards grabbed Alton roughly under his arms. "I'll tell her you died at the hands of your fellow interns when they discovered your true identity. *Cockroach.*"

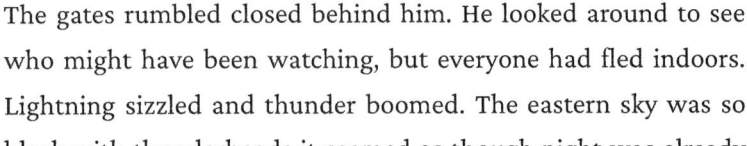

The gates rumbled closed behind him. He looked around to see who might have been watching, but everyone had fled indoors. Lightning sizzled and thunder boomed. The eastern sky was so black with thunderheads it seemed as though night was already upon them.

He had to be in the classroom in twenty minutes. He hustled to the Med-Shell as the wind whipped droplets in his face. Simon wasn't there, so he double-timed it to the barracks. Not there either. He fought down his panic.

He was frantic by the time he finally found Simon alone in the chow hall with a cup of tea, writing a letter. He looked up as Alton slid in across from him, breathless and disheveled.

"You need a tranquilizer, my friend?"

"Lance is blackmailing me into helping him escape tonight," he sputtered. "He'll have his men ready to charge the gates as soon as I give the guards some pretense to open them."

"And it's a perfect night for chaos with that bastard storm coming," Simon said.

"He told me to hold class so that everything seems normal until they're ready to pounce. But I have an idea how we can avoid helping him *and* not get swept up in this."

"I'm listening."

"I know a way outside of camp."

Simon raised an eyebrow. "And how long have you been sitting on this particular nugget?"

"We can't escape that way, or I would have already told you about it. It leads to a sheer cliff drop. But we could *wait* out there, then sneak back when it's all over. Claim we were hiding somewhere inside the camp."

When Simon didn't respond, Alton said, "Unless you're really thinking of helping them?"

Simon sighed. "No. But what if Lance calls off the attack when you don't show up and they can't get into the compound? We'll be the only two missing."

"I think he *will* try something, no matter what. If he misses this window, he can't join Hagen for the final battle or whatever. He's not going to pass up that chance at glory. It's all he lives for."

Simon rubbed his whiskers as he took it all in.

"I understand if you'd rather not chance it," Alton said. "But I have to. They're going to kill me otherwise."

"Have you considered that your safest course of action might just be to help the Aryan bastard? Run for cover as soon as it kicks off?"

"And be responsible for his reunion with Hagen? No way."

Simon nodded. "All right then. What do you need from me?"

"Skip class tonight. Gather any rain gear you can find. We might be spending the night in the storm. When class is over, wait until everybody is gone and meet me in the Ed-Shell. Don't be late. Once I don't show at the gates, Lance is going to come looking. We need to be ghosts."

Simon slid the letter into an envelope and sealed it. "Let me post this to the wife first," he said. "In case our ghost condition becomes permanent."

CHAPTER 11

ALTON STOOD IN front of the class clutching *The Quiet American* in an attempt to still his trembling hands. He tried to look normal, but Oliver's expression suggested he wasn't succeeding. Alton smiled at his friend to conceal his regret that he hadn't thought to warn him. But it was too late to say anything now.

The door flew open, and a few tardy regulars filed in, then some new faces, then Crow, and then, to Alton's shock, Lance, who pushed the door tight against the brewing gale.

"I've heard such good things, Prof. Had to come see for myself!" Lance bellowed.

They were a pulsing mass, primed for rebellion. Alton felt trapped, claustrophobic. "Then why don't you get us started?" he said, finding his courage. "And summarize this week's novel."

"Sure thing, Prof!" Lance said. "This story is about choosing sides."

Could he actually have read it, or had Crow just briefed him? "That's a bit reductive, but yes, that's one theme," he said. "Can you show evidence of that from the book?"

"*Re-duck-tiv?*"

"It means overly simplified. Like the idea that some groups are inferior to others because of their skin color."

Lance slapped his forehead. "Prof too smart sometimes."

The class cracked up. Alton made a *ha-ha* face and was about to move on, but Lance said, "Wait, I marked it." He motioned for Crow to hand him a tablet, then read, "'*Sooner or later . . . one has to take sides. If one is to remain human.*' He says it a few times throughout."

"Who says it?"

"Fowler."

"Remind the class who Fowler is."

"The limey. The newspaper reporter who wants to stay in Vietnam for that yellow ass."

"What's a *noozepaper*?" One of the new guys blurted out.

"It's a holofeed but printed with ink," Alton said. "And raise your hand to speak, please."

Damien raised his hand.

"Damien?"

"Pyle chooses a side too," Damien said.

"And who's Pyle?"

"The American. The spy."

"And what side does he choose?" Alton asked.

"The white side. I mean . . . the right side."

"Same difference!" Lance sang out, and the class howled.

Oliver shot his hand up. "Pyle chooses to try to enlist local fighters, a 'third force,' to fight the communists," he said. "But the cost is the innocent Vietnamese people who die and are maimed in the bombing, not to mention everything that happens in the war afterward. Greene is definitely saying that this is the *white* side, but he is not by any means saying that the white side is the *right* side."

Alton jumped in before Damien and Oliver could get into it. That was the last thing he needed right now. "How does Fowler react to Pyle?" he asked. "Zane?"

"He kills Pyle," Zane said.

"Why?"

"For that yellow ass. And so he can keep smoking that pipe!" Zane said.

"Wish we could get some of that primo dope up in here," someone said.

"And some primo slush!"

They roared. Alton was losing them, but it didn't matter anymore. The minutes were ticking down to Armageddon. He raised his voice above the din. "Are those the only reasons Fowler lets Pyle die?"

"He hates white people," Damien said. "He hates *himself*."

"I don't think he would have thought about it like that. But he does criticize Western countries for being morally compromised. As well as ignorant and shortsighted. He wants to hold them accountable. For thinking they know better than other people, for thinking that they're *superior*." He wished Simon were here to say it instead of him, so it didn't sound as much like preaching.

"But we *do* know better," said Damien. "Pyle was defending America. Just like we are."

"Pyle wants to stand up for his race. Fowler doesn't. He's weak and a traitor," said Lance.

"Now, *that's* fucking reductive," said Oliver.

Alton shot him a look. "Maybe Fowler has a moral code higher than loyalty to a particular race or nation," Alton said.

Lance was shaking his head. "There is no higher code," he said. "And anyway, he says over and over again that he doesn't have a code."

"Not even at the end?"

"In the end, he just wants the slush. He doesn't care who dies."

"That's a pretty nihilistic reading."

"I'd say realistic."

Before Alton could respond, the door opened, funneling a blast of wind into the shell, and four heavily armored guards entered. "Is there a problem?" Alton asked, startled.

"Just a little extra security," said the commander. "Carry on." They flanked the room, two at the back of the class, between the students and the bookshelves, and two at the entrance. They held web guns across their chests.

Alton met Lance's eyes. The big man's face was tight, but there was a gleam in his eye. He nodded to Alton to continue.

With nothing to lose, Alton decided to crank it up a notch. "All right, then, Damien," he said. "Since you brought it up, why do you think white people are superior?"

He shrugged. "We were just made that way."

He glanced at the guards, but they remained impassive. Behind their armor and face shields, their racial identities were hidden.

"Where's the evidence for that?" Alton asked.

"It's self-evident," said Damien, and the class murmured its agreement.

Now, Oliver spoke up. "Do you know that every human's DNA is all but identical to every other human?" he said. "We share DNA with all life on Earth, even plants. We're just atoms arranged together. How can that be superior?"

Crow looked thoughtful, as though he might finally contribute something, but Lance cut in before he had a chance.

"It's about superior values. About character. About tradition. About what those atoms *become*," Lance said.

"We raise our hands, Lance," Alton said. "When we want to speak."

"Sure thing, Prof." He smiled and stood, raising his arm in an unmistakable Nazi salute. "I've got a question. It's one I asked you before that you never answered," he said.

Alton swallowed. "Go ahead."

"Why is your soft ass in this maximum-security camp? You're not a fighter. You're not anything."

The last comment stung. "That's off topic."

"I'm changing the topic to one that's more relevant."

"Because I volunteered," Alton said. "I thought I could do some good here, help these men see that the world is bigger than what you and Hagen have brainwashed them into accepting. Give them a chance at something different."

"That's bullshit."

"What's your theory, Lance?"

"I think you're a spy, like Pyle. Except not for the right side. For *them*." He jerked a thumb at the guards. "It would explain a lot after we learned about your identity this week."

Identity. For all his assured talk, he really couldn't say what his was. He looked down at the book and smiled despite the impending doom. He loved the way Greene's stubborn romanticism clashed with his cynicism, yielding the occasional passionate outburst of idealism. He might have even described himself this way.

In the charged silence, his voice felt disembodied as he looked to the guard commander and said with complete calm, "They plan to rush the compound after class."

The class exploded, immediately overwhelming the two guards behind them. But the door sentries had time to react. Alton saw a flash, felt his arms and legs seize up as though restrained by invisible ligatures. Whenever he moved, the web glowed, restraining him further.

Everyone not wearing a vest was immobilized. The two free guards pulled their battered colleagues out from under the pile of glowing, twitching limbs. Their masks had been yanked off to reveal one face with a nose gushing dark blood, the other with two black eyes already swelling shut.

The one with the broken nose started kicking at the pile. Even through the shouts and cries, Alton could hear crunching and cracking.

"Enough!" the commander shouted. "Grab Lance. And this one." He pointed at Crow. "And this one." He indicated Damien. "And the professor. Keep the rest webbed until we can get the camp locked down."

"What?" Alton cried. "I haven't done anything!"

But they dragged him outside with the others into a deafening downpour. The guards adjusted the webs so that the prisoners' hands were bound behind them, then marched the men through the black torrent toward the Central Compound.

Alton could hardly see in front of him. But as they neared the compound, he could just make out that the gates were already open. This was odd, but he didn't have time to wonder about it as packs of rabid Nibelungs rushed in from all sides. They surged onto their captors, beating and tearing. Lightning slashed, revealing berserk faces, dark blood washing off them in the rain.

The webs fizzled out, and Alton was free. Before he could react, he was seized again. "Go back and free the others!" Lance yelled above the fray and shoved Alton toward the gates. He hadn't needed Alton's help to get them open after all.

Then Alton saw why Lance hadn't needed him.

Simon stood just inside, near the bodies of the two gate guards that had let Alton through earlier. He held two used syringes, likely the two Alton had seen on his desk that night in the Med-Shell. He must have filled them with poison, then convinced the guards he was giving them flu shots.

As though reading Alton's mind, Simon gave him a contrite shrug. All things being equal, his friend seemed to suggest, he would have preferred a different course of action. Under the circumstances, however, there was little else he could have done.

CHAPTER 12

IT WAS AN oddly familiar feeling, the board tilting down, his head wedged between the two restraints, almost like he was waiting for the dentist. Crow made sure that Alton was secured, then began inspecting the other devices in the room.

He motioned for two Neebs to drag some equipment away from a wall lined with rusty shackles, then he went out again. Alton waited, the blood draining into his face, feeling almost relaxed. At least now the end was known.

Crow returned after a minute, followed by Lance, who wore a blood-splattered web vest stretched to breaking over his massive frame. Two more Neebs dragged a limp body between them, which Crow shackled to the wall. Alton could only tell that it was Miller because of his uniform. His face was an unrecognizable bloody-black welt.

Lance's upside-down face suddenly filled his vision, big-eyed and grinning. "I've never been on this end of it," he said. "Should be fun!"

The blindfold slipped over his eyes. He heard a tap running, a receptacle filling with water, then footsteps and a faint sloshing as it was carried over.

There was no taunt, no clever remark, no warning.

Water splashed on his face, then flooded his nose and mouth. He sputtered and hacked and wheezed, but he couldn't get it out. His brain went red as the alerts started flashing. He tried to flail and claw, but his arms were strapped to his side. His lungs felt like a cave-in.

The pouring stopped as abruptly as it had started, but there was still too much water. His body heaved, his throat and lungs raw and burning as he gagged and sputtered and fought to turn on his side so that he could drain and spit it out. But he was tied too tightly.

Then an echoing voice, hard-edged and cold in the musty chamber.

"You still haven't answered my question."

But no question followed, just another assault. This time, he made the mistake of trying to scream through it, which only opened deeper hollows for the water to fill. The red in his brain faded to black, and he was sure he was going to go under for good, but then the board raised, allowing him to suck in precious air.

He tried weakly to spit, but a puddle of mucus just slopped down his chin. As they tilted the board down again, he retched and gurgled something incomprehensible.

"What's that, Prof?" Lance's mouth was in his ear. Alton heard the first part of the laugh, but the rest was drowned out. Some distant part of him marveled at how cold water could turn his lungs to fire. When it was over this time, he didn't try to talk or move. He could feel the fight leaving him. His ears popped painfully, and he heard Lance saying, "... don't let him go under yet."

The sopping blindfold was pulled off, and the board was tilted up far enough so that Alton's feet touched the ground. As he regained his bearings, spewing water from his mouth and lungs, he saw Miller gaping in fear. The commandant now had a deep gash on his forehead along with the bruises.

Lance came around the board to stand in front of him, nose to nose, and Alton winced at his putrid breath. "Are you a fucking spic spy?" Lance asked. "For that cockroach, Áquilar? That's why she came here, wasn't it?"

Spit slavered down his chin, but he managed to say, "Fuck you."

Lance turned to Crow. "Bring it."

Crow unwound a heavy cable from a cylinder and began to drag it over. Alton thought it looked like a python slithering toward him, thick and slow. He winced as the icy metal teeth bit into the flesh of his left ankle.

"You're soaked through," Lance said. "If he throws that lever, they'll see you light up all the way down in Salt Lake."

Okay!" He realized he didn't really want to die, especially not like this. "My father is Mexican American. That part is true. But I'm no spy. That clueless asshole didn't even know about it." He jerked his chin toward Miller.

"Then why did they bring you here?" He squeezed the clamp deeper. "Why are you in this fucking camp? Last chance!"

Alton felt warm blood seeping from beneath the rusty teeth. He winced as the clamp bit the bone. "You might as well do it," he said. "Because you'll never believe the truth."

"Try me."

"I know Hagen."

Lance stopped squeezing. "What do you mean, you *know* him?"

"We were friends as kids. Somebody must have found out, arrested me, but they never asked me about it. I swear I don't know why." It suddenly occurred to him that maybe Áquilar and her people had been sitting on his secret all along, waiting for the right time to use it.

"Bullshit." He motioned to Crow.

"Wait! Ask Miller! When Áquilar came that night, he was in the room with us."

They looked over at Miller, but he had lost consciousness. Or died.

"What's Hagen's name?" Lance asked. "His real name? You get it wrong, and he flips that switch."

"Alex! Alex Weber."

"You went to school together? Where?"

"North Hollywood."

"Anybody could find that out." He squeezed the teeth of the clamp, and Alton was stunned that he could still find the strength to scream.

"Ki . . . Ki . . . Kiara," he finally managed. "His girlfriend was Kiara Cunningham." He was feeling faint, struggling not to vomit. Her name clutched at him even in that state.

Lance took a step back. He looked genuinely shocked. "Holy shit," he said. "Were you the one he told me about?"

"I have no idea," Alton sputtered. "Maybe."

"What did that bean-eating bitch want with you?"

"She wants to capture Alex alive so she can put him on trial. She wants my help bringing him in."

"*Your* help? What could *you* possibly do?" He laughed like it was the most ridiculous thing he had ever heard. Then his face changed as though an idea had dawned. But before he could articulate it, a claxon began to blare. "They're here," he said. "You two, bring the commandant as a shield. Crow, watch the professor."

The Neebs unshackled Miller while Lance pulled the squelchy

blindfold over Alton's eyes. The alarm blared, piercing and persistent, while Alton lay blind in a haze of pain.

He didn't know how long had passed when he felt the pressure let up, then some of the pain, as the teeth released his ankle. Next, the straps were unbuckled.

Finally, the blindfold came off, and Crow motioned for him to climb down, which he did unsteadily. Crow was holding a guard's sidearm.

Alton put his hands up slowly, not sure if Crow planned to escort him out or shoot him.

But the other man simply lowered the gun and nodded toward the exit.

Alton looked around. Was it a trick? The room was empty except for the two of them.

"W . . . why?" Alton asked him.

"Sooner or later, one has to take sides," Crow said. "If one is to remain human."

CHAPTER 13

OUTSIDE, HE BENT over and gagged up the last of the water, which was swallowed up by the pouring rain. Nibelungs with stolen weapons and gear bolted past him toward the landing platform at the north end of the compound. Even through the clamor, he could hear the excitement in their voices, the elation of newfound freedom.

Their euphoria lit him up too. After years in a depressive haze, he was surprised by how fiercely he wanted to live. And he knew exactly what he wanted to live for: to get out of here, find Alex, and kill him. He would do whatever it took to achieve this. It felt invigorating to finally have a purpose in life.

The Nibelungs, hell-bent on their mission, failed to notice him snake along the wall of Intake, then slip past them back toward the camp. He passed the bodies of Miller's men—pale and bent and oddly clean-looking, the blood and viscera washing away in the storm—and stopped to pull the web-vest, rain jacket, and helmet off one of them. With the rain out of his eyes, he could clearly see the lights of incoming ships no more than a few minutes away. *Shit, I'm out of time.* Just as panic began to seize him, an insane idea struck.

He hobbled toward the weightlifting area on his mangled ankle, grabbed a small barbell plate, then looked around to make sure no one was watching. He spotted the Civvies huddled together in barracks alcoves, gazing anxiously toward the compound. He hoped they would be okay.

He also hoped he would never see them again as he splashed through freezing mud to the equipment shed. He didn't pause to measure the distance as he approached, just clutched the weight with both hands and smashed it down onto the heavy lock until the pieces fell away into the muck.

Inside, the top setting on the helmet lamp blinded him, but a middle setting cast a soft glow. He wrapped as much of the rope piled in the corner as he could around his chest. Next, he hung a grappling hook from his belt. As he did, two enormous *boom*s rattled the camp. A third boom almost knocked him over. No time to find more toys. He needed to go *right now*.

He hit the main drag to find the Nibelungs raising an unholy din of fear and rage as they fled a phalanx of stun-drones. Every instinct told him to retreat, but if he didn't reach the Ed-Shell before the battle engulfed him, he might not have another chance. Just as he took off again, another explosion sent him sprawling.

He raised his head, spitting mud, and was transfixed by a phantasma of light and motion. Electric webs crackled, and blue stun energy lifted men off their feet and *whomp*ed them onto the ground again. Sprays of burning aspirate caused the men to claw at their eyes and skin.

Three Nibelungs had climbed up onto a barracks roof, and Alton watched as they sprinted across it and leapt toward a hovering drone. One missed it entirely and went hurtling into the fray, but the other two grabbed hold, and their combined weight began to force it down.

When it neared the ground, more crazed Neebs pulled it in and hammered it to pieces. The drone had one last defense at its disposal, an earsplitting alarm that forced the men to stumble back and clutch the sides of their head.

Alton jammed his fingers in his ears, but from out of nowhere a hot white blast obliterated the drone. A moment later, Lance emerged from the smoke, wielding an enormous railgun. He spotted Alton, and their eyes met just as the skirmish closed in around him again.

Seeing Lance propelled him to his feet. He lurched through the entrance to the Ed-Shell, not altogether sure in his dazed state if the man he saw before him was real.

"What?" Alton yelled.

"Your leg!" Simon yelled back.

He looked down to see that he had fallen onto the grappling hook. A barbed spear had plunged deep into his left thigh, and his pants were dark with blood. Simon sat him down and peered at the wound. Then he went over to the American flag on its stand in the corner, yanked it down, and tore a huge strip from it.

"Bite down on something."

Alton stuffed a fistful of the nylon rope into his mouth as Simon twisted the spear down and out. Cold air rushed into the wound, and Alton was surprised it didn't hurt more. Maybe he was just getting used to pain.

But then Simon cinched the wound with the strip of flag, and his howl was deafening. Simon wiped the blood from his hands on the tattered flag and heaved it away.

"I have to get out of here," Alton managed to say.

"You need real treatment. More than I can give you here," Simon said. "But I don't know how we can get to the Med-Shell through this madness."

Rage gave Alton the strength to yell. "Madness that *you* caused! Why did you help him?"

"The bastards took everything from me, Alton. I have the moral right to take it back."

"But you murdered those men! You betrayed everything you swore to uphold!"

"It's not murder when you're at war."

"Funny, that's exactly what Lance said."

But before Simon could respond, the door exploded, and then his chest cavity. The blast sizzled over Alton's head, along with an enormous flood of viscera. Had he been standing, he would have been cut in half as well.

He wiped thick blood from his eyes and spat out Simon. He might have vomited, but there was no time because Lance was lumbering through the wreckage with the railgun. Once inside, he stepped over Simon's split-open rib cage and pointed the comically huge weapon at Alton.

"Where are you going with that?" he asked, nodding toward the rope. "You're going to *him*, aren't you?" He leaned into Alton's face, his red eyes bulging. "*Aren't you?*"

Alton threw himself flat on the ground.

"Coward," Lance said. But only because he hadn't seen the drone silently appear in the crater that he had blown into the building. A bolt of cobalt energy launched him into the east wall, his vest and armor crackling as they absorbed it.

Figuring he was next, Alton rolled away, sending crippling pain through his thigh as he did. But he stopped when he realized that the drone had become wedged in the crevice. He was riveted by how alive it seemed, its roving eye scanning for targets as it tried to free itself.

Lance meanwhile had flattened himself against the north wall, out of its sight, and was edging back around with his railgun. But the drone registered his presence and hosed the area with burning aspirant.

"Motherfucker!" Lance screamed as the mist enveloped him. He lurched forward and fired blind. One blast opened a gaping hole in the ceiling; the other hit the drone square.

The roving eye pulsed and strobed, then went dark as the dead craft slumped into the breach, crumpling the shell underneath.

Lance dropped to his knees, hacking and coughing, clawing at his eyes.

"It's burning through your armor! Take it off; take it off!" Alton cried.

Crazed and blind, Lance ripped away his vest and armor, shedding his weapons and gear as he did. As soon as he dropped the web gun, Alton grabbed it and fired. Lance fell back in helpless agony, unable to move his arms to reach his burning face, while Alton exchanged the web gun for the railgun, staggering under its heft.

"Cockroach!" Lance raged. "You tricked me."

"And you killed Simon."

"At least the doc finally did something for his people," Lance said. "It's more than they'll say for you." He spat glistening orange phlegm.

"Simon had nothing but contempt for you. He was just desperate to go home." He winced at what was left of his former friend, imagining his widow alone in the world somewhere. "And I've got a different legacy in mind for myself." He turned to go.

When Lance next spoke, it was in a beseeching tone that Alton had never heard from him. "I *have* to get to him," Lance said. "*Please* take me with you. You'll be rewarded."

He turned back. "After what you did to me?"

"I didn't know you knew him!"

"What the hell difference does that make? I'm a human being, Lance, which is more than anybody's ever going to say about you."

"I don't want to be left behind," he whimpered. "Please."

"What about your army of children? Going to leave them behind to face the fallout on their own?"

"They fought for the cause, and they'll be remembered with honor."

"Cause, my ass. This was never anything but a means to get your*self* out."

And then he was outside the camp heading for the cliff edge in the raging storm.

PART II

CHAPTER 14

"HURRY UP," SAID Lena. "Do we have to go through this every Saturday?"

"I'm ready!" Alton protested, emerging from his room and slinging his backpack over his shoulder.

She gave him one of her looks. "What's in the bag?"

"Stuff I got at the Stalls."

"Leave it here."

"Why?"

"Because God knows Bernardo has more than enough for both of you."

You mean don't let his mom see how shitty my stuff is.

"And stop pouting." She looked at him as though she didn't recognize him anymore. "You're getting too old for toys anyway."

It was already fiercely hot in the Valley at seven o'clock in the morning as they made their way through the crumbling, trash-strewn streets, trying to avoid the ever-sprawling encampments. Because they were poor and he was getting old enough to realize that his mother was unlikely to lift them out of their situation, Alton sometimes feared they might end up here. The thought made him pick up his pace, as though lingering there might seal their fate.

As he hurried along, sweat leaking down his neck, he glanced with envy at the new freeway system soaring above them. The rich, like Bernardo and his family, floated above the city; everybody else took the Hyperloop, which they arrived at after a few more minutes of walking.

They pushed through the crowded station, shuffled down two flights to the platform, and queued up for a pod, which accommodated thirty-five and left every two and a half minutes. When their pod arrived, they settled into their seats near the front of the long, cylindrical cone. His mother seemed dispirited as usual, but Alton loved riding the 'loop. There were no windows, so you couldn't estimate speed, but the descent into the dark and the vague feeling of floating let him pretend that he was sailing through the solar system. Also, the pods were air-conditioned.

They emerged after a brief journey into a lush neighborhood. Beyond the pleasure he took from the ride itself, Alton looked forward to visiting the big house in the nice area of town where his mother worked, which he had done almost every Saturday for the last few years.

At fourteen, he was old enough now to stay at home by himself, but he liked to visit Bernardo, his only friend. And he enjoyed coming to East Los Angeles, with its clean streets empty of tents, bright refurbished murals, and bustling businesses with their cheerful storefronts.

The 'loop station let out near Belvedere Park Lake. Lena had sometimes let Alton play by the lake when he was younger, until she had had enough of the well-off mothers giving them disapproving stares. Lena, still young and slender with long sandy hair, was keen to avoid other kinds of stares as well. Alton was old enough now that both kinds of looks made him feel ashamed.

They walked to the east side of the little lake, shimmering in the oppressive morning sun, and then hastened south down Atlantic to Sixth Street, where the old neighborhoods had been "relocated" so the new estates could be put in near the new City Hall and the growing government complex.

Transplanted trees towered along the avenues, creating lovely shade and privacy that contrasted Alton and Lena's sunbaked tower, with its congestion and noise and foul smells and sense of despair.

When she had first started to bring him along, Alton had asked her a few times why they couldn't live over here. "I wouldn't live here even if we *could*," she snarled. He had been bewildered by her response.

When they came up the sidewalk to the Torreses' estate, three stories and set back from the street on a half-acre of landscaped grounds, Bernardo was already playing out front. When he saw them, he pushed his thick glasses up his nose and waved. Alton waved back.

As they climbed the steep drive, a mini-rocket spurted straight up, hissing and spiraling through the trees. At its apex, the capsule lifted off, sprouted a parachute, and came rocking down. Meanwhile, the rocket itself began a flight down its original path, slowing, then settling onto the platform Bernardo had unfolded onto the lawn.

"Whoa!" Alton said. Bernardo grinned, beaming, and pushed his glasses up again. It was surprising how often they fell down his nose, considering how bulbous it was. "I just built this one," he said.

"Do it again!"

But before he could, Bernardo's mother, Camellia, appeared. She was still draped in a silky robe, open at the neck, but had applied elegant makeup and brushed out her dark, lustrous hair.

"Breakfast first, Bernardo," she said.

Bernardo struggled to his feet on ungainly legs. Alton suppressed a smile. He loved the kid, but he was such a doofus.

"What about Alton, Mom?"

"Are you hungry, Alton?"

"He's not *hungry*," Lena said. "But if he would like to join Bernardo, that's fine with me."

While Lena polished the cherrywood balustrade in the foyer, the boys sat at an island in a palatial kitchen. Alton marveled at the platter of glistening orange slices, kiwi, and strawberries. The only time he saw fruit this fresh was at Bernardo's house. The fruit hawked at the Stalls was as crummy and ancient as everything else.

"Hello, Alton!" Bernardo's father, Fernando, boomed as he entered the kitchen. Alton noticed how handsome he looked in his sleek suit. "How's things?"

Alton mumbled a shy response.

"My dad's company gave him a prototype of the new augmentation," Bernardo said, eggs spilling from his mouth. He nodded toward some glasses on the counter.

"Yeah, check this out," said Fernando. He put on the glasses, and images immediately flitted across the kitchen. Fernando made some adjustments to center the image, then cycled through content, which blazed in a riot of high-res color and 3D motion. He paused on a video of a dog farting and jacked the volume. He and the boys cracked up. Camellia sighed.

Alton was impressed. "Is everything inside the glasses?"

"No, it's tiny silicone implants," Fernando said. "Just inside of the skin, so they're easy to remove. I can access and see everything in my own vision. The glasses are just for projection. But the engineers told me that a few versions from now, my *eyes* will be able to do the projecting. It will be virtual reality without the hardware. Pretty cool, huh?"

"If you think becoming somebody's Frankenstein experiment is cool," Camellia said, sipping her espresso from its tiny mug. "What happens if something goes wrong? I hope you don't expect *me* to support you."

"Dad said I can get them too!" Bernardo exclaimed, and Camellia gave her husband an evil eye.

"In time," said Fernando. "The implants can't be made until your brain and eyes have mostly stopped growing. By that time, you'll be almost old enough to make your own choices."

"I want to get it!" Alton blurted out.

"It's very expensive," Camellia said.

Fernando gave her a look. "But maybe someday. All right, I have to go!"

"Aren't you forgetting something?" she asked.

"Oh, right! Bernardo, since I'll be traveling on your birthday, I want to give this to you now."

He put the glasses back on and projected a holo-vid from Cosmost, which played dramatic launch footage followed by grinning space tourists floating weightless through their kitchen.

After a minute, the CEO of the company appeared on-screen. "Hello, Bernardo. We can't take you to space until you're sixteen, but for your fourteenth, we'd like to invite you to view a launch here at Cosmost. Happy birthday!"

"Wow!" Bernardo squealed. "Thanks, Dad!" He ran over and hugged his father. As it was the only reality he had known, Alton didn't often think of not having a father in his life. But he felt the absence now as he watched them embrace.

"Can Alton come?"

"Of course!" said Fernando. "I expected he would!"

"Back to the launchpad!" Bernardo cried, and the two ran out of the room before Alton doubled back, remembering that he should thank them.

As he neared the kitchen, he heard Camellia say, "Should you really encourage them?"

He stopped and listened.

"Bernardo needs friends," said Fernando. "And Alton is a good kid."

"They'll be at different schools next year."

"You and I were living in different states when we started dating."

She sighed. "I'm just saying, sooner or later, Bernardo is going to run in his own circles. Private school, college prep. Clubs that require parents to *pay* for trips, equipment."

"We can worry about that later. For now, please ask Lena if he can go. I'm sure she'll be fine with it."

"Of course she will," Camellia sniffed. "It's free."

"Jesus, Cami. I remember when you used to resent your mother for that kind of snobbery."

"She's not perfect, but I've come to realize that she recognizes the natural order of things."

"I'll never understand how you can think that way after what happened to you."

"It's *because* of what happened to me that I think that way," she said. "The gringos are simply reaping what they sowed. It's our turn now."

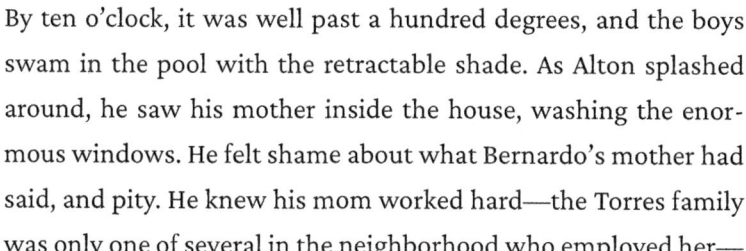

By ten o'clock, it was well past a hundred degrees, and the boys swam in the pool with the retractable shade. As Alton splashed around, he saw his mother inside the house, washing the enormous windows. He felt shame about what Bernardo's mother had said, and pity. He knew his mom worked hard—the Torres family was only one of several in the neighborhood who employed her—but he also felt resentment for what they didn't have.

When she had begun working for the Torreses two years earlier, Alton had switched to the junior high in the neighborhood, which was attended by mostly upper-middle-class Hispanic kids. He had been an outcast.

Even though he was from one of the wealthiest families in the neighborhood, Bernardo was also an outcast. He was teased because he was unathletic, because he could be slow on the uptake, because his defective genes forced him to wear glasses when most kids could get laser, and because he had befriended Alton, the outsider.

One day at recess, when the bullying was especially bad, Alton escaped to the empty fields behind the main buildings. Kids were supposed to stay in sight of the teachers, so Alton was surprised to see the typically obedient Bernardo at the far end of the field, his back up against a fence, engrossed in his VR set. Alton went and stood over him. "How come you never leave your room when my mom brings me over?"

Bernardo shrugged but didn't look up. Alton could see the images flitting across the insides of the glasses as Bernardo worked the console controls.

"What are you playing?"

"It's called Urban War," he said. "You can play in all these different cities. Damascus. Peshawar. Caracas. Chicago."

"It looks cool."

"Or..." He took off the glasses and handed them to Alton. "You can put it in AR mode and create your own battlefield."

Alton slid them on and broke into a grin. Bernardo had overlayed the game onto the school grounds and made the other students into enemy fighters. Some of their most hated classmates lay in puddles of their own blood, limbs askew.

"They make fun of me for wearing glasses, but I've been able to scan them all," he said. "Then I just program the scans into the game. You want to watch me waste these dicks?"

"Hell yeah I do," said Alton, and he squeezed in beside Bernardo.

CHAPTER 15

LENA AND ALTON arrived home in the late afternoon. Lena went straight for the vodka and disappeared into the bathroom for an hour. Alton went to the window and stared into the brown haze. Their twenty-story garden tower, one of a cluster in North Hollywood, had been built for low-income families who agreed to maintain the gardens that grew between floors.

In theory, it had been a great deal for residents. Spend a few hours working the gardens each week; take enough food for your family; send the rest to market to generate revenue for the city, and keep the operation running. Technologically, it had been a snap; logistically, less so. The process of delivering all the materials efficiently—as well as harvesting, collecting, packing, delivering, and transporting the crops—was not as well thought out. Nor were issues of labor organization and training.

Then there was laziness, theft, and the inevitable black market once floors became devoted to growing strains of MJX. The law had shut it down, leaving the faint stench of rotting vegetation even fifteen years later.

The floors were chained off and forbidden, though one day, when the lifts were out, Alton had been taking the stairs and came across an open floor. He knew he shouldn't hang around, but he was entranced by the graffiti that gang members and street artists had plastered across the concrete walls.

The sun glowed orange against the color and detail, layer against layer of language and symbol that he didn't understand, except of course for the swastikas. Everyone knew what those were.

Bernardo had been to the building just once, when he had come to collect Alton for some activity. Lena, of course, had freaked out, jumping at the sound of the buzzer and flicking on the monitor to reveal Bernardo and his driver, Ron, standing in the breezeway.

"You told him to come up? Why didn't you just go down to the street?"

He felt the familiar fear of not understanding why she was angry.

"God damn it," she said. "Get your stuff. He's not coming in."

Lena buttoned the neck of her shirt and opened the door, blocking the entrance. "Hey, Bernardo," she sighed. "Ron."

Ron nodded at her behind his sunglasses. He ran security for the Torres family, and Alton was sure he had escorted Bernardo upstairs because of their neighborhood.

"Come *on*, Alton!" Lena said, and she turned to reveal their unit. Alton would always remember how Bernardo's face changed when he glimpsed the tiny, dank interior, the ungenerous light, the secondhand furniture, the untidiness bordering on uncleanliness.

His friend wouldn't say anything about it. He was too polite. But from that day on, Alton would see his home through Bernardo's eyes: shabby and woeful—a place where poor white people lived.

"What are you daydreaming about now?"

He turned from the window to find her in her robe, unwrapping a frozen pizza.

"Nothing."

"I don't want you going to that launch viewing with Bernardo."

"What? Why not?"

"Because I'm tired of them treating us like a charity case."

"But, Mom, I didn't even ask to go! It's his birthday! He wants me there!"

"Tell him you can't make it. And don't argue with me. I don't have it in me right now."

You never have it in you, he thought. He started to stomp out, then spun back. "Dad would have let me go," he said.

She slid the pizza into the wall-cooker. "If your dad had stuck around, you would have never *met* Bernardo," she said. "Because I wouldn't have had to work as their fucking servant."

Alton slammed the door to his room and fumed for a few minutes. He lay in bed and thought of how he could run away, where he could stay if he did. Would he end up in an encampment on the street below? And if he did, would it really be that much worse than living with *her*?

He got out of bed and pulled a dusty case down from the top shelf of his closet. The vinyl was cracked and peeling. The rusty hinges squeaked as he opened them. Inside was an ancient trumpet, the platinum-colored brass tarnished and flaking. It was the one thing he had from his father.

He still had no idea why his mother had given it to him when she had purged everything else of him from their lives. He inspected it again for clues, wondering, as he so often did, where the man was and why he had abandoned them.

He closed the case and put it back, then flopped on his bed. He wouldn't argue with her, he decided. But he was going to the launch viewing, one way or another.

CHAPTER 16

A WEEK LATER, he and Bernardo reclined into air-conditioned luxury behind deep-tinted windows as the Torres family cruiser took the steep onramp up onto the new 111 freeway system. Alton had only been on the RFF—Rich Folks' Freeway, as it was unaffectionately known—a few times, but he loved skimming the friction-lite plasphalt™, as their fellow travelers flashed by in silvery blurs, almost as if underwater. The near silence completed the effect.

He had told Camellia that Lena had given him permission, and scheduled Ron to pick him up after Lena had left for the day. She would discover his deception soon enough, but he didn't care. This was worth being grounded for a couple of months, even if he did have to sit around the apartment with her all day.

Now, they sped northwest up and out over the Valley. As they began their descent on the far side, the deep blue of the ocean came into view, glimmering to the horizon. Once his eyes adjusted, he could see that Cosmost spread out almost to the sea. Several rockets, topped with glinting crew capsules, perched between sleek towers designed to redirect lightning.

Ron dropped them out front and told them to meet back no later than 5:00 p.m. This would give them time after the viewing for burgers and to browse the gift shops so that Bernardo could spend his birthday money.

They dashed into a vast lobby crowned by a shaded skylight a hundred feet up. Floating holo-projections advertised Cosmost tourist experiences. There was the "bargain" suborbital trip, which would stay just within Earth's atmosphere, as well as an Orbital "Loop," which provided patrons one full turn about the planet. Then there were tiers of ever-pricier orbital vacations, including an inflatable orbiting "hotel" that allowed tourists a week or more in space.

The most expensive—because of the fuel costs and the bragging rights—was the Rocket to the Moon, a jaunt around Earth's satellite and back, which lasted just under a week. This was the Everest of space tourism for the heartiest and most in-shape of adventure junkies. Alton gazed at the expeditions in awe and vowed to do them all one day. Today, though, they were there to watch, and Bernardo was tugging him toward the viewing section.

"Didn't your dad say you were supposed to check in with somebody?" Alton asked.

"I think that's for lunch tickets or something. We'll do it later. Come on!"

There was an elevator, but they sprinted up the carpeted ramp instead, circling past a bustling cafe until they were out of breath, giggly, and dizzy. At the top, a bony twentysomething greeter scanned their virtual tickets and pointed down the hall to two viewing rooms. "You can choose either one," he said. "I'll be down before the launch to give a short presentation."

They charged down to the first entrance to find four rows of seven seats situated in front of a viewing window. Alton was dismayed by how far away the launchpad seemed. He wanted to breathe the fumes, to be close enough for ignition flames to singe his nose hairs, but this wasn't much better than watching the holo-projection at Bernardo's house.

Worse, the place was full of old people, and the codgers had their sweaters and lunch bags draped everywhere. Alton looked at Bernardo, who seemed equally annoyed. "Let's try the next one," he said.

But an even more obnoxious sight greeted them: the same setup, this time overrun by a gaggle of little kids romping over their parents.

"What the fuck?" Bernardo said, his voice squeaking into a higher register. Alton was taken aback. He had never heard Bernardo drop an f-bomb before. He pulled his friend back into the corridor.

"Some birthday," Bernardo said. His eyes moistened behind the Coke-bottle glasses.

Alton wasn't going to pout about it, but Bernardo was right. This was not worth whatever draconian punishment his mother would dream up for his lying to her. If this was to be his last hurrah for a while, they needed to go out in style.

As he thought about options, his eyes drifted down the corridor. "I wonder where this goes," he said, nodding to where the corridor continued on the other side of some theater ropes.

Bernardo shrugged. "Let's find out."

They ducked under the ropes and followed the hallway around in a long curve. Just as it seemed without promise, they came to a door emblazoned with a sign that made them both smile: *To the Roof.*

It was two narrow flights of clattering metal steps to a hatch. Bernardo climbed out first. When Alton stuck his head into a blinding burst of hot wind, he wondered if the rocket was already taking off.

But it was just climate-change-baked Los Angeles in late spring. As his eyes adjusted to the glare, he saw Bernardo leaning over a guardrail. He joined his friend to find a ladder that led down onto a platform. Another ladder hung over the far edge of the platform.

"I bet that second one goes all the way to the tarmac," Alton said.

Bernardo again went first. As Alton straddled the rail to follow, the roof hatch burst open and a security guard emerged, "Hey!" he yelled.

"Go!" Alton cried. He clambered down a few rungs and then leaped the rest of the way. Ignoring the pain blazing up his shins, he sprinted after Bernardo, easily overtaking him. He was down the next ladder in a blur but had to wait for his friend. Security intercepted them before Bernardo even reached the ground.

The guards took them to an office in the main building, where they sat facing a broad desk. Bernardo looked rabbit-scared. "My mom is going to be so pissed," he whispered. Alton didn't even want to think about how his own mother might react.

After a few unbearable minutes, a sinewy middle-aged man in a sky-blue Cosmost flight jacket entered. He sat and appraised them from across his desk. "You boys trying to get sucked into an engine?" he asked. "That's a good way to go home in a coffin."

"Actually," Bernardo said, without looking up. "I think we would just evaporate into a fine mist."

The man suppressed a smile.

"We were just trying to get a better look at the launch, sir. We didn't mean any harm," Alton said. "It's his birthday," he added, as though that should explain it.

"Well, I think you can do better than that."

"We know, sir. We're sorry." Alton was starting to feel annoyed. This was Bernardo's trip. Why was he doing all the apologizing?

"No, I mean, I think we can get you a better view than that. As long as it's his birthday."

Alton and Bernardo exchanged glances.

"I'm Clay Prendergast."

Bernardo found his voice. "You're the man my dad asked us to meet."

Prendergast nodded. "The real birthday surprise," he said, "is that your father arranged for you two to be on a suborbital launch today. That's why you were supposed to meet me first instead of tear-assing around the complex."

Alton initially didn't process what the man was saying. Slow-on-the-uptake Bernardo reached comprehension liftoff first. He sprang out of his seat. "We're going into space?"

Prendergast smiled and nodded. "Well . . . suborbital space. If you want to, I mean."

"I thought we had to be sixteen?" Alton said.

He handed them each a badge with their name and picture. "Today you *are* sixteen."

CHAPTER 17

WHEN HE WAS older and understood more about how the world worked, Alton wondered how Bernardo's father had contrived such a thing. Because Prendergast was risking his career by breaking age statutes for space travel, Alton doubted he had been persuaded by a simple bribe.

More likely, Fernando had promised political connections to Cosmost for the coming years. It wasn't yet public knowledge, but Fernando was facilitating the reelection campaign of a young state congressman by the name of Maximillian Guerrero.

Like the sleek vessels out on the platform, Guerrero's career would have a rocket ascent. He would run for governor of California within the decade and eventually be in the position to help Cosmost get the biggest private piece of the Mars colony missions.

But even if Alton had had an inkling of how their passage had been arranged, there was no time to think about it. They needed to get geared up ASAP so they didn't hold up the launch and further inconvenience the other tourists who had paid a premium.

And so Prendergast's ponytailed blonde assistant, Emily, whisked them to an equipment room where she gave them jackets and helmets fitted with bite straps and chin guards. The jackets were sleek and satiny like the one Prendergast wore, adorned with

Cosmost patches on the breast and shoulders. But these were dark navy, almost black, so that the blue showed only when the light caught them just so.

The jacket took Alton's breath away. The feel of it. The look of it as he admired himself in the mirror, turning this way and that. But mainly the *idea* of himself in it. As he drew himself up to his full height and set his jaw, he very much liked this vision of himself.

He caught Emily smiling at him, and maybe she was mocking his preening, but he didn't care. For once, he wasn't embarrassed. For once, he didn't feel inferior to everybody else in the room. This was somebody that even his father might want to know.

Once provisioned, they hustled down the corridor to the briefing room, where a balding man with astronaut wings on his lapel waited in front of a holo-projection of the words *Your Suborbital Spaceflight* revolving around a three-dimensional Earth.

He introduced himself as Commander Chuck, and he started with the safety portion: where to sit, and how to sit, and where to put your hands, and how to be careful while floating about the cabin when they reached zero g, and what to do if you needed to puke (just let it out, and a ceiling vacuum would suck it out of the cabin). He identified the emergency exits and gave instructions on what to do in case of smoke, fire, loss of cabin pressure, sea splashdown, etc.

Alton was far too excited to process much. And he was mesmerized by Commander Chuck's astronaut wings, which glittered in the shifting light of the projection. He could only imagine how smart a pair of those beauties would look on his Cosmost jacket just above a patch embroidered with his name. But they wouldn't be merely cosmetic. They would be earned during a brilliant career as a space explorer.

He paid more attention when Commander Chuck got to the technical details, even though he and Bernardo had memorized most of them long before. The ship would shoot to 150 miles above sea level, traveling at 1.7 kilometers per second. Alton knew they would technically be in space once they reached sixty-two miles above sea level—a boundary known as the Kármán line.

But that altitude, though affording an impressive view, wouldn't display the curvature of the Earth that astronauts got (the International Space Station, then in its second iteration, orbited from about 250 miles up). Due to advances in rocket technology, space tourism was less expensive than it had once been, but it was by no means cheap. People who could afford it expected the vistas to be sufficiently awe-inspiring.

When they reached the intended altitude, Commander Chuck continued, the engines would cut, but the thrust would keep moving them upward for about ten minutes. During this final phase of ascent, they could float around the zero-g cabin and take advantage of the capsule's generous viewing ports to admire the curvature of the Earth against space, the sun, and distant stars.

The moon, alas, would be out of sight behind Earth, but they were more than welcome to book a future flight! They were also welcome to take as many pictures and videos as they wanted, though onboard cameras would take plenty as well (available for extra charge, of course).

Once the ship neared its apex, the floating and viewing portion would end, and they would strap in for their free fall back to Earth. Except, instead of the rocket melting and falling into the sea like Icarus, the rocket booster would fire up again and lower them gently to the landing area.

"If only Daedalus had used a staged combustion cycle instead of wax," Commander Chuck said, grinning. A few of his audience chuckled.

"But seriously," Commander Chuck said. "You have nothing to worry about, even if I pass out while we're up there, which I have never done. The world's best AI runs the whole show."

The briefing thus concluded, the tourists signed another round of liability waivers. Giddy and terrified, they followed Commander Chuck and Emily out of the room and down a long corridor at the end of which blinding light poured through double doors.

It was so bright that Alton, like Icarus, felt beckoned into the heart of the sun itself. His heart pounded in fear and awe. His mouth was dry, and he was seized by the impulse to flee back to the safety of the museum and the cafe.

But he was being carried along now, not just by the momentum of the group but by forces of destiny, he imagined. And who was he to subvert the will of destiny? This was the first step, after all, if he wanted his own astronaut wings, if he wanted to travel to another world.

Just before the exit onto the tarmac, they pit-stopped at the "last bathroom on earth" to relieve their anxiety and morning fluids. And then, before Alton even knew what was happening, they were loaded into a waiting transport that sped them across the sunbaked asphalt to the launchpad, the rocket looming ever larger as they approached. The snub-nosed craft was nothing compared to the skyscraping grandeur of the Saturn V, still one of the largest rockets ever built.

But it was imposing enough for Alton to decide that this was a very stupid thing they were doing. He looked over at Bernardo, who didn't appear frightened at all. In fact, he was absolutely beaming. And if that four-eyed trundle-bum wasn't scared, Alton wasn't about to admit he was.

Then they were up the elevator and being led across the glinting metal catwalk one at a time to the open capsule hatch. When Alton stepped over the threshold, he was alarmed by how small the space was. This was not a place you would want to be trapped with eight other people.

Fortunately, the six floor-to-roof windows calmed his claustrophobia. He took his seat, which was reclined almost to the floor, attached to a metal scissor mechanism that he remembered would dampen the g-forces as they hurtled back to Earth.

As the others filed in and began to situate themselves, Alton located all the sills and handholds to grab as they floated about in zero gravity. He was suddenly afraid of being completely helpless up there—of being the one fool who couldn't even get weightlessness right.

The impulse struck him again to flee to sturdy ground. But everybody was onboard now, and Commander Chuck and Emily were strapping them in.

"I think these are too tight," he told Emily, his mouth so dry he could barely get the words out.

"Take deep breaths," she said, which was impossible, as she was tightening them even further. "It's not much different from being on an airplane."

But he had never been on an airplane. It wasn't something his mother could afford, not that they had anywhere to go.

Still, he wanted to please Emily and her reassuring smile, and so he concentrated on breathing, realizing as he did that the tightness was not from the harness but from his chest heaving against it—and for all he knew, the heart that was slamming against that. He tried to focus on the soothing blue LED lighting.

He suddenly remembered that Bernardo was with him, and he looked across the capsule to see him grinning like a maniac. *He's too dumb to be scared*, he thought, then chided himself for his unkindness. Alton was just angry at himself for his own fear. He forced himself to feel gratitude instead. Bernardo and his family were making this possible, after all.

Once she had cinched them in, Emily wished them a wonderful voyage and ducked out. The hatch sealed behind her bobbing ponytail, and they sat in silence. Alton noticed that even Commander Chuck was completely still in his seat. At a certain point, he supposed there was nothing to do but give it up to God.

After a while, his eyelids grew heavy, and just as he felt he might slip into sleep, the ship rumbled slightly. The gentle harmony of whirring and beeps and hissings that followed fully awakened him again. The cabin lights dimmed to a faint glimmer, and a soothing voice came over a speaker: "Passengers, prepare for liftoff."

Thinking back on it, Alton couldn't remember if he felt it or heard it first: the roar of the rockets as they blasted off or the sensation as though a sumo wrestler had plopped down on him. It was a moot point in the moment because he could only lie there, pinned, and feel the immense propulsion, the *whoosh* and thunder of the engines, his stomach seizing up, and a vibration deep in his loins. He was utterly at the mercy of forces beyond him but knew he could do nothing was, conversely, freeing.

As the sense of peace overtook him, he became aware of his environment and the other passengers. He became conscious of the light outside the windows: blinding white, then aquamarine, then violet, then the blackest black he had ever known.

They continued upward, a stretching and blurring of experience so indeterminate that he later realized that he lost his sense of time. The launch could have been a minute or an hour or a year. It could have been forever. And in the way that it untethered him from reality, he wished that it had been.

Objectively, the joyride to the heavens lasted just over eight minutes and then abruptly terminated. If it had felt calm and quiet as they waited for liftoff, it was nothing compared to the utter silence and stillness once the engine cut. It was almost as though he could feel the vacuum pressing in on them.

Then he began to hear little noises in the craft. He was aware of a retching sound and then a faint whirring as someone's vomit was sucked out of the cabin. This visceral human response revived his senses enough that he became more aware of where they were and what they were doing.

He turned his head to face the window to his right and began to make out stars in the inky depths. He was transfixed by their proximity. On the ground, they were something he could never hope to touch, bound as he was by Earth's soil, choked as he was by her dust. Here, they seemed awake and alive.

He was so mesmerized, it was a moment before he realized that Commander Chuck was hovering next to him, his big white face in his helmet rising over Alton like the moon. He gestured to Alton's harness.

At first, Alton didn't understand, but when he saw the others rising from their seats like tentative ghosts at a first haunting, he nodded, and Commander Chuck unstrapped him and drifted away.

Alton's arms began to levitate, then his butt was off the seat, and it was like floating in a still lake without water. The others had lifted their face shields, and as he did the same, he could hear their expressions of wonderment.

He pushed his hands downward in a backward swimming motion until he was able to grab a ceiling handhold, then maneuvered himself into a vertical position, overcorrecting so that he gently bumped the window behind him.

Once he felt confident enough, he pushed off and went gliding to the other side. He bumped a few of the other passengers on his journey to the opposite windows, but they just laughed and met his eyes and shook their heads in amazement.

Alton began to feel gratitude, which deepened as he floated to the side facing Earth. He drank in the glowing orb, the vague clay-colored shape of a continent half-shrouded by clouds, and the blue line of the precious atmosphere protecting the most valuable thing in the universe.

He thought for a moment of his mother down there in their tiny, drab apartment, the ugly, aimless sprawl of greater Los Angeles, the restrictions and limitations on his life.

He forced it from his head. He would be back there soon enough and wanted to be present in the moment. He turned to find Bernardo had bobbed over with a giant grin. Alton held up a hand for a high five, and they cracked up when the lack of gravity made them miss by a foot.

Alton suddenly felt an immense love for this kid who had befriended him when no one else had, who had stood up for him, who had never once judged or criticized him, who was giving him this greatest of all gifts.

He vowed to think better of his friend, to no longer secretly call him unkind names, or be impatient with him, or to feel superior when, deep down, he knew he had no reason to. *Things are going to change now*, he thought. *Everything will change.*

Now, Commander Chuck was indicating where they could see Mars, and Alton and Bernardo fluttered over a few windows to find a glowing orange speck against the black, just a little bigger than it was from the ground.

Let's keep going, Alton thought. They had no supplies, no food, no fuel. Still, he prayed as hard as he could. *Please just keep going.*

But when he opened his eyes, it was time to strap in for the return trip. As he placed his palm on the frigid window to say goodbye, he felt crushed by grief. He was too young to understand his feelings in the moment, but as he thought about it over the years, he realized that space was the ultimate fresh start, a place where disappointments and failures and unmet expectations had absolutely no meaning. A place where not having a father might not matter that much.

CHAPTER 18

THE RETURN HAD been more uncomfortable and more frightening. The heavier g-forces now felt like four men squatting on his chest instead of just one. Orange flares swelled into molten lava outside their window until he was certain they would burn to a crisp. He felt disappointed and disoriented as they staggered from the capsule into the blinding white-hot afternoon, sickened by the smell of spent fuel.

He remembered very little of the rest of their day. They had visited the café, where he sipped a ginger ale, too nauseous to eat, then drifted through the gift shop. He was surprised to find himself unenvious as Bernardo scooped up birthday loot. No model or glossy volume could ever hope to approach the transcendence of their journey.

It was only when they were heading home, spent from adrenaline, that Alton began to think of his mother. He knew he should be worried, especially because it was almost 7:00 p.m., but how could she be anything other than thrilled for him? Surely, she wouldn't begrudge him one of his most deeply hoped-for experiences, not once she learned what had happened.

Maybe she would be pleased to see him as he now saw himself: closer to manhood. He looked down at the jacket he had been allowed to keep, ran his fingers over the Cosmost patch.

But when he came in, she glared, shaking her head in disdain as her eyes went to the jacket, then returned her gaze to her show. He walked by, feeling relieved she hadn't said anything. But then he thought it might be better if he tried to show some accountability.

"I know I messed up," he said.

She shook her head again. "You went into *space* without my permission? You're fourteen years old!"

Alton controlled the urge to roll his eyes. "It was perfectly safe."

She leaped up, her drink sloshing everywhere. "Give me the jacket." She didn't shout, but her voice shook with fury, which scared him more.

He recoiled. "What? No!"

"Alton, hand over the jacket, or so help me, I'll call the cops and tell them you stole it."

"I earned this!"

Her laugh was short and derisive. "Doing *what*?"

"Training to be an astronaut." But even as he said it, he felt like a fool.

"Give it here," she said.

He folded his arms across his chest, but she pried them open, yanked a sleeve from one arm.

"Ow! All right, stop! You're going to rip it."

He wriggled out of the other sleeve, and she snatched it away from him.

"It doesn't matter. You're not going to be wearing it. And you're not going to see Bernardo anymore either."

His mouth dropped open, while she disappeared into her bedroom and stashed the jacket away somewhere. Then she went to the kitchen and ordered the fridge to mix her another drink.

"Don't you even want to know what it was like up there?" he asked her.

"No."

His mouth curled down in utter hatred.

"I bet my father would," he said, but even as he did, he knew he was overplaying this card.

Was it his imagination, or did her tone soften a little when she said, "Not if you knew him, you wouldn't."

"Tell me where he is."

"I honestly have no idea."

"*You* drove him away."

"Please," she said. "That man's family had money. I would have milked him for all he was worth."

"Then why did he leave?"

She whirled around to face him. "Because he never meant to stay! He was just slumming with me."

"What does that mean?"

"He didn't think I was good enough for him."

"He was right."

She slammed her drink down on the kitchen table. He recoiled, thinking she was coming for him, but she pushed past him back into her bedroom. He heard her rustling around for a few moments before she emerged carrying the jacket and went into the hall. Before he understood what she was doing, it was too late.

He fled past her in the corridor as she was returning to the apartment and banged open the garbage chute. His one hope was that the jacket had caught on its way down. But the chute was empty as far as he could see, which meant that it had slid twelve floors to their in-house landfill, to which there was no entry, as it had been sealed to deter scavengers.

An automated truck came once a week, slid a conveyor down into the pit, and vacuumed everything into its maw. There was no human to appeal to. Once something went down the chute, it was gone.

Still, he had to try, and so he took the elevator to the lobby, then descended the basement stairs and pushed open the heavy door.

A dank space housed equipment and tools, heavy-duty cleansers on blackened shelves, piles of rusted old parts, tangles of cords and wire, a few ancient ladders, and—in the middle of it all—a hulking steel dumpster.

There has to be a way in, he thought. *Some kind of maintenance hatch or something.* If he could stand the stench long enough to find one. He covered his nose and mouth with a forearm, trying not to gag.

As his eyes adjusted, he could make out the garbage drum more clearly. Though it bore its share of dents, it revealed no cracks, fissures, levers, or hatches. A sign on the far wall read, *Caution: Keep away from the compactor while in operation.*

Beneath the sign, he found a control panel with two buttons. When he pressed the green one, the bin lid began to whir upward. His eyes widened until it stopped again, and he realized it wasn't designed to rise more than a few inches.

Still, a few inches might be all he needed. He dragged over one of the creaky ladders and climbed up to where he could peer into the squalid abyss. There, among the shitty diapers, moldy food, and dead cat, lay his precious jacket.

He climbed down and searched for a hook or something, but there wasn't much to work with. His best option was the long handle on a push broom, which he unscrewed and carried back up.

He had to poke around for a few minutes, but eventually he was able to position the pole under the jacket and drag it toward him. It took him a dozen tries before he was able to get it so that it wouldn't slip off as he brought it toward him.

When it was within reach, he grabbed a sleeve between two fingers and began to carefully pull it through the narrow gap. He jerked in surprise as something small and black skittered out and went clattering onto the concrete. His flailing tipped the ladder, smashing him into the button that started the compactor again. It whirred downward, splintering the broomstick and clamping shut.

Grimacing in pain, he jabbed at the buttons, but it was no use. It must have had some kind of fail-safe shutdown. He reached up and pulled on the protruding sleeve. But the jacket was sealed in. He worked the sleeve back and forth until the threads started to rip, and it came free. He could keep the shoulder patch at least.

As he made his way out, his eyes fell on the thing that had skittered out of the dumpster and scared him. It was an ancient thumb drive, which he picked up and put in his pocket.

He didn't want to go home yet, so he went to the abandoned garden floor he had discovered, the one with the swastika. The door was pulled shut this time, but no one had replaced the lock, so he leaned against a graffiti-covered wall and slid down to the floor.

He smoothed the shredded sleeve, fingering the contours of the patch, then closed his eyes, alarmed to discover that the day already seemed like a fast-fading dream. He looked out into the night, hoping to evoke memories of the experience, but the sky was a sulfurous haze. The lights of the city intruded from everywhere.

Bright beams sliced through the mesh screens and lit up the

grotesquerie of painted faces on the walls. The cold, dark purity of space felt farther away than ever, and his mother had destroyed the one thing that would have reminded him of it.

He was filthy and starving. His back throbbed where he had fallen off the ladder. He wanted a meal and a shower and his bed, but more than that, he wanted to make his mother worry, so he committed to suffering there for a while longer.

Thinking of her reminded him of the thumb drive he had found. It was old, but his wrist device could still scan it and upload the data. Once he had it, he projected a holo-vid and watched it, his eyes widening as he did.

CHAPTER 19

HE SHOWED IT to Bernardo at school on Monday. In it, a very young Lena threw her arms around a handsome man about her age, while friends around them drank and laughed. The group was up at Griffith Observatory at night. Behind and below them, the lights of Los Angeles glimmered to the horizon.

"Holy shit," Bernardo said. "Is that him? He's pretty dark." He studied Alton with a blank expression, as though looking for resemblance and not finding it.

In the video, the man picked up a trumpet and trilled a melody, while Lena did a sassy little shuffle. Someone off-screen yelled, "Hot stuff!"

"It must be," Alton said. "My mom must have tried to throw it out with the jacket, to destroy all evidence of him, I guess. But I have that trumpet. I don't think she remembered she gave it to me."

They watched a while longer. More startling to Alton than the man's complexion was this sunny, relaxed, and playful version of his mother. He felt a pang of pity for her, for what she had become, but forced it from himself. She didn't deserve his sympathy after what she had done.

"So, now what?" Bernardo asked as the video ended.

"I'm going to find him. He left before I was born, so she probably never even told him about me. I'm sure he'll want to find out I exist."

"How are you going to do that with your mom around?"

"I can't. I need someplace to stay while I search. And then I'll go live with him."

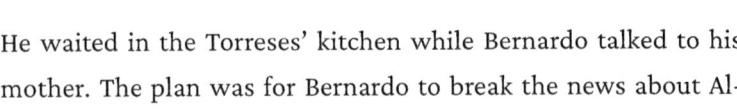

He waited in the Torreses' kitchen while Bernardo talked to his mother. The plan was for Bernardo to break the news about Alton's true identity, then ask if Alton could stay with them while he looked for his father. Lord knew they had plenty of extra room.

The housekeeper offered him a snack, but he was too excited to eat as he imagined the ways his new identity would raise his status. He remembered what he had overheard Camellia say about Bernardo needing to start running in his own circles and smiled. *Maybe I'm in his circle now.*

After half an hour or so, Camellia came into the kitchen and sat at the table with him, dismissing the housekeeper with a flick of her hand.

"Bernardo told me what you found," she said with a pitying smile.

Alton just nodded.

"Are you sure it's true?" she said. "Maybe that man was someone else she was dating. Or even just a friend."

He didn't like the insinuation that his mother was some kind of slut. But he couldn't deny that he didn't know for sure.

"I'm pretty sure," was all he could say, but he could hear how unconvincing he sounded.

"Well," she said, patting his hand. "I don't think it matters one way or another."

He was stung. "What do you mean?"

"The world is changing, Alton. My mother taught me that sometimes it's easiest to just accept your station. If I had learned that earlier, it might have saved me some pain."

She gave him what she must have considered a consoling smile. A few minutes later, she and Bernardo left to go shopping. Bernardo said he needed a new suit for a cousin's wedding, but he didn't look Alton in the eye when he said it, and Alton suspected they just wanted to avoid an awkward situation.

But he couldn't face going home yet, so he sat on a bench in the cavernous foyer as evening fell. The light took forever to fade, deepening the gloom slowly and darkening his mood with it. The balustrade his mother had polished shone in the fading sun. He sat so he wouldn't have to look at it and be reminded of their "station."

Eventually, darkness fell completely, and soon after, the front doors slid open. It was Fernando, home from work, striking in his dark suit. He paused at the threshold and squinted. "Alton?"

"Hi, Mr. Torres."

"What are you doing alone in the dark? Are you okay?"

When he didn't answer, Fernando said, "Go on into the sitting room."

He did so, and Fernando entered a few minutes later, tie loosened, with a bottle of beer for himself and a soda for Alton. Alton took a grateful gulp.

"Camellia told me about your discovery," he said, taking the wing chair facing Alton. "That's quite a thing to learn. Especially at your age."

"You believe me, don't you?"

"Of course I do."

"I don't think Mrs. Torres does."

"She does. She just doesn't want you to get your hopes up. It's not easy to track down a missing parent. And even if you could..." He trailed off as though not wanting to spell it out.

"Did you lose a parent?"

"No... but Camellia did. Both of them, actually."

Alton sat up. If that was true, why hadn't she been more sympathetic to his cause? "What happened to them?"

"There was a civil war in her country a few years after she was born. Her family was on the wrong side of it. They had to flee. They came up through Central America and Mexico to try to get to the United States. It was a very hard journey. When they got here, they were arrested, and she was separated from her family and put in a prison for children."

This shocked him. "How old was she?"

"She was six."

Alton didn't know what to say. It sounded awful, but at the same time, he couldn't imagine the imperious Mrs. Torres as a frightened and vulnerable child.

"The government either lost track of her parents or didn't care to reunite the family," Fernando continued. "So, she went into the foster system and was eventually adopted. But that was a few years later and not before horrible things happened to her. Thankfully, this was after the ICE massacres, or she might not have made it out at all."

"Did she ever find her parents?"

"She was too young to remember much, but once we started dating, I helped her search. Turns out, her mother had gone back home and remarried. A rich man this time. On the right side of politics. She had more children with him. When we located her, she insisted that she had tried to find Camellia, although between you and me, I don't think she made much of an effort. They do have something of a relationship now, though they're not close."

"What happened to her father?"

"We never found him."

Alton felt the sting of that.

"But we've come a long way," Fernando continued. "I've worked hard to help ensure that nothing like those government camps will ever happen again in this country. Nobody should be locked up just because of who they are or where they come from. Or, God forbid, their skin color."

Alton wondered what the exact nature of Mr. Torres's work was, but knew he shouldn't ask. They sat for a few moments, sipping their drinks.

"You're at a hard age, Alton. In a few years, you'll be better equipped to make some of your own life decisions. Right now, you have to stay with your mother. You may feel like you want to leave, but being on your own is not easy. And besides, she's worried about you."

Alton shook his head.

"Of course she is. I've already spoken with her. But it's more than just that, Alton. Your mother needs you. If you leave her, she'll be all alone. And she's already been abandoned by your father."

He considered this. He desperately wanted to find his father and a better life. But he did find it difficult to imagine leaving her, despite everything. Mr. Torres was right that she didn't have anybody else.

"What happened with the launch was my fault," he said. "I just assumed that Lena and Camellia had worked it out and I didn't hear anything about it because we were trying to keep it a surprise. I should have double-checked. Anyway, I've already apologized to your mother and taken responsibility. That should make it easier for you to go home."

"It's not that."

"What, then?"

"I just don't feel like I belong there." He felt humiliated by the hot tears that came into his eyes. "I don't feel like I belong *any*where."

Fernando gave him a compassionate look. "You're going to be fine, Alton. You just have to be yourself."

But he had no idea who that was.

CHAPTER 20

For weeks after he began at North High that fall, Alton wandered the immense campus in a daze.

The junior high he had attended with Bernardo had small classrooms and flesh-and-blood teachers. North felt more like a military base. Though it served thousands of students, no instructors were actually on-site. There were only proctors that monitored vast windowless auditorium pods while armed security patrolled the spaces between them.

Inside the pods, tiered seating for one thousand ringed enormous 3D holograms of a lecturing teacher that was simulcast across Los Angeles County. Students submitted questions and answers through tablets embedded in their seats. AI teaching assistants would reply on the tablets, but with so many students, the lecturer would only occasionally address a question live.

Alton had never imagined anything could feel so impersonal, but since few of his classmates were paying attention, he guessed it didn't matter.

He wouldn't have minded the crappy learning situation as much if he hadn't felt so lonely. He missed Bernardo, whom he hadn't been allowed to see since the "incident" and who now attended a private school. Their messaging had grown infrequent, and Alton worried that he was losing Bernardo to new friends.

Alton had hoped that he would find his father, who would then pay for him to join Bernardo at the elite Hidden Valley—surely he wouldn't deny his newly discovered son the best possible education. But Alton had made no progress in his search.

In the absence of the real man, he had begun to obsessively study himself—his eyes, his face, his voice, his manner—to find some evidence of his father in him. Maybe this would help him feel more certain of his identity. But after months of looking, he could see nothing different.

This, along with the painful fact that he was still waiting for his growth spurt, made him extremely self-conscious. Staring in the mirror so much lately had made him realize how scrawny and undeveloped he was, especially around older kids who already had facial hair and pumped-up physiques. He stepped carefully around these Goliaths, not that they noticed him.

Even though—or perhaps because—North was more diverse than his former school, the students had largely organized themselves into racial and ethnic cliques. Groups of Mexicans, Hondurans, Koreans, Guatemalans, Chinese, Azerbaijani, African Americans, and white kids claimed the shadowy breezeways and sections of the cavernous cafeteria. He envied them as they ate together, laughed and joked and flirted, watched each other's backs, strutted with the confidence of numbers.

The Mexicans had the largest presence, but Alton didn't think they would accept him, even if he had an idea of how to approach them or prove that his pale appearance concealed a biracial identity. Of course, there were mixed-race kids in every group, and Alton wondered, given their varying skin colors, what gave them license to belong. The white kids, meanwhile, didn't give him a second glance, not even a contemptuous one. He guessed they didn't want the responsibility of taking care of a weakling. Their numbers were small enough. *Or maybe I really am that invisible.*

Just as Alton began to give up on improving his status, a new kid swept in one day. His face and skin were pale, and his straight blond purple-tipped hair fell into his cobalt eyes. He was skinny but tall and strapping. He looked older than the other tenth graders, which made Alton wonder if he had been held back.

But mainly he stood out because he dressed like a hoverskater, with the tapered shorts and long sleeves and high-topped rubber shoes, a rare fashion for the Valley. You typically only saw them where the beaches used to be, down around Venice and Santa Monica.

Alton had been down there a few times and seen the Hov'skaters. When the tide receded, they would glide along above just a few inches of water, sending up a fine spray on either side. The most skilled kept jets of seawater shooting behind them for miles as they zipped down the surfwalk.

It was an endangered sport, however. The seawall under construction would soon end it. As the water rose against the wall, their turf would disappear forever into the lower depths.

Hoverskating was mostly a white sport. In an inner-city school, the kid was making a statement about identity, however unconscious. And it wasn't lost on anyone. Some mean-looking dudes glared at the new kid, but to Alton, at least, he seemed thoroughly untroubled.

A few weeks after he had appeared, Alton was in the back of the cafeteria, as usual, with his back to the wall for safety, when the kid sauntered down the aisles, scanning each table, ignoring—or pretending to ignore—the hush that had fallen.

Alton watched until the kid locked eyes with him and started over. *No way,* Alton thought. But he strode up and slid in across the table, blowing white-blond, purple-tipped hair out of his face as he opened a carton of chocolate milk.

"I'm Alex," he said and downed the whole carton.

Alton hesitated. Other kids were looking at them. *Many* other kids. Maybe most of them. But those piercing cobalt eyes demanded a reply.

"Alton."

"*Alton?* Really?" Alex chuckled. "Place is a dump, huh?" He shook his head as though wherever he had come from had been worlds better.

"It takes some getting used to," Alton said.

"Seems like you're on top of things here."

Now, Alton understood. Alex was here to put him on. Why not? He was an easy target. But then Alex said, "You finish your classwork first almost every day."

He wondered if he should be flattered or concerned that somebody was watching him. "Maybe I just don't care if I do a shitty job," he said.

Alex seemed taken aback for a second, as though this was something he hadn't considered, then he broke into a smile that was charming, relaxed, and persuasive all at once, tinged with just enough indifference to make sure you knew he wasn't fully invested in you.

That smile reeled you in, made you yearn for full investment, for sincerity, for validation. It was a smile that Alton later supposed let Alex get away with things.

"Nah, you *have* to do a good job." He looked around. "What else do you have going for you?"

This was not a nice thing to say, but Alton appreciated the

honesty. Anyway, it was obvious. Being a good student was one of the few things he could control.

"My dad says I need to get really good at writing and public speaking if I'm going to help him out with his work eventually," Alex continued.

"What does your dad do?"

"He used to be a cop. Now he's a . . . community organizer." He reached over and stuffed some of Alton's 'tater mash into his mouth with his bony fingers.

"And he's liable to kick my ass if I don't start doing better here than I did at my last school." The hair fell into his face again, and he used his greasy hands to tuck it behind his ears.

"Does that happen a lot?" Alton asked.

"Does what?"

"Your dad kicking your ass."

A distant look came into his eyes as though he was trying to determine what constituted "a lot."

Finally, he said, "Maybe you could help me." He flashed that smile again.

"Why not just use AI?"

"Because it might not always be available, especially if the world goes back to the way it used to be, which some people are kind of hoping that it will."

"The way it used to be when?"

A glimmer of impatience flickered across his eyes, and he looked away for a moment, something Alton would later realize he did when he didn't know the answer to something.

"My dad just told me not to trust it and that I needed to be self- . . . self- . . ."

"Self-reliant?"

"See, you're helping me already! I knew I was right about you."

No one ever complimented him, and the rush made him feel giddy. Of course he would help. After five minutes, Alex owned him emotionally, which wasn't hard. He was sick of being alone. He was *angry* about being alone.

The other kids watched them walk out together. He wondered how far and for how long he would follow his new friend, even if it became—as he suspected it would—dangerous. All he knew in that moment was that he was no longer invisible, and this thrilled and vindicated him more than he could have imagined.

CHAPTER 21

AFTER SCHOOL THEY took the 'loop to Reseda, got off on Sherman Way, and walked down Wilbur to Alex's neighborhood. He lived in a dilapidated house set back from the road and a dense tangle of oleanders and bougainvillea.

"My dad found out that Germans settled in this area," Alex said as they went up the street. "Said once upon a time, Los Angeles was Weimar on the Pacific."

Alton had no idea what this meant. He didn't even know how he would identify a German.

"Obviously, there aren't many of us left around here," Alex said, as two young Latinas crossed the street in front of them.

At his front door, he scanned the palm pad, and two deadbolts slid open. Inside, sunlight fell in dusty stripes across a room crammed with two couches, a love seat, and a handful of folding chairs.

Alton thought it looked more like a dentist's office than a home. On the wall opposite the door hung a framed picture of an illustrated fist against a red background. Bolts of lightning radiated behind the fist. It looked like propaganda posters Alton had seen in history class.

"My dad holds meetings here," he said when he saw Alton looking around the room.

"What kind of meetings?"

"Come on. But be quiet. He might be sleeping. He works nights."

In the kitchen, Alex opened the fridge.

"Is your mom at work?" Alton asked.

"Shit," he said. It was empty of everything except beer. "I need to order groceries."

Since Alex had eaten half his lunch, Alton was ravenous. He winced, thinking of having a fat snack at Bernardo's after school. Those were the days.

They squeezed through a tiny hallway into a musty, cluttered living room, where Alton was surprised to find a small man reclining in a tattered armchair in a white T-shirt and boxers. His blond hair stuck up in tufts, and the gray stubble and deep bags under his eyes made him look older than Alton guessed he was.

"Alton, this is my dad, Kurt. Alton is going to help me with my homework, Dad."

The man appraised Alton coldly. "Well, somebody better," he said.

As they went into Alex's room, the man called back. "We're meeting tonight. Get some food in the house. And more beer."

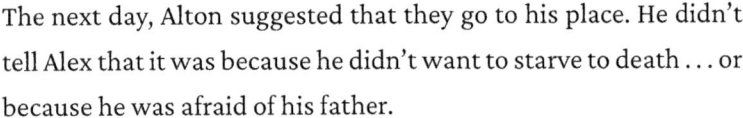

The next day, Alton suggested that they go to his place. He didn't tell Alex that it was because he didn't want to starve to death... or because he was afraid of his father.

"I'm cutting school early today," Alex said. "Got some shit to do. But I'll meet you at your place later. Ping me when you get home."

On the 'loop after school, a group of five Hispanic students Alton didn't recognize sat across from him. He pretended not to notice, but their stares were intense. He was relieved when one of them finally broke the tension.

"You better tread carefully," the kid said. "That Hov'skater could be bad for your health."

Alton resisted the urge to raise an eyebrow. The kid was smaller than Alton. But when you had big friends, you could say what you want, Alton supposed.

"I'm just helping him with his homework. We're not best friends or anything."

"Still, you need to be careful who represents you."

"I'll keep that in mind."

At this, one of the bigger kids, muscular and tattooed, stood up in a threatening manner. He was barely out of his seat when a blue light began strobing silently inside the pod. If the AI detected a crime, or even suspected a threat, it would alert station security to meet the pod when it arrived.

The older kid backed off, and Tiny just smiled and shook his head as if to indicate how lucky Alton had been. "Not much can stop Bouncer here when he's feeling feral," Tiny said.

They arrived at the station. As the passengers unloaded, Alton was relieved to find security waiting. He hurried past them and sprinted up the stairs and out of the station into the suffocatingly hot day, pinging Alex as he did. He wove his way through the afternoon crowds and hustled down an alley, checking behind him to make sure no one was following.

The second he stopped to catch his breath, "There he is!" came bellowing down the alley, and he turned to see the gang tear after him.

He squeezed through a rusted gate at the end of the alley, cursing as he burned his arm on the hot aluminum, and fled down a sloping path. The underpass that led to his building was within sight, but he would have to make his way through a dense shantytown of tents and shelters to get there.

He typically avoided the encampments like the plague, but seeing no other choice, he bent low and began snaking through. Going too fast, he stumbled, skinning his knees and forearms on the hot, gritty asphalt. The pain was intense, but adrenaline and the sounds of their shouts at the edge of the encampment kept him moving.

He lurched ahead, stinging sweat forcing his eyes shut. Half blind, he ran into a large appliance box wedged between two tents. He didn't have time to find another way around, so he held his nose and plunged into the humid carton.

Inside, a shirtless, emaciated man lay on his back wearing VR goggles. At first, the man didn't speak or even move, but as Alton clambered around him, he made a sound, some reaction to whatever he was immersed in. Alton felt relieved, not so much that the man was alive but that he had some means of escape from his miserable existence.

Outside, he could see the heads of his pursuers looming like scarecrows not ten yards away, and again his impulse was to duck into an open tent.

This one sheltered two women and a baby, their faces streaked with grime and sweat. The tent overflowed with junk and old clothes and stank of spoiled milk. The woman holding the baby moved into the corner. The other edged in front of them, her eyes wide with fear.

Alton crouched near the entrance and tried to control his breath. He tilted his head toward the voices outside and held up one finger to indicate he would be gone in a moment.

The moment lasted a long time. The scrapes on his arms and legs burned like crazy. The heat amplified the stench, and it was all he could do not to gag. But he decided that would be the ultimate insult, and he was already invading their home.

When the voices subsided again, he crawled out and dashed toward the concealing shadows of the underpass. He was almost home free when he stumbled against another tent and set a dog inside to yapping.

There was no place else to hide, so he leapt up and bolted.

He turned to see one of his pursuers catch a leg on something and take a tumble, but the other four closed fast. His building was just a few streets over, but they would catch him before he got there, so he pulled up short and turned to face them.

"Caught the snitch," Tiny said.

"I didn't call security!" Alton gasped.

"It's still your fault for mouthing off in the first place," Tiny said, grabbing his lapels. Alton tried to wrest free, but Bouncer went behind him and wrenched his arms back, causing him to cry out.

"Now listen, *Bolillo*," said Tiny, showering Alton with sweat and spit. "Final warning. Your boy is dangerous. His kind is a serious problem."

Alton didn't have a chance to ask what that problem was, or what distinction they were making between Alex and Alton when it came to *kind* because Alex was charging them with a steel pipe.

"Get the fuck off him!" he yelled, swinging the pipe in a wide arc. Their antagonists leapt backward but held their ground.

"Five of us and one of you," Tiny said.

"Been skipping math, field rat? There are *four* of you." Alex smirked, but as he did, the kid who had taken a spill appeared behind him and wrenched the pipe from Alex. As it went clattering away, Alex kicked the kid hard in his bloody knee. He dropped, but the other four were on Alex in an instant.

"Go!" Alex yelled.

Alton started to backpedal. "Do you want me to call the cops?"

"Fuck no!"

Alton ran, looking back just once to see a jumble of flailing legs and fists.

He waited for what seemed like forever outside his building, panting, his gut gurgling with dread. What if his new friend was a pile of broken bones? Wouldn't that be Alton's fault? But just as he began to talk himself into going back, Alex appeared. His nose was a faucet of blood, one eye was swelling, and he clutched his side. But he was grinning.

In the lobby, the elevator took an infuriatingly long time. Alton expected the gang to burst in at any moment, but finally they were headed up to his floor.

"Thanks," he said. "You saved my ass."

"Of course," Alex said, tilting his head back to slow the blood. "We have to stick together."

We do?

"Also, neber call da cops."

"I thought your dad used to be a cop."

"That's why I know not to do it."

In his apartment, Alton gave Alex an ice pack and an old hand towel for his nose, then went into the bathroom to wash the dirt and blood out of his own wounds. When he returned, Alex was sitting upright, the nosebleed stanched. Alton disposed of the bloody towel, then pulled out half the contents of the fridge and started slapping sandwiches together.

Sitting in the quiet air-conditioning, as they stuffed their faces and guzzled energy drinks, Alton thought of the man in the box and the little family in the rancid tent. Despite all his resentment and complaining, maybe he didn't have it so bad after all, especially compared to Alex, who was a mass of purpling welts. "Do you think anything is broken?" he asked.

"Naw, but something *might be* if my old man finds out I got my ass whooped by a pack of cholos."

After they ate, they slumped onto the couch in front of a projection. Alton awoke to the sound of his mother coming in.

"Is your friend okay?" she asked as she put her stuff down. "His nose is bleeding." She spoke in a tone of sympathetic urgency Alton had never heard from her before.

Alex woke up. "Shit," he said, jumping off the couch. "I'm sorry."

"Mom, this is Alex. Alex, this is my mom, Lena."

She smiled. Alton had never seen this smile before either, but he knew what it meant. He finally had a friend. A *white* friend. An *older* white friend. Probably also didn't hurt that he was good-looking.

"You look like you're in rough shape, Alex," she said. "Let me patch you up a little bit."

Were his own wounds invisible?

She took him into the kitchen, and when she was done, he had new bandages and his nose had stopped bleeding again.

"It's getting late. Where do you live?" she asked him.

"Reseda."

"Your parents must be worried."

"My dad is at work. He doesn't know I'm not home."

"What about your mom?"

He hesitated. It was the first time Alton had ever seen Alex look anything but confident and carefree. "She left when I was young," he said.

"I'm sorry," she said. "That must have been really hard."

Alton glared at his mother. In fourteen years, she hadn't once said anything like that to comfort him about his father. But she wouldn't return his gaze.

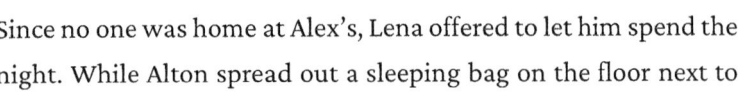

Since no one was home at Alex's, Lena offered to let him spend the night. While Alton spread out a sleeping bag on the floor next to his bed, Alex poked around his room.

"I've never seen so many real books," he said. "These must be old as shit."

"I get them at the Stalls," he said. "This one guy sells to me all the time. There's no way he makes any money. I think he just likes to talk about them."

"Why not just read on a device or holo-proj?" Alex asked.

Alton came over and gazed with Alex at the collection of creased spines and tattered covers. "I don't know." He shrugged. "I just like to hold them. There's something about the fact that they were *made*."

"That's dumb," Alex said.

The remark hurt, but Alton ignored it and left the room to grab a couple of pillows. When he returned, Alex was staring at a poster of a rocket launch, an arc of streaking light against the midnight sky.

"I went to space," Alton said proudly. "Not a full orbit or anything, but I was up there for a few minutes."

Alton was again stung when Alex seemed unimpressed, but finally he said, "Could be cool. You want to be an astronaut or something?"

"Maybe."

"Good luck. They don't take too many of our kind anymore. It's all chinks and ragheads now. But who knows, maybe by the time you're old enough, things will be like they used to again."

Alton cringed at the language but stayed silent. He tried to avoid responding whenever Alex mentioned "us" or "our kind." He wasn't sure how his friend would feel if he knew what *kind* Alton really was. Or how Tiny and his friends would feel, for that matter. One thing was certain: everybody seemed obsessed with kind. "We should probably go to bed," he said.

Alton lay awake in the dark for a while. He wasn't sure if Alex was asleep until he heard, "Dude, your mom is pretty hot."

Alton groaned.

"She must've had you young."

"Very."

"What happened to your dad?"

"He left before I was born."

"Do you know where he is?"

"No. And my mom has no interest in helping me find him. What about your mom?"

"My dad kept me when they split. I was like eight or something. I don't know what happened to her after that. He wouldn't let her see me."

"He wouldn't *let* her?"

"Yeah. She wasn't down for the cause. And in my dad's world, if you're not with him, you're with the enemy."

CHAPTER 22

WHILE ALTON WENT to school the next day, Alex stayed at Alton's house to convalesce and eat most of what was left in the fridge. He spent the next night there as well and then disappeared. At first, Alton thought he might be recovering from his wounds.

But after more than a week of silence, Alton wondered if maybe Alex's dad *did* kick his ass or maybe pulled him from school. Maybe this sort of incident was why he had transferred to North in the first place.

Alton felt disappointed but decided it was probably for the best. Tiny and his friends had stopped harassing him, and he figured shit was squashed. He felt lonely and HoloTimed Bernardo. They made tentative plans to hang out at some point, but Bernardo seemed distant. He was taller and skinnier and looked and sounded like another person.

Alton was reluctant to tell him about Alex or the fight, and they didn't have much else to say to each other. When they timed out, he felt lonelier than ever.

Just as Alton was getting used to invisibility again, Alex showed up at lunch, just like he had that first day, though dressed differently this time, in baggy clothes, despite the heat. Alton thought maybe he had decided to ditch the Hov'skate threads and the unwanted attention.

Alex waved and smiled when he saw Alton, then slid in across the table from him as though nothing had ever happened. The only difference from the first time he had invited himself to Alton's table was that he had two chocolate milks with him rather than one.

Alton didn't return his smile. "I thought you transferred schools again," he said.

"Naw, just had some things to take care of." He opened one of the milks and downed it.

"You couldn't have kept in contact?"

"Are you my mother now?"

"Maybe if you had one, you'd know how to treat your friends."

Alex gave him a stony stare, then broke into a rueful grin. "Good one," he said. "You're right, though. I'm sorry. I went somewhere that was kind of . . . secret. I couldn't tell you about it."

"Can you tell me about it now?"

"Better. I'll show you. After school. Meet me at the 'loop." He grinned again, grabbed the unopened milk carton, and went straight for the table where Tiny and his friends sat.

Alton was too far away to see exactly what happened, but suddenly the milk exploded with incredible force like a water balloon dropped from the roof, showering everyone in the vicinity.

Tiny's crew leapt from their seats, initially too shocked to react. When they finally did lunge after Alex, the security lights in the cafeteria began whirring. Alex gave a bow and slipped out. His milk-sodden victims stared after him with lethal intent.

This guy is going to get me killed, Alton thought.

Against his better judgment, Alton met Alex after school. "You put a bomb in that milk?" Alton asked as Alex walked up.

"Something like that," Alex chuckled.

The pod arrived, but Alex said, "Wait for the next one," and nodded toward Tiny and his posse as they came through into the hub.

"No thanks," Alton said. He stepped toward the pod, but Alex restrained him with one hand. The strength of his grip was startling. "Why are you trying to stir shit up again?"

"Trust me."

There were seven in Tiny's gang now. They came onto the platform and stared at Alex in disbelief. "You loco, white boy?" Bouncer asked.

The next pod slid into the station, and the doors hissed open. "After you," Alex said and stepped back to give them room.

Tiny shook his head. "It's your life, *ese*," he said.

Alton turned to go. "I don't want to be part of this."

Alex clutched his shoulders more gently this time. Alton was surprised to see a weak pink light glowing from beneath his long sleeves. But before he could ask, the doors sealed behind them and they were off. Tiny and company had occupied the rear so their backs weren't exposed.

Alex and Alton sat opposite them. No one was between them on the pod. Alton was hardly breathing. This was reckless even for Alex.

"Everything was chill," Tiny said. "Why come back?"

"Unfinished business," Alex said.

"I guess we'll finish it then, once we get out."

"Why wait?"

"You know why." Tiny looked up, indicating the security alarms.

"Oh, is that all?"

The car instantly went black, leaving only the incandescent pink light that illuminated Alex. The light allowed for a little visibility, but the disoriented gang didn't have time to adjust.

There was a sizzle of electricity, and two of them were launched, as if by an invisible force, against the sides of the pod.

Alex punched another, and there was a sickening cracking sound. He hurled the next kid against the two behind him, and all three spilled on top of Tiny, who yelped. The thumping of bodies rumbled through the small space.

While Alex was preoccupied, Bouncer scrambled over the tops of the seats, his body skittering against the wall of the pod like a gecko. At first, Alton thought he was coming for *him*, but then he saw the terror in the pink glow of his face and knew he was trying to escape. The door opened, and Bouncer sprang out. Alex turned to see him flee.

"No!" Alton yelled, but Alex was after his prey in a flash.

As soon as he was gone, the pod lights flickered on again, and Alton got a full view of the sprawled and moaning teens. There was blood everywhere. Tiny quavered under his pile of friends, then looked up at Alton in abject fear.

"I'll try to stop him," Alton said.

He looked around frantically, but they were nowhere in the station, so he took the stairs two at a time up to street level and ran past people who had stopped in their tracks, heads turned.

Following their gaze, he sprinted out of the pavilion, scanning side streets and alleys until he saw the pink light shining in full bloom.

He ran down an alley to find Alex pinning Bouncer against a dumpster. He seemed to be holding him in place with just one hand around his neck. Bouncer clutched and pawed to no avail. His eyes bulged from his bloodied face.

Alton shook off his shock. "That's enough!" he yelled, running over.

Alex held his victim a beat longer, his face twisted in hateful satisfaction. Then he smiled and relaxed. "Sure, boss," he said. Bouncer went to his knees, drawing ragged breaths.

Alton helped Bouncer up. "Go on, get out of here," he said.

As Bouncer staggered away, Alex gave Alton a disappointed look.

"Are you trying to start a war?" The words raked Alton's throat. He was surprised by the depth of his fury.

"War's already started," Alex said. "See?"

Alton looked up to see the fleet of drones buzzing in their direction.

"Ditch your watch," Alton said, starting to take his off.

"Don't need to. The augmentation prevents tracking. They're running blind."

I knew it, Alton thought. But didn't only soldiers get augmentation? And they had it removed when they were discharged. It was highly illegal for a civilian to be augmented. And as far as Alton knew, it was almost impossible for a civilian to even find someone to augment them.

"They'll find us soon enough!" Alton said. "Let's go!"

"We can't go to your place," Alex said. "They'll look for us there."

"Trust *me*," Alton said.

CHAPTER 23

THEY MADE IT to Alton's building, looking over their shoulders the entire time, and took the elevator to the empty garden floor.

"Damn it," Alton said, fingering the padlock. "This wasn't here before."

"Move." Alex punched down on the lock, and it smacked to the ground, echoing down the empty hall. Alton looked to see if anyone had noticed, but the floor was abandoned as usual.

Inside, Alton said, "Nobody will think to look for us here. And you should feel right at home." He gestured toward the swastika graffiti.

Alex looked affronted. "If you think that's what I stand for, then why help me?"

"Because I was on that pod too!"

"I killed the cameras, the brain, everything. And not just in the pod. In the station. No one saw or recorded anything."

"Are you going to kill the witnesses too? If you haven't already, I mean?"

Alex looked down and appeared to notice for the first time how much blood was on him. He gave a little laugh.

"You're psycho," Alton said. "Just wait here for a minute."

He left and returned with a pile of clothes, soft drinks, snacks, and a solar fan. While Alex dressed, Alton inspected the augmentation. It seemed crude. Slim black wedges protruded from slits in his armpits. "How does it work?" he asked.

"Nanocrystalline alloy. These things in my arms go under the flesh and fuse to the bone and muscle. The pink light means it's activated. When I squeeze my fists, they generate a thin but superstrong alloy all the way down to my hand."

"That's why the punches are so loud."

He grinned. "Yeah. I basically have steel fists. The best facilities seal it all inside the body, but my operation was a little more homemade."

"What even is the point of this? I thought everything in the military was drones and virtual."

"There are places drones can't reach. And what good is virtual warfare in a cave where nothing is plugged in? Sometimes they have to get an actual person in the field. This gives them the best chance."

"The best chance of what?"

"Mission success," he said. "Whatever that may be." He turned his head and lifted his hair to reveal ragged black stitches across his scalp. "Nano-neural interface technology allows me to generate electromagnetic force to move and control things in my immediate vicinity. I used electromagnetic pulses to cut the electricity to the pod. Other functions include infrared vision, quantum sensing and receiving, machine-learning interface ability, secure server and database access, hacking abilities, embedded VR access—I can't remember everything now . . ." He opened a sports drink and guzzled it down.

The swollen, stitched gash was making Alton feel sick. He turned away as he said, "All to get back at some bullies?"

"They provided some motivation," Alex said. "And some practice. But this is something that's been in the works for a while."

"Does your dad know?"

"Of course. I couldn't get access to something like this by myself."

Alton was incredulous that Kurt would make his teenage son into a weapon of war. What the hell had Alton stumbled into here?

Alex, seeing the aghast expression on Alton's face, just shrugged. "I have every right to protect myself. *And* my friends."

Despite himself, Alton felt a little quiver of pride at the word *friend*. "That wasn't protection," he said. "That was revenge."

Alex sighed and went to sit against the wall. "Things are getting worse," he said. "My Dad says this Mexican who's running for governor, Guerrero, is a big problem."

Alton wondered if Alex had heard this at his father's "community meetings." He slid down next to him and switched on the little fan. "California has had other Mexican American governors," he said. "What's the big deal?"

Alex snorted. Alton assumed it was at the word *American*.

"My dad says that people haven't seen it yet because it's in the early stages, but Guerrero will run on an anti-white platform. Targeting people like my dad for exercising their civic rights."

"Whites have been the minority in LA for a long time. Why come here in the first place if he has such a big problem with it?"

"Because we'll soon be the minority everywhere. And we have to take the fight to them. Otherwise, we'll always be hiding. Always be running."

"What's so bad about being in the minority?"

Alex looked at him as though he had no idea who he was, which, of course, he didn't, and Alton suddenly realized he was afraid to reveal his true identity. The most he could admit to was his friendship with Bernardo. "My best friend is Hispanic. He's a good guy."

The words tumbled out, betraying his fear of how Alex might react.

"I'm not saying there aren't exceptions," Alex said. "But the ones that want to replace us or blend us into their gene pool—and that's most of them—have to be dealt with. This was our country once. But we stopped fighting for it. That's why I did this." He lifted his arms. "And that's why I want you to help me. Not just with my writing but with other stuff too. You're smart. And my dad wants me to become a leader for the cause."

"Aren't you kind of young for that?"

"I'm not as young as you think. We moved around a lot when I was a kid, then lived off the grid for a while. I started school late. Besides, it's never too early or too late to do what's right."

Alton stared at the pile of bloody clothes Alex had shed. "What's *right*?" he said. The words surprised him as they came out. He wasn't sure if he was talking to Alex or himself. All he knew was that he needed to end his association with Alex before anything worse happened. He hoped it wasn't too late.

His mom had been out the last few weeks, dating some new creep he hadn't met, so he hoped to sneak in late without getting the third degree. He yelped when she grabbed him hard around his skinny bicep.

"The cops were here," she said. "And they said it was serious. What the hell have you guys been up to?"

"It wasn't me, Mom. I promise!"

"What happened?"

"We got chased down by some kids a few weeks ago. That's why Alex had those bruises and stuff."

"I figured that much. Why was he roughed up and not you?"

Alton paused, suddenly feeling ashamed.

"Tell me!"

"Because he fought them while I escaped."

She nodded as though this was exactly what she had expected to hear. "Who were the kids?"

"Just some kids from school."

"Black kids? Mexicans?"

"What difference does that make? Ow, let me go!"

She relinquished her grip. "Down," she said.

He sank onto the couch, rubbing his arm. "Alex went after them. Things got a little out of hand."

"Payback?" she said.

"Something like that."

She crossed her arms. "I guess they had it coming," she said.

He looked at her, appalled.

"They can't prove it was us. Alex fixed it so there was no recorded evidence. It's our word against theirs."

"Is that what you're going to tell the cops?"

He thought about it. "I didn't hurt anybody. Maybe I should just tell them the truth."

"And let your friend get arrested?"

"I'm not sure he's my friend, Mom."

"Of course he is. Do you think Bernardo would have done that for you? That little pussy would have curled up like a worm and cried for his daddy."

"That *little pussy*," he spat, "wouldn't have gotten me into this in the first place."

CHAPTER 24

ALTON WAITED UP all night, sick with dread, but nobody else knocked on their door. On the way to school the next day, bleary-eyed with exhaustion, he stopped to check on Alex. Curled up on a pile of clothes, he looked younger and more innocent, and Alton felt some of the anger drain from him. It wasn't Alex's fault that his dad was a mean bastard who had stolen him from his mom. Under the right influences, maybe he could change.

Alton could barely keep his eyes open in class, but he jolted awake when security entered and circled around to his seat. They escorted him to the school lockup, where they shut him in a tiny airless room that reeked of heavy-duty cleansers.

It must have been at least an hour before they arrived: a middle-aged Black woman and a crew-cut younger man having a heated discussion in Spanish through his earpiece, both in suits.

The woman sat across from Alton and scrolled through her notepad. After what seemed like forever, the man joined them, scowling and shaking his head.

"I'm Agent Taylor," the woman said. "This is Agent Sandoval."

Alton nodded, his mouth too dry to reply. *Agent* didn't make them sound like cops.

Taylor reached into her pocket for two sleek metal balls, which she tossed into the air as though releasing pigeons. They sprouted tiny wings and buzzed up and behind Alton.

Alton swallowed. "What are those?"

"Those are police business," Sandoval growled.

Taylor gave a tired smile. "We record everything, Alton. For your sake and ours."

"Why two of them?"

"It's important to get all angles. Just like we want to get all angles in this case."

Alton forced himself not to roll his eyes.

"Do you know why we're here?" she continued.

"I . . . I think so."

She waited.

"Tiny and his crew got roughed up yesterday," he said.

"Tiny? You mean Jorge Ramirez?"

She turned the pad so Alton could see.

"Yeah, that's him."

"How do you know about the incident?"

"Some cops talked to my mom last night. Then I asked around this morning and heard what happened."

"And what was that?"

"Somebody jumped his crew after school yesterday."

"*Jumped* is putting it lightly," Sandoval said. "The city had to scrap that entire pod car."

Alton winced. He knew it had been bad but not *that* bad.

"Do you know why we're asking you about this?" Taylor asked.

"I guess because we've had problems with those kids."

"Who are *we*?" Sandoval asked.

"Me and Alex."

"Alex Weber?"

"Yeah."

Taylor showed him the pad again. "That him?"

The picture was of Alex with his father. He couldn't tell where they were. Alex wore a headband that pulled the hair back from his face and made him look older. Alton had to look twice before he could say for sure it was him.

Sandoval pressed on. "What kind of problems did you have with Jorge and his friends?"

"They didn't like the way Alex dressed. I guess they have a problem with Hov'skaters."

Sandoval raised an eyebrow. "Is that all?"

"They said I shouldn't hang around Alex because he was trouble. They chased me one afternoon after school, and Alex took a beating from them so I could get away. But we didn't have anything to do with whatever happened yesterday."

It all spilled out before he knew what he was saying. Was he trying to stay out of trouble himself or protect Alex? Did he feel like he owed Alex? Or was he afraid of what Alex would do if Alton betrayed *him*?

"Who could it have been then?" Taylor asked.

Alton shrugged. "I'm sure they have plenty of enemies."

"Why?" Sandoval glared. "Because they're brown?"

"No." Alton swallowed. "Because they're bullies."

"Did they say why you shouldn't hang around him?" Taylor asked.

"They said he was dangerous, but I didn't know what they meant."

"Two of them are in the hospital today," said Sandoval. "Maybe *that's* what they meant."

Alton tried to look concerned, but his heart was hammering. *Shit*, he thought. *What if they died?*

"One of them can't talk yet," Taylor said. "But the rest of them say it was Alex who attacked them and that you were with him. The cameras were cut, but witnesses saw you at the North High hub at the same time."

"We take the 'loop home every day. We saw them, but we got the next car. We didn't want to mess with them anymore."

"About five hundred people witnessed that milk incident in the cafeteria yesterday. Seems to me like he was all *about* messing with them," said Sandoval.

Alton chided himself for forgetting. "I don't know why he did that. He can definitely be a punk. Sometimes he thinks he's smarter than everybody."

"And *better*?"

Alton lowered his gaze. "I guess."

"Better how?" Taylor pressed.

"He's made some comments."

"What kind of comments?"

"Comments about people who aren't... white. Can I have some water?"

"When we're finished," Sandoval said.

Taylor made a gesture and the recording pigeons floated down just at the edge of Alton's peripheral vision, an intimidation tactic, he guessed. "The victims say they got on the North High 'loop," she said. "You and Alex climbed in behind them. The lights went out, and Alex attacked. Allegedly, he did this."

She touched the pad and turned it toward Alton. The carnage actually looked less vicious than what he had seen firsthand, but he gave his best shocked look.

"How could he have done this by himself?" Alton said. "He got his ass kicked by fewer of them than that before." The lies were coming more easily now.

"If that's true, why would they make up a story like this?" Sandoval asked. "It makes them look pretty weak. Why not say they were jumped by another gang?"

Alton shrugged again. His mouth was insanely dry.

"Do you want to hear our theory?" said Sandoval.

Taylor set her pad down. "Let's get some water in here first," she said.

The door opened and someone who had been outside listening handed out three bottles. Alton wanted to guzzle his but thought it might make him look desperate, so he forced himself to sip.

"All better?" Sandoval said with a smirk.

Alton nodded.

"Terrific. You want to hear our theory about what happened?"

Alton was too terrified to breathe. *They know*, he thought.

"Our theory is that your friend Alex got himself augmented," said Taylor.

"Augmented? You mean like . . . like in the army?"

"Yeah," Sandoval said. "But not the regular army. The Special Forces. It's extremely rare."

"How would a high school kid get that?" Alton asked, his voice squeaking up a register.

"You tell us," said Jones. "You two have gotten pretty close as far as we can tell."

"Not really. We hung out yesterday, but before that, he had disappeared for a few weeks."

The agents exchanged looks.

Idiot, he thought.

"Disappeared?" said Taylor. "Disappeared where?"

"I don't know. He didn't contact me. I honestly didn't expect him to come back."

"Two weeks is just about how long it takes to have the process done and recover," said Sandoval.

"I mean... how... how would he even do that?" Alton said.

"You're the one that got a firsthand look," Sandoval said. "He must have been dying to brag about it, show off all the fun little details."

Alton shook his head, but his nerve was faltering. He felt like he was going to cry.

"Have you met his father?" Taylor asked.

"Once," he said. It came out barely more than a whisper.

"This him?"

Alton took a long look at the pad, grateful to have a few seconds to regain his composure. The person in the photo wore a sidearm and some kind of uniform. He didn't look much like the small man in boxers that Alton had seen drinking beer in the tattered recliner.

"I... I think so."

"Kurt Weber," Taylor said. "He's ex-military, ex-contractor, ex-cop, ex-who-knows-what. Tied to some serious white extremist groups. FBI, DHS, and ATF files on him are pretty long."

Sandoval said, "Sound like the kind of guy who could get somebody augmented if he wanted to?"

The fear had crept from Alton's chest into his throat. He wasn't sure if he could keep this up much longer, especially given his dizzying fatigue.

"What about this person?" Taylor asked, flicking the screen. "Recognize her?"

Alton stared at the pad, then up at them, then at the pad again. Were they messing with him?

"Of course I do. It's my mom."

"This her too?"

He couldn't believe what he was seeing. She was with Kurt, their arms snaked around each other's waists. Her smile looked similar to the one she had flashed with his father at the Griffith Observatory. It explained who she had been out with lately, though not how the two of them had met.

"This is not good for her," said Taylor. "She works for Fernando Torres, right? Whose company provides government security?"

"Is that what he does?" He hadn't known for sure.

"This gets out and she'll lose her clearance," said Taylor.

"And then you'll be really fucked," said Sandoval. "You're not exactly living high on the hog now, are you?"

They had him. He couldn't be responsible for his mother losing her job. He had a chilling vision of the two of them subsisting in the camp near the underpass.

Taylor leaned back in her chair and looked at her partner. "How about a Coke for Alton?"

"Sure thing, boss. Twinkies too?" He snorted and left the room.

When they were alone, she said, "We're just starting here, Alton. We'll find more evidence, more witnesses. Somebody always records something. Eventually, we'll find out whatever you're not telling us. And then maybe you'll end up in the California Youth Authority. You know what they call that place?"

"No," he croaked.

"They call it Gladiator School. Alex could probably do okay there. He's older; he can handle himself. But the state splits up crime partners when they're sentenced. So, whatever facility you wind up in, he won't be there to protect you this time." She let this sink in, then said, "But it doesn't have to come to that."

"It doesn't?" He could hear the pleading in his voice.

"You grew up without a dad, and you've gotten in with some of the wrong people. But we know you're a smart kid, Alton. A good kid. We know you tried to stop Alex from hurting those guys."

His eyes burned with sudden tears. He didn't think of himself as a good kid. He never had.

Sandoval came back with the Coke. The burn of cold carbonation was exactly what Alton needed. He guzzled half of it, then rubbed his red eyes. He felt like he would say anything if they would let him go home and sleep.

Taylor beckoned, and the drones whirred toward her, folding their wings inside as they did. She plucked them out of the air and returned them to her pocket.

"It doesn't have to come to that if you're willing to do some good for us," she said. "There's a big rally in the desert next weekend. Supposedly, some kind of music festival. But its primary purpose is recruitment."

"Recruitment of what?"

"White Warriors," said Sandoval, curling his fingers into quotes.

"We think Kurt is one of the organizers," said Taylor. "All you have to do is get yourself invited, stay close to Alex, and report back whatever you see. Shouldn't be that hard."

"Will my mom be there?"

"Maybe."

"I don't want her to get in trouble."

"She won't," said Taylor. "At least not because of us. We just want to head off this activity before it escalates any further."

"Escalates to what?"

"Domestic terrorism," Sandoval said. "Maybe even a good old-fashioned race war."

"Race war? But that's history, right? Haven't things changed?" But even as he said it, he thought of the swastika graffiti in his building.

"Alton," Taylor said. "Take it from us. Some things *never* change."

CHAPTER 25

WHEN ALTON LEFT for school a few days later, Alex was waiting outside his building.

"Dammit," Alton said. "You scared the crap out of me."

"I don't want to risk any electronic messages."

"Where have you been?"

"Just laying low."

"They've got half of LA out looking for you."

Alex shrugged, smiled a little as though he was proud of it. "Listen, my dad wants to thank you in person for having my back. For helping me out lately."

Alton froze. Kurt must have known about his interrogation, that he had caved and agreed to spy. "Right now?" He swallowed. Were they going to snatch him off the street? He looked around for a car.

"No, not right now," Alex said. "It's seven o'clock in the morning. What are you so nervous about?"

"There's a... big test today."

"So sad I'm going to miss it. Anyway, there's a heavy metal show out in the desert outside of Lancaster next Saturday. Dad's got a VIP setup. Tents and shit. There'll be good grub there. Can you make it?"

"I should be able to."

"Check your calendar and get back to me."

Alton gave a nervous laugh.

"Saturday night, take the 17 'loop as far north as it goes, to the Angeles Forest. I'll have somebody pick you up at the station around seven." Alex paused. "And try not to look so excited."

Alton managed a smile. It felt utterly unconvincing, but it didn't matter. If this was a trap, there was nothing he could do about it now.

Save for him, the pod was vacated when it finally hit the end of the line. He took a deep breath and climbed the stairs to the desolate platform. It was hot but not as hot as in town. He could just make out the lights of LA blinking on in the purple dusk.

A voice said, "Hey, bud."

Alton whirled around to find a young dude with a blond goatee and ponytail waiting in the shadow of a black dune buggy.

"Here for the festival?" he said.

Alton nodded. He didn't know what else he could possibly be here for. The scrubby desert stretched in all directions.

"I'm yer ride."

They climbed into the vehicle. It was little more than scaffolding strapped around tires and bucket seats, but Alton was more mesmerized by the young man's ropey arms, sleeved with phosphorescent tattoos that depicted wide eyes and mouths distended to unnatural degrees. Whether they were faces in delirium or ecstasy or despair, Alton couldn't tell. They stretched together in a deformed orgy of expression.

"Ever wear a four-point belt?"

"Yes, actually," Alton said with pride, remembering Emily strapping him into the suborbital capsule.

"Cool, cool. Put this on too." He handed Alton a clear mask that covered his eyes and mouth. The mask lit up around the edges and sealed tight. The cool air that rushed in was so fresh and pure, he wondered why smog-huffing Angelenos didn't wear them day and night.

The driver retrieved a small container from the center console. Inside were thumbnail-sized patches. He slapped one onto a forearm, and it dissolved into a gaping phosphorescent mouth.

He held out the container to Alton. "MJX?"

"Uh, maybe later." His voice seemed trapped inside the mask, so he shook his head as well.

"Suit yerself." The driver stowed the box and waved his hand over the dash, illuminating a virtual touch screen. A snap of his fingers kicked on the throaty engine and triggered the piercing headlights. Ethereal electronica began to seep from behind the seats.

Alton was surprised to see an old-fashioned gear shift—long and flat black with a chrome knob—extending from the floor. He pointed to it. "Isn't this self-driving?"

"Sure, but where's the fun in that?"

To prove his point, he toggled through the gears and punched it, lurching them northeast into the brushland. They bounded over slopes and through ditches, the shocks like down pillows. Alton's stomach jumped into his throat as they flew up a hill and caught air for several long seconds. He held on as they plunged to earth, but the vehicle hit its stride effortlessly.

They emerged from the brushland into a flatter, sandier stretch. At first, only the sulfur-yellow high beams were visible through the dust, but then a 3D topo-gram blazed onto the windshield, allowing them to navigate with ease. The holo-light made the phosphorescent tattooed faces float in and out like a bolero of the damned.

The map extinguished as visibility returned and the lights of the festival appeared. Just as Alton began to relax, another pair of headlights sliced in from the east. As the driver adjusted their course, the second vehicle did as well so that they were headed toward each other on a *V*.

Alton wondered if he should point out that they would collide, until he realized that was the point. With no warning, they shot forth like an old rocket car screaming across salt flats. The g-forces mashed Alton against his seat, though he managed to raise his arm enough to grip the roll bar.

Their opposite number blasted forth as well, blue plasma streaking from its backend and lighting up the billowing dust.

Just as a collision seemed inevitable, the vehicles straightened on a dime. They were so close that Alton could touch the other driver if his arms weren't pinned in place. The vehicles edged in front of each other, trying to take the lead, when out of nowhere, a third buggy lurched in front of them both. Alton's driver stomped the brakes, and they spun out four or five times in a tide of earth and sand.

A few moments of deathly silence passed before the three drivers leapt from their buggies and charged each other. Alton waited for the blows to start, but their raised fists met only in high fives as they laughed and whooped it up.

What the hell have I gotten myself into, he thought as he staggered from the vehicle. As his adrenaline subsided and his senses returned, he felt the deep thumping of subwoofers and wrinkled his nose at the stench of overflowing porta potties. His instincts told him to turn back, but there was nothing to turn back *to* except the dark desert.

Maybe it was all a test, he decided. Those who could white-knuckle it through the octane-boosted joyride, then cross the gauntlet of shit, were worthy enough for whatever waited for them.

CHAPTER 26

INSIDE, JUST BEYOND the main entrance, he passed several head-banging acts playing on small stages. The tuneless throat shredding all sounded the same to him, though the performers' primary goal seemed not musical but to whip their fans into a convulsing frenzy.

Everybody here was white, more white people than he had ever seen together. There were skinheads, ripped lumberjack types with dense beards and hard expressions, pockmarked pencil necks with beady eyes and tiny mustaches, rabbity meth-heads that seemed primed for violence. They all sported ink, phosphorescent or traditional. The dress was combat boots, leather, chains, studs, but Alton also spotted a few preppies and frat-bro types. Almost all of them were young men in their twenties.

There weren't many women, perhaps not surprising given how erratic and dangerous the masculine presence felt.

He thought it was plain to see he didn't belong, but nobody seemed to notice. They moved within their own worlds. It helped that they all seemed pretty intoxicated. He thought he might feel less out of place if he was at least holding a beer, so he stood in line at one of the refreshment stands, crossing his arms, then uncrossing them, trying to determine how one was supposed to pose while waiting in line for beer. Most events now delivered drinks via drone, but the facilities here were decidedly low-tech, probably to keep prying digital eyes out, he thought.

He ordered his beer and drifted through the crowd. He took a sip and almost spat it out in disgust. He suddenly felt angry. What was he supposed to be looking for? Couldn't the cops have guessed that it would be like this? And where was Alex? He had said that his dad had some kind of VIP tent set up.

There was nothing like that nearby, so he headed toward the main stage with its two huge flanking screens, the desert mountains silhouetted in the distance behind them. Many others had begun to migrate in that direction as well. Something was about to begin.

He came to a huge space jammed with hundreds of people and stood near the back as the lights dimmed. The two enormous screens shimmered on and began playing a slickly produced video: purposeful-looking white people, American flags, eagles and trucks and guns, golden prairies, purple mountains' majesty, towheaded children, small towns, all set to deafening country-metal. People around him danced and hooted and hollered.

The video sizzled out, and the lights dimmed further. After thirty seconds of heightened silence, the main stage appeared on the screens and erupted in a blaze of pyrotechnics. The crowd exploded around him.

Alton expected a band to emerge, but out of the billowing haze, backlit to give him an entrance, strode Kurt. He came to the microphone, and his severe face filled both screens. Alton instinctively shrank back. The small man had clearly learned how to make his presence feel enormous.

"Welcome, my brothers and sisters! So glad you could join us on this important night!" Kurt's voice rang out, deep and clear. A great cheer arose.

"Thank you for traveling so far. I know this isn't an easy spot to reach. Unfortunately, despite our supposed First and Second Amendment rights, we aren't welcome to assemble peaceably near our homes without the police state, the surveillance state, inviting themselves into our midst. Just one of the many ways this country has turned against its original masters."

Scathing hissing and booing rippled across the crowd. Alton felt transfixed, rooted in place by seductive energy as much as his own fear. He realized he was holding his breath.

"A wise leader once said, 'The white community is entitled to take such measures as are necessary to prevail, politically and culturally, in areas in which it does not predominate numerically.' That was wisdom from the last century. But it is no longer just 'areas' in which we don't predominate numerically. It is this entire country! And so, matters dictate that we move beyond the political and cultural. That we take more decisive action for our survival. This is the beginning of that. We will usher in a new era before it truly is too late!"

The crowd noise was deafening this time. The eyes of those around him blazed with pride and purpose, as well as something he would one day learn to recognize as bloodlust.

"This Guerrero running for governor is a new kind of radical. One who wants to see us diminished even further. And believe me, he has ambitions. Presidential ambitions. He and his party are a direct threat that must be stopped!"

More roaring from the crowd. Alton scanned the crowd for Alex but still couldn't spot him.

"We won't go into details now. Obviously, we don't know who's listening." Alton froze. It seemed like Kurt was addressing him directly. "Just know that you will be asked to step up for your people at some point. So, be ready! In the meantime, we're here to enjoy ourselves!"

As Kurt stepped away, the sounds of a drummer counting out four beats reverberated through the space, and a band erupted over the giant speakers. Of course, Kurt hadn't been singling him out, but he remained frozen to his spot, half-expecting someone to drag him away.

In his thirst, he took a sip of beer. It was funny how every sip tasted less awful than the last, but still, he wanted a Coke, and that was enough to get him moving again.

Wandering around, he began to relax a little. He had almost never been out of the city, and despite Kurt's chilling rhetoric and the noise, he couldn't help thinking what a beautiful night it was. The last bit of indigo dusk was on the horizon, and a cool breeze drifted over the grounds.

Slightly buzzed, he forgot for a moment why he was there. And then, out of nowhere, he heard his name. *Shit*, he thought. *I'm caught.*

Somebody glowing pink with a pink mohawk was beelining toward him. He squinted through the dusky light and was stunned to realize that it was Alex, wearing a tank top that didn't hide his augmentation.

Yet even this spellbinding sight wasn't enough to keep Alton's eyes from going to the person with him. She looked younger than

Alex, maybe fifteen or sixteen. She was stunningly beautiful with long chestnut hair and sharp, even features. Her smile as they approached appeared so genuine and untroubled, he couldn't help but smile back.

"Hey, man!" Alex yelled. Alton was even more stunned when Alex wrapped him in a hug. He winced as the augmented armpits jabbed him in the shoulder blades.

Alex released him and turned to the girl. "This is Kiara."

"Alton, right?" she said.

"Uh, yeah, that's me."

"Very original name!" she yelled over the pounding of the music. "I love it!"

He hoped the darkness hid his blushing.

"You're drinking beer?!" Alex exclaimed. He seemed very excited, almost euphoric, Alton thought, like a teenager at a concert should be and not whatever his dad was making him into.

Alton fumbled the can from one hand to another. "I love your new hairstyle," he said.

Kiara threw her head back and laughed, startling Alton. Nobody ever thought he was *that* funny.

"Ha-ha," Alex said. "Blood kept clumping the sides, so I just got rid of it."

He turned his head to show thick black stitches settling into an angry laceration. Alton flinched.

"I get that ... but pink?"

"It matches my augmentation!" He squeezed his fists, sending the hot pink glow radiating down his arms.

"I cannot get over how fucking wicked that is," Kiara said. Alton wondered how wicked she would think it was if she had been in the blood-splashed pod that day.

Alex took Alton's warm beer can from him. "Hey, why don't you guys get to know each other while I get some refills?"

"Wait..." Alton said. But he was gone, leaving Alton to conquer his shyness.

"So... um, having fun?" he asked her. Glow sticks and neon collars bobbed and shimmered throughout the darkening concourse, making it feel like raves he had seen in holo-vids.

She shrugged. "It's not really my scene."

He was relieved to hear that. They already had something in common.

"How about you?" she said.

"Alex invited me. Well, his dad did."

"That's right," she said. "You're Alex's writing tutor."

He had never thought of himself as such, but he liked the sound of it. "How did you meet Alex?" he asked.

"Oh, we've known each other since we were little. Our parents were friends."

So, maybe not a girlfriend then, he thought, his heart hopping. "Do you live in LA?"

"I do now! I was living way north, in the mountains. Trinity County. Ever heard of it?"

He shook his head, smitten. Thinking back on this moment later in life, he would realize that part of his initial attraction to her was that she seemed so utterly guileless.

"Most people haven't," she said. "There's, like, ten people in the nearest town, and I just got tired of living in the middle of nowhere. So, my grandparents let me move down here to stay with my aunt and her wife. My aunts are weird, but it's got to be better than being a hermit."

"The mountains sound kind of peaceful actually," he said, thinking of his apartment tower in its cocoon of smog.

"Peaceful and boring."

"I guess you'll love LA then. What school are you going to?"

"North Hollywood. With you!"

He offered a high five, an excuse to touch her hand, which was rougher than he had been expecting.

"I guess Alex won't be attending anymore," she said.

He hadn't heard for sure yet whether Alex would ever return after the incident, but this was the best news possible. He could get to know Kiara without the bastard always hanging around.

"So, where are your parents now?" he asked.

Her face darkened. "They died when I was young."

"Oh . . . I'm . . . I'm sorry."

He kicked himself for the bluntness of the question. Fortunately, Alex was striding up with two beers and three shots. He handed a beer and a shot to Alton.

"No thanks," said Alton, returning the shot.

Alex shrugged and downed them both. Kiara downed hers and shudder-grimaced.

"Oh, look!" she exclaimed. They turned to where she was pointing. A rocket had just launched to the southwest and was streaking up toward the stratosphere.

"From Cosmost," Alex said.

She was enthralled. "It's so beautiful! I never see anything like that up north."

"Alton wants to be an astronaut," Alex said. "He's been to space."

Alton was surprised to hear Alex talk about him as though he was interesting. He certainly hadn't seemed interested before.

Kiara's mouth dropped open. "Amazing!"

His insides slithered like eels through a cloud of plankton. No girl had ever been so nice to him.

"Yeah, he'll tell you all about it, but we should probably go see my dad before it gets any later," Alex said.

"Before you get any drunker, you mean," Kiara said, and the two of them laughed.

Alton had actually begun to have fun, but now his abdomen swelled with dread.

CHAPTER 27

THE VIP AREA WAS at the northern edge of the festival, about a hundred yards behind the stage, with the open desert stretching to starry darkness on the other side. With the speakers pointed toward the masses, it was quieter here, if spookier, Alton thought.

As they made their way toward a large tent, they passed unsmiling men adjusting generators, servicing vehicles, hustling supplies back and forth, or just standing guard in front of various structures. Alton was alarmed to see that they were all wearing sidearms, which required an insane permit process to get in California.

Whatever was going on back here was surely the sort of thing that Jones and Sandoval wanted to hear about, so he tried to pay attention to as much detail as possible, though he strained to do so through the darkness and the fog of his fear. He also felt irritated that Alex and Kiara were laughing and joking while he felt like he was walking toward his executioner.

They came to the tent where two sentries recognized them and let them through. Inside, a few dozen people mingled in the dim light cast by a central hanging lamp. There was a bar against the far wall and a few tables piled with food.

Alton felt a chill when his gaze fell on a gun rack loaded with assault rifles. No permits allowed those, he thought. His chill turned to shock when someone stepped aside to reveal his mother standing next to Kurt.

In his anxiety, he had completely forgotten she would be here, and for a moment he wondered if it was even her. She wore sandals and short shorts that showed off her slim legs, and maybe it was just the dim light, but she looked younger.

She inhaled from a vape pen, then offered the pen to Kurt, who declined. As he did, he made some comment that sent her into gales of laughter, clouds of luminescent vapor billowing from her lungs.

Alton stood in horror until finally she saw him and exclaimed, "Baby!" He was completely mortified as people turned to look. She hadn't called him *baby* in years, and certainly not at this volume. She began to unsteadily come toward him, but instead of greeting him, her eyes fell on Kiara. "Oh my Lord," she said. "Who is this beauty?"

Kiara smiled and blushed. "Hi, I'm Kiara; nice to meet you." Lena did an awkward curtsy and almost fell on her butt. Kiara put her hand over her mouth to hide her smile. "I'm starving," she said and departed for the buffet.

"Jesus, Mom," he said. "Can you give me a break?"

But she was beaming and seemed completely unperturbed.

"How did you two meet?" he asked, nodding toward Kurt.

"What? Oh, yeah! Remember when Alex spent the night? He was nervous about going home the next day after you left for school, so I took him to smooth things over. We started seeing each other after that. Sorry, I should have told you."

He was taken aback. She never disclosed any details about her dating, let alone apologized for not doing so.

"And what about your . . . past?" he said. "I'm sure he knows all about it, right? And me?"

"Of course he knows about you, sweetie. You're my son." She tried to awkwardly embrace him, but he pushed her away.

"No, Mom. Does he know who *I really am*? Who my *father* is?"

Her smile disappeared. This was the first time he had even indirectly broached the subject of his mixed race with her. She put an unsteady finger to her mouth as though to shush him, and then fear came into her eyes as she saw Kurt approaching.

"How did you find out?" she asked.

"Don't worry," Alton said. "I'm not going to screw things up for you." *I'd have to care first.*

Kurt extended his hand as he walked up, and Alton shook it. Even in the desert, it felt like ice.

"Thank you for being a friend to Alex," he said. "Supporting Alex is supporting the cause. And it couldn't have been easy."

Alton, flustered, just nodded.

"Don't be modest. A young guy like you with no experience withstanding professional interrogation, and *almost* not folding under pressure?"

So, they had known, Alton thought. *Of course they had.*

He motioned for an assistant to hand him a sheetbook. As Kurt reached for it, his hand smacked the hanging lamp, throwing abrupt shadows in every direction. Alton felt paralyzed by the stony faces floating in and out of the swinging light, which now revealed that everyone in the tent was staring at him.

He shivered and looked over to Alex for help. His friend seemed merely embarrassed, while Kiara just stared at the ground. Alton felt grateful that she refused to witness his intimidation. He had one ally in the room at least.

Kurt tapped the sheetbook, and holograms of Taylor and Sandoval sprang from its surface. Staring straight ahead with no expression, they looked dead already. He cast a glance toward the rack of assault rifles. Would he be next? Would Kurt execute him in front of his own mother?

"They're treacherous people," Kurt said. "And it's not easy when they have you cut off from your own. That's why we want you to know that you have a place with us. Support. Solidarity. Do you know what that means?"

Alton nodded.

"Of course you do," Kurt said. "You're smart! Anyway, you won't have to worry about them anymore." He handed the tablet back to the assistant.

"Why . . . why not?"

Kurt smiled and patted Alton's shoulder. "The less you know about that, the better," he said.

Alton sucked in his breath. He was ragged with thirst. He looked to the bar, but Kurt wasn't finished.

"You've been a friend to Alex, and we appreciate that," Kurt said. "But coming here under false pretenses is something you'll need to atone for," Kurt said.

He scanned their faces again and felt rage. He wanted to tell him that they had no idea the depth of his false pretenses. That his mom had been with a man of color and that—somewhere inside that he couldn't identify yet—he was a person of color too.

He wanted to laugh at them and call them fucking idiots because they thought they had some kind of purity sense that would sniff it out. Because they thought they were special when they were just trash.

He snapped back to reality. "What . . . what do you want me to do?"

"I don't know yet. But you are to be ready when you're called upon. That could be at any moment. Do you understand?"

"Yes . . . yes, sir."

"Good. Now, go have some fun."

Avoiding his mother's eyes, Alton went to the bar and gulped down an icy beer. It fizzed in his belly as Alex and Kiara joined him.

"Sorry about that," Alex murmured.

Alton didn't think he sounded very sincere, but even a bullshit apology from Alex was a monumental event. He looked back at Kurt and his mother, their arms around each other, and then again at the lethal sheen of the guns on the rack. "How did they know about those cops?"

"Probably that guy," Alex said, gesturing at a compact, unsmiling man with severely parted black hair and pasty skin. "He does tracking for my dad, including DNA tracking."

Alton could feel the man's malignant energy from across the room. "DNA tracking? Like ancestry-type stuff?"

"No, like if they have your DNA, they can pinpoint your location anywhere in the world."

"I've never heard of it."

"That's because it's highly illegal. The ultimate in surveillance."

But that means . . . they tracked my DNA to figure out who I was with during my interrogation, he thought. *And that either you or my mom provided it.*

"Fascinating stuff," said Kiara. "But can we chill someplace else?"

Yes, Alton thought. *Anywhere but here.*

"Sure," Alex said. "Let's say bye to my dad first."

Waiting for them outside the tent, Alton realized he had never felt more isolated in his life. Even his own mother wasn't on his side. He stared up at the desert sky and watched the afterburn from the earlier launch fade into the violet stratosphere. Somewhere just beyond them, the ship rocketed away from Earth. He desperately wished he could reach escape velocity along with it.

He suddenly wished that Kiara was escaping with him, that they were hurtling to the stars and a new life together. Alex, of course, would remain back in the dust. Where he belonged.

PART III

CHAPTER 28

WHEN ALTON AWOKE, he knew immediately that he wasn't in his bed. The mattress was firm but supple, the comforter clean and soft, the pillows deep. The room was quiet and cool, the walls white and clean, and it was mostly empty, save for the bed and some blinking medical equipment.

There were two doors, one of which presumably led to a bathroom, and one to places unknown. There was a window, but the shade was down. Not being able to see out, he guessed he must be somewhere in the Central Compound.

With effort, splinters of memory began to tear at the gauze swaddling his brain. Rifts opened and images flitted like the shadows of fast-moving clouds across a canyon floor. He was splashing through muddy puddles . . . drone fire dancing blue through the camp like an electrical storm . . . Lance in bulky armor, cradling a big gun . . . himself frantically clutching and clawing as he descended into a valley, fathomless and indistinct like a never-ending bad dream.

These can't be memories, he decided. They must be drug-induced hallucinations. And yet . . . somebody had brought him here. Somebody had given him medical treatment. *Something* had injured him.

His mouth was very dry. He took a cup from a tray and sipped water through a straw. As he started to feel more awake, he began to sense his own body. He felt no pain, likely because of drugs. But he did feel an acute stiffness in his left leg.

Moving stiffened it further, almost as if it were encased in something. Fumbling around, he found the button that raised the bed and then tossed off the covers as his leg inched toward his body. He peered at it closely. It appeared to be sheathed in some kind of hard cast.

He swung his legs around and eased himself to the edge of the bed. There were no crutches, so he led with his right leg and then pushed gingerly onto his left. He was surprised by how strong it was, supporting him with no problem. He took one small step and then another. The cast was very flexible and easy to move in. This was impressive work, even for Simon.

He went to the window and passed his hand over the shade, raising it. The blazing light blinded him. He was stunned by how orange it was, especially for late October at Gypsum, when the sun struggled to reach mid-sky as it scattered feeble white particles across their short days. This was more like summer light.

Had he been in a coma for months? The thought sent a jolt of fear through him, but then his eyes adjusted. Below the window was an expansive stone courtyard ringed with landscaped hedges. A path led from the courtyard to a tangled grove of incense and camphor trees, oleanders and bougainvillea, beyond which lay buildings in the hazy distance. Tall buildings. A city skyline.

One that he would never not recognize, no matter how much it changed.

He turned toward the wall behind him, then toward the ceiling, to make sure the skyline wasn't being holo-projected. It wasn't.

He was in Los Angeles.

He tried to determine the series of events that could have brought him here. But as he gazed out, absorbing that particular quality of light against the familiar backdrop, the spinning wheel of his brain slowed, its spokes gummed up with nostalgia and grief and regret for the childhood he had had here. For the childhood he had wanted but couldn't have. For those long days and nights of yearning. For praying to be free but not having any idea how to achieve it. For lost friends. For mistakes and failures. For Kiara. For Bernardo, for . . . Christina.

"Hi," a voice said. "How are you feeling?"

He spun around to find a young woman in scrubs smiling at him.

"What happened to me?" he asked. "Where am I?"

"Someone will be along to answer your questions," she said. "Do you mind getting back into bed so I can take your vitals?"

He looked toward the open door, then back to her, then went to the bed. It had been a long time since he had been so close to a woman. Thus distracted, he didn't notice until he looked up that another woman had appeared in the doorway, sleekly attired in black jeans and boots and an open-necked shirt. Her raven hair was tied in a bun. The wisps spraying out the sides glowed in the sunlight.

"Hello, Alton," Áquilar said. "Feeling okay?"

He squinted to make sure it was her. "How long have I been out?" he asked.

"A few days."

That much was a relief at least. "When do I get this cast off?"

The deputy secretary and the nurse exchanged glances, and the nurse nodded. "He's in pretty good shape," she said as she left.

Áquilar crossed to the window and adjusted the shade so that the room wasn't so bright. "How much do you recall?" she asked.

"I remember that you wanted something and you were willing to put me in danger to get it."

"Things were urgent. I felt you needed more... convincing."

He sat bolt upright and regretted it immediately. "And you were okay almost getting me killed to do it?" He sank back into his pillow, starbursts crackling in his vision.

"You know what's at stake here," she said. "We need to get to Hagen before Guerrero does. And before Hagen follows through on his current agenda."

"I don't give a shit," he said. "I'm gone as soon as you remove this cast."

"It's not a cast."

He stared at her.

"It's your new leg."

He continued to stare.

"You had a number of injuries to your old one, including a compound fracture after your fall."

He gaped at it in horror. "You couldn't have set it?!"

"Time is of the essence. and it was much faster to remove it and give you a prosthesis. Also, we put a DNA scrambler in it so no one can track you."

He tried to shrink from it and felt utterly trapped because he couldn't.

"We can switch it out later if you don't like this one," she said. "There are sleeker models, models that are more... leglike. Either way, you'll be faster, stronger. Frankly, we should all get them."

He wondered where his old leg was. Had they incinerated it? Was it decomposing in a slimy bag somewhere? If he saw it separated from his body, would he recognize it as his?

"I'm sure it feels like things are being done against your will," she said. "But you made your choice when you escaped Gypsum."

"It was hardly a choice!"

"Well, unfortunately, that's the world in which you currently live," she said, her tone reflecting impatience for the first time. "Would you like to help me try to change it or not?"

"Fuck you. Send me back."

She went to the window and passed her hand over the shade until the light of the outside world dwindled and died. "There is no going back," she said. "Because no one knows you're here."

She returned to the foot of his bed and looked down on him. "You disappeared during a violent riot that left dozens dead," she said. "For all anyone knows, you may have even masterminded it. If they realize you escaped, you'll be right near the top of everybody's shoot-on-sight list. As a terrorist *and* former close associate of Hagen's, any possibility of a new life will be erased."

He lay there, seething, refusing to look her in the eye. She sighed and went to the door.

"We leave soon, Alton, so find some motivation," she said. "Even if it's just revenge against me."

He tried to stay angry, but lightheadedness and fatigue overwhelmed him, and he slept. He awoke in some pain, but he felt more clearheaded, the memory fragments stringing together into a narrative now. *They must have stopped the drugs*, he thought.

His lungs felt raw. He touched his hand to his chest as he remembered his torture and, with a sickening jolt, Simon's brutal death. He remembered believing he was going to die strapped to that board, drowning, almost blacking out, then being freed by Crow, of all people.

He thought of Oliver and his other friends at camp. Things would be more punitive for them now. They would be even more cut off from their loved ones. He couldn't imagine himself living free while they continued to suffer. Even more reason to cut off the head of the snake. End this insurgency so they could go home too. *There's your fucking motivation*, he thought.

But he didn't think their mission could succeed. None of them knew Alex like he did, knew the depths of his god complex, his utter indifference to the lives of people he felt were beneath him.

If this had a chance to work, he needed some kind of advantage when the moment of confrontation with his old friend came. And he had an idea what that could be.

He was starving. They had left a nutrition bar on the bedside table, but it tasted like electrical tape, so he dressed and went into the corridor.

His first thought was that this was a very strange hospital. The hallway was dark and burnished and lined with expensively framed portraits. It led to a landing that overlooked a space that was more gallery than living room, everything arranged just so on gleaming porcelain tile, incandescent in morning light through bay windows.

He descended the spiral staircase, slow and unsteady like the actress in that old movie about Hollywood. French doors led to a courtyard, where the deputy secretary and two others sat around a wrought iron table beneath green and gold citrus.

Her guests were Hispanic, fit, and attractive, with buzz cuts and coal-black eyes. Alton recognized them immediately as the two officers who had flanked her during his midnight interview at Gypsum.

Áquilar was smearing a plump bagel with cream cheese whipped to a decadent froth. She looked up as he emerged. "Hungry?"

He stepped forward, his eyes going wet as he surveyed the spread. A cast-iron skillet overflowed with bacon, eggs, and fried potatoes. Avocado, strawberries, and orange slices spilled from a centerpiece. The aroma of rich, strong coffee buckled his knees.

He wiped the drool from his mouth. "I could eat."

CHAPTER 29

THE TABLE, LADEN with its rich bacon and glistening fruit, reminded him of Bernardo and their childhood breakfasts around his parents' kitchen table. Alton stopped chewing as grief and regret gathered in his throat. Áquilar's house—its size and opulence and layout—also reminded him of Bernardo's, which he realized probably didn't exist anymore after the bombing. He had never gone back to find out. He couldn't face it.

Then he realized. "We're in East LA."

Áquilar had stepped away for a moment, and neither Eli nor Valeria, as they had been introduced, responded, so he got up and wandered to the northern edge of the courtyard. Through the branches and leaves, the skyline was just visible, dominated by a large complex of new-looking buildings several miles away, including a squat alabaster edifice he could just make out. In the near distance, two fighter jets streaked by. His mouth dropped open as he realized he was looking at the temporary White House.

DC had been evacuated after Alex detonated the dirty bomb in its suburbs, and temporary relocation of the Capitol was necessary. But choosing a traditionally Hispanic neighborhood in an American metropolis that was 80 percent Latin only further fueled the grievances of the white minority.

President Guerrero's experts made arguments about the location's security and environmental stability. Climate change had compromised the East Coast well before the bomb, they said, while East LA was far enough inland *and* under the protection of military bases in the region.

The move made some white people, steeped in victimhood even when they had been the majority, claim even greater marginalization. Alton thought it was curious that Alex hadn't returned earlier to take advantage of their outrage to recruit or launch renewed attacks.

Then it occurred to Alton for the first time that perhaps Alex was finished fighting and had something different in mind for his next move. Had the message imploring his followers to rise up simply been misdirection? Or was he really preparing for his last stand?

When Alton returned to the table, Áquilar was back, the food had been cleared, and they were getting down to business. Eli projected a holomap of a residential area and said, "We've been through Kiara's place several times. But not through Alton's eyes. I suggest we go back there with him."

Áquilar looked at Valeria. "What do you think?"

Valeria studied the map for a moment, then said, "If she left voluntarily, maybe she indicated where, possibly without realizing it. If someone kidnapped her, maybe she managed to leave some sign, something only he would recognize. Beyond that, I can't imagine what the gringo might be good for."

"We still have the same questions, Alton," Áquilar said. "If she did go with Hagen willingly, why now? And why, after two years, has he chosen this moment to come back, beyond the possibility that he has simply recovered his strength?"

"Could there be something symbolic?" Eli asked. "An upcoming event or an anniversary maybe? What about some recent development that presents a new strategic opportunity?" He looked at Alton and crossed his muscular forearms, causing the EV bio-matter to shimmer pink in the sun, making Alton think of Alex and that horrible day on the 'loop.

Alton considered mentioning that the Mars Colony Launch might be a target but didn't want to look foolish for stating the obvious. Surely, they'd already considered this, so he just shook his head.

"See what I mean?" said Valeria. "Useless."

"If you think being here is my idea, read the whole dossier next time," Alton said.

Áquilar gave Valeria a withering look, then said to Alton, "Try to think."

He massaged his forehead. "There was this Nibelung lieutenant in camp with me, Lance, who had been hiding the fact that he had been with Alex somewhat recently—like six months ago. Just before the riot, he told me they had been planning a big operation, but I never found out what it was."

"Some skinhead trying to look like a big shot in prison," said Valeria. "He probably never even met Hagen."

Alton shook his head. "If he just wanted to brag, he wouldn't have kept it a secret until *after* Alex made his grand reappearance. Whatever it was, I think he at least believed it was real." He remembered Lance's desperation, how he had abandoned his men mid-battle and begged to escape with Alton.

"Another dirty bomb?" Eli asked.

"Or a nuke this time." Valeria scowled. "Maybe we shouldn't be sipping espressos a few miles from ground zero."

"I didn't get that sense, but she has a point," Alton said. "If we find him and you don't alert the military, and he wipes out a city when you had the chance to put him down..."

"It's a risk I believe worth taking," Áquilar interjected. "Before Guerrero consolidates more of the wrong kind of power. Before this country slides even further into authoritarianism and we're forced into the same battles my grandparents' generation had to fight. And their grandparents before them. Except this time with one of our own at the helm."

"Why do you think it's acceptable for you to choose that risk on behalf of everybody?" Alton asked but received only silence in response.

"Much as I hate to say it, the gringo is right," Valeria said. "I say we waste Hagen on sight."

"He's still a citizen with rights," Eli said. "And a human being."

"No. He's the fucking devil," Alton said, surprising them with his venom. He wiped the spit from his lip. "He's a master manipulator and propagandist. *If* we somehow capture him, has it occurred to you that a trial in front of the whole world could get him even more support?"

"That's why we argue against his values in the court of public opinion. Like you're supposed to in a democracy. And we lift this system back onto the rails."

"And what's Guerrero going to say about that?" Alton asked.

"Once we have Hagen in custody, what's he going to do, blow up the prison?"

"No, but he could just dump him in a black site," Eli said.

"And he'll fire you for sure," Valeria added. "Maybe even bring you up on charges."

She shrugged. "It will be a slap on the wrist. I've already won three terms in Congress. I'll run for something else."

Like POTUS, Alton thought.

"But at least our side gets to make a case for who we are," she concluded.

Our side. Did she mean all Americans who shared her values? Or just non-whites? He supposed that even if it was the latter, no one could blame her for not wanting to go down in history the way so many generations of Anglo-Americans had.

"I'll help you," he said. "But I want something from you first."

"Clock is ticking, Alton."

"I don't give a shit. You took my leg. You owe me."

"What then?"

"Augmentation."

"Completely out of the question."

"I'm not going into the lion's den unprotected."

"The team will protect you."

"Yeah," he said, casting a side-eye at Valeria. "They seem totally committed to my safety."

"I can't implant a civilian, Alton."

He sat back and folded his arms. "I guess we'll find out how bad you really need me then."

She rolled her eyes and sighed. "You can have everything but EVs. They're too dangerous. And they take too long to implant and recover from. I want to go tonight, as soon as you get the procedure."

"I'll be less capable than the rest of the team without EVs." *And less able to kill Alex on sight.*

"It's a highly trained special-ops unit. You'll be less capable no matter what."

CHAPTER 30

ÁQUILAR WOKE HIM at midnight. They took a pilotless stealth chopper, black and sleek, the cramped interior aglow in sulfur-yellow. As they sliced toward downtown, he reclined as best he could and gazed out. The glowing grid of the Inland Empire stretched behind them, but the metropolis seemed truncated to the northwest as if part of it had been lost.

"I haven't been home in years," he said. "Why does the Valley seem... smaller?"

"It's just the blackouts. They've been common for years but seem to be happening even more lately."

"Why?"

"Heat. Fires. Weather events. Cyberattacks. Offshore grid siphoning. Gremlins." She shrugged. "It's not always easy to pinpoint the cause."

He must have looked worried because she said, "Don't worry. They've got plenty of juice at the augmentation facility."

He had been debating whether or not he should bring it up, but finally he asked, "Why is Valeria so hostile toward me?"

Áquilar hesitated, then said, "She sees the camps as a necessary evil and would be perfectly happy if they stayed open indefinitely. Her family suffered badly during the ICE wars. And for many years before. We all did."

"It doesn't worry you? Or that she openly stated her preference for killing Alex rather than capturing him?"

"We're not looking for dogmatists, Alton, just professionals. And few are as professional as she is. You can trust her to follow orders."

They swooped down into the high-rises, the streets a mosaic of light far below, and set down on one of the highest rooftops. Security led them inside and down several echoing stairwells to a fortified door that whooshed open to reveal an industrial laboratory two stories high and full of elaborate equipment.

Panels blinked against the far wall, illuminating stainless steel tables and medical lockers. Straps and tubes and cords protruded from a reclining chair. Alton felt as though he had entered some kind of steampunk dentist's office.

A lightly bearded middle-aged man came toward them, his shirtsleeves rolled up to the elbows. He nodded to Áquilar. "Dr. Reynolds, deputy secretary. It's an honor." He turned to Alton. "This must be the guinea pig."

Alton looked at Áquilar, and Reynolds laughed. "Just kidding," he said. "Okay, so he's getting the basic package, no EVs, right?"

"And don't put him under, even if it hurts," she said. "I need him sharp."

"You got it," Reynolds said. "Okay, Alton, first things first." He pointed to an assistant holding an electric razor. Without ceremony, the assistant began to shear him like a sheep.

"Shouldn't take longer than two hours. If he survives," he said and laughed again.

When he was finished, they brought him to the roof, dressed in dark clothes. His shaved head tingled in the hot breeze. Within a few minutes, the stealth chopper set down to retrieve him. Áquilar was gone, replaced by Eli and Valeria wearing black TALOS.

"Popped your cherry, huh?" Eli said once they were in the air.

"It doesn't feel much different."

"That's because you didn't get the EVs. They make you feel really funky," he said.

"You only felt funky because you got pink ones," Valeria said.

"Val holds some fairly regressive views on gender roles," Eli said. "I got pink because it's my son's favorite color."

"How old is your son?"

"He'll be five next week. It would be nice to be home for his birthday, but I'm not holding my breath."

Alton murmured a response, but his mind was on his old apartment buildings as they came into view to the east, dark husks protruding from the earth. Despite his difficult relationship with his mother, he'd been glad when she'd finally gotten out of there. The complex had only become more run-down and dangerous.

They continued west over parks and preserves, Mulholland Drive snaking beneath them through the darkened domain of the ever-wealthy. Soon they slowed and began to descend amid trees and well-kept streets.

"It's a good night for a blackout," Eli said. "Makes our job easier."

"Where are we?" Alton asked.

"Near Calabasas."

"She's moved up in the world."

The chopper hovered silently over a park and then touched the ground. Eli killed the engine, and they climbed out. He waved his hand like a magician, and the chopper disappeared.

"What happens if someone bumps into it?" Alton asked.

"The cloaking device is also an electrified field. They won't know what hit them and won't hang around to find out. Anyway, we won't be here long."

They strode through the silent park, past the sleeping homeless, then crossed the street to a newish townhouse complex, the units staggered at different levels in the popular style. Kiara lived on the ground level. Valeria passed her hand over the lockpad, and the front door opened into a low-lit space.

Kiara had once favored a quirky aesthetic that was nowhere in evidence here. Of course, Alton was remembering the bright, chaotic bedroom she had occupied at her aunt's house during high school. Her temporary apartment in DC had featured a more muted style, so perhaps her move here was a natural evolution.

But he doubted it. Her DC apartment had been sparse because she hadn't intended to stay, not because she had changed. Looking around the immaculate front room, he suspected she had spent even less time here. The kitchen was equally unlived-in. Opening cupboards and drawers, he doubted a meal had ever been prepared.

He turned to Eli and said, "Either she never intended to live here or never got a chance to."

They went down the hall to the master bedroom to find the bed made. The walls were bare except for a large framed black-and-white photo that hung over the bed, depicting a mountain landscape in the style of Ansel Adams. Professional clothes hung in the closet. Alton began flipping through them.

"Doesn't look like she had a chance to pack," Eli said.

Alton went to the chest of drawers. The top drawer was swept clean. The middle drawers contained a few more items but seemed light.

"She packed," he said. "No underwear or socks. Only a few T-shirts."

"Glad we brought the panty detective," Valeria said. "How do you know she didn't just like to freestyle it?"

"Because even when she stayed one night, she brought six pairs of everything."

He opened the remaining drawers, then checked the top of the closet and the hall closet as well. "She was a big hiker," he said. "And there's no evidence of that here. No pack, boots, gear."

"Maybe she gave it up?" Eli said.

"Maybe," he said, eyeing the framed photo of the mountain. "But she lived and breathed that shit." For a few years after high school, it was practically all she had done.

Eli stood beside him, and they regarded the picture together.

"Is there a way to tell where that is?" Alton asked him. "Can you scan it or something?"

"*You* can," Eli said. "Just fix it with your eyes and say 'scan.' Once you become more practiced, you won't need to say it out loud."

He stood at the foot of the bed and focused on the poster. "Scan," he said. "Location."

Suddenly, a screen appeared before his eyes offering a selection of capabilities: night vision, infrared and other spectrums, mapping and location services, medical imaging, composition imaging. The program fixed the image and outlined it, waiting for him to choose. There were menus and submenus. He didn't know where to begin.

"Move." Valeria nudged him out of the way and peered at it, while Alton kept trying to work out the functions.

"It's white granite," she said. "It says it's in the Trinity Alps, a subrange of the Klamaths. Way up northeast of San Francisco."

It hit him with a jolt. *Trinity County. Where Kiara had lived before moving to LA.*

Alton must have hit all the functions simultaneously because the photo began to rotate in and out of various outlines and colors, making him dizzy. Now it was transparent, then in X-ray, then pixelated. The scans were flitting by too quickly for him to get a good look, but one of the iterations caught his eye.

"Wait. Stop," he said. "Go back. Stop." After another pause, he said, "Holy shit."

"What is it?" Eli asked.

"Can I project this thing?

"Just say 'project.'"

"Project."

A beam of soft, translucent light emanated from behind his eyeballs, enveloping the picture and revealing a small image at the base of the mountains. Three figures stood together.

"Enlarge."

They could all see it now, shimmering in the hologlow: Kiara, Alex, and Alton grinning for the camera. He didn't remember exactly when or where it had been taken—he thought he looked about sixteen—but it was obviously before things had taken a turn for the worse.

Kiara was sandwiched between them, her arms around their shoulders, sunlight illuminating her chestnut hair. He drew in his breath, remembering how it had felt just to be around her, even despite the crushing weight of his desire.

"This wasn't taken there," he said.

"Obviously," Valeria said. "She overlaid it onto the poster. For *you*, white bread."

"What do you think she wanted to tell you?" Eli asked.

"Probably where they are," he said. "Roughly, anyway."

"The Trinity Alps?" Valeria asked.

"I think so. Her grandparents lived in the region. They might still."

"If she planted this, she wants us to follow," said Eli. "Áquilar was right. Bringing you was a good move."

He could practically feel Valeria rolling her eyes, while his eyes remained glued to the image. It was one thing to trash the fading printout of Kiara in his locker at camp, the one from their time together in DC, when her heart had been hardened and she was not altogether present during their brief affair.

But seeing her young again like this, he didn't know if he could turn away after all. What if he really could help ensure Alex's peaceful capture? Alex would live, and Áquilar would get her glory, but maybe it was a fair price to pay to make sure Kiara was okay. But then something occurred to him.

"I've been locked up for two years," he said. "How did she even know I would see this? What if it's a trap?"

Valeria shrugged. "I'll take that action over sorting through underwear any day," she said.

CHAPTER 31

KIARA'S AUNTS, SALLY and Lorna, lived in the same Reseda neighborhood, sprawling over with ancient junk and dried-up vegetation. Alton and Eli stood on their porch and rang the doorbell just before 8:00 a.m. Sally, a big-framed woman of about sixty with tight, close-cut curls, answered in sweats and a T-shirt. She squinted for several seconds trying to recognize him, before he remembered his head was freshly shaved.

"Alton!" she exclaimed finally.

"Hi, Sally."

Her eyes filled with tears. She stepped forward and gave him a hug.

"Kiara told us you had been . . ."

"Two years," he said, misting up despite himself. He let go of the embrace and said, "This is Eli. Can we talk for a minute?"

"Is this about Kiara?" she asked.

Alton nodded.

She hesitated as she looked Eli over but stepped aside and let them through. Lorna, short and slight, her straight, shoulder-length hair gone gray, stood inside.

"Hi, Lorna," Alton said.

She nodded but kept her distance.

"Lorna was just making our morning pot," Sally said. "Let us get you a cup."

She led them to wicker seats all but buried in the cluttered living room and settled into the love seat opposite them.

"Did they treat you okay?" Her eyes shone with pity.

Alton gave a thin smile.

After a minute, Lorna came in and handed around steaming mugs, then joined Sally on the love seat.

"Is she okay?" Sally asked.

"We're not exactly sure," Alton said. "When was the last time you heard from her?"

Sally looked at Lorna. "It's hard to say," she said. "It's been a long time since she checked in regularly."

"It's been a couple of months at least," Lorna said. "She's with *him*, isn't she?"

"We think so. But we don't know if it's . . . voluntary or not."

"Of course it is," Lorna snapped.

"You don't know that, Lor," Sally said. But her voice was resigned.

Eli's wicker chair crackled as he leaned forward. "Why do you say that?"

"Because being with him is the only thing she's ever cared about," Lorna said.

Alton felt the truth of that. And the pain.

"I'm sure you're aware of his grand reappearance," Eli said. "Do you think whatever he came back for involves her?"

"How the hell should we know?" Lorna said. "She's never let us in on their plans."

"Do you have an idea where they are?" Sally asked.

"We're pretty sure they've gone north," Eli said. "Trinity County."

Sally and Lorna exchanged glances.

The mug was burning Alton's hand. Every space was covered, so he set it on the floor in front of him, then asked, "Are her grandparents still alive?"

The two women looked at each other again, confused.

"Grandparents?" Sally said. "My mother is still with us, but she lives in Ohio. Why?"

"Wasn't that who she lived with up there? Before she moved down here with you?"

"Those are her *parents*," Lorna said. "My sister."

Alton was taken aback. "She told me they live out in the boonies," Alton said. "That she couldn't stand it up there and wanted to be in the city." *Why would she lie about something like that?*

"That part is true," Sally said.

"Are you in contact with them?" Eli asked.

"Not really," Sally said. "They used to come down here every so often for a visit, but it's been at least two years since we've seen them."

"Can you tell us how to find them? Maybe they can help us locate Kiara," Eli said. "This is a very urgent matter."

Lorna cast him an evil look. "Who is *we*?"

"All I can tell you is that *we* want to bring in both Alex and Kiara safely," Eli said. "Before anyone else gets to them."

"What does that mean?" Sally asked.

"I think you know that Alex has no shortage of people who want to harm him."

"We're not about to send the government to our sister's front door," said Lorna. "She's off the grid for a reason. It's bad enough you brought them this far, Alton."

He tried to look penitent, but he was busy wondering what their reason for getting off the grid had been.

"Okay, this is all classified," Eli said. "So, please keep it in this room. President Guerrero failed to get Alex before. There's declining political support for the camps. Election season is ramping up, and the president is desperate for a victory. We have no doubt he will blitz that whole mountain range if he thinks Hagen is up there. Your sister's place could end up as collateral damage."

Lorna raised an eyebrow at Alton. "And just how did you get yourself involved in all this?"

"I think Kiara is trying to get in contact with me. I think she wants me to come find her. I promise if we do find her, I'll do everything I can to get her away from him."

Lorna looked at Sally, who nodded grimly and went into the back room. She returned a minute later with a piece of folded-up paper.

"There's no address," Sally said. "Just these directions. Don't put them into anything that can be tracked. And please let us know when she's safe."

"Of course," said Alton.

At the door, Lorna said, "One more thing."

"What's that?"

"If Alex doesn't make it out, that's okay."

CHAPTER 32

THEY TOOK OFF a little after noon in a transport ship that seemed too big for the small crew and modest equipment. In addition to Eli and Valeria, there were seven other commandos. There had been brief introductions, but Alton hadn't bothered to remember their names. He hoped he wouldn't know them long enough for names to matter.

They flew at twenty thousand feet, low enough for him to get a good look at the landscape. North of LA, the expanse of Cosmost, with its control facilities and giant hangars and spaceport, spread out to the sea.

Just inside the northern end of the complex lay the two cavernous openings of the old underground Hydro-channels that had once diverted water to the region from the northern mountains but had been abandoned since the advent of affordable desalination. Nobody had bothered to fill them in, and they lay gaping like the mouths of giant worms.

The Mars Colony ship was docked at the northwestern edge, near the ocean. It was at least twice as tall as the other vessels, and it had short wings and a snub nose, not unlike the old space shuttles, but was much bigger.

As they flew by, he admired the sleek silver-and-white craft with its orange trim. Because the plan was to have exterior cameras film the voyage, the world would gaze upon that gorgeous body for months. He felt a little foolish when it passed out of sight and he realized his face was pressed against the window.

They next flew over vast facilities that removed carbon from the air, slowly converting it to stone in huge underground caverns, then endless fields of wind turbines that spun silvery-white in coordinated spirals like schools of fish. He watched them, transfixed, until he nodded off.

When he awoke, the landscape had changed. Blackened and charred land crisscrossed clay-colored tracts of tentative saplings in a jagged patchwork. The countryside was so ruined that he was surprised when an enormous complex suddenly came into view.

"Wait... is that...?"

"Yes," said Eli, who sat across the aisle from him, next to Sergeant Martinez. "One of the first and the biggest. It houses about ten thousand interns, multi-gender, plus children."

He was dumbfounded by its sheer holding capacity. Gypsum had been small, almost like a summer camp. This was more like a city.

"They just dropped them right into that hellscape?" Alton felt a chill.

"Safest place for them. All the fuel in the area is already burned."

"Yeah, I'm sure they're completely safe," Alton said, thinking of his own experiences at Gypsum. For a moment, he wondered if maybe Alex wasn't wrong to fight any government responsible for this.

From a few seats up, he heard Valeria say, "Come on, gringo. Don't you miss your camp just a little? Three hots and a cot, all on the taxpayers?"

He refused to take the bait and just said, "This is wrong. Those people are innocent."

"Val doesn't think white folks *can* be innocent," Eli said, and he and Martinez chuckled.

As they passed over San Francisco and its gleaming bridges, the unit began to gear up. Everybody was in a TALOS now, slate gray and skintight, even Alton. He thought he looked like a seal, but the suit was surprisingly comfy and breathable.

Just as he began to wonder where they would land the lumbering transport, a transparent shield descended from the roof. There was a hissing of gas as the shield sealed, then a terrifying jolt as the seams of the plane seemed to split. Their section detached from the transport and rocketed back for a few moments, pinning Alton to his seat.

Next, they seemed to float, as though bobbing in water, then the detached craft began to travel under its own power. As they banked, Alton saw the body of the transport disappearing into a tower of clouds.

Rain spattered the windows, and the dropship rocked in the wind as they descended. Valeria, unfazed, went to the front of the craft to brief them. Alton tried to ignore the fact that she looked utterly smashing in her dark TALOS, fresh buzz cut, eyes glowing like coals.

"We're over the Trinity Alps," she said. "The targets live at the base in a forested area far from any town or road," she said. "We've determined a landing area five kilometers out. We'll scatter down the hill toward the domicile, flank the house, and advance from three sides. Sat-birds haven't spotted anything to worry about, and these people aren't professionals that we know of, but stay sharp. This is their territory."

Alton's raised eyebrows must have been more conspicuous than he realized because she said, "You got a problem with my orders, Civvie?"

Everyone turned to look at him, and he shrank in his seat a little. "I'm sure you know what you're doing," he said.

"You're here to advise," Eli said. "Tell us what's on your mind."

"Well," Alton said, "they moved off the grid to avoid this kind of thing. If they detect us, it's going to spook them, maybe send them into hiding. And, like you said, they know this area a lot better than we do..."

Val turned her palms up. "So?"

"So, let me go in first, alone. I've never met them, but at least they'll know who I am once I introduce myself. And, as you keep pointing out, I'm a civilian. The rest of you can be nearby if something goes wrong."

She gave Eli a dubious look.

"He makes good points," Eli said. "I think it's worth trying."

"Fine," she said. "If he's wrong, it's your responsibility."

They set down in a glade snugged by firs. As the others unloaded, Alton stepped away from the ship and deeply breathed the cool mountain air. The occasional bird hooted or cawed, and water dripped from branches, but otherwise the forest was quiet and still. He closed his eyes and absorbed the serenity until he heard footsteps and turned to find Eli handing him a pack.

"What's in here?" he asked, struggling to get ahold of it.

"Stuff to keep you alive for at least a couple of weeks," Eli said. "In case we get stuck up here or you get separated from us."

"Stuck up here?"

He shrugged. "Shit happens."

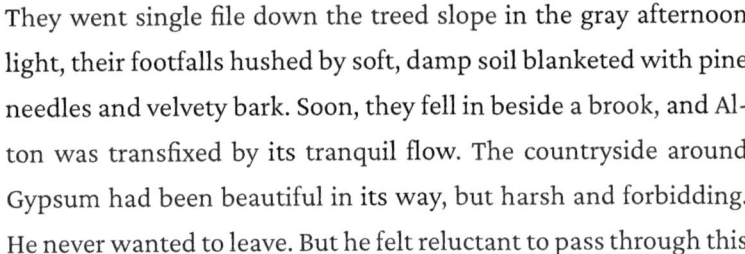

They went single file down the treed slope in the gray afternoon light, their footfalls hushed by soft, damp soil blanketed with pine needles and velvety bark. Soon, they fell in beside a brook, and Alton was transfixed by its tranquil flow. The countryside around Gypsum had been beautiful in its way, but harsh and forbidding. He never wanted to leave. But he felt reluctant to pass through this place.

The path leveled out after about thirty minutes. The brook turned away from them, and the soil at the base of the mountain became firmer and less wet. They walked for another twenty minutes until their route intersected a faint trail curving out of sight through the trees. Valeria turned to Alton. "You're up, Civvie," she whispered. "Don't fuck it up."

Alton gave her a sarcastic salute, then proceeded past them along the trail, glancing back to see the squad evaporating into the gloom. The light was almost gone, and it became even darker as a canopy of branches enveloped the path.

After a few minutes, the path let out in a meadow. He could just make out the house against the base of the mountain, maybe a hundred meters from him, secluded by dense pines that pricked the dusk-mottled sky with charcoal tips.

There were no vehicles, signs of people, or any lights. Perhaps Kiara's parents had made a run to town or maybe no longer lived here at all. Or maybe they had spotted their ship and fled, as Alton had feared they might.

He went carefully across the glade, overrun with poppies and larkspur. He wondered if Kiara had played here as a child, though its tangles of wild flowers and grasses seemed to suggest that humans had barely touched this place.

Later, Alton would think that this was exactly the idea being cultivated since it made him put his guard down and think he could walk up to the front door. Instead, the energy shield sprang up around him in an instant, a translucent box no bigger than a wardrobe. He tried to neutralize it with his augmentation.

"Shield down!" he yelled. "Penetrate! Energy field off!"

"It doesn't work that way," said an older male voice. "Even if you knew what you were doing, which it don't seem like you do."

Through the energy field and the very last of the light, Alton could just make out a tall man holding a rifle. A white dog stood at his side, growling.

"But even if you do get out, you're gonna taste a few barrels of rock salt."

"Mr. Cunningham," Alton said. "I'm here to . . ."

His muscles seized up as the box began to compress. He resisted crying out.

"I know why you're here. I guess I should be grateful it's taken your lot all these years to pay us a visit. But we're not going to one of those camps." He shouldered the rifle.

"I'm Alton Lucas. I'm just here to find Kiara," he said through gritted teeth. "She's missing."

"Don't you say my daughter's name."

Alton fell to his knees as the cube sizzled around him. His body balled up and quivered. His head felt like it was being crushed by a mountain troll.

"I'm a friend of hers! I'm just here to try to help... Arrrghhh!"

"Tell me where the rest of your team is, and I'll make it stop."

Alton opened his mouth, but his lips were pulled tight against his teeth, and he couldn't speak.

The edges of his vision blurred and blackened.

Now, a female voice said, "That's enough, Howard."

Howard kept the gun leveled at him.

"This is Alton, Howard. The one that was locked up in the camp for two years."

The energy field fizzled away. Alton slumped over on his side, his face in the cool dirt, the sound of crickets in his ears. The dog came over and sniffed him.

"I'll shoot you if you try anything," Howard said. "Camp or no camp."

CHAPTER 33

IN THEIR WARM kitchen, the woman, Geraldine, boiled water for tea in a copper kettle. It was a smart kitchen like any other but with antique touches—cast-iron pots and pans, wicker baskets piled in the corner, a wood-burning stove—as though they had adopted the best parts of the new world but preserved the old. As a young person craving excitement, Kiara had wanted to get away from here. Maybe now that she was older, she would recognize the balance they had achieved, not to mention the inviting coziness.

Alton watched Geraldine as she prepared the tea, trying to see Kiara in her. She was not as old as he had imagined. Maybe in her early sixties, small and trim like her daughter but with short gray hair.

Her father sat across the table, the rifle still pointed in Alton's direction. He appeared to be older than his wife, maybe seventy, with a gaunt face and Kiara's high cheekbones and white hair that stuck straight up. The dog, sandy white with rough-looking fur, was his doppelgänger.

"When did they let you out?" she asked him, as she set milk and sugar and spoons on the table.

"They didn't," he said. "I escaped. A few days ago."

"On the one hand, good for you," said Howard. "On the other, we're none too pleased that you came straight here."

"What was it like?" Geraldine asked.

Alton gazed around the kitchen. Fresh-baked bread cooled on the counter, and a tin of cookies sat above the stove. Three or four well-used throw pillows filled out a window bench. The place smelled of mint leaves and tomato soup. "You miss the little things," he said, absently rubbing his crew cut. It was a strange thing to get used to.

She brought three mugs over and joined them at the table. The warm aroma of the tea made him feel a little less brittle after his virtual electrocution.

"You get that done in there?" Howard asked.

"My augmentation?"

"Yeah."

He shook his head. "I got this done in Los Angeles yesterday."

He looked taken aback. "Yesterday?"

"Yes, it was mandatory for me to join the team." He looked down as he stirred milk and sugar into his tea in case Howard could tell he was lying.

"Where is the team?" Howard said.

Alton took a sip, eyed the rifle over the rim of his mug. "Not too far from here."

"How many?"

"Ten total."

Howard looked at his wife as if to say, *What did I tell you?*

"But we're not here for you. We just want to find Kiara. She may need rescuing."

Howard snorted, and Alton got the gist. *Kiara never needed rescuing in her life.* Geraldine gazed without expression into her mug.

It had started to rain, and the drops pattered against the darkened window. The dog scratched its ear.

Finally, Howard said, "You didn't bring a special ops unit to our front door just to rescue our daughter."

"We're after him too. But to bring him in, not to kill him."

Howard shook his head. "He'll never let that happen."

"I don't think so either. Believe me, this wasn't my idea."

"Whose then?"

Alton hesitated, then said, "Rose Áquilar's."

Howard scowled, and Geraldine shook her head as though not surprised.

"I thought she and Kiara had a good relationship?" Alton asked.

"Maybe once," Geraldine said. "But that woman used Kiara. Held her career back. Not that it matters now."

Alton caught Howard shooting a look of warning at his wife, and he was struck by an intuition. "She's been here recently, hasn't she?" he asked.

Geraldine nodded. "A few weeks ago."

"What did she come for?"

Her face darkened. "To say goodbye."

"Geraldine!" Howard banged his hand on the table, sloshing tea from the mugs. The dog looked up with a start.

"Not that she said it outright," she said. "But it was pretty obvious that wherever she's going—wherever *they're* going—it's meant to be permanent."

"His team is out there listening!" Howard said.

Now, it was her turn to raise her voice. "Good! Tell them everything, and maybe we'll see her again!"

"That's not what she wants!"

"She doesn't know what she wants! She's always been under the sway of that boy."

"No," said Howard. "She's just as smart and calculating as he is. *More*."

Alton's mind raced. Had Alex and Kiara planned some sort of suicide mission, some doomed lovers' final hurrah? Did they think they might not escape the radius of their next bomb? Was Guerrero finally closing in on them? Then he remembered what Sally and Lorna had revealed.

"Kiara told me that she was raised by her grandparents, that her parents were dead," he said. "I believed that for years. Do you know why she would lie about something like that?"

Geraldine had brought the kettle over to refill their cups. On her way back to the stove, she deftly plucked the rifle from the table and leaned it in a corner. "Because we *were* dead to her. For a while," she said.

"What happened?"

She looked at her husband, who sighed and reluctantly began to speak. "Kurt and I were close when we were young," he said.

Alton remembered Kiara telling him that she and Alex's parents had known one another.

"Then he went into combat," Howard continued. "That skirmish over the Yellow Sea, back in the thirties. The war ended quickly, but something happened to him over there because he was completely changed when he came back. Started to get into all kinds of secretive, paranoid shit. Then he met a girl and got married, and they had Alex. He seemed to be back to his old self. For a while, anyway. A few years later, when we had Kiara, they moved near us so we could raise the kids together. It ended up being a bad idea."

"Why?"

"Alex and Kiara ran around that neighborhood thick as thieves when they were kids. It was a reasonably happy time. But Kurt got restless again. He started to get weird visitors, military types, ex-cons, motorcycle gangs, white priders, who knows what all, and we could tell that Darlene—that was his wife—was scared."

He paused, seeming lost in the memory, and Geraldine took over. "One day, she was up and gone," she said. "Kurt swore she had left him for another man, but we knew that wasn't true. We still have no idea what really happened to her."

Alton nodded, remembering what Alex had told him in his bedroom that night when they were kids. *No place in their home for nonbelievers.*

"So, how did you end up here?"

"Kurt kept trying to get me involved in his activities. But I'm not like him. Live and let live, I say. I don't care about color, nor creed. This garbage has been going on forever. I want this nation *healed*."

"And we didn't want Kiara in that environment," Geraldine added. "With those crazies. And Alex not having his mother."

"It must have been tough for her to leave her best friend to move up here."

They looked at each other. "Which best friend?" Geraldine asked.

"Alex."

"Son, Kurt is my *brother*," Howard said.

Alton's mouth fell open. *Alex and Kiara are first cousins?*

"It was easier to overlook how unnaturally close they were when they were kids," Geraldine said. "But as they got older, not so much, and we could see where things were headed. So, we got her out of there."

The rain had become more insistent on the window. They sat, listening to it for a few moments while Alton absorbed the news. He thought of that summer evening at the launch, Alex and Kiara on the picnic blanket in a deep embrace. They had seemed to devour one another.

"She wouldn't forgive us," Geraldine continued. "Wouldn't take to this new life. Not that it was much of a life for a young girl. I can see that now." The regret was stark on her face.

"She started threatening to run away the moment we got here," said Howard. "We knew she would go to him. When Kurt and Alex relocated to LA, at least it worked out that we could send her to live with Sally and Lorna. Thank God for those two."

It had started to feel late. He wondered how long they had been sitting there. His head throbbed, and he was suddenly very tired. He noticed the dog had left the room, probably to curl up somewhere. How nice it would be to follow it upstairs to some dusty loft—maybe even Kiara's old room—pull the comforter up around his eyes and hibernate among her old secrets. Let those fuckers spend the night in the wet cold.

But the fuckers had different ideas. And if the dog had been sleeping, he wasn't now because he began to bark. Howard jumped up much faster than Alton thought he could at his age and snatched the rifle from the corner.

"Wait!" Alton yelled and ran out in front of him. He opened the door in a whoosh of cold mist to find a dark figure standing there.

"Get down!"

He wasn't even sure who had yelled it, but he leapt aside and onto the hardwood floor just as Howard fired right through the screen door. He heard the grunt of the wind being knocked out of somebody and then a heavy toppling, like a bag of baseballs being thrown down some cellar stairs.

The ragged screen door was ripped entirely from its hinges, along with part of the frame, and Valeria, glimmering arctic blue, stepped through the threshold. She wrenched the rifle from Howard and sent him tumbling across the room with the flat of her other hand. As though the gun was a Styrofoam prop, she broke the rifle in half over her knee and hurled the pieces into the rain.

Next, she turned on Geraldine, but the older woman had grabbed the dog and was clutching him in a corner. When Valeria saw that they were neutralized, she went out again.

Alton scrambled through the splintered frame after her to find Eli blown off the porch into a jumble of ferns. Two of the team were helping him up. He appeared to be fine, as the TALOS had deflected or absorbed the blast. His chest was dusted with crushed rock salt.

When Alton saw that he was okay, he turned to Valeria. "What the fuck?"

"You're having tea while we get pissed on in the bushes."

"I was getting the info we need!"

"Too slowly," she said, stepping back inside. Geraldine had shut the dog in the kitchen and was attending to Howard on the floor. Valeria leaned over them, glowing like a cobalt demon.

"Where are they?" she snarled.

"Jesus," Alton said and got between her and them. He crouched down. "Is he okay?"

Geraldine looked grim but nodded. Alton helped her get him up onto a sofa. Eli had entered along with several of the other commandos. Cold rain was pouring into the front room.

"Can somebody close that?" Alton said.

Valeria slammed the door. "Everybody all comfy, now?" she asked. "Then how about some answers?"

Geraldine looked up, defiant. "We don't know where they are, and we wouldn't tell you if we did."

From her wrists, Valeria launched web cuffs onto Howard. When he tried to stand, she launched another pair around his ankles, and he sank back into the couch.

"Goddamnit," Alton said. "They were helping!"

She turned on him. "Ask Eli how he feels about their *help*."

Eli's face was drained, and he was still too short of breath to respond.

"We got more than enough to pack you off right now," she said. "Collaborating with the enemy, for starters. I haven't been in one myself, but I'm sure white boy here can tell you the camps aren't exactly tailor-made for old folks."

Geraldine scowled at her. "Maybe my brother-in-law was right about you people," she spat.

"*No*, Geraldine," Howard said. "That's not who we are."

Eli stepped forward. "Come on, Val," he said, still trying to get his wind back. "Let's not get carried away."

She shook her head in disgust but extinguished Howard's cuffs.

"Do you mind if I sit down?" Eli asked, rubbing his chest. He lowered himself into an old wooden rocker and said, "As I'm assuming you know based on his recent transmission, Hagen—Alex, I mean—looks ready to drop his next cataclysm on the world. We would really like to stop him before we all find out whatever it is together."

Howard leaned forward, massaging his wrists. "You're wasting time. If you think he's up here, why not send a battalion?"

"If the president finds out, he just might."

"What do you mean *if* he finds out? Didn't he send you?" Geraldine asked.

"Christ, they're a damn splinter cell," Howard said.

"That's right," Eli said. "Some of us would prefer not to desecrate American soil with yet another battlefield if we can help it. Our group is trying to prevent that."

Howard nodded.

"We want to capture him and let the courts do their jobs," Eli continued. "The hope is that by doing this with minimal violence, we can leverage enough public and political will to close the camps, start doing some healing."

Healing. It was the second time the word had been uttered that evening, and it struck something unexpected in Alton.

"Why wouldn't Hagen's men just keep on fighting without him?" Howard asked.

"That's a possibility," said Eli. "But let's start with the head of the snake and see what we can accomplish."

"They're up in the mountains somewhere," Geraldine said. "We've never known exactly where."

"You've *never* known?" Alton asked. "How long have they been up there?"

"Kiara didn't want to have anything to do with us when she first moved away," she said. "But the summer after high school, and whenever she had a break at college, she would base camp here for a few days, then backpack up into the mountains."

That would have been just after the attack on the Torreses' compound, Alton thought, when everybody was hunting Alex—LAPD, FBI, ATF, DHS, probably other acronyms he didn't even know existed. They hadn't found him because he'd been way up in the backcountry. Alton was back East at college by that time and had no idea what was happening with either of them.

Eli wrinkled his brow. "Base camp?"

"Visit with us. Have meals. Pretend we were a family again. But it was all just to keep things civil between us so she could use this place as a jumping-off point to get up there, which she would do for days or even weeks at a time."

"And she was going to see him?" Eli asked.

Howard nodded. "She must have been. Even though she claimed to be camping alone."

"And you were okay with that?" Alton asked. "It's got to be pretty harsh terrain back there."

"Like I said before, Kiara does what she wants. And she was an adult by then."

"You've known all this time where he was, and you didn't report it?" Valeria said.

"You don't have children," said Geraldine. It wasn't a question.

"Doesn't change the fact that you have blood on your hands."

Eli gestured at her to back off. "I have children," he said. "I get it."

"Anyway, we only suspected where they were," Howard said. "That's not the same as knowing. There's five hundred thousand square acres of wilderness back there."

"All we can do is point you in the direction she went on those trips," Geraldine added. "We have no idea how far back they are."

"Will you do that for us?" Eli asked.

They looked at each other and came to an unspoken agreement.

"Bring him in if you can," Howard said. "It's time for all this to end."

CHAPTER 34

TWO OF THE team stayed behind to watch Geraldine and Howard in shifts, to make sure they didn't try to warn Alex or Kiara or alert some other authorities to their presence in the area. That left eight of them to start up the wet, dark mountain. A meager force, and woefully insufficient for what likely lay ahead, Alton thought, as they picked their way into the black woods behind the house where Kiara had set off on her journeys to meet Alex.

He imagined what it was like for them, fleeing the world, just the two of them, the sky and the stars and the snow. Kiara would have known what Alex was capable of by then, after Bernardo. Clearly, she was all in by that point. But if she was willing to overlook Alex's moral culpability, Alton had been just as willing to overlook hers when the two of them later got together in DC. *People will justify any desire,* he thought.

He felt sick at the thought of his own selfishness but not as sick as he felt thinking of them together up here, making love at the top of the world. It was crazy, irrational thinking, but it did make him wonder again how much of his hatred for Alex was based not on outrage but envy, jealousy, and regret.

He shook it off and put one foot in front of the other as they ascended the steep grade. Drones would be detected, so this was purely a walking gig, and a mostly blind one at that. One of the team, Gagné, of French Canadian descent—preferred pronouns *they/them*—knew mountain country well. They led the way, mapping the terrain and transmitting the route back on a closed channel into the team's virtual map feeds. Built-in night vision allowed the group to see what was in front of and around them, but they still had little idea of where they were going without Gagné guiding them.

Even then, the route Gagné created was only a guess drawn from a slightly worn path that may or may not have been human-created. The team's augmented hyper-senses were attuned to sounds and even smells that might point them in the right direction. But Alex had been disguising his tracks for years, with help from animals and weather and changing seasons.

"We could be out here for weeks doing this," Alton groused. He had fallen behind, and Eli had fallen back with him.

"Yeah, so much for my kid's birthday," said Eli, kicking a rock.

Alton looked up the path to make sure they were relatively alone, then said, "We don't have anything to worry about with Valeria, do we?"

"Like what?"

"She said she wanted to kill Alex at Áquilar's. She believes in the camps. After what happened back there . . . I mean, do you think she might go rogue or something? Put us in danger?"

"We're already in danger, and we've already gone rogue too. I suppose she could go double rogue?" He chuckled. "She can be a hothead, no doubt. But I wouldn't worry about it."

"Did something happen to her?"

"She doesn't talk about herself much, but she doesn't have to," Eli said. "Things have been better for our generation, but all of us have family who were second-class citizens at some point. She's probably still carrying a grudge for somebody."

One that she might like to vindicate by taking out the world's most famous white supremacist, Alton thought, along with his former friend.

After an hour or so, the rain began splattering against the mountainside in sheets, driving into their face shields. Logically, he knew he was mostly dry, but he *felt* wet. And nothing—no augmentation, no industrial weatherproof fabrics—kept him from feeling cold. Except his prosthetic leg. It could convey pressure, which allowed him to move, to have a relationship with the earth, but it didn't seem to feel temperature. He wondered what it would feel like to have an entire body like that—so much less sensation but also so much less pain and discomfort.

They struggled up an ever-steeper grade until they came to an overhanging bluff that offered some protection. After conferring with Eli for a moment, Val nodded reluctantly, then gave the signal for them to unshoulder their packs.

Eli came over. "No use going farther," he said. "We're unlikely to find better shelter."

Alton sighed with relief and found a dry space near the back of the overhang. The others had already begun to unload, producing handkerchief-sized squares of material, which they attached to nozzles protruding from their packs and inflated into sleeping bag/mat combos. Alton found his, and Martinez helped him set it up.

"There's food in there too," said Martinez.

"Nutrition bars?" Alton made a face.

"This is a special ops unit, man. We do better than that." He pulled out packets of dehydrated soup and coffee.

Following the lead of the others, Alton went to the edge of the overhang and filled a receptacle with rain, then screwed it onto a tiny heating device. It didn't seem to generate any heat at all, but within a few minutes, the area was aromatic with simmering soup.

When his soup was ready, he settled onto his bag/mat, his back against the stone, and sipped it, the luxuriant steam opening his sinuses and warming his face. There wasn't much of it, but it was surprisingly rich and filling—the height of lab food technology, he guessed.

By the time he had prepared coffee with the remaining water, he felt too tired to drink it. But he wanted to enjoy feeling relaxed for the first time in a while, so he sipped it while peering out into the black, the shapes of trees barely visible, the rain still steady but less fierce, soothing even.

Most of the others had disappeared into their bags or lay on top of them. Several were already snoring. Only Eli, Valeria, and Gagné—huddled around a heating element and talking in hushed voices—had yet to go down for the night.

Something flashed, and Alton saw that Eli had produced a flask and was adding a touch of something to their coffee. It occurred to him that if he wanted to escape, it would be the perfect moment to slip into the rainy blackness and head back down the mountain.

But he had made himself a promise to kill Alex if he could. For Bernardo, for Simon, for Oliver and the others. And after meeting Kiara's parents, witnessing their love and their worry, he had begun to feel tenderness toward her again as well. *Who knows,* he thought, *maybe there could still be a chance for us. Especially if Alex is gone for good.*

He awoke in a gray-white light, otherworldly in its dull glow. The rain had ceased, but water dripped from everything, and a mist snaked through the trees. The others were already packing, and some had coffee going again. Still groggy, he sat up, massaging the crick in his neck from sleeping on the uneven ledge, and began to stow his things. When they were ready, Valeria huddled them up.

"I'm sending the CAMSETS based on what we know of today's terrain and weather," she said. All at once, the group shimmered as each TALOS blurred from charcoal to grayish soot like watercolors bleeding together. Alton hadn't seen this trick yet, and he marveled at the effect. When they had transformed, Gagné stepped forward.

"Satellites worked up an up-to-the-minute topo map of the area," they began, casting a hologram into the center of the group. "Obviously, it doesn't tell us where they are, but it almost certainly eliminates several directions. Heading directly east leads to this cliff face, a sheer drop down the side of the mountain into farmland. Northwest brings them too close to these towns here and here," they indicated, "which I'm guessing they have been avoiding."

As they moved their hands, the hologram glimmered in their red hair. "Northeast, down through this valley, and then up again into the core of the Trinity Alps—these high, white granite peaks here, known as the White Trinities—is our best bet," they continued. "Not only is it relatively easy to get there through the valley, but once up and inside these granite slabs, there would be any number of places to hide, establish a base, or whatever. They're almost certainly back there somewhere." They extinguished the map.

"I would have thought satellites, drones, and every other surveillance technology would have exposed everything there is to expose," Alton said.

"There are still remote places on Earth," Eli said. "Kind of comforting, really."

"Speaking of exposed, isn't that what we'll be, moving through that valley?" Martinez asked.

"This whole thing might be a trap," Valeria said. "So, don't daydream out there."

Gagné cast a more regional map. "The risk will be minimized if we stay under the tree line here on the west side of the valley, until we get to the base of the peaks. Then we can disappear into the mountains just like they presumably did."

"And when, or I guess I should say, *if* we find them?" Martinez asked.

"This is still a target extraction," said Eli. "We can't formulate a more specific plan until we know what we're dealing with. We just have to be flexible."

"Let's move out then," said Valeria.

Some members of the unit looked at one another, some at their feet.

She glared at them. "Is there a problem?"

A commando of Jamaican descent, Jones, said, "We've been in some sketchy shit before, but this is totally slapdash. There could be a whole battalion waiting for us inside those mountains."

"There probably is," said Martinez.

"Val was handpicked for this by the deputy secretary," Eli said.

"That's just it," said Martinez. "How do we know she's looking out for our best interests and not some politician's? What if she's got some secret orders? Maybe we're expendable."

"And having a Civvie along?" Jones added, gesturing at Alton.

Valeria ordered them all to attention, then went nose to nose, first with Jones, then Martinez.

"Nobody's expendable here," she said. "But if you question me or my orders again, you'll be at the worst fucking internment camp I can find, ladling gringo diarrhea out of latrines. Understood?"

Their eyes were hard as they met hers, but they barked, "Yes, sir" in unison. Alton noticed Gagné concealing a smile.

"Good. Then move. The fuck. Out."

As the unit dispersed, Alton heard Eli say, "Don't worry. You know I've got your backs."

CHAPTER 35

IN DAYLIGHT, OUT from under the low overhang of the bluff, Alton could see that their efforts from the night before had brought them almost to the ridge. Another twenty minutes of strenuous ascent, and they reached a plateau that allowed them a sustained stretch of easy walking over level terrain. It was cool and misty and almost pleasant, Alton thought, the pines and firs giving them comforting cover, the silent trudging of the group creating a reassuring rhythm.

He didn't even notice they had begun a gradual descent until it became much more apparent after another thirty or forty minutes. Then it was tougher going, clambering over and around boulders as they approached the valley floor. It was a weird sensation, having only one quad ache, having only one knee squeezed by the pressure. But he could lean on the prosthetic when he needed a rest.

The final stretch was crumbling dirt and rock that had broken up over the ages and slid down to the base of the mountain. They had to carefully pick their way through so they didn't lose traction, turning sideways, and even sliding on their butts in places.

When they reached the bottom, the trees parted to reveal the glacial valley before them, vast and silent, the lake in the center glittering silver-gray in the overcast light of high morning and stretching forever. Valeria pointed to the other side, where the Alps shot up in jagged slabs from the earth.

"That's where we're headed," she said.

Alton stared and squinted until he remembered he had telescopic vision as part of his augmentation kit. He brought up his menu screens. Not having figured out how to manage the commands internally, he had to whisper them. A few of the others chuckled as he tried to hide his efforts. But once he accessed the vision app, the mountains appeared up close in all their rough-hewn gray-and-white granite glory.

"No snow?" he asked, remembering the poster in Kiara's bedroom.

"Maybe thirty years ago," Gagné said.

He realized the mountains must have retreated for many miles and felt a wave of despair. How on earth would they find anyone in there? It made him think of flying over the country and realizing just how much sheer unnavigable acreage lay between highways and population centers, even after two centuries of paving everything over. Alex had gotten deep into that acreage, and it was no mystery why he'd been able to stay hidden for so long.

After a water break, they set out across the valley, careful to stay under the line of red and white firs that ran along the western shore. The sun emerged in the early afternoon, burning away the last of the mist and rendering the lake a stunning ice-blue. When the time was right, someplace like this would be perfect to escape to, Alton thought. Water and sun and silence.

The group had spread out as they walked, with Alton again falling to the rear. After a while, Martinez and Jones fell back too. When they flanked him, Alton realized they had fallen back intentionally.

"How you holding up?" Jones asked him.

"Fine," Alton said, trying not to sound out of breath.

Martinez said, "Hey, we're curious about something."

"Yeah?"

"What is it with you and Hagen? He stole your girl? Is that what this is all about?"

Why were they asking about this now? And isolating him to do it?

"I thought you had been briefed," he said.

"Not the personal stuff."

"She was never my girl," he said after a pause.

"So, what then? You wanted her to be?"

"Yeah, but that's not . . ." He didn't know how much he should tell them.

"We just want to know who we're up against," said Jones. "So we have the best chance. Who's the guy behind the scenes, know what I mean?"

As they walked, he was suddenly aware of how big and powerful the two commandos were. He had a flashback of being escorted by camp guards to the Central Compound and figured he should give them something.

"We weren't friends for long," he said. "But I feel like I should have done something to stop him before everything got this far."

"That all?" Martinez asked. "I'm sure a lot of people who knew him feel that way."

The sun suddenly felt hot on Alton's face. He hoped someone would fall back and save him from this grilling, but nobody even turned their head.

"It's possible he may feel that he owes me," he said. "Áquilar was hoping we might be able to leverage that."

"Why would he owe *you*?" Jones asked.

"I did him a . . . favor that resulted in a friend of mine getting badly hurt. It wasn't supposed to go down that way. Alex fucked me over. He lied to me."

"And you think a sociopath like him feels guilty about *that*?" Martinez asked.

"No, I don't. But I could have turned him in, and I didn't. That's what he owes me for. For letting him get away." He swallowed, then managed to say it out loud: "If it wasn't for me, he might never have become Hagen. The insurgency, the dirty bomb, the camps, none of it might have happened."

He felt the burn of that in his chest, his throat, and in his mind's eye, he saw the fire and the blood at the Torreses' house that night, the bodies strewn over the grounds.

They trudged on in silence for a bit before Jones said, "Things ain't that cause and effect, know what I mean?"

"Yeah, don't feel too bad about it," Martinez said. "This war was coming one way or another."

CHAPTER 36

IT WAS LATE afternoon when they finally reached the foot of the Alps. The sun was still bright on the far side of the valley, but shadows had fallen on the western half, and it was growing cold. The landscape was eerily silent. No breeze, no birds, no insects. Alton had felt an increasing dread all afternoon, and he sensed the others—grim-faced and tight-lipped—shared it.

Except for a light spotting of spruce and hemlock, the mountains were like a moonscape but not so steep at their base that they couldn't begin their ascent on foot over the crunchy gravel. They adjusted their TALOS camouflage to blend in with the ash-colored slate and managed to climb for an hour up and across the wide slopes.

When they reached a series of flat slabs that jutted straight up out of the mountain face and could go no farther, the others began to remove and open their packs. Alton unshouldered his as well and sorted through it. But save for some rope and a few random carabiners, he found no harness, belays, or repelling equipment.

Just as he looked up for help, Eli was reaching into his pack, retrieving a streamlined-looking metallic device about sixteen inches across. Except for the four small turrets poking out of the bottom, it looked like a titanium boomerang. Eli handed it to him and kneeled to adjust something near the bottom of Alton's pack.

As Alton held the device, he realized it was responsible for much of the pack's weight.

"What is this?" Alton asked.

"Independent Propulsion Delivery System."

"Huh?"

"Jetpack."

Alton smiled as he looked it over. *Bernardo would love this,* he thought, remembering how they had fantasized about jetpacks as kids. Of course, they were bigger and bulkier in those days than the sleek gadget he now held in his hand. This was the epitome of cool.

Eli affixed it low on the outside of his pack, the turrets facing down, and then pulled out what looked like a soft wrist cast, which he slid onto Alton's left hand, pulled tight, and sealed. "The controls," Eli said. "You wear them instead of holding them so that you can't drop them when you're a hundred meters up."

"Is now a bad time to mention that I'm scared of heights?"

"Then don't look down," Eli said. "Now, watch; this is simple. Touch your thumb to your forefinger to start and stop. Don't worry, the sensors won't allow it to cut out while you're in the air as long as you have the safeties on, which you will. One is on the device, which I activated. The other is on the back of the wrist pad, here."

He turned Alton's hand so that the palm faced up. "Okay," he said. "Thumb to your middle finger creates propulsion. Thumb to your ring finger retards propulsion. That's your up and down basically. Thumb to your pinkie allows horizontal movement. That's your side to side. The palm pad allows for all kinds of variations in direction, but don't worry about that right now. Got it?"

"Um."

"Good. We're going to levitate over these slabs. If there's a plateau up top, we'll touch down and keep walking to save fuel. If it's a steep drop or it's too jagged, we may stay in the air for a while. Just stay close to me and follow my lead."

Alton had many questions, but the others were already lifting off. Valeria shot straight up in an elegant *whoosh*, then disappeared over the top of the slab. Gagné followed. Then the others. They all moved much faster than seemed safe.

"Okay," said Eli. "Thumb to forefinger."

Alton touched them together and felt the sensation of the device powering on, sending a low vibration through his pack and into his lower back.

"Now, thumb to middle finger. Just touch it once at first because each time you touch it, you'll gain speed."

He brought the two fingers together and felt a gentle push as he lifted off. He was ten feet in the air and then twenty, and suddenly felt a desperate need to be back on the ground, but Eli was saying, "You're doing fine! Just keep it steady!"

He felt like he was too close to the rock, so he kicked his feet, which did nothing. Then he remembered that the pinkie finger moved him horizontally. He touched it with his forefinger and began to fly straight into the mountain. "Shit!" he yelled and dialed the palm pad, which immediately sent him shooting in the other direction.

Eli was on him, grabbing his arm and dialing his palm back toward the wall. "I'll stay with you until you get the hang of it," he said. "But it's important that we stay close to surfaces to keep us concealed. Fly too high and we'll be visible."

Alton nodded, trying to focus.

"So, as soon as you get to the top, touch your thumb to pinkie again, but this time slowly palm-dial right once you get over the mountain. If there's nowhere to land, then it's ring finger to descend. Stay close to the side, and try not to float out into space."

But Alton was hardly listening as he elevated along the granite face. His fear of heights hadn't bothered him as he escaped over the cliff at Gypsum because of the dark and his adrenaline. Now, he felt panicky and disoriented. But maybe it was almost over, he thought, maybe they were approaching another plateau. *Just don't look down.*

But it wasn't another plateau, and he had no choice but to look down because the top of the slab ended in a jagged point with no place to land, and the canyon between the peaks was hundreds of feet below them and thousands of feet across. He sucked in his breath at the utter immensity and started to kick again, but Eli was at his side.

"I got you," he said. "Thumb to ring finger and let's start moving down along the face toward the bottom."

"Bottom good," was all he could muster.

After getting his paralyzed brain to remember which was his ring finger, he touched it twice with his thumb and began to descend. With Eli alongside him, holding his arm, he felt less afraid enough to take in the depth and majesty of the canyon, blazing in the late afternoon sun.

As his eyes adjusted, he saw the others far below, floating like butterflies along the canyon floor, which was crumbling and craggy and rust-colored in the bronze light. It was almost as though *this* was Mars. Seeing that the others had made it down, Alton began to relax somewhat until Eli said, "Shit."

"What?" This was *not* the time or place for *shit*.

"Somebody might be back there."

"Back *where?*" He craned his head but couldn't turn around well enough to see anything.

"I'm going to check it out," Eli said.

"What? No, wait! Don't leave me!"

"You know what you're doing now," he said. "Just go slow and join the others." Eli gave him a reassuring squeeze on the wrist and disappeared.

I can do this. Take a breath. But then a granite shelf appeared out of nowhere, jutting from the side of the peak. He turned the palm dial to move out and around it but in his haste, cranked the dial the wrong way again and hurtled toward the wall.

He dialed it back just as he went sliding against the stone, a sharp edge tearing through the sleeve of his TALOS and searing into his flesh.

Crying out, he cranked the dial as far as it would go in the other direction and zoomed out over the canyon. He took a deep, shuddering breath, realizing he had cleared the shelf, but now he was hurtling across the gorge.

He found the presence of mind to return the dial to its starting position, and now he was floating. There was a momentary sensation of peace until he looked down and saw the canyon floor far below. He realized he was completely exposed, just what Eli had told him *not* to be. Alarmed, he began pinching his thumb to every finger in an unthinking flurry of movement.

He felt the sensation under his crotch subside first. The soft purr of the jets extinguished, and the space around him went still as a vacuum. Then he was spilling through empty air, straight down, ass over teakettle, kicking and flailing at nothing, the sky and landscape spinning into a disorienting jumble.

Just as he began to understand he was going to die, a blur of slate-gray whooshed past. He felt a painful pressure around his real ankle, then looked up to see that someone had him. A few seconds later, there was another whoosh. Red hair fell into his face as Gagné and Valeria each took an arm.

"Hold him," said Valeria. Gagné clutched him under both armpits, while Valeria adjusted his pack. Within a few seconds, the jets were streaming again, and he felt the air firm up underneath him. Valeria kept a tight hold anyway, one arm around his waist, one on his shoulder. He leaned into her, shaking.

"Where's Eli?"

"I . . . I don't know," he said. "He said he saw someone, left to check it out."

"He didn't relay anything to us." She looked at Gagné. "Go see."

Gagné jetted off, and Alton and Valeria floated for a while, his head buried in her shoulder. When he finally looked up, he saw that they had glided to the canyon floor and the others were waiting for them among the slag. They landed, and Valeria began to attend to his bleeding gash.

He knew if he tried to talk too much, he would throw up. "Sorry," was all he could muster.

"It's not your fault. He should never have left you."

He was taken aback. It was the first time she hadn't taken the opportunity to let him know what a piece of garbage he was.

He followed the gaze of the others to the two figures zooming toward them. Valeria was barking at Eli before they even touched down.

"I thought we were being followed," said Eli. He turned to Alton. "I'm so sorry, man. I thought you had it. This is on me."

"Goddamn right it is," said Valeria. "Both his safeties were off! How the fuck did that happen?"

Alton felt a chill spread over him. He really *had* almost died. "It was me," he said. "I just started wildly hitting all the controls. I must have shut them down."

"It's designed *not* to do that," she said, still glaring at Eli. "It's designed to do the *opposite* of that."

Eli looked contrite. "It was a fuckup," he said. "It won't happen again."

"A *major* fuckup," she said. "And it better not. He's the whole mission."

Also, I'd like to live if anybody cares, Alton thought.

She turned to the unit. "Light is dying, but I want us to make it up and over that far peak before we quit for the day." To Eli, she said, "Since we had plenty of time to topo-scan while you were back there fucking around, we found a plateau at the top where we can camp."

Eli strode over to Alton, but Valeria stepped between them.

"I've got him the rest of the way," she said. "Move out. And keep the formation tight this time."

CHAPTER 37

THEY REACHED THE peak at the western end of the canyon just as the sun drained from the valley, leaving a faint amethyst twilight. Alton was afraid they would encounter more of the same rocky pinnacles, but to his great relief, they floated up onto the promised plateau, mostly level and flat and dense with trees, which he scanned and identified as foxtail pine, mountain hemlock, white fir, and weeping spruce.

They immediately set up camp underneath a spruce canopy. The slender drooping branches dusted the ground beneath them with soft silver-green needles. In another context, it might have felt like a forest in a fairy tale.

After the long, difficult day, the unit chowed and settled into their sleeping gear right away. Alton was too amped from his ordeal to sleep, so he lay on top of his bag/mat and stared up at the stars peeking in between the branches, hard and white in the midnight blue.

After the previous night's drizzle, he was grateful for clear skies, although at least the clouds and humidity had locked in a little heat. Without them, high in the Northern California mountains in early November, the temperature was already below freezing. He adjusted the thermostat on his TALOS, which toasted him up a bit, although his hands and feet and face were still cold. He would do anything for a bourboned-up cocoa and a steaming bath.

Eli and Valeria were having a quiet but intense exchange near the ridge until he turned and went away with a resentful look.

Alton thought about going over to thank her for saving his life, but she probably relished a few moments to herself. Anyway, he didn't want to be reminded again that his value to them was strictly based on the mission, or that she thought he belonged in a camp, or that he was just some white-bread betrayer of the Mexican race.

The mission. The day had been so grueling and terrifying that he had hardly thought of it. Were they close? Had they gone in the right direction? Or were they still miles away? Was Alex spying on them now, prepared to set upon them? If he did, would he spare Alton? It seemed likely, or why else would Kiara have led him here? But in the vast silence of the dark, frigid mountain range, away from all help, this gave him little comfort.

He was flailing into the abyss. With supreme effort, he managed to twist himself around in the air and see the person floating far above him. As soon as he did, he was suddenly secure in the jetpack, hovering, but he had merely switched places with the person above him, and now that person was falling.

Looking down, he gasped to see Bernardo plummeting toward the hard earth. Alton reached out, but he knew he couldn't save him.

He shot straight up in his bag, heart racing, then peered into the darkness for some time until he got his bearings. *It wasn't real.*

You're fine. But he didn't feel fine. He felt intense dread. He tried to shake it off as he slipped out of his bag to go relieve himself.

Ducking under the canopy, he jumped when he ran into a black form just outside the camp.

"You okay?"

Alton's eyes adjusted, and the black form resolved into Eli.

"Just half asleep," said Alton. "You on watch?"

"Yeah."

"Going to piss," he said.

On the plateau, it was icy, clear, and very still. The vista of mountains and night sky was so immense and pristine that it was easy to imagine there was nothing wrong in the world. At their high elevation, the stars shone even more intensely than they had at Gypsum.

He was grateful because they illuminated the ridge not twenty meters from him, marking the border on the other side of which was the headlong plunge back the way they had come. He almost laughed. *What is it with me and cliffs?* Not wanting to get too close, he stood behind several boulders.

As he did his business, gaping at the sky, he thought of the Mars vessel, scheduled for liftoff soon. It had been announced as a night launch. If they were still up here, and he knew where to look in the sky, he might be able to glimpse it as it departed, especially with his new telescopic abilities. He brought up a news app to check the launch time. The expedition was set to go in four days at 9:30 p.m.

Next, he accessed a sky map to check where the stars and planets would be. This was probably unnecessary, as he had more or less memorized the sky during his time at Gypsum. But as he was inputting the day and time into the app, it suddenly went black.

He tapped the side of his head twice, as he had seen the others do on occasion, then whispered, "Constellation map." It didn't reappear, and neither did anything else.

Somehow, his augmentation had gone dead, shorted out perhaps, or he had switched it off without realizing it. Given his lack of training and his debacle with the jetpack, he supposed it was the latter.

As he returned to camp, he thought Eli appeared to be looking at something. Or perhaps *for* something. Eli also tapped his head several times, as Alton had done, then lowered his hand when he saw Alton.

"Everything okay?" Alton whispered.

"Yeah, just doing a multiscan. Making sure we're alone out here."

"My whole setup just went dead. I can't access anything."

"That happens sometimes before you've got the kinks worked out. I'll help you reboot in the morning."

"Damn."

"What?"

"It's so clear up here, I was hoping to get a look at Alpha Centauri. It's supposed to be very visible this time of year. But my system went down before I got the chance. Can you tell me if that's it?" He pointed at a bright star above them.

Eli looked mildly put out but fixed his gaze in the direction Alton had indicated. "That's it," he said quickly. "You were right."

Alton smiled. "I knew it. Thanks."

"Sure," Eli said. "Get some sleep."

Under the canopy, moving stealthily, Alton located Valeria and lightly shook her shoulder. She woke immediately.

"Something's wrong," he whispered.

CHAPTER 38

HER BLACK EYES focused. "What is it?"

"Is your augmentation working?"

She tapped her head and looked puzzled. "No," she said.

"I don't think any of them are."

She sprang to her feet. "Wake everybody," she whispered, slipping into her boots. "*Quietly.*"

Alton roused the others. Within seconds everyone was up and alert.

Gagné was tapping their head. "I've gone dead," they said.

"We all have," said Valeria. "Bring it in. EVs are offline too, so ready your sidearms."

They produced slender pistols from their packs, then moved into a tight circle.

"What should I do?" Alton asked.

"Get your gear ready in case we have to pull out fast."

"Where's Eli?" Gagné asked.

"He's on watch," Valeria said. "Go get him, Martinez."

When Martinez had gone, Alton, keeping his voice low, said to Valeria, "Something's not right with Eli."

"What are you talking about?"

"When I saw him just now, he seemed to be looking for something. And he lied to me."

"About what? Hold on—"

Eli and Martinez were ducking back under the canopy.

"I'm offline too," Eli said. "We should run a unit diagnostic."

"Not a minute ago, you told me yours was working," Alton said.

"It was," he said. "It just now died."

"No, I think yours was dead *before* too," Alton said.

"Yeah, well you're not exactly a wiz with technology."

"You lied to me."

It came out louder than he meant it too, and they all stopped to listen.

"Why do you think he lied?" Valeria asked.

"Aww, come on, Val," said Eli. "You're not going to listen to this shit, are you?"

"When my constellation maps went down, I asked him to scan Alpha Centauri for me," Alton said.

"And I did," said Eli.

"That was Jupiter. Alpha Centauri can only be seen from the Southern Hemisphere. You were just telling me what I wanted to hear because you were already offline."

Alton could feel the spike in tension. He was very conscious that they were all holding sidearms.

"I told you what you wanted to hear so you'd stop pestering me."

"No, you were offline. *And* you knew everybody else was. You were looking for somebody out there. I saw you."

Eli turned to Valeria. "What is this idiot talking about?"

"I have no idea," she said. "You tell me."

"There's nothing to tell! He was in a black site prison for terrorists a few days ago, and now we're supposed to trust him?"

Jones had maneuvered near Eli and Martinez. Out of the corner of his eye, Alton saw Gagné clench their pistol grip.

"Why are we offline?" Alton asked. "Is it Alex? Could he do that from afar?"

"Maybe, but I doubt it," said Valeria.

"Only the military has the tech to remotely incapacitate secure augmentation," said Gagné. "Only they could decipher our individual codes, which are constantly in flux. But they would have to know where we are. They would have to know *exactly* where we are."

"And they should have no idea we even exist, let alone our location," said Valeria, looking directly at Eli. "Unless somebody transmitted our coordinates."

"Maybe Kiara's folks got word out somehow," said Martinez.

"Or Áquilar. She got cold feet. Betrayed us," said Jones.

"Maybe betraying us was her plan all along," Eli said.

"No," Alton said. "It was you. Just like it was you who killed the safety on my pack." He suddenly remembered Eli squeezing his left wrist before he flew off. Alton had thought that squeeze was meant to be reassuring. He realized now it was meant to be disabling.

"Why the hell would he do that?" Martinez asked.

"No me, no mission," Alton answered. "Everybody gets to go home."

Valeria made eye contact with Gagné, and everything happened in less than a second. Gagné had their pistol at the side of Martinez's head, and Valeria had hers pointed between Eli's eyes. The others leveled their pistols at Jones.

"Weapons down," said Valeria. "Or you'll *never* see home."

Alton stood frozen amid the standoff, waiting for the shooting to start. But Eli said, "Put them down. It doesn't matter. It's just about over anyway."

Jones and Martinez lowered their weapons, and the others quickly disarmed them.

Valeria stepped toward Eli and pointed her gun between his eyes. "What do you mean?"

"You're right," he said. "A unit will arrive soon to relieve us of duty."

Her face twisted in disgust. "*Why?*"

"Why do you think? Because this is a suicide mission. And for what? So we can bring Whitey to trial? Who cares? Hagen has an army out here somewhere! He's sitting on a nuke! Why walk into certain death?"

"Because it's your sworn duty," said Gagné. "Because in this unit you're supposed to be the most loyal, the most honorable, the most willing to sacrifice."

"But this won't end dishonorably," he said. "Far from it! They'll be able to dust him now because of *us*!"

"Not to mention ferreting out this little fifth column for Guerrero," Martinez added.

"Yes, turning in that traitor Áquilar makes us even *bigger* heroes," Eli said. "No way to lose here."

The sinewy muscles of Valeria's TALOS-sheathed arm trembled, and Alton thought she might snuff out their little insurrection right then and there.

Eli must have thought the same because he visibly swallowed. "Come on, Val," he said. "How can you not be on board? You were against this fuck-scapade from the beginning. You're the one who said they all belong in camps!"

Was Alton imagining it, or was there remorse in her expression?

"And you're right!" Eli continued. "Let 'em rot. You won't be held accountable because you were just following orders. Shit, you'll probably get promoted. And now you won't be *dead* either."

"And you won't miss your kid's birthday," said Alton.

Eli smiled. "Damn right."

It seemed to Alton then that the trees moved, that every other trunk took a synchronized step forward, as though part of a performance. It took him a moment to realize that it was the promised military unit, outfitted in stygian-black TALOS, armed with assault rifles and web guns, fanning into the camp from the dense grove behind them.

No one did anything for several beats, then the leader pointed to Alton and said, "That's the one. Eliminate the rest."

Eli's face was in horror and confusion. He put his palm up. "Wait! That's not—" he said before his hand separated from his body in a sluicing red spray.

The next moment, his head exploded.

In the half moment after that, Valeria unloaded on the leader, blasting him multiple times.

Then the firing came from every direction. Alton dove out of the sleeping area and sprinted toward the two boulders. He skidded to a stop behind the first, gasping as he skirted the edge of the ridge, gravel flying off into the abyss, then huddling as weapons-fire thundered across the echoing silence.

He stuffed his fingers into his ears, but every sickening sound got through: petrified shouts, a gurgling, high-pitched scream. It was impossible to imagine they couldn't be heard from leagues away, and he permitted himself a foolish hope that somebody out there would raise an alert, save them.

But he knew that wouldn't happen and he'd better do something to help them fast. Then he remembered what was in his bag. He unslung it from his shoulder just as Valeria burst from the trees.

"Over here," he shouted. "Look out!"

Valeria turned as two pursuers erupted from the foliage behind her. She had seized one of their assault rifles, and she laid down a carpet of fire as she high-stepped backward toward Alton.

But the men in their TALOS absorbed the blasts and tore off a pummeling fusillade in return. She yelped as the projectiles bounced off her thighs and shins. As she came careening behind the boulder, Alton wrapped her up so she wouldn't slide over the ridge, then held her as she shuddered in rage and pain.

She had been hit dozens of times, and her TALOS was mottled everywhere. Her left sleeve was shredded, and her hand was slick and dark with blood. He gasped as she turned toward him, and he saw that a chunk of her right ear had been blown off. The blood was pooling on her neck and shoulder, thick and syrupy. He tried to conceal his shock.

"Whe . . . where are the others?"

She slumped hard against the rock. "I think Gagné got out. Everybody else is down." She took deep, convulsing breaths.

He fought down his mushrooming panic. "What the hell is going on? Why would the military want *me*? Why would they kill their own?"

"Those have to be Hagen's men," she gasped. "I don't know how they got here first. Maybe they scanned us out here somehow. But more likely somebody tipped them off."

"Who?"

But three, then four, more men were charging them, their volleys igniting the night. Valeria slid the barrel of the assault rifle around the side of the boulder and ripped into them.

"You have to get out of here," he said. "Take this." He shoved his pack at her.

"I'm not leaving a Civvie," she said. "Or abandoning this mission." Three of their four assailants were moving again. She tore off another burst in their direction.

"They said they were here for me," he said. "Which means they're not going to kill me."

Hopefully, he thought. He thrust the pack into her chest. "Get the fuck out of here! Regroup!"

She agonized for a moment, then snatched the pack. They would be overrun in moments, but she had the jet out and affixed with lightning speed.

She strapped it on and lit it up, then took out her sidearm and jammed it into Alton's hand.

"Cover me," she said.

He waved the gun above his head and fired a few shots, which they answered with a shattering salvo. Alton and Valeria covered their heads as boulder chunks showered them.

As Valeria slid toward the edge, she said, "I'll come back for you."

He stuck the pistol up again, but they were already wrenching it from his grasp just as Valeria took a diving leap into the blackness.

They fired down on her location, the bursts booming across the gorge. One of the commandos pitched forward, bellowing into the abyss as she got him, but another took his place instantly. This one had a web gun.

Alton lurched forward, trying to stop him, but the others viciously restrained him. He saw the yellow glow of the web, heard her cry out, and then was pulled away before he could see anything else. Like Bernardo in his dream, she fell. And as in his dream, he could do nothing about it.

They wrestled him up as a craft touched down in front of them, its lights blinding him. The men shoved him up its ramp and into a drop seat, then cinched him with straps until he could barely breathe.

A few others shuffled in behind him, banged up and limping, one bleeding from a forehead gash.

"Christ, you guys got creamed," the pilot said.

"Just fly," somebody barked, and he brought the ramp up and lifted off the plateau.

There was a deathly silence inside the shuttle. It was obvious they knew they were lucky to have made it out. Alton tried to take a deep breath but couldn't. "Can you loosen these a little?" he croaked.

"If we loosen those straps," one of them said, "it will be to dump you overboard."

CHAPTER 39

AS THEY LIFTED up and over the mountains, the pilot cut the lights and put them in drone mode, but not before Alton finally saw snow on the peaks. They must have been close to the highest part of the range, and the most remote, he thought.

He strained to make out details in case he needed to remember how to return, but it was too dark, and the tilt and shiver of the craft was making him feel sick. He closed his eyes and saw the image of Valeria web-bound and plunging. He hoped against hope that she had managed to survive.

They were in the air for maybe fifteen minutes. Then, as the first gray seam of dawn split along the horizon, they began to descend between the peaks. Below them, just visible in the faint illumination, were more of the endless slabs of jagged slate, dotted at this elevation with only tundra and the heartiest alpine flora.

Just as Alton began to wonder where they would land, he felt the craft shake, then saw the windshield mottle and blur. In the next instant, a facility appeared in the valley below. A landing pad, metal installations jutting from the rock, a huge door carved into the mountainside, all became visible inside the stealth shield they had just penetrated.

He would have thought a shield of the capacity to conceal an entire base for this long was the sole purview of the military. And yet, as with the ability to remotely neutralize their augmentation, Alex appeared to have it. He must have raided more military installations than even Lance had suggested. Or maybe insiders had helped him, disgruntled spies willing to smuggle him weapons and tech, perhaps even some of his father's old connections.

Alton couldn't help but admire Alex's dedication, trudging back and forth through the frigid outback to construct this fortress. Still, even the most committed efforts on foot wouldn't have begun to haul a fraction of the materials necessary to erect what he saw before him, never mind whatever lay inside the mountain. And a steady airlift would have been spotted and shut down a long time ago.

If this had been his primary base for all these years of waging civil war and then hiding for the last two years, how had he managed to transport people and equipment without being discovered?

The craft alighted softly on the pad. The instant the engines ceased, the men untethered him and dragged him down the ramp and over a narrow catwalk toward the massive steel door.

On the journey here, with its hardships and distractions, finding Alex and Kiara had seemed purely theoretical. But now that he was being steered into a dimly lit tunnel, a profound dread welled up at the prospect of facing them at last.

He needn't have worried about it for the moment, however, as the room along the corridor into which they thrust him was empty of people.

The heavy door boomed and bolted behind him, and he stood frozen in a murky space. Shadowy shapes, a damp chill, and a chemical stench sent his adrenaline racing. He would eventually realize this was his torture reflex, a permanent physiological response to strange, dark places with nasty-looking machines.

But as his eyes adjusted, he relaxed a little. It wasn't a torture chamber, at least not a conventional one. A long stainless-steel table occupied the center. As he took in his surroundings, dully gleaming under an iron-colored light, it began to look familiar.

He had seen more contemporary versions of these displays and interfaces, buckets of parts, canisters and bottles of liquid metals, rusty first-aid cabinets, and shelves stacked with sinister-looking tools, scalpels, and other blades. He looked into each shadowy corner until . . . yes, there it was. A reclining chair with tubes and wires like that of a . . . what had it brought to his mind? *Steampunk dentist.*

He was in an augmentation lab. Although this one was grimier and more sinister than the sterling studio in which he had been augmented a few days earlier. He shivered, wondering what had been done in here. And to whom.

He was spared from having to imagine the worst when the door swung open and three men came at him. Two held his arms, and the third jammed a nasty-looking syringe into his neck. He couldn't muster a single objection before the world slipped out from under him.

CHAPTER 40

THE BEDCHAMBER WAS steeped in a faint copper glow. The corners receded into darkness, but Alton could tell that a figure sat cross-legged in one of them because of the huge, gnarled shadow thrown against the opposite wall.

He moved a little in the rickety bed, then threw off a coarse Afghan to find bandages swaddling his arms and right leg. His left leg—the prosthetic—was coated with some kind of shimmering material. He tried to reach out, but his puffy-bandaged arm was too heavy, as were his eyelids, which closed around the sight of his fingers dropping back to the bed.

When he next awakened, he was more cautious with movement as he let his mind filter toward awareness. He was startled to see the figure still in the corner. He hesitated to rouse its attention, but thirst savaged him.

"Water," he rasped. The figure stirred, then left the room. A minute later, it returned with a thermos. A hand removed the top and flipped up a plastic straw. "Drink this. It's a nutrient-electrolyte solution."

He was weak, and the thermos rolled onto the floor. The figure kneeled to retrieve it, and in the burnished light, it looked like Kiara. Her eyes floated in and out of deep shadows, making her seem like an apparition. She placed the thermos gently into his hands, then brought the chair to his bedside. It had been her watching him from the corner, throwing that monstrous shadow.

"It's so good to see you, Alton," she said, her eyes moistening.

Hearing her voice made his mind race back over the years. Grief clutched his chest.

"How . . . how did you know where I was?"

"I'll let him give you the details," she said. "Are you in pain?"

He thought about this. He was always in pain, couldn't remember a time when he wasn't in pain. But this seemed a little melodramatic, so he just grunted.

She nodded toward the bandages. "You'll get those off shortly," she said. "I apologize for the . . . invasiveness of the surgery. I wanted to talk to you about it first, but you know he does love the grand gesture." She shrugged as though it was all out of her hands.

"Don't worry; I'm used to it." He could feel what they had done to him but didn't need to consider the ramifications just yet. At least nobody had removed a limb this time.

"We were also going to implant a DNA scrambler until they found that you already have one."

"I'm guessing everyone here has one?"

"Of course." She leaned in and touched his forehead, then his cheek. "No fever," she said.

Pride told him to brush her hand away, but it felt too good.

"I'm sorry for what happened to you," she said. "The camps."

He did pull away then. "You don't seem to have a problem with the person responsible for them."

"He's not responsible for them, Alton. Guerrero is." She sighed. "Alex has always fought for the rights of our people. Minority rights now."

Our people. It was the first time he had ever heard her utter such a thing.

"And where has your holy crusader been these last two years while I was wasting away? Not fighting for *my* rights, that's for damn sure."

"I know it's hard to accept, but what he's preparing has taken a lot of time. You'll soon see that it's all been worth it."

She was more beautiful than ever. Her chestnut hair was cut close around her ears now. She was dressed simply but elegantly in light cotton pants and a navy fleece, dusty hiking boots laced up the ankles. Her eyes were still lustrous, even in the drab light, though perhaps flintier than they once had been.

"I met your parents," he said. It was hard to tell from the shadows on her face, but he thought he saw sadness flicker there. "They seemed to think they were never going to see you again."

She stood. "I'm glad you made it here, Alton. We don't have much time left."

"Deciphering your clue was easy enough, but how did you know I would find it there? How did you know Áquilar would come up with the idea to use me in the first place?"

"Because it wasn't her idea. It was mine." She let this sink in, then said, "I suggested she enlist you in tracking Alex before I slipped the grid."

He stared at her. *How long had they been planning this?*

"You almost got me killed," he said. "More than once."

"Some things are worth the risk."

"If only people would let me decide that for myself."

She stood and went to the door. "Someone will come and remove your bandages, get you cleaned up. Once that's done, I'll take you to him."

He stood naked in the cramped shower receptacle and stared at himself in the plexiglass reflection. Shaved head. Augmented eyes. Scars. Prosthetic leg. Newly fused electric veins shimmering like rivulets of mercury beneath his limbs.

He had struggled his whole life to figure out his identity, torn between one parent who refused to acknowledge his existence and one who openly resented it. Confronting this bizarre hybrid stranger did nothing to clarify his confusion, although he almost smiled at the thought of standing before his class in Gypsum. What would his students make of him now that he was like them?

He increased the water temperature and let the steam cloud over his unsettling image, then luxuriated with his eyes closed. Being in camp had made him realize that a lot of things had let him down in life but never a hot shower.

After twenty minutes, the water shut off, and he climbed out and carefully dried himself, wiping the towel back and forth over his forearms, feeling the funky substance underneath.

There was only the faintest of lines where they had lasered the incisions. He thought of Alex's first set of EVs, the back-alley crudeness of them, the pipes sticking out of his elbow joints. What he was looking at now was as smooth as could be, just the faintest metallic sheen underneath the flesh, not heavy at all. If anything, his limbs felt lighter, more mobile, more flexible.

Nothing was activated though. His augmentation had yet to be restored. And the EVs were not yet operational. He wondered what color they would be. Just one more thing he'd had no say in.

And yet part of him had begun to accept that he was being swept along now. He had been at the mercy of others for so long, the concept of choice had become as foreign as the concept of requited love. Given the opportunity to pilot his own life, he had to admit he had little idea where he would start.

They had confiscated his TALOS, and so he dressed in the clothes they had left for him and went out into the corridor to find Kiara waiting. The shock of seeing her seized him fully now that he was more awake: the warm, breathing reality of a person whose memory he had both fetishized and resented for so long.

They fell into step without speaking, and she led him through the dark tunnels. He was conscious of brushing against her in the close space, their sleeves softly rustling, and his heartbeat quickened as he remembered their nights together in DC. When they came around a curve and a faint light began to seep in, he stopped and put a hand on her shoulder.

"I came here for you," he said. "Come back with me before it's too late. What good end can this possibly have?"

"Alton, I'm with him till the end. You know that."

The old familiar pain welled up in him, and he looked away. "I always thought we had a special connection." He wanted to tell her how her picture in his locker had kept him going in camp but thought it would make him sound pathetic.

"Of course we did," she said. "Why do you think you're here?"

She smiled at him—equal parts sadness and pity, he thought, with maybe a pinch of gratitude. It made him want to smash something.

"Because I've been your third wheel my whole life." He almost spit.

"I promise you that won't always be the case."

He didn't know what she meant, but he let her lead him out onto a catwalk, where he stared, dumbfounded.

The massive cavern was at least six stories high and five hundred meters in circumference, so vast he could hardly see the other side. Steel girders held up the floors, and gantries with guardrails crisscrossed between them. Far below, human figures were scattered among industrial equipment and machines. A vehicle that resembled a lunar rover crawled among them.

He gawked but couldn't get his mind around it. They couldn't have dug this out in half a century. This was an International Construction Consortium kind of job. Army Corps of Engineers.

"How did you manage...?"

"We didn't," she said and led him along the catwalk to show him what was directly beneath them: two massive hollows, side by side, carved into the granite wall.

He shook his head, uncomprehending.

"Hydro-Channels," she said. "This was their origin point, guzzling up all the fresh runoff from the peaks to send downstate. But they were abandoned after desalination. No point in maintaining the expense anymore. This place has been deserted for..."

"Twenty years," he said. He remembered seeing the termination points of the tunnels just at the edge of Cosmost when the team had been flying out of LA.

"Give or take."

"And he's been here all this time?"

"No. Alex was expeditioning in this wilderness for a long time before he found it. I helped him when I could get away. But discovering the tunnels was just blind luck."

He marveled. "These tunnels span almost the entire length of California."

She nodded. "It took him a few years to repurpose the infrastructure, to create exit points along the way for operations—"

"You mean raids."

"But once he did, transport was easy. Men, weapons, supplies. There's no way he could have grown the movement so big without it."

"My God. No wonder nobody caught him. He's literally been underground. They wouldn't have *begun* to know where to look."

The corners of her mouth turned up in the hint of a smile. A smile of pride, he thought. "Come on," she said. "Tour's just beginning."

But why was she showing him all this? Was he to be some kind of witness to their final crusade? Was he supposed to document everything for history? Or was this just to be one final cruel betrayal? He thought of Bernardo and sucked in his breath.

A little farther along, the catwalk branched off into a set of rickety metal stairs leading down to the next level. They took the steps down to a platform lined with monitors and controls, a kind of observation terrace that extended out over the cavern.

A bony bald man supervised several technicians, while another man, who seemed to be security, lingered nearby. Kiara went up to the bald man and put her hand on his shoulder. The man turned and broke into a huge smile. It was several full seconds before Alton, astonished, realized it was Alex.

CHAPTER 41

ALEX LOOKED HIM up and down, his eyes wide and bright. "The prodigal son returns," he intoned, then enfolded Alton in a delicate embrace. His skin felt papery, the embrace anemic. The broad shoulders of fifteen years earlier seemed shrunken. Alton felt revolted.

Alex released him and ran his hands down Alton's arms, squeezing and massaging them. It seemed embarrassingly intimate until he rolled back Alton's sleeves and Alton realized he was just inspecting the EVs.

"A long way from the back-alley job I had as a kid. Remember those?"

"Of course," he said, thinking of the bloodied Hyperloop pod, the mangled kids. "But at least yours worked." He protruded his arms in a limp display.

"Let's do something about that, shall we?"

There was a whirring sound, and Alton felt a buzzing in his head as his augmentation powered up. His limbs shivered, and he looked down to see the mercury-like material radiating faintly.

"Light up your interface. See the app in the top right corner of your menu? Access it."

He did, and suddenly the platform was suffused with a deep red glow. It was so dazzling, a moment passed before Alton realized *he* was casting it. He brandished his arms, tracing crimson streaks in the air. "A little garish, don't you think?"

Alex laughed. "It was her idea."

Alton looked at her. "Why red?"

"Because you've always been so angry," she said.

He was taken aback. He had never thought of himself as especially angry. Cynical, maybe sad, but he had felt too impotent for anger.

"So, now what?" he asked. "I can blow things up real good?"

"Sure, why not?" Alex said. "Lunch break!"

The workers didn't need to be told twice, high-tailing it down the clattering steps. Although some still had the forehead tattoos, Alton noticed they were older than the Nibelungs in camp, and less . . . rabid-looking. Maybe Alex kept the more stable ones near him. When only the three of them and the security man remained, Alex said, "Okay, light 'em up!"

"Light what up?"

"Point your arm at the terminal. See how the crosshairs populate your interface automatically?"

"Yes." A 3D augmented-reality targeting system appeared. Red crosshairs filled his vision.

"Tell it to 'engage target.'"

"En . . . engage target," Alton said, and the crosshairs turned green.

"Now, tell it to fire."

"Are you sure?"

"Do it!"

"Fire!" Alton barked. A seismic bolt of energy instantly escaped his left arm and annihilated one side of the terminal. They all jumped back as sparks and material showered everywhere. An emergency klaxon began to blare.

"Hahaha, *yes!*" Alex bellowed.

Kiara swore and ran back up the steps.

The klaxon abruptly cut out, and Alex announced, "Nothing to worry about, folks. Just a little accident on Level 6." His voice echoed throughout the subterrane.

Kiara returned with a fire extinguisher and thrust it into the arms of the security guy, who began to hose the burn.

Alex was grinning ear to ear. "Feels pretty fucking good, right?"

Alton had to admit it did. The most amazing thing was that there had been almost no recoil at all. He remembered how the railgun at camp had thrown him back ten feet. Loosing that powerful energy without a kick made him feel invincible.

Alex was still excited. "Blast something else!"

"Don't you need this stuff?" The terminal he had destroyed was still smoking. The air was acrid with the smell of melted metal.

"This place will be a memory in three days." Alex smiled at Kiara and added, "A very distant memory."

Alton looked down at the killing machine into which they had transformed him. "Why did you do this?" he asked.

"Because you're going to need it eventually," Alex said. "And the facilities where we're headed can't do work that sophisticated. At least not at first."

Alton took a step back. "What are you talking about? I'm not going anywhere with you."

He looked at Kiara, then at the guard, who watched him closely, then back at Alex, still grinning. Alex was so thin, frail almost. The image of the strapping warrior he had broadcast to the world two weeks earlier had been fake after all. It would take little to waste this version of him. He wouldn't even need the augmentation. He could just wring his neck. How good would that feel?

A sudden memory seized him: the young Christina, her pulse faint, her pretty dress soaked in blood, the wreckage pinning her arms and chest. Here was a chance for revenge he never thought he would get. He would be a fool not to take it.

As though reading his mind, Alex smiled and said, "Go ahead then, if that's what you came here to do."

"Alex . . ." Kiara said. Her voice was tight.

The security man had set down the extinguisher. His gold EVs glowed faintly.

"Don't worry about him," Alex said, catching Alton's glance. As he said it, the guard's power fizzled out, and his arms went limp.

"You could reduce us to ash," Alex continued. "Probably get back out to the landing platform before anybody knows what happened. From there, I don't know, but at least you'd have a chance. And the world would be rid of me, wouldn't it?"

He pried open his jacket with both hands as though to expose his heart as a target.

"Alex!" Kiara cried. "Stop this now."

For a long moment, no one moved. Alton saw that he had raised his lethal appendage and pointed it at Alex without even realizing it. He fought to still its trembling.

"You would be completely justified," Alex said. "But I'd like you to consider this first. What if I could give you something you've long craved even more than my death? Two things, actually. A package deal, if you like."

Alton reflexively glanced at Kiara.

Alex raised his eyebrows. "Ah, such things do exist, don't they?"

Alton lowered his arm a few degrees.

"Come on. Let me show you," Alex said. "For old times' sake."

Alton looked at Kiara again, met her eyes. "This isn't a trick," she said. "We didn't bring you all the way here for nothing."

They went down and strode along the narrow catwalk that circumnavigated the second level. Alton felt like he was in the cheap seats of some giant stadium, the main stage a mile away.

Alex spoke to him over his shoulder, his voice echoing. "I never did get a chance to thank you for not turning me in," he said.

"I only did it for Kiara."

"And she wants to repay you, especially after what you've suffered through these last few years."

"How?"

But Alex said nothing as they made their way around to the other side. Alton noticed that no weapons were visible, and the place seemed generally emptied out. Had he already staged his men and equipment near the next battlefront?

They came to the other side, almost exactly opposite of where they had been, and Alex led them into a little dining alcove with a full kitchen. Someone appeared and began making them food while they sat overlooking the enormous chamber.

Alton's mouth watered as onions and peppers began to sizzle. "It doesn't look like you're making bombs here," he said.

Alex didn't answer as he went to a small bar and poured them bourbons. It was small-batch, and it glowed a magnificent amber. Alton took a long swallow. It flowed through him like a river of molten gold.

"Life's little pleasures are crucial," Alex said. "Which is why we're taking several cases with us. We'll distill our own, but of course it will be a while before we can make anything this good."

"Taking it where?"

"Utopia Basin."

Alton laughed. "Seriously?"

"A perfectly named place for the life we plan to establish, don't you think?" Kiara said. "We launch in four days."

Alton set his glass down. "Four days? That's . . ." He surveyed the floor, spotted the moon rover.

"I already told you where these tunnels lead," she said.

He thought again of the flight out of LA, the abandoned Hydrochannels not five kilometers from the spaceport. The tunnels let out *inside* Cosmost grounds.

His mouth dropped open. "You're going to try to *hijack* the Mars colony ship?"

"We prefer to think of it as . . . reappropriation," said Alex. "For what was rightfully ours in the first place."

Kiara refilled their glasses. "To our future," she said.

CHAPTER 42

AFTER THEY HAD eaten, Alex took Alton down to the operations floor. Alton felt woozy from the bourbon and clung to the guardrails as they descended.

"There's not much to see at this point," Alex said, gesturing around. His bald pate shone in the overhead light. "Most of the equipment, the radiation suits, even some of the crew are already staged near Cosmost. Or headed that way. Anyway, most everything we need is already on planet. They've been kindly delivering equipment and supplies for a couple of years now."

"The ship will have remote override systems," Alton said. "Even if you get off the ground, they'll just kill the engines, turn you around."

"That's the beautiful thing about not having to worry about shelter and supplies. We've been able to focus on training and getting past their encryption, waiting inside every system and program for zero-day exploits."

"Which they will undoubtedly have fixes for."

"Yes, but by the time they patch their vulnerabilities, we'll have transferred control of the systems to our custom and much better encrypted programs."

"Their AI will anticipate that."

"Fortunately for us, they still don't fully trust AI for this yet.

They have a redundant AI system in place for emergencies, but we've managed to skirt it. An intelligent, self-driving system was the one thing that could have recognized and prevented what we were doing."

"But they don't want to risk it going HAL 9000," Alton said.

"Exactly. Not after that South China Sea debacle, not with the Chinese already established on the other side. Nobody wants another world war, let alone two of them."

"They'll just shoot you down then."

"Nope. Because three of the original crew will be with us and the whole world will be watching."

"Hostages?"

"And we know which three to grab, based on their expertise." Alex grinned. "You see, I really have thought of everything."

Alton shook his head, both disgusted and impressed. "They'll come after you."

"Eventually, but how is that different from my life now? At least once we're dug in, we'll have the advantage. And some time to stretch our wings. Plus . . . *we'll be on fucking Mars*."

Alton squeezed his eyes, trying to focus through the creeping hangover.

"I've been planning this for a decade," Alex continued. "As soon as the Chinese announced their colony mission. I've recruited scientists, engineers, coders, hackers, even former astronauts."

"White supremacists in every field," Alton said. "Gotta love it."

"Not everybody joined up for the cause. A few were just generally disaffected or didn't want to wait around for climate change to finish us off. A few knew it was their only chance to be part of the mission rather than just help plan it."

Now, Alton knew why the men he had seen earlier on the platform hadn't looked like Nibelungs. It was because they weren't.

Alex led him over to a large metal husk that looked like a hunk of fuselage from a small jetliner. He patted it, and it resounded with a dull metallic echo.

"Once Cosmost announced a three-year launch target, we started to really prepare." We did zero-g training here, radiation shield tests there." He pointed across the cavern to a chamber behind thick plexiglass. "And you saw our rover," he said, smiling. "That wasn't easy to get our hands on. But here's the main thing," he said, picking up a pair of slim headsets.

"VR?"

"Every training program. Controls. Take off and landing. Emergency procedures. How to take a dump in zero g. Everything. We've been studying this for the last year."

"Won't you be leaving an awful lot of your disciples behind?" Alton said. "Not much they can do about it once you're 144 million miles away, I guess."

He thought of Lance's desperation to flee Gypsum and realized that he must have known about the planned voyage. That's why he had been so frantic to escape with Alton. *I don't want to be left behind*, he had said.

"They'll be happy to have played a part in spreading our way of life throughout the solar system," Alex said. "For the twenty-nine signed on so far, this will be the greatest adventure."

"What do you mean 'so far'? Aren't you supposed to be leaving in three days?"

"We saved the last seat."

"For whom?"

"Who do you think?"

Alton began to vigorously shake his head even as he was still processing it.

"You used to dream about this when we were kids, and *I've* made it happen," Alex said. "You were the one who got me thinking about this in the first place. Don't you dare back out now."

Alton felt sick thinking that he could be responsible for yet another of Alex's blows against civilization. If successful, the long-term consequences of this could be the most devastating yet.

"But I came here to kill you," he said, knowing how weak it sounded.

"No, you didn't," he said. "You came here for her. Don't let her down now."

He couldn't wrap his mind around any of it, so he returned to his room. He tried to sleep, but his thoughts were racing. Stealing a colony ship and getting away with it seemed insane, impossible.

But they did have two big advantages. First, nobody would ever expect it. Second, they had a way to sneak onto the Cosmost grounds from inside. If the timing was right, Alton believed they might take control of the ship, even take off. But getting all the way to the Red Planet was another thing entirely.

But if they did make it... how would he feel if he had a chance to go and stayed behind? Only a few weeks earlier, his future had been mud, literally. In the wintertime, Gypsum was sloppy with it. Now, he had his greatest dream within his grasp.

He thought of his trip into orbit with Bernardo, remembered how he had looked out at Mars from inside the capsule and prayed for their ship to take him there. He would have never believed in a million years that it would one day be a possibility.

Who cared if they failed? He had nothing else to return to. Even if Áquilar kept her promise and set him up somewhere, he would still be alone, probably in some remote location. It wouldn't be much different from being in camp. And after what they'd done to him—and thousands of others—this government had no moral authority at all.

You know that doesn't justify anything. He sat up in bed, angry with himself. Even if the plan was guaranteed to succeed, there was no way in hell he would willingly join any colony led by a psychopathic killer who was also his sworn enemy. He felt claustrophobic and desperate for air. After wandering the corridors for a bit, he found someone to let him out onto the platform.

The icy air bit at him as he clutched the guardrail and stared into the abyss. The canyon walls surrounding the platform were pitch black. Far above, a circular patch of stars shimmered through into the canyon, slightly blurred by the cloaking shield.

The only other illumination came from the dimly glowing catwalk extending to the smaller adjoining platform where the ship was docked. He had no idea how far the fall was from that gantry to the bottom of the canyon, and he didn't care to find out.

After a while, the exquisite stillness of the night, along with the cold and his exhaustion, began to drain some of the anger from him. He looked for Mars to give him a sign about what he should do, but it was not visible from where he stood.

Alex had said not everybody going was on board with Nibelung ideology. *Maybe there will be others like me who don't really believe this bullshit*, he thought, *like the three hostages*. Maybe there would be an opportunity for nonbelievers to break off into their own colony once they had been established for a while.

But he knew Alex's ego would never allow that. He would kill anybody who tried to make an example of them.

He shivered and exhaled a gust of frosty breath. He was about to retreat inside when the massive door groaned open and Kiara emerged. She crossed the platform, her exquisite silhouette backlit from the tunnel lights, and stood shoulder to shoulder with him. She touched his hand with hers, and he let it linger there. It took everything he had not to wrap her in his arms.

"It will be what you always dreamed about," she said, looking up.

"What about the people who died to make this a reality? The people who will still die?"

"You're a student of history, Alton. You know that sometimes bloodshed is the price of justice."

"Justice?" He recoiled slightly, but couldn't bring himself to break away from her entirely. "I can't believe you're on board with his bullshit now. We used to feel sorry for him!"

"You know I'm not racist, but you can't deny this country has changed. And this government is a monstrosity," she said. "Look what it did to you. Don't you want to get away from all that?"

"Of course I do."

"We'll be starting a new civilization on a new world," she said. "Slate wiped clean."

"That's what I'm afraid of. All of this German mythology bullshit. Being worshiped like some kind of god. It will only get worse once he goes all the way upriver. There'll be no one to stop him from putting our heads on spikes if he feels like it."

"There's no one to stop him from doing that now," she said. "But I don't think about that."

"What do you think about then?"

She lifted her arms to the sky. "That my child will take her first steps on pristine red soil! That all of human history has been pointing toward this, and *we* could be at the forefront, Alton! Some poor kids from North Hollywood!" She laughed in amazement.

He looked at her, stupefied. She hadn't just drunk the Kool-Aid; she was marinating in it.

She leaned closer to him. "I'm sorry about leaving you so abruptly in DC," she said.

Her breath was suddenly hot in his ear. He shivered again, but this time not from the cold. He resisted turning toward her. "I thought we had something," he said.

"We did, Alton." She took his hand and caressed it with her thumb. "Our time together has always been important to me."

"But you left me without a word!" He pulled away then. "And then you went back to him like always, no matter how much he takes you for granted." His throat felt raw. His head was throbbing, and he was ragged with thirst.

"He's always had my heart, Alton. I can't help that." She paused, then added, "Still, you never know what the future holds."

"What does that mean?"

But she was silent.

"What happened to him, anyway?" he asked. "Why is he so skinny?"

"He was sick for a while," she said. "It was hard to get the kind of treatment he needed up here. But he's fine now."

He could get lunar rovers but not a doctor? That sounded like bullshit.

She rested her hand on his trembling forearm. "We need you. We need your intelligence and your imagination. And your moral compass."

He snorted.

"I care for you, Alton. We both do, regardless of what you may think."

She was weakening whatever resolve he had left, and he gripped the frozen rail with both hands until he could hardly feel them. "He's a narcissist. He doesn't care about anybody but himself." He wanted to add *including you*. But he suspected she already knew that.

She turned him toward her and locked eyes with him. "I promise you won't regret coming."

"How can you promise that?"

"I can't tell you right now. But please just trust me."

Searching her eyes brought back her radiance at the festival the night they had met. The purple twilight and the sweet desert air. Her invigorating laugh. The feelings of lightness and purpose she gave him, even in that terrible place full of hateful small men.

Most of all, she gave him hope that his future might open up in ways he hadn't dared to dream. That intoxicating girl in the desert was permanently associated with everything he ever wanted, even if the person she was now would never—*could never*—give it to him.

He released his grip from the rails and looked down into the abyss. "I'll never trust you," he said. "But you know I'll give you what you want anyway."

CHAPTER 43

AND THEN HE finally slept—for how long he had no idea—until he sat straight up in bed, heart pounding. At first, he thought he was having nightmares. But once fully awake, he distinctly heard the shouts, then the weapons fire. Light sliced into the room, temporarily blinding him. When his eyes adjusted, he saw Kiara backlit in the doorway.

"What is it?"

"Don't know yet," she said. "Just stay here."

"Fuck that," he said and leapt out of bed. He threw on his clothes and boots, then looked around the room for a weapon before remembering that he *was* a weapon now. He powered on and brought the sight up, as Alex had shown him. The room flooded crimson.

Now, Alex appeared in the corridor wearing a hiking pack that dwarfed his feeble frame.

"Time to go," he said. "Final evacuation has begun through the tunnels."

Alton was alarmed. "Who's out there?" he asked. "Guerrero's men?"

"Can't be."

"How do you know that?"

They braced themselves against the wall as a shockwave rippled through the chamber.

Shit, he thought. *Can it be?*

"I'll meet you down there," he said.

"If you're not there by launch time, you'll be left behind," Alex said. "*Way* behind."

"Understood."

He ran down the corridor and crouched with Alex's men just inside the entrance. Blinding energy bolts lit up the dark as they exchanged fire. He couldn't see anything, then remembered to engage his night vision.

When he did, his suspicions were confirmed. Valeria was out on the landing platform, firing at them from behind the shuttle on its little platform. Alton wondered why they didn't just charge her—they were ten to one—when several blasts crackled like lightning down the mountainside. Someone hidden up there had them pinned.

"Let me through," Alton said and pushed his way to the front.

He waited for a pause in the firing, then shouted, "Val! Val, it's me! It's Alton!"

A few moments of ringing silence lapsed, and then she was in his head on a secure channel.

"Are you wounded?" she asked.

"I'm okay," he said.

"Where are they holding you?"

He paused. "They're not."

"They're not what?"

"They're not holding me."

"You need to clarify, Civvie. What is your situation?"

"Hang on," he said and muted the channel. He stood. "I'm going out there."

"No way," said one of the men.

"I can get them to stand down," he said. He had no idea if he could or not, but he knew the men had no other choice. Some were stealing apprehensive glances back down the corridor, perhaps worried that their supreme leader would abandon them.

He unmuted his coms channel. "I'm coming out," he told her.

"What do you mean you're *coming out*? Why are they allowing that?"

"Just trust me, please. Tell your partner to cease fire."

He edged out onto the larger platform, expecting to be fired upon anyway, and hastened across the catwalk to behind the shuttle, where Valeria yanked him down next to her.

Her wounds weren't gushing, as they had been on the plateau, but her face and head were bruised and mottled. Someone—whoever was hiding up the mountain, he guessed—had shaved around her ear and field-stitched the gash. Alton winced at the frightful job. He also noticed she was wearing her propulsion pack.

"Holy shit . . ." she said, gawking at his EVs, until her shock gave way to suspicion. "What the fuck is going on?"

He ignored her. "How long before reinforcements?"

"There are no reinforcements. It's just Gagné and me."

"Why didn't you call for backup?"

"Why do you think? This mission is secret. The whole point is *not* to tell everybody we're here."

"What about Guerrero's unit? The one that Eli said was en route?"

"No sign of them," she said.

"Then what—"

"We came back for *you*, Civvie, like I promised!"

He looked up the dark mountainside. "Get out of here," he said. "I can stall them long enough. You can take this shuttle."

"What are you talking about? Let's go while we have the chance!"

"I'm not leaving Kiara," he said.

She looked at his EVs again. "You're with them, aren't you? You fucking Nazi. I should have known. This was all a ploy to reunite you with your comrades."

He turned to bolt, but she was too quick. He hadn't even seen the web gun beside her until the blast cinched his torso, just as it had that fateful night at Gypsum. His augmentation sizzled out, and then she was dragging him up the shuttle ramp and heaving him inside.

"We're coming, Gagné," she said. "Keep these fuckers at bay."

As they took off, Gagné tore off a fusillade of fire to give them cover. Val rotated the ship's gun to help, ricocheting rapid-fire ammunition off the massive steel portal as Alex's men dove back inside.

Valeria maneuvered the shuttle close to the mountainside, and Gagné leapt in from the ledge they had been perched on.

Alton's face was mashed to the floor, but he turned his head enough to see the air outside muddle and smear as they exited the cloaking field.

Gagné went to a panel and brought up several displays. Just as they said, "They're not following," all the juice inside the craft, including their augmentations and the web binding him, fizzled out. Except for the faint cast of the predawn moon, everything was black.

"Shit," Gagné said. "Electromagnetic pulse." They punched at the controls, but it was useless. "We're going down."

"There's only enough fuel left for one pack!" Valeria yelled. "Only two of us can go."

"Take him," Gagné said. "I'll glide this thing in."

Even Alton knew this was bullshit. There was no place to glide among these jagged peaks. The shuttle would smash into the mountains any moment.

"Fuck that," Val said. "Let's leave him."

"No, Val. Mission first. Always."

Valeria looked stricken. She grabbed the manual release on the door and wrenched it open, then fired up her pack and grabbed Alton roughly under the pits. "It was an honor and a privilege, soldier," she said to Gagné, who saluted in return.

Then Valeria leapt from the craft, and she and Alton were falling toward the mountains in the first flush of dawn.

She adjusted the jets to slow them and produced two straps that she hooked to his belt with carabiners. Her hands thus freed, she concentrated on guiding them through the icy wind. Their combined weight dragged them down but not with such speed that they would plummet. Still, they needed to find a place to land before gravity handled it for them.

Without warning, the granite curtain parted, and Alton was stunned to see they were out of the mountains. The Trinity River coursed sleek and dark through the firs and pines that stretched to the horizon. Mount Shasta loomed over the region like an ancient god, the first rays of sun falling on its sleeping face in heavenly shafts.

Alton sucked in his breath at the glorious vista, then expelled it in shock when the titanic boom echoed through the mountains behind them and Gagné met their end. He could feel Valeria's body stiffen, then shudder. After the echo subsided, only the distant cry of an eagle pierced the silence.

Valeria directed them through the treetops and toward a glade, which they hit harder than he would have liked, tumbling together in a tangle of smacking elbows and barbed pinecones.

She unhooked him and stumbled to her feet. Her face tightened as she looked back towards Gagné's final resting place.

He remained on the ground in disbelief, realizing that Alex would have ordered the EMT pulse to take down their craft even though he knew Alton was aboard. *But then what choice did he have? He couldn't risk everything to spare me. He warned me not to miss my chance.*

He got to his feet, brushing off a crust of pine needles. "I'm...I'm sorry," he said.

"Fuck you," she spat.

"Don't blame me for that. I told you to leave me back there."

She wheeled around and gave him a murderous stare. "How did you get those EVs?"

"They implanted them against my will."

"Why would they do that?"

"I have no idea. Probably so they could use me as some kind of weapon."

"Bullshit. You're one of them. You always have been."

"I've been teaching anti-racist literature for half my life!"

"As cover," she said. "This whole thing was just an elaborate ploy to spring you from camp and reunite with them. But why now? What are you planning?"

He started to protest again, but she was on him quick, grabbing him by the shoulders and shaking him. "What are you planning!"

She shoved him square in the sternum with the flat of her hand and he went down, smacking his tail bone on the cold, hard ground.

"Motherfucker," she said, standing over him. "You let Hagen know our coordinates on the mountain. You're responsible for the deaths of my unit."

"Are you crazy?"

But she was wrenching him up so that she could slam him against a tree. His head smacked the thick bark. Pain hammered his skull, and he saw double for a few seconds.

"I should waste you right here," she said, putting one hand around his throat.

"I would never have put them in that kind of danger! Even if I had any idea how to transmit our location. I swear to God, I wanted to kill Hagen as badly as you did. I still do!"

"Then why didn't you when you had the chance?"

"Because of Kiara." It was half true anyway.

"You seemed perfectly content to let her die when we interviewed you at Gypsum."

"That's before I saw her for the first time in years." He tried to give a convincingly pained look.

"Bullshit," she said and lifted her other fist to his face.

"Go ahead," he said, "I'm not telling you shit about where they are until I know Kiara's safe."

He waited for the blow to come, but she let him go and went and slumped on a fallen log. "It wouldn't matter if you did," she said. "I can't do a fucking thing about it right now."

"Is there any way we can get back online out here?"

"Not unless you can plug into a tree. That EMP drained us dry."

The slow light of dawn was confirming the obvious. They were in the middle of nowhere. The old-growth forest was deep, silent, and still.

"We have no way at all to contact somebody?" He asked.

"Nope."

"So what do we do?"

She made a Herculean effort to stand.

"We walk. And when we get back, they'll strip those EVs and throw your ass right back in camp. Hopefully for good this time."

I'll never go back there, he thought. *But how the hell am I going to get to Cosmost before they launch?*

CHAPTER 44

THEY HIKED SOUTHWEST for a few hours. Having not eaten since lunch the day before, Alton was already starving. But at least the path through the forest was reasonably flat and not too strenuous. The exercise kept him from shivering, but the late November sun—white and diffuse and low in the sky—provided little heat. He could only imagine how cold it would turn once darkness fell.

But that would feel like nothing compared to the sickening recognition that he had likely lost his one chance to join them. He had been torn before, but now that it had slipped his grasp, he knew for sure that he wanted to be part of their adventure, even despite the moral cost.

But even if he could somehow make it to LA before the launch, he didn't know how he would 1) escape Valeria. 2) breach Cosmost security from the outside, or 3) find Alex and Kiara even if he could manage 1) and 2).

He spat in disgust. His love of space had been nothing but a curse. If he hadn't chanced to befriend a lonely rich kid, maybe he would have focused on more terrestrial concerns and not grasped for an impossible dream.

He and Valeria hadn't spoken since they had set out, but he could suffer his own thoughts no longer. "How did you find me, anyway?" he asked.

She was a few paces ahead, and she spoke without looking back at him. "We located you once your augmentation powered back on. There was plenty of leftover fuel after my team got iced on the plateau. But we used most of it to get to your location. That's why we only had one pack remaining."

He let a little more silence elapse, then asked, "What are you going to do with me when we get back?"

"You mean *if* we get back? It's not up to me. I'm sure Áquilar has some black site to dump you in."

"Your fidelity to the Constitution amazes me."

"Fuck the Constitution. Ain't nothing but a white man's charter."

This surprised him. He knew she was cynical but not sacrilegious when it came to her oath.

"Hispanic people have more power in this country than ever," he said. "More than I've ever had."

Now, she stopped and spun to face him. "And that's supposed to make up for centuries of injustice? It's only been recently that we've gained more power," she said. "But we still can't be *too* dark or *too* steeped in our culture. Look at what Native Americans still deal with."

He knew she was right but stayed silent.

"And it's not just the gringos who've shit on us. My grandparents and even my parents were persecuted for being too brown in South Texas. Their own people, light-skins, looked down on them, even though everybody had the same last names, the same ancestors."

So, that's why you hate me, he thought. *I'm a half breed that looks white.*

"Why did you join the military if you feel that way about the Constitution?" he said.

"Because I hated school, and it gave me a passport out of that dusty-ass pueblo pequeño. Once I realized I was good at it and got into special forces, there was no reason to leave."

"But you still fight for the United States."

"I fight for my unit, for the soldier beside me." She crossed herself. "I fight for what I want this country to be, not for what it is."

And yet you came back for me, he thought but kept this to himself. He didn't want to push it.

They came to a stream and watered themselves and then continued on into the deep shadows of late afternoon. Alton had begun to tip all his weight onto his prosthetic leg, which easily bore it, but the subsequent painful misalignment of his hips and back forced him to quit for the day.

"We still have light," she said.

"What's the point? We don't appear to have gotten any closer to civilization."

"Sit on your worthless ass, then. I'll build a fire."

"You have a flame?"

"I graduated from SERE school. I could get a spark rubbing polar bear nuts together."

She finally got a fire started after many failed attempts. He kept it going while she gathered some berries and a few wild mushrooms, but if anything, they just whetted his appetite. He understood the meaning of the word *ravenous* for the first time.

After she had exhausted her search, she slumped down across the fire from him, her eyes hollow as they stared into the flames. Her head wound was deep purple in the soft light. The stitches seemed to be unraveling.

"Are you doing okay with that?" he said.

"It's just pain, Civvie. You learn to deal with it."

"At SERE school?"

She looked up, surprised at the joke. "Among other places." She smiled a little.

He had heard that torture was part of SERE training. He thought about mentioning his own experiences with torture, but he didn't feel like comparing notes on suffering just then. She probably wouldn't believe him anyway. Or care.

"What happened after you dove off the mountain?" he asked instead. "I saw them nail you with the web gun."

"The web wrapped me up, but it only kills electrical signals. The packs run on fuel. I was trapped in the web, floating, but I could still manipulate the pack with my hand controls. So, I descended slowly, making sure I didn't impale myself on a tree, and got to the ground."

"How did you get out of the web?"

"They run out of juice after twelve hours."

"You were tied up and bleeding in that thing for twelve hours?"

"At least I had my TALOS to keep me from freezing." She rubbed her arms at the memory and inched closer to the fire.

"Then what?"

"I had to scale the cliff to get back to our camp. Took me about half a day. Gagné was waiting there."

He stared at her.

"What?"

"You are a complete badass."

She shook her head. "My team is dead, and I survived. It should be the opposite. I failed in every way possible."

He considered saying something consoling, but he knew that would only make it worse, so he stared at the fire for a while. The crackling of orange and blue plasma made him think of rocket ignitions and Bernardo.

"You said I have no connection to the culture, but my best friend when I was a kid was Hispanic," he mused. "I spent a lot of time with him and his family."

"Remind me to put you up for a heritage award."

"It's ironic that the Nibelungs in camp would have killed me for being half Hispanic, while you refuse to accept me as anything but white. People see what they want to, I guess."

"Tell me *anything* about your Mexican side. And food doesn't count."

"My dad was gone before I was born. I didn't have a chance to pick up much."

"You couldn't have bothered to learn about your father's family in all these years? I thought you were an educator!"

"Maybe I should have made more of an effort," he said. "But I lost the desire to after I met him."

They sat in silence. The breeze gusted through the trees, showering the forest floor with pine needles. Amethyst lightning forked across the distant sky.

"Do you think that's headed toward us?" he asked.

"Maybe. It seems pretty far away, for now anyway."

She stirred the fire a little more, which just sent the smoke billowing into her face. She tossed her stick into the flames and came over and sat next to him. "So, what happened with your dad?" she asked.

He looked at her. "You really want to know?"

"Not really, but anything is better than thinking about how hungry I am."

PART IV

CHAPTER 45

TO ALTON'S SURPRISE, the misery of his childhood lifted somewhat in his senior year of high school. He had become involved in a few activities and made some casual friends. Advisors had identified him as college material and begun helping him prepare.

But of course, most of his joy came from Kiara. Alex was long gone from the school, and she and Alton rode the 'loop to campus, ate lunch together, even formed a book club with a few of their classmates. The little group ran riot through the Stalls every Saturday morning, breathlessly unearthing fresh analog treasures.

Periodically, there was news of an attack that seemed like something Kurt's group might be responsible for. Especially after what Alton had seen out in the desert, he wondered if they were ramping up their activity, but he didn't want to know the details.

Besides, it didn't matter. The fact that he had forged such a strong friendship with Kiara was worth everything he had endured because of Alex. He knew that Kiara saw Alex alone and that they were likely intimate, but his friendship with her was enough.

Then Alex ruined it, just like he always did.

Alton was taking the 'loop to meet her now, when a hand fell on his shoulder, making him whirl around in his seat. "Damn it, can you ever just ping me first?"

"Can't be too careful anymore," Alex said. "We need to talk."

They went up to the street at the next stop, where Alex led them to an empty bench in a wide-open pavilion. "You're looking good, man," Alex said, as they sat down. "Have you gotten taller?"

If Alton hadn't been shielding his eyes from the 4:00 p.m. sun, he would have rolled them.

"I'm glad you and K have become close," Alex continued, nodding as though it was some plan he had set in motion. "Anyway, I'm guessing you know why I'm here."

Alton's annoyance was building. He was supposed to meet Kiara for pizza. He had been looking forward to it. "No. I don't."

"You promised my dad you would be available at some future time of his choosing."

Alton's stomach dropped. He must have looked funny because Alex raised an eyebrow in amusement.

"You remember, don't you?"

"I remember not having much of a choice."

"Do you think you do now?"

Alton almost laughed at the nerve. "What does he want me to do?"

Alex waited as a Hispanic couple with a black Lab glided past on hover skates. Alton could tell Alex was glaring at them behind his shades.

"This candidate for governor, Guerrero, is having a big fundraiser a few weeks from now," Alex said.

"Yeah... and?"

"It's being hosted by Fernando Torres."

The name sent a jolt through Alton. He hadn't heard it in a while.

"My dad wants security access to the Torreses' compound that night."

"No way," Alton said. "I'm not going to help you hurt them. Anything but that."

"It's not that kind of mission. Guerrero's security is too good to crack remotely, and we want to get our hands on some hardware so we can get dirt on his campaign."

"How am I supposed to help?"

"We need you to be our inside man. You know the place well."

"I used to. But I haven't been over there in years," he said. "It would seem suspicious if I suddenly showed up." He thought for a moment. "Why not ask my mom? She still works for Torres. She helps out at every big event."

"She's not talking to my dad since they split."

So, that's why she's been so down, Alton thought.

"What exactly am I supposed to do?"

"Someone will contact you within a week. You'll work out the details with him."

"I still don't know how I'm going to get in there."

"That's where you need to get creative. Kiara's always telling me how smart you are. Let's see you put it in action for once."

The *for once* stung. Alex always knew how to twist the knife.

"Is this really what you want?" Alton said. "To be drawn into your dad's war? Hiding out all the time? What about *your* future?"

"There won't be a future if we don't act now, Alton. It's disappointing that you can't see that."

He sat across from Kiara in the dingy pizza joint, untouched slices slapped onto greasy paper plates in front of them. Their VR table headsets projected a waterfront bistro in Venice, a profoundly realistic simulation, right down to the bird turds splattered on the wrought-iron railing.

Normally, with the faint harpsichord and the fake soft light on the fake canal, Alton would have enjoyed a romantic fantasy. But today the mood was bleak.

"I thought he was just trying to scare you that night," she said. "Teach you a lesson or whatever. I never thought he would force you to actually *do* something."

"It's such bad timing. I'll be back East at college in the fall."

They watched a gondola float by, the burnished bow glinting in the virtual afternoon sun.

"Are you going to go through with it?" she asked.

"What choice do I have?"

"You could run away. Just leave. I doubt they'd come after you."

"I'd miss you too much," he said and met her eyes. She looked away, and he was disappointed.

"It wouldn't have to be forever," she said. "Maybe just for a little while? You know they're going to arrest Kurt for something eventually."

"Yeah, maybe... but where would I even go?"

He arrived home late a few nights later to find some creep loitering outside his building. He was shocked to see that it was the man from the music festival, with black hair and pasty skin—the one Alex had said did DNA tracking for his dad. The man tilted his head as Alton approached, indicating he should follow him around to the unlit side of the building. Alton paused, feeling the same chill he had in the tent that night, then plunged into darkness.

Up close, even in shadow, the man wasn't just pasty but desiccated, with sunken cheeks and ancient acne scars. He looked to make sure that no one had followed and then spoke with an accent that Alton thought might be southern European. He dropped a small plastic nodule into Alton's palm. "Earpiece on an encrypted channel. You can contact me if you need to, but try to keep the channel clear on the night of the event."

Alton looked it over. It was as dry and creepy as a dead insect.

"Your mother won't be issued an event security badge until after she arrives; is that right?" the man asked.

Fear gripped him, and he fought his instinct to escape back into the well-lit street. "Yeah, they . . . they give her a new one for every event."

"Go in and get her security badge and bring it out to me. I'll be waiting on the corner by a transformer, wearing a Century Utility uniform. There will be a van there as well."

"How am I supposed to do that?" His fear was giving way to annoyance. "You think she's just going to hand it over and I'm going to breeze out past security?"

The man shrugged. "Go when guests are starting to arrive so there will be more distraction and cover."

"I'm sure that will solve everything."

"Look kid, Kurt told me you could handle it."

"You know her badge has her picture on it, right?" His annoyance was growing.

"Don't worry about that. I just need the components, not the shell."

"Then what?"

"Then you get out of there and don't look back. Your debt will be paid."

"You make it all sound so easy. What if I can't manage it?"

"This is the most painless way to do this," the man growled. "For you *and* for the people there. That includes your mother and your friend. If this fails, subsequent methods become more painful."

Alton shook his head and resisted the urge to spit. These people were complete scum. But his disdain made it easier for him to say what he said next, the thing he had been fearing the most. "I'll figure it out," he said. "But I want something from you too." He resisted the urge to call him "Crater Face."

"That's not the deal."

"I don't give a shit." His trembling now was more from anger than fear. "You're the guy who does DNA tracking, right?"

"I don't know where you heard that," he said and turned to go.

The words spilled out of him. "You're going to find somebody for me. Otherwise, you can explain to Kurt why you fucked this up when I don't show and the cops do."

The man gave him a menacing look, his features gnarled in shadow. Alton's blood ran cold, but he stood his ground.

"I could end you here, and nobody would have any idea."

"But you won't," Alton said. "Because you only do what your supreme leader commands."

The man seemed bemused by this. "If that's true, what makes you think I would track someone without his permission?"

"Because he'll never know about it. And I'll feel a lot more motivated to do your dirty work."

"Who would I be looking for?"

"My father."

"When's the last time you saw him?"

"I've never seen him. Not in person anyway."

"I've got to have DNA to do DNA tracking, kid."

Shit, he thought. *That part never even occurred to me.* But then he had an idea. "Just wait here," he said.

He ran into the lobby, took the elevator to his darkened apartment, his heart pounding. In his room, he pulled the trumpet case down from the top of his closet and tore out of there again. Back in the alley, gasping for breath, his hands fumbling from adrenaline, he unlatched the case and removed the metal mouthpiece. "What about this?" He held it toward the dull light.

Crafter Face produced a handkerchief and took the mouthpiece by its tip. "How long since he played it?"

"Before I was born."

"I doubt there will be usable genetic material here, but give me the case. I'll see if my guy can lift anything. But you're not getting it back."

"That's fine," Alton said, re-latching it and handing it over. *If this works, I won't need it anymore. And if it doesn't, I'm done trying to find the bastard.*

CHAPTER 46

ALTON TRIED TO concentrate on normal life, but the possibility of locating his father—along with the dread of what he would have to do if he couldn't—made that impossible. Then, a few mornings later, as he set the earpiece on the edge of the bathroom sink to get in the shower, it began flashing green. He grabbed at it, knocking it behind the toilet. He didn't even bother to stand, just jammed it in his ear while leaning on the bowl.

The message played. "All right, kid, we couldn't get anything off the mouthpiece, but lucky you, there was some residue inside the . . . what do you call it . . . spit valve. Your dad spent all of yesterday at the Golden Gate Trade Plaza in San Francisco. The address is . . ."

Alton yelped and leaped up, smacking his head on the edge of the sink. But he was too elated to feel pain. He stuffed a few things into his backpack and tore off to school to tell Kiara.

"He's in San Francisco!"

"Oh my God," she said as they stood in the white morning sun outside their first-period auditorium. "I'm so happy for you!"

"I know! He could have been dead! He could have moved to Peru! Who knows what . . ."

"So, are you going to try to call him?" She shivered a little in the crisp March air, and he wanted more than anything to pull her close.

"Nope." He grinned. "I'm going to surprise him in person."

Her muted response wasn't what he was hoping for. "What is it?" he asked.

"What if... he doesn't want to see you? Or he's a giant asshole or something? Maybe don't leap so far just yet?"

He felt almost angry at her. "I'm in trouble, and he has a chance to help me. What father wouldn't want to do that? Besides—you said it yourself—I have to get out of here. I can't wait around for him to call me back."

She gave him a weak smile as the first hour bell rang. "Come on," she said.

"I'm leaving right now," he said, shouldering his backpack. "I've already booked the CHSR."

"Now?"

"Yeah! This is it!"

"Just be careful, okay?"

"I will," he said. "Shit, I don't know when I'll see you again." Now, they did embrace, and she let it linger a moment. He wished more than anything in the world that she would come with him, that they could discover a new life together and never return. Let Alex wonder where they went. Let *him* feel the hurt of rejection for once.

"Message me when you get there," she said. "Let me know you're safe."

He shook his head. "Kurt might send someone after me. The less you know about where I've gone, the better."

"Come on," she said. "Do you really think *I* have anything to worry about?"

"You know what happened to Alex's mom."

A shadow crossed her face. "Right," she said. "You're either with them or you're the enemy."

CHAPTER 47

A FEW HOURS LATER, Alton was on the CHSR, rocketing past green and brown swaths of Central Valley agriculture.

The final leg of the high-speed bullet train from San Diego to Sacramento had been completed in the mid-2030s. Controversial at the time for its massive cost and endless delays, it had since become one of California's crowning achievements. The original machinery, including the seats, was still working and intact.

Which meant that it wasn't a terrifically comfortable ride, but he was too hyped to relax anyway. He felt fear and excitement in equal measure. He did believe, as he had told Kiara, that Kurt would come looking for him eventually.

But perhaps Edwin had the resources to help spirit him away while it all blew over. With everything he was up to, Kurt was bound to be arrested or perhaps even killed before too long. It occurred to Alton that maybe he shouldn't get his father involved in something this dangerous, but then he thought, *I'm sure he can take care of himself.*

Besides, he owes me.

And then he almost laughed out loud as he realized he only knew the first name. But how many Edwins could be at the Golden Gate Trade Plaza? He used his watch to scroll through listed companies and found it almost right away: *Aerotech MicrotechniX, Edwin de La Cruz, Chief Data Officer.*

Damn, Alton thought. *I'll bet he's rich.*

He stared at the accompanying profile pic. The man was graying at the temples and wore a dark business suit. It was hard to see evidence of the playful young guy who had flirted with his mom in the vid. For the first time, he considered the possibility that he had the wrong person. Maybe Crater Face had sent Alton on a wild goose chase.

But he had to check for himself, so he pulled a snack from his bag and began to plan. He had taken the 10:45 train, which would put him in downtown San Francisco by 2:00. From there, it was only about twenty-five minutes to the plaza by trolley. He assumed that Edwin kept regular hours. As long as he arrived by 5:00, he should get there before his father left for the day.

He had never been to the City by the Bay, but in his mounting dread, he all but ignored its sunlit splendor once he arrived. He boarded the electric trolley from the transit center and stared straight ahead, biting his lip. He began to wonder if he could go through with this after all but reasoned he couldn't go back and had nowhere else to go. So, he huffed up a hill, then followed the GPS down to an elegant glass tower at the plaza's south end.

Feeling a perverse pride in the impressive digs, he entered. He was early, but he didn't want to intrude or make a scene, so, holding his breath, he gave the name Edwin de La Cruz to the security desk and told them Edwin had asked him to wait. He thought for sure they would flag him as an impostor immediately. But the guard barely looked up as he nodded toward a reception area across the lobby.

He sat rigid and still for twenty minutes, waiting for someone to tell him to leave, then finally sank his aching back into the cushiony sofa. He watched the sky darken with clouds through the big windows and marveled at the otherworldly contrast from sun-blasted LA. He felt drowsy, so he drank sickly sweet coffee from a machine until his bladder ached and he could practically see double.

After 4:00, people began to trickle down and out. Near 5:00, a mass exodus began. By 5:20, Edwin still hadn't emerged. Maybe Alton had missed him when he had made a bathroom run? Had Edwin even been in the building?

It occurred to him that, in his hope and excitement, he had made a lot of assumptions. For all he knew, it was Edwin's day off. Or maybe he usually worked from home. He fought down his panic. But at 6:05, just as he began to consider messaging Kiara for advice, a tired-looking man emerged from the elevator.

Alton recognized him immediately but remained frozen while the man crossed the cavernous lobby, the slapping of his shoes echoing to the far corners. He was suddenly terrified that Edwin would recognize *him*, but the man seemed occupied by his own thoughts and didn't look up. It was only after he pushed through the doors into the gray evening that Alton found the urgency to pursue.

Outside, in the shivery dusk, he had another fear. What if Edwin called him crazy or a liar? Alton looked nothing like his father and had been considered white his entire life. Suddenly, he was going to claim to be Edwin de La Cruz's son?

At the very least, if he was going to be told to fuck off, he had to know where his father lived, what his life was like, where he could look for him again. So, he decided to follow.

The pursuit was more involved than he expected. First, Edwin took the trolley to the light rail, then the light rail to the ferry. Fortunately, Edwin remained oblivious to the nondescript white kid on his route. But just to be safe, once they boarded the ferry, Alton went up to the deck while his father entered the bright cabin.

Cold bit into Alton's arms, and he hugged himself as they glided out onto the dark water. Now, he did take time to survey his surroundings, what little he could make of them in the gathering dark and fog, and he felt a little spooked. Pics of San Francisco were always of sunsets illuminating the bridge, green hills against the horizon. This reminded him of movies set in Victorian London. It seemed an odd place to find the jaunty jazzman who had courted his mother. But, he reminded himself, that was a few seconds of footage from a lifetime ago.

They docked after half an hour, and then he was tailing Edwin among the disembarking commuters, too nervous to feel the cold any longer. He became alarmed as he realized that Edwin was headed for the parking lot. *Idiot*, he thought. *Where else would he be going?*

He accessed a rideshare app and queued up a self-driving vehicle. It was only a minute away, which made sense, as they were likely waiting here for commuters.

But he couldn't just instruct an AI to "follow that car" without an address. He quickly searched Edwin de la Cruz, but of course, he wasn't listed. Now, he was disappearing across the emptying lot, approaching a Jaguar, smooth and sleek in its ebony contours.

When Alton saw he wouldn't make it before Edwin got in the car, he removed his backpack and heaved it toward the passenger side. It hit the asphalt with a rough thump, and Edwin looked up to see Alton approaching.

"Everything all right?" he asked, though the tone was one of suspicion rather than concern.

He met Alton's eyes, and Alton's stomach lurched as he realized *this might be it*. But there was no recognition in his eyes. Alton felt disappointed that some kind of magical genetic frequency didn't confirm their connection.

"Sorry. I dropped my backpack," Alton said.

When he reached down to grab it, he unstrapped his watch and buckled it around the side mirror, then stood, holding the bag for Edwin to see.

"Got it," he said.

Edwin gave a tight-lipped nod and disappeared into his car. Once he was pulling out of the lot, Alton turned on the location-finding app on his phone to track his watch.

When it came up on-screen, moving with Edwin's car, he broke into a huge grin. He couldn't wait to tell Kiara how clever he had been.

CHAPTER 48

ONCE EDWIN ARRIVED home, Alton got the coordinates, and soon he was gliding up through lush hills into a wealthy enclave. The warm lights of dinnertime seemed to beckon through passing windows, deepening his feelings of loneliness.

When the car reached its destination at the back of a darkened cul-de-sac, Alton found himself standing alone and asking himself for the first time just what he thought he was doing.

The neighborhood was still, silent, dark, and damp in the fine rain and the pooling fog. He had lost his nerve to ring the bell, so he crept around to the side of the house through the dense mesquite and manzanita, careful of the sharp branches and thorns, where he could find some concealment and shelter.

Edwin's house was a split-level beauty of glass and stone and smoky metal. Despite himself, Alton thought of his mother and felt sorry for her. This was everything she had feared, everything she had resisted discovering about the man: that he could have kept her from the humiliation and exhaustion of a life of servitude.

For the first time, Alton felt angry at his father instead of his mother. How could he abandon them like this? Not send support when he so obviously could have?

His anger provided the motivation he needed to go up to the front door, but just as he began to disentangle himself from the brush, something hard and freezing gripped him under his armpits. Then he was being lifted and shoved through the brush, thorns tearing at his clothes and branches scratching his face.

"Ow!" he yelled, as he was pushed toward a vehicle that had appeared in the cul-de-sac, its electric motor hush-soft, a top light faintly illuminating the word *Security*.

He wrenched his head around to see who had a hold of him, only to discover that it was some kind of floating metal clamp. He didn't know what enraged him more, the pain or the fact that this security system was designed to sweep him up without alerting the neighborhood. Making poor people invisible was the shit he and his mother had dealt with their whole lives.

But this time, he'd be damned if he would go quietly. He began to shout his father's full name wildly and at the top of his lungs until his throat was raw.

Doors began to open, illuminating the mist, as neighbors appeared to see what was happening. But just as he was being folded into the back of the vehicle, the device unlatched from his back and floated to the top of the car, where it reattached.

Suddenly, Edwin's voice boomed across the grounds. "Who are you, and what do you want?"

He turned to see his father standing underneath the portico. As he wiped the rain from his eyes, he realized that three other people had emerged with him: a woman in her thirties and two children who looked to be about eight and ten.

His mouth dropped open when he realized that he might be looking at his half sister and half brother.

"What do you want?" Edwin repeated. "Cops are on the way."

"I want to talk to my father."

"You've got the wrong house."

"*You're* my father," he said. "I'm your son. I'm Lena Lucas's kid."

Edwin appeared to notice his neighbors for the first time. "I'm sorry to disrupt your evening," he said to them. "Thank you for your concern, but I have it under control."

As they began to disperse, some casting disapproving looks, Edwin turned to his family. "Go inside," he said.

"What's this about?" the woman asked, not taking her eyes from Alton. "Who is Lena Lucas?"

"He probably just wants money. He was trying to get into my car at the ferry station. Go inside. I'll take care of it."

She looked at him now. "Shouldn't we just wait for the police? What if he's dangerous?"

"Go inside, Oleta."

She scowled. "Come on, kids."

When they had gone, Edwin came down to meet Alton. "For the last time, who are you, and what do you want?"

"I just told you who I am." Alton held his ground, trembling.

"That's impossible." He looked him over, clearly finding none of himself in this boy. "Did Lena put you up to this for money? I'm surprised she waited so long."

"I've got your DNA," Alton said. "That's how I found you. How hard do you think it would be for me to prove it?"

Edwin's expression changed as he seemed to recognize the truth, though what he was feeling, Alton could only guess.

"So, you do want money then."

"No, I don't want *money*," Alton spat. "I want *my father*."

Edwin seemed at a loss for words. After a moment, he gestured back toward his house as though things were out of his control. "That's impossible," he said again.

Then it was Alton who didn't know what to say. He just stood there shaking in the cold, his sides aching from the clamp, rain, and blood from a scratch streaming down his face. He felt humiliated and defeated.

"Just wait here." Edwin sighed. "I'll be right back."

Just when Alton thought Edwin might not return, the garage door opened, and the black Jaguar emerged. The car pulled up, and the gull wing lifted to reveal Edwin. "Get in," he said.

Alton rescued his watch, still hanging from the mirror, then climbed in across from his father. This model had no option for a driver, so the cab was like that of a limo with facing sofa benches and various amenities. Edwin flicked open a drawer and retrieved a towel for Alton.

"Would you like some hot cocoa?" he asked.

Alton mopped his face with the towel, streaking it with blood. "Sure."

His father made two cocoas and added a healthy splash of whiskey to his. Only after Alton had begun to warm up and relax somewhat, did he realize they were traveling.

"Where are we going?" he asked.

"That's up to you," he said. "I can book you a room for the night if you want."

"Right, gotta keep the white trash out of the mansion."

"You just gave my family a shock," Edwin said. "There may be a time for a visit, but now's not it."

"What about the cops?"

"I never called them."

"Why not?"

"Our private security service is far more responsive. Also, I wanted to see what you had to say."

"Well, I said it," Alton said and went sullen. He turned in his seat to stare out the window but the dark and the fog and the deep-tinted windows obscured any view.

"So, would you like to go to a hotel? I can put you up for the night, and you can contact your mother or whoever in the morning."

Alton felt the grief pooling in his chest, and then the anger. "Just take me to the Transit Center," he said. "I'll get a train home."

"Los Angeles?"

"What do you care?"

They rode in silence for a while. Alton had always dreamed about regaling his father with his space adventure. But now he found he had lost all desire to share anything with the man. Instead, he asked, "Did you know about me before you left?"

He hesitated, then said, "I knew you were coming."

"So, why didn't you stay?"

"Your mother and I were young," he said. "We were just having fun. It was never meant to last."

"Why not?"

"My family is very . . . traditional."

"They wouldn't have accepted her?"

"No," he sighed. "They probably wouldn't have."

"Because she was white?"

"Mostly because she was poor."

"So, that's why you left?"

"It wasn't the only reason. Believe it or not, I always meant to do right by you."

"She's had a really hard life," he said.

Edwin nodded but said nothing. They both knew an apology would be meaningless.

Their silence resumed. Alton wanted to know about his heritage and his father's family. He wanted to know where they had all come from originally. He wanted to know how they had suffered before things started to get better for Latinos.

Mostly, he wanted to know what it meant to be half Mexican: how he was supposed to act, how he was supposed to feel, how he was supposed to not feel so goddamn lonely all the time.

He wanted to know all kinds of things but didn't know how to breach the distance between them.

They arrived at the station after another forty minutes or so. The car stopped, and Alton gathered up his things.

"Of course, we'll work something out financially," he said. "Have your mother contact me when you get back."

"No."

Edwin was taken aback. "Why not?"

"She'll never know I found you, that you gave your new family everything you denied us."

He nodded, tight-lipped. "Then let me at least pay for your train." He tapped his watch a few times, then held it out for Alton to touch faces.

"Well, take it easy, Pops," Alton said and climbed out.

"Wait," his father called after him.

But Alton didn't stop or turn around, and his only regret was that he couldn't slam a gull-wing door.

Edwin had deposited $1,500, far more than Alton needed, so he bought a first-class ticket and some food and boarded for a 10:30 departure. The car was mostly empty, and he was able to stretch out. He thought he might even be able to sleep on the return trip. But before he did, he wanted to message Kiara.

Coming home.

She responded almost immediately.

Did you find your father?

Yes. Tell you about it later.

But you're coming home?? What about Kurt?

I'll figure it out.

She signed off with a worried-face emoji that floated up out of the screen and dissipated into thin air.

What he knew but didn't tell her was, *I don't have to worry about it because I'm going to help him. I'm going to do anything he wants me to.*

And then it popped into his head, unbidden but with a certain undeniable transgressive thrill, and more than a measure of self-loathing. *Fucking Mexicans deserve what's coming to them.*

PART V

CHAPTER 49

HE GOT UP in the middle of the night, shuddering to the bone in the cold wind, and went to piss. He didn't understand why their fire was still smoking when it had smoldered to embers before they had even fallen asleep.

But as he rubbed his eyes, he realized that the smoke he saw was in the distance. Back at their sleeping spot, he felt an overwhelming urge to slide in next to her for more slumber. But he sensed that would be a mistake, and he tapped her shoulder. As always, she sprang up in an instant.

"Somebody's campfire?"

She squinted into the dark.

"No way," she said. "We're in the middle of nowhere. You saw that when we were coming in."

"Then what?"

"Probably started by that storm," she said. "It looks to be in an incipient stage. But if it blows up, we could be fucked with this wind."

Alton thought of the fire at Gypsum that had threatened to overrun them before the transport had vacuumed the men into its titanium belly. It ultimately hadn't burned their way, but he remembered how fast it had moved in the direction that it did burn and how futile the efforts had been to squelch it.

"So, what do we do?"

"We move our asses."

"It's still completely dark."

"Well, we could wait for the fire to light our way. Except that it might also, you know, burn us to death. Not that it could be worse than this cold."

And so they moved out, at first haltingly, then gaining speed with the help of a bright moon. They made decent progress until they became entangled in a thicket of trees and brush that obscured the faint light, causing them to lose the path.

"I need my holomaps," Valeria said. "I don't know how people ever survived without augmentation."

Alton hadn't been augmented long, but he was forced to agree.

They fought their way out of the thicket and pushed on south, but the effort ate up a good hour of forward progress, not to mention much of his faltering energy.

He kept looking back, half hoping to see smoke or fire rising into the sky that would motivate him to keep moving. But there was nothing yet.

Even through his dread of fire, something had been gnawing at him. His better instincts told him not to bring it up, lest he give away Alex's intentions, along with his own dwindling chances of joining him before the launch. But he really wanted to hear Valeria's thoughts.

"Something's been bothering me," he said.

"I'm guessing it's not your conscience."

"When you arrived at the compound and started shooting—before I knew it was you out there—I asked Alex if it might be the military. And he said he *knew* that it wasn't them."

"Yeah, so? He must have seen us on scanners or something."

"Maybe. But then why did his men ambush us so soon after Eli radioed the military? How did they get there so fast?"

"Maybe he'd already been monitoring us. He's been dug in those mountains for a long time. He knew where to place his surveillance. Or the timing could have been a coincidence. We were getting close to him, after all."

"But did a military unit ever show?"

"I was over that cliff for eighteen hours before I made it back to our camp spot. They could have come and gone."

"And left all those bodies? Plus, wasn't Gagné waiting there for you?"

"Are you saying Hagen's men got to us first because somebody inside the military tipped him off?"

"I'm saying I don't think the military was *ever* coming. I think Eli thought they were, but somebody up high not only never sent them but informed Alex of where we were."

"That would mean that Hagen's contact, whoever he is, is pretty far up the chain."

"Very far up. Wouldn't that also explain why they've never sniffed out his location despite supposedly searching for him all those years?"

She stopped. "We have more pressing problems at the moment."

It was faint, but he could detect traces of charcoal. The air had also warmed.

"Let's go up this rise and see what direction it's headed," she said.

It was ten minutes of hard climbing, but once they cleared the tree line, they had a good view of the valley and of the fire that had begun to blossom orange and yellow across it.

"Of course, the wind has to be blowing south," she said. "Fuck, we can't catch a break."

"What do we do?"

"Let's go west, see if we can skirt it."

A ruddy dawn cracking across the horizon improved visibility. Soon she was tearing along, and it was all he could do to keep up with her. His hand throbbed and leaked blood where he had torn it on some thorns, and he couldn't spare a strip of clothing to wrap it because it was still so damn cold. His insides were in agony: he couldn't tell where the raw pain of his hunger ended and the burn in his lungs began.

When they finally stumbled across a stream, he had no choice but to stop. He plunged his bleeding hand into the brook until he couldn't feel it, then slurped the freezing water until it numbed him from the inside out.

"How far have we gone?" he managed to ask.

"We gotta go," she said. "Come on."

It was the first time he had ever heard worry in her voice, and he forced himself to his feet.

They kept moving. His adrenaline was long spent, and only autopilot kept him going. In his disoriented state, he only gradually realized that the intensifying light was now due less to the rising sun and more to the hyperreal glow of the fire.

Smoke, meanwhile, had begun to chase them through the woods like sooty apparitions. He wondered how much longer they would be able to breathe comfortably.

Twenty meters ahead of Alton, Valeria stopped short. When he caught up, she was looking skyward. He followed her gaze to see two fireships gliding in overhead.

"Thank God," she breathed.

Then one of the transports came into view, trailing behind the fireships, and hope flared in Alton. It must have been heading toward some mountain town or other populated area they hadn't noticed during their predawn flight. Or maybe it was just standard procedure to send one to every fire. Either way, they had a chance of rescue.

After another half hour, smoke was rancid in their gills, and Valeria stopped again. The elevation had increased, and they had a better view of the region and the conflagration now headed toward them.

He couldn't tell if it was sweat or tears or both streaking through the grime on her face, but it didn't matter. He knew what hopelessness looked like.

"We're not going to outrun this," she said.

"So, what do we do?"

"Dig in somewhere. Hope for the best."

"I have an idea," he said.

"I'm all ears," she said, then touched the side of her head gingerly. "Well, I'm one ear anyway."

He used his hand to shield the glare and squinted toward the horizon. Several more fireships had arrived to spray impotent streams into the burning maw. The transport ship hung nearby like a bloated kidney.

"Instead of running away from the fire, let's run toward it."

"I can snap your neck if you want to end it," she said. "It will be a lot less painful."

He told her about the fire in camp, the transport. "It's got to be scanning for people," he said, pointing to it. "Maybe we just need to get closer."

"Just when I thought this couldn't get any more fubar," she said.

She stripped off the top of her TALOS, ripped it in two, and handed half to Alton. "The material is designed to be breathable but filter out toxins and particulates." She tied it around her nose and mouth. Alton did the same, and they advanced toward the orange glow.

Now, the smoke blotted out the daylight. His skin was uncomfortably dry, and his lungs felt squeezed. They couldn't hear each other over the roar of the firewind and the crackle of wood. He was fighting every cell in his body, screaming for him to turn and flee.

He scanned for the evac transport, but the sky was completely obscured. The ship could have been hovering directly above them, and they wouldn't know it. He realized, too late, that this was a bad idea.

Then, all at once, the flames were upon them, snaking around charred trunks and racing toward them through the spitting grass. Sparks and embers churned as though from a grinder's wheel.

"We need to get to higher ground," she shouted and yanked him east toward where they had come down the rise earlier.

They skittered past waves of flame and began to clamber up the slope. He could feel the hair on his forearms shivering away, the skin beneath puckering in the heat. For a moment, he thought this might be the end, but when he looked back, he saw the wall of fire roar by them along the foot of the hill.

They scrambled up, Alton leaning into his artificial leg to provide as much leverage as possible. The rise steepened, and soon they climbed above the first tree line and came upon a wide dirt path zigging up the mountain. The path had been swept clean of all trees and other obstacles, and they were able to move much faster.

After a few minutes, the first section of the path terminated at a plateau, and Alton sank to his knees in exhaustion. He could hardly breathe through his face wrap, and he foolishly removed it only to hack and gag on the smoke.

Valeria pulled her mask just far enough from her mouth that she could be understood.

"A crew cut this line recently," she said. "There must have been another fire, or they were anticipating one. But we can use it to get to the top. Maybe they'll see us up there."

He nodded as though to say, *Give me a second*, but she was already pulling him up. Visibility improved some as they climbed. Alton could see fireships battling the blaze not too far from them. But there was no sign of the transport.

"It's gone!" he shouted.

She turned to look. "Maybe it's on the other side of the mountain. Come on!"

He followed, though he knew he couldn't last much longer. Then he felt a strange sensation, as if from a sudden pressure change, and his ears popped.

A moment later, a roar filled them as a tidal wave of fire began to charge up beside them, almost parallel to their path. He almost jumped off the ridge, but she grabbed him.

"Stay in the fire line!" she shouted. "It can't burn where there's no fuel!"

Alton thought there was no way she believed this. The tsunami of flame hurtling up the slope could devour *anything*. This puny path wasn't going to stop it from engulfing the entire mountain.

But then he did a double-take. Was it his imagination? No. The fire had begun to burn along a different fuel path, away from them.

"Look!" he shouted.

Now, it was her turn to slump to her knees, utterly spent. He joined her, and they clutched each other's shoulders for stability. With the fire turning away, they could rest for a few moments before the final push to the top. He closed his stinging eyes, trying to weep out some of the smoke and ash.

Then he heard her say, "NO!"

The wall of flame had licked up and around the peak and now was charging back toward them down the fire line like somebody had dumped molten lava onto a waterslide.

There was nothing left for them to do but jump, which they did, plunging toward the brambles and jagged rocks below. *This is it*, Alton thought, as blackness and silence enveloped him.

But instead of losing consciousness, he remained aware of the blackness and the silence and then began to realize that he also felt much cooler.

Was this the afterlife?

He heard a sucking sound, and they levitated upward before being deposited into a large, shadowy bay. A hatch behind them sealed shut. Above their heads, propellers whirled on, sucking the smoke out. Alton tried to see where the smoke was coming from until he realized it was coming from them.

He stood on unsteady legs and pulled her up beside him. They regarded the bay with its blinking lights and modern equipment, as two beds slid out of the wall and two oxygen masks dropped from above.

"It worked," she gasped as they lay down.

Then he was breathing exquisite refrigerated air through a mask, and fluids were pumping into him through an IV. He felt his skin burn in places, and as he passed out, he realized medical bots were treating his wounds.

He awoke feeling much better. His torn hand was bandaged in clean white strips. The bed next to his was empty, and he looked to see her staring out a port. He pulled off his mask and IV and joined her.

"Holy shit," he said.

A colossus of black smoke rose at least a mile into the sky. It looked like the mushroom cloud from a thermonuclear explosion. The only solace was that the transport was moving in the other direction.

"Pyrocumulus," she said. "Jesus Christ, it grew fast."

He stared at it, horrified. *At least on Mars, there's nothing to burn*, he thought.

"When I was in one of these ships before, there was—" he turned his head to the ceiling before concluding his sentence with more emphasis "—food."

Two drawers slid out of the wall near them, yielding nutrition bars, which they hardly bothered to unwrap before shoving them in their faces.

CHAPTER 50

IT WASN'T LONG before the transport began to descend and the floor hatch unsealed, letting them out at a forestry station deep in the wilderness.

After they had showered off a metric ton of grime and soot, an EMT checked their wounds again, and they were given clean clothes and shown to a bunk room.

Now, Valeria sat on a bed, digging through a bowl of nuts and fruit while Alton stood at the window, flexing the wrap on his hand and taking in the staggering pyrocumulus cloud.

But he wasn't thinking about the fire at all. He was thinking that their miracle escape meant he still had time to get to the colony ship before launch time the following evening.

After almost dying several times in the last few days, he knew for sure now that he wanted this, even though he also knew it was morally wrong and a mistake to put himself at Alex's mercy for the rest of his potentially short days on the desolate frontier of human civilization.

"Take a breather, Civvie," Valeria said. "We're safe." She chucked a banana peel into a trash receptacle.

"At least until I get to the black site, right?"

When she didn't answer, he went and sat on his bunk. "'*Civvie* ...'" he said. "Did you know that's what the Nibelungs call white people who don't claim affiliation with the cause? They called me that in camp all the time."

"The first and last thing I'll ever have in common with them."

"Really?" he said. "Because they tortured me too."

"Well, that don't sound too fun," said the stout man with the graying mustache and ropey arms who had appeared in the doorway. "I'm Station Chief Rodgers. How are you feeling?"

Alton stood. "We appreciate everything you've done for us," he said. "But we really need to get out of here. If you could spare somebody to—"

Chief Rodgers held up his hand. "Out of the question. Every available resource is on this fire. As you can see, it ain't nearly enough."

Alton looked out to where several fireships were parked at odd angles on a narrow tarmac. A small helicopter perched near them. "What about those?"

"They're refueling. And they'll be back in action the second they're ready."

"Then we'll call somebody to come get us. If we can just—"

He was already shaking his head. "Airspace is closed for miles around. Except for the supply craft, and one's not scheduled until tomorrow afternoon out of Sacramento. You can go back with them."

"We're on a very important military mission," Alton said, turning his bare arms over and showing his dead EVs as evidence. "Time is of the essence."

"I figured something like that," Rodgers said. "But we can't very well ask the fire to hold off on account of it, now can we? I'm afraid you're stuck here for the time being. There's plenty of coffee, and you can join the crew coming off the fire for steaks at around six.

I grill 'em myself, and I don't mind telling you I know what I'm doing." He tipped his Smokey the Bear hat and left.

"Oooohh, steak," Valeria said. "Yum."

"What about 'mission first'?"

"The mission failed. Hagen's long gone. Until you spill what you know, there ain't shit I can do."

"I just want to make sure that Kiara is safe, that she doesn't become collateral damage. Then he's all yours."

"Give me something I can use. *Anything*."

He took a deep breath, then said, "They're headed south."

"How far south? LA? México? Buenos Aires?"

"I'll tell you when we're on the way there. But if we don't get there by tomorrow, it will be too late."

"Too late for *what*?"

"Please just trust me. You'll get your man," he lied. "And save a lot of lives."

"You're playing a dangerous game, Civvie. You mistime this and those deaths are on you. You'll never leave that black site. If I don't take you out first."

"I accept that."

"We'll have to get back to our shuttle. Boot up, re-juice. Collect my men if they're still waiting there."

"How?"

She lowered her voice. "We steal a plane, but we can't do that until after dark. Which means we can have a steak. Or two. Wake me at chow time." She lay back and shut her eyes.

He sighed in relief. He had to admit, despite her constant insults, he felt gratitude, even kinship, after what they had been through. She had saved his life.

But it was also because of her that he had lost his chance to be with Kiara right now. If he got another chance, and Valeria stood in his way, he wouldn't make the mistake of helping her again. Even if *she* became collateral damage.

CHAPTER 51

BELLIES FULL, THEY pretended to turn in, waiting until the refueled ships took off and the incoming ships were gassing up. Then they slipped out. No moon was visible, but they didn't need one with the glowing orange horizon. *It's almost too bright for this*, Alton thought. *But it's now or never.*

They snuck around the barracks to the fuel depot. She indicated for him to wait in the shadows while she went to the pump and shut it off. Then she motioned him onto the tarmac.

They crept to the plane, where she pulled the fuel hose from the tank, eased it onto the ground, then twisted the cap back on. Next, she pried open the door of the cockpit, wincing at the sound of the creaking hinges. They climbed inside.

"Doors aren't locked," he said.

"Who's going to steal a plane out here? Which means . . . yup, won't even need to hot-wire it." She ran through a series of controls, and the engines began to sputter.

"Jesus," he said, looking back toward the station. "That's loud."

"Lock your door and buckle up," she said over the noise.

She rotated the nose around and slowly taxied. Just as they began to pick up speed, two rovers sped past them on the tarmac, honking horns and flashing lights.

They swung in front of the plane and squealed to a halt, blocking the way. Chief Rogers and a few others leapt out and sprinted toward them.

Alton cried, "We won't have enough runway to take off!"

She punched a few buttons and threw a few switches. There was a deep rumbling followed by the sound of thrusters kicking on.

"Runway is helpful for gaining speed," she said, "but not strictly necessary."

There was a loud banging sound. Alton jumped at the man at the window trying to pry open the door.

Then, suddenly, they were levitating. She eased back on a lever, and they began to hover upward. The man released his grip on the door handle and slipped off.

"Vectored thrust," she said.

"Huh?"

"Vertical takeoff and landing technology. Makes total sense for fighting fires. Much more maneuverable."

He looked down. The men and vehicles were already fading into the darkened landscape. Once the plane reached sufficient elevation, she accelerated. They flew for ten minutes or so in silence before a staggering sight came into view.

"My God . . ." he said.

She nodded. "Incredible."

A million points of light glittered in the valley below. It was as though they had come upon a small galaxy ablaze with stars. Or a stadium of fans holding flickering lights aloft in benediction to some rock god.

As they flew closer, he realized they were actually seeing countless embers still glowing from where the fire had raged through earlier. *Nature is astonishing even in its devastation,* he thought.

She turned southwest, and the sight disappeared behind them. He craned his head around to catch one last glimpse. "Doesn't look like anybody is following," he said.

"It's a ranger station. They can't exactly scramble fighters. Most they can do is call it in. We'll be at our destination by then. It's not far by air."

"Speaking of which . . . where are we going to land?"

He remembered how they had squeezed their small shuttle into the glade in the woods near Kiara's parents' property. There was no way they were putting this crate down anywhere near there.

"We're not."

He looked at her.

"Don't worry. I got it covered."

It was maybe thirty minutes before she started their descent. Alton reflected on how long it had taken them to walk, climb, and jetpack most of that distance less than a week before.

"Hold this," she said, letting go of the wheel and climbing out of her seat. The plane instantly started to tip.

"Gimme some warning!" He lunged across and steadied the wheel as she disappeared into the back.

She popped back a few moments later. "All good," she said. "Strap in."

She punched a few buttons, and the plane took a steep dive. He was alarmed by the sound of creaking and crunching metal.

"Don't worry," she said. "This thing is ancient. It's just the vertical thrusters rotating downward."

"Who's worried?" he said, gripping the sides of his seat.

"There it is," she said. "A little to the east."

She turned the plane slightly and then began their descent. He squinted through the dirty cockpit windows. At first, it was too dark to see anything, but then he recognized the moonlit glade outside the Cunninghams' house and then the house itself.

She brought the plane straight down until it was hovering maybe thirty feet over the field, thrusters whipping and churning the tall grasses.

"Go wait by the cargo door," she said.

The door was sliding open as he approached it, and he could see the ground nearing fast.

Then the plane shuddered and began to ascend again, and she was leaping into the bay from the cockpit. She grabbed a rope ladder, hooked the handles over the edge of the door frame, and let it unfurl toward the ground.

"Go!" she said.

"Shouldn't we—"

"NOW."

He crouched and jutted his legs over the edge, then squirmed around until he was lowering himself over the belly of the plane. She held his arms until he had hold of the first rung, and then he was scrambling down the dangling ladder, going mostly by feel in the darkness, further disoriented by the heat and the howling of the thrusters.

He reached the last rung only to discover that it was still about ten feet from the ground, then fifteen, as they continued to rise.

"We're too far!" he yelled.

Then he was yelping in pain as her boots stomped on his hands and he let go, plummeting into the high grass. A moment later, she plunked beside him.

They lay in the cool meadow catching their breath as the plane lifted into the sky and buzzed back the way they had come. She propped herself up on an elbow and watched it depart. "I programmed it to return," she said.

"And you're sure it will get there?"

"If not, *e* for *effort*, right?"

And then, like déjà vu, he was once again met by the sloppy snout of a white-haired dog as Kiara's parents, along with the two commandos Val had left to babysit them, hustled up to their position.

The commandos—Ramos and the one they just called Wombat—helped Valeria to her feet, leaving Alton to struggle up on his own.

Ramos looked around. "The team?" she asked.

Valeria said, "You're looking at who made it."

Ramos scowled at Alton. "They're gone and he survived. That's pretty messed up."

"At ease, soldier," Valeria said. "If it wasn't for Wonder Bread, I wouldn't be here either."

"What about Kiara?" asked Geraldine. "Did you find her?"

"I did, and there's still a chance to get her back, but we have to go *right now*," Alton said.

"Go where?" Howard asked. "Where has the bastard taken her?"

Valeria looked at Alton. "Time to spill," she said. They were all staring at him.

"He knows, and you haven't forced it out of him?" Wombat asked. He took a step toward Alton.

"Do you find it acceptable to question my methods, soldier?" Valeria barked.

"No, Lieutenant," he said, snapping to attention.

"Do you remember where we parked?" she asked Ramos.

"Yes, Lieutenant," Ramos answered.

"Then let's move out."

California's dark expanse stretched beneath them as they cruised south.

They had returned to their dropship and decloaked. Valeria juiced up and re-auged right away, then slid into a new TALOS.

"God, that feels good," she said as the new material sheathed around her and her revived EVs glowed like glacial frost. She looked fiercer than ever.

"My turn," he said.

"No way," she said. "No power for you. Now give me a destination before I beat it out of you. No more fucking around."

"Los Angeles."

"I figured that much."

"You did?"

"Of course. He's going after the ultimate target."

"The ultimate target?" Alton swallowed.

She nodded to Ramos, indicating for her to answer.

"The new White House," said Ramos.

"You got it," he said.

Relief flooded through Alton. They didn't appear to have considered Cosmost a target at all. The hijacking would be a complete surprise, just as Alex had predicted.

"I've already had the staff and surrounding area evacuated," she said. "Áquilar is erecting a stealth perimeter with a few small units so he doesn't detect us. Also, if he's sitting on another bomb,

I don't want to get an entire squad killed."

"It's not a bomb," he had said. "I can tell you that much."

"It better not be. For your sake."

Now, Alton and Valeria sat together in the cramped cockpit. He stared out at the blackness, contemplating what would—one way or another—be the end of their shared adventure.

"Did you mean it when you said you wouldn't have made it without me?" he asked.

"Your pack allowed me to escape when Hagen's men attacked us in the forest."

"I guess that's true," he said.

"And it was your idea to head into the fire to attract the rescue ship. Even though we almost got vaporized." She laughed.

"Yeah, that was close."

"I know you're not one of them," she said.

He looked at her, surprised. "Thank you," he said.

"But I also know you're up to something. And if you get in my way, I'll take you down just the same. And her too."

He nodded.

They sliced through the dark a while longer. He had started to doze off when she said, "You never finished telling me what happened after you found your dad."

"If I tell you the rest of that story," he said. "You might think I'm one of them after all."

PART VI

CHAPTER 52

He went back to school on Monday as though his journey to San Francisco had never happened. He told Kiara about how the reunion with his father had been a big letdown and that he had decided, after all, that he could manage Kurt's "request" without much risk to himself or harm to others.

It was all bullshit. Inside, he was seething and looking forward to a chance to do some damage. Of course he didn't care about Kurt and his worthless "cause." But maybe the neo-Nazis were right that Hispanic people *had* gained too much power too fast.

The outcome was that white people like him and his mother had become a kind of underclass that people like his father, the Torres family, and candidate Guerrero could afford to ignore, if not outright stomp on.

Then he would feel guilty about being racist and remind himself what he had learned from reading: that it's only about power. *Anytime a group gets it, they become the enemy of the people. It's just a historical fact. It has nothing to do with heritage, culture, language, or certainly not skin color. One group of people is never inherently, biologically superior to another. We're just atoms arranged together.*

But to convince himself of that, he had to pretend he wasn't seeing Hispanic people with a new resentment. And that he wasn't catching sight of himself and feeling a twinge of satisfaction that despite wanting to manifest some outward evidence of his father's genes for as long as he could remember, he was now secretly happy that it remained invisible.

When the day came, he was jumping with nerves and couldn't stand to stay home anymore. He took the 'loop down to the East side and sat in the park with the lake until it was time.

He thought about how his mother, in her foul moods, had dragged him away as a child when he wanted to linger in this pretty place. It made him think about how long she had sleepwalked, with bent back, through a life with no ambition, and how she had kept him down too. He knew she might lose her job should any of what he was about to do be traced back to her. She might even be arrested, but he felt no sympathy. After all, she had given him little sympathy after his arrest.

Everybody gets theirs today, he thought.

First guests were to arrive soon, and so he swallowed his dread and started on his way with the sun behind him and low in the sky. The heightened security was evident as he came onto the street. Long black vehicles with tinted glass clogged the curbs, drones hovered above the treetops, and men in black suits and sunglasses patrolled the area. Two stopped him before he even reached the house.

"My mom works here," he said. "She's been with the Torres family for years. She forgot her meds and can't leave while she's on duty, especially during an event." He shook the bottle of pills he had brought as a prop.

"Give us the meds, and we'll see that she gets them," the taller security guy said.

Alton lowered his voice. "My mom is kind of . . . embarrassed by her condition," he said. "If I give these to someone else to give to her, she's going to rip me a new one."

"Well, that's the only way they're getting in there today."

"And count yourself privileged that we're allowing even that," said the shorter one. With his sprouts of hair and jutting nose, he resembled a kingfisher. "We shouldn't pass anything from outside. Could be a bomb, for all we know."

Alton held up the translucent pill bottle between his thumb and index finger, as if to say *In this?*

"I've seen all kinds, kid," Kingfisher said. "All. Kinds."

Alton started to panic a little and cast a glance behind him, wondering if Kurt's creepy henchman was watching or listening, poised to immediately report his failure to the *Gruppenführer*. Then he had an idea.

"I'm an old friend of the Torreses' son. Let me give it to him to give to my mom."

Kingfisher's eyebrows shot up behind his oversized glasses. "Their son?"

"Yeah, Bernardo. Just tell him that Alton Lucas is here. He'll let me in."

They looked at each other, and the tall one smirked. "Sure," he said, then went up the walk a ways, speaking into his earpiece as he did. After a moment, he motioned for Alton to follow.

Two sentries let him through the electronic security field, and then he was standing in the foyer for the first time in years. It hadn't really changed at all. The balustrade his mother polished was still as rich and lustrous as it had been in his childhood, a gleaming monument to all her labor.

He waited, trying not to tremble where he stood. He felt certain that someone suspected his true intent and would detain him at any moment.

But it was just a teenage girl who appeared, wearing a white cotton Mexican crochet dress with multicolored bands stitched across the chest and knees. She had shoulder-length dark brown hair with bangs. Glitter sparkled underneath her eyes.

Alton gave a polite smile and then looked away, not wanting to stare.

But the girl stared at him, then began to approach with an unmistakable gait. He knew that gait. Their eyes met. He knew those eyes too.

"Ber . . . Bernardo?"

"I'm Christina now," she said.

"Since . . . since when?" He tried not to gawk.

"It's been more than a year."

Alton felt his cheeks flush. "Oh, wow. I'm . . . I'm sorry that I haven't been in touch for so long."

"It's okay," she said. "I could have reached out too."

The glitter under her eyes seemed to pop and fizz. Or maybe it was just dust motes floating through rays of setting sun. Everything felt so surreal all of a sudden.

"They said you asked for me?" she said.

He shook himself out of it. "I just needed to see my mom. They wouldn't let me in because of all the . . ." He gestured vaguely behind him.

"Oh, I thought you wanted to say hi."

He winced at her disappointment. His guilt for being there, already weighing him down, threatened to cripple him. They had always been unlikely friends, destined to grow apart, but he could have thought to check in once in a while as they got older. Now the gulf between them seemed uncrossable.

Not because she had changed, he realized in a sudden rush of insight. *But because he hadn't.* Because he was still so preoccupied with getting his own needs met but didn't know how.

"It's okay," she said again when the silence had stretched on too long.

"But what's new with you? I mean . . . uh, what else is new?" *Idiot*, he thought.

She brightened. "I'll be attending USC in the fall. Biophysics!"

"Me too!" he blurted. For once in his life, he felt like an equal. "I mean, not USC. But college. I'm going to college back East. I got a scholarship."

She smiled broadly. "That's really great news, Alton. I'm so happy for you."

He almost turned to go but then said, "I still think about our trip to space almost every day. It changed my life. I don't know if I ever really thanked you."

"It changed my life too," she said. "I'm glad we shared that together."

"I was so terrified. I remember resenting you for being so calm about everything."

"What? I was just as terrified! But it's good to know I was hiding it." She laughed.

He laughed a little too but felt choked by regret. What was he doing here after everything this family had done for him? He had let his hate consume him. He would be no better than Alex if he went through with this. He would be *worse* because he knew it was wrong.

He should leave now, accept the consequences. Who cared what happened to him? Even if he died, he would deserve it. But he would get the badge first and throw it away so those assholes couldn't get their hands on it.

"I have to help my dad finish setting up," she said. "But I saw your mom back by the laundry earlier. It was really good to see you, Alton."

He felt panicked all of a sudden, as though he had to say the right thing before she left or that he had to make up for lost time somehow. "I never had any idea about this," he said. "I'm sorry if I was oblivious when we were kids."

"I didn't really have any idea back then either. It was something that awoke in me as I got older."

"Do you feel like you know who you are now?"

"I think so," she said.

"What does that feel like?"

She shrugged. "I can't imagine anything that would feel better."

As he watched her leave, he felt certain that he would never know that feeling for himself.

He found his mother in the laundry room, folding towels. The reek of cleansers burned, and he wondered how she had stood it all these years.

"Alton," she said, startled. "What are you doing here?"

"I came to see you."

Confusion came into her watery eyes. "You know I'll be home in a few hours."

"It can't wait."

He hadn't taken a good look at her in a while—he had, in fact, avoided looking at her—but he was unsettled by how spent she looked in the unflattering fluorescent light. There were black gouges underneath her eyes, and her forehead was lined. Not even forty, she was starting to look aged.

"I need your badge." He nodded at where it was magnetized to her shirt.

She touched it protectively. "Did Kurt put you up to this? He's a bad man, Alton."

"Oh, are you just figuring that out? How long were you together? A year?"

She lowered her gaze.. "You should just stay away from him."

"That's great advice, Mom. If only you had spoken up that night in the desert, I might have a choice in the matter."

"We were all alone out there. What was I supposed to do? Once I saw he was going to let you leave, I decided to let it alone."

"You never even checked in with me after that to see if I was okay!"

"I realize I've been a shitty parent, Alton, even without you constantly reminding me."

"Well, hey, speaking of shitty parents, I never told you the big news. I wasn't going to, but since everything's gone to hell, why not?"

"What are you talking about?"

"I found him."

"Kurt?"

"*Edwin.*" It came out more savage than he meant.

She blanched, steadied herself against the counter.

"He lives in San Francisco. He's rich. Everything you were afraid of."

"Did you go see him in person?"

"Yeah, he doesn't want to have anything to do with me. Turns out you were right about something after all." He could hear what a bastard he sounded like, but he couldn't stop.

"That's awful, Alton. I'm sorry."

"It's too late for that now."

"How did you find him?"

"His stupid trumpet. I traced the DNA."

She seemed surprised, or maybe impressed, but Alton didn't want her to feel that kind of pride in him.

"You probably forgot you gave that to me, didn't you?" he said.

"I didn't forget."

"Why was that the one thing you wanted me to have when you threw away everything else?"

"I used to love to hear him play it," she said. "He was a different person when he gave himself to the music."

He thought of the video, of her in her youth laughing, of Edwin being silly and carrying on. How much better would his life have been if *those* two people had raised him?

"If you want to help me for once, just give me the badge."

"They'll trace it back to me."

"Make something up then. Tell them you lost it. They'll believe you."

"Camilla won't."

She was probably right, but he was running out of time to argue. He thought about ripping the badge from her shirt, but he knew guilt was his more effective tool.

"Well, I hope all they do is break my legs," he said, turning to go. "Adios if this is the last time we see each other."

She took it off and passed it to him, her hands shaking as she did. "When Kurt asked me for it, he told me no one would be hurt," she said.

"That's what they told me, too, but you might want to get clear of here just in case. Long past time you moved on anyway."

Did a look of resolve cross her face, as though maybe she agreed? He never found out, and it would all soon be moot in any case.

CHAPTER 53

Evening had deepened. Tastefully attired guests were arriving, sleek and luminous beneath the saffron glow of the Japanese lanterns. While security was busy checking them in, he slipped out unnoticed and hurried down the wide lawn onto the tree-shrouded streets.

He felt unexpected nostalgia. For so long, he had wanted to forget his childhood, move on, never think about it again. But hanging out with Bernardo at that house *had* been great times. He had felt secure and welcome there. Cared for, even.

He prayed that whatever Kurt had planned would be minor, superficial. *Nothing violent*, Alex had promised him. Alton admitted to himself for the first time since he had decided to go through with this how unlikely that was. If not today, there would be violence eventually. There always was.

It's not too late, he thought. *Throw this thing away and face the consequences.*

He fingered the smooth contours of the badge in his hand and looked around for a place to dispose of it. As he did, guests streamed by him toward the event entrance. It was a glorious spring night, and they seemed so carefree, these well-to-do people assembling to plan their future in support of their candidate, Guerrero, who was promising ever more radical departures from the ways of the past. There was a verve to their step, a lilt to their laughter.

Alton felt conspicuous, even illicit, standing among them, but no one gave him a glance. Or perhaps they chose not to see him, just as his father had done.

The rage consumed him again, along with the grotesque humiliation he had felt when Edwin had paid him off so he would go away. The desire to hurt them, to punish them all, superseded everything.

And then he was approaching the Century Utility van almost without realizing it, parked where the black-haired creep had said it would be. And the creep himself was loitering in the alley in his utilityman disguise. Alton handed him the badge and turned to go.

"Hey, kid."

Alton froze, expecting the worst.

"Did you find your father?"

Alton hesitated, then said, "The man I found wasn't my father."

He didn't get far before the blast wave from the first explosion juddered through the neighborhood like an earthquake, sending him sprawling into the gravel of a nearby yard.

He was shocked by how quickly it had occurred. The creep hadn't even needed to get inside. He must have used the badge to reverse-engineer their security and kill it remotely.

Alton stayed on his hands and knees as two more explosions followed in quick succession. A moment later, two drones hurtled overhead. Assuming they had been the assailants and it was over, he leapt to his feet, ignoring his stinging knees as he tore off.

You bastard, he thought. But as he sprinted back toward the house, he wasn't sure if he meant Alex or himself.

He remembered a shortcut they had used as kids, a pair of houses that led them to Bernardo's street. He reached the first one, bolting into the backyard, past the pool, then leaping over the gate into the adjacent property.

Out front, he faced a scene of mass chaos and hysteria. Black smoke poured from behind the Torreses' house as screaming people peeled away in all directions. *No . . .* he thought. He had told his mother to leave, but she would have had so little time.

The grounds were strewn with debris, but as the last of the guests dispersed, he was able to make his way to the front doors, which stood agape, the electronic security neutralized. The two sentries that had let him through earlier were slumped in dark pools of blood. He tried not to look as he stepped over them into the foyer.

The front of the house wasn't in flames, but acrid smoke billowed throughout, and he could hear the snap and crackle of burning. Broken glass and puddles of champagne reflected everywhere in the toasty light.

He hurried to the laundry room. It was empty and undamaged, and his heart flared with hope. Maybe she had gotten out. But what about Christina?

He chugged up the stairs toward Bernardo's old room and recoiled in horror. The back wall of the second story was blasted out, leaving a gaping hole, the edges of which were ragged and smoking. Rivulets of flame cut across the backyard.

One bomb had blown shrubbery and dark soil everywhere; another had annihilated the swimming pool area he had once enjoyed, shredding the furniture and umbrellas and even melting the decking. A few inches of muddy water gurgled and steamed at the bottom. Bodies were strewn among the devastation.

Then he heard moaning. He crossed the landing to the bedrooms, the walls of which had collapsed into each other, and followed the moaning to a pile of rubble. He could hear a person coughing and hacking up smoke and fine drywall dust that sifted through the room like first snow.

He saw vivid color first, splashes of crimson on white, and his mind went numb. *Please, no.*

Christina was pinned under a ragged jumble of wall and ceiling and splintered furniture. Her white dress was so soggy with blood that he couldn't tell where the wounds were.

He knew nothing about how to locate a pulse, but he thought he might try to comfort her, so he knelt on his skinned knees and tried to find a hand to hold. Both hands were pinned, so he touched her face. He was mortified by how clammy she felt. He knew he needed to get aid but was afraid that if he pulled away even for a few moments, she would die before he returned. Blessedly, he could hear voices downstairs entering the house.

"Hang on," he said. "Help is coming."

But it was taking forever, even after they had come upstairs. He could hear them rooting around, voices low. "We're in here!" he yelled. "Hurry!"

The voices and movement stopped, and rage tore through him. *What the fuck was taking them so long?* "IN HERE!"

A figure finally entered. "In the back," Alton yelled, his voice hoarse and phlegmy.

Alton could see boots moving toward them, and then he was shocked to see Alex looking down in genuine surprise.

He was attired in some kind of paramilitary outfit, his EVs faintly glowing beneath, carrying drives and other technology he had looted. He looked much older. Alton found it hard to believe they had ever been in high school together.

"What are you still doing here?" Alex asked him.

"You said nobody would get hurt!"

"We're in a war, Alton. What did you think was going to happen?"

"Can you help her? Just lift this off at least."

He smirked down at them. "Is this your girlfriend? Finally got tired of chasing after mine?"

Even through everything else, the remark stung.

"This is my friend from childhood who I told you about." He looked down, but Christina's eyes were glazed and uncomprehending.

Alex's eyebrows went up and he chuckled. "This is Bernardo?"

"Please help me lift this off her."

"No can do."

Panic was engulfing him. "Why not?"

"Do you know what this whole event was about?" he said. "It was *them*—" he jabbed his finger at Christina "—planning to end *us*."

"She's just a kid..."

"No. They're all complicit. Every. Single. One."

"I'm going to tell people everything I know about you and your father," Alton said.

"No, you won't. Because it will be the end of your freedom. And your mother's."

"We deserve it."

"When Kiara finds out you've betrayed me, she'll never speak to you again. Are you prepared to lose *her*?"

"When she finds out what you've done here, *you're* the one she'll never talk to again."

"No, Alton. She knows I'm here right now. She's known all along what was going to happen."

He shook his head. "No, she's a good person. She doesn't believe in your bullshit."

"Maybe not, but she believes in *me*."

"But you're . . . you're a monster."

He meant it as a savage condemnation, but the words that came out sounded weak and far away. He could feel his own pain being eased by a frigid hollowness, a hollowness he sensed would always be with him.

"The history of civilization is the history of monstrous actions committed in the name of preserving what's important," he said. "Today we took a big step toward restoring that civilization."

At the door, he called back across the rubble pile, "Alton is a really stupid fucking name, by the way. I always wanted to tell you that." And he was gone.

PART VII

CHAPTER 54

A LONG SILENCE rang in the cockpit as the lights of Southern California came into view. A faint dawn was blooming in the east. Eventually, Valeria asked, "Did she live?"

"After a year of recovery. Seven people died that day, and thirty-four were injured, but the Torreses were okay. My Mom got out too. And you know what happened with Guerrero."

"Yeah. It's not hard to see why he erected the camps."

"I was going to say that anger over the incident let him win his first term as governor easily. But you're right, he's been great at leveraging violence for his own political ends."

"Violence? Or survival?" But then, in a softer voice, she said, "You were a kid. You were scared. You had nobody to help you. They had you over a barrel. You're not responsible."

"I could have sacrificed myself, and I chose my own survival instead."

"Few can make that kind of a choice."

"Gagné did." He thought of the shuttle hitting the mountain, remembered the stupendous boom.

"Yeah, well, Gagné was special."

The lights were closer now, and they had begun a slight descent. They unstrapped and went into the back with the others.

"Can I charge up my EVs now?" Alton asked.

She shook her head.

"If I don't do it now, I won't have enough time," he said.

"Doesn't matter. You're not going."

"What? I thought we agreed that I go in first to make sure Kiara is safe?"

"Please. I was never going to let a Civvie get anywhere near this and especially not you. When we land, you'll wait on the ship with Wombat until it's over. Then Áquilar can decide what to do with you."

"More babysitting?" Wombat whined. "I want to shoot somebody."

"Well, you might get your chance," she said. "Don't let him out of your sight."

"No problem." He patted his sidearm.

"I will retrieve Kiara if I can," she said to Alton. "But if it's not possible, she made her bed on this one a long time ago."

They set down on the deserted concrete bank of the LA River about five miles from the White House, and Valeria and Ramos set out at the first light of day to rendezvous with Áquilar's units.

In the ship, Wombat paced, grousing, while Alton measured the time and distance to the weapons locker.

"Why don't you just let me go?" Alton said. "Then you can join your unit."

"I've got my orders, Civvie."

"I just want to go visit my Mom before they lock me up again or worse. I haven't seen her in years. She's over in North Hollywood."

Wombat shook his head.

"I'm not going to interfere with the operation. I promise."

"That's enough."

"When's the last time you saw your mom?" Alton asked. "Don't you miss her?"

"I said that's enough."

"Can I just show you a picture?" Alton said. He walked over, as though palming a device.

"Christ, Civvie..."

"Just look," he said.

Wombat looked into his empty palm. "Look at what?"

But Alton already had his sidearm and had retreated. "This thing on stun?" Alton asked him.

"Civvie!" he roared and took a step forward.

Alton raised the weapon. "I suggest you tell me," he said.

"Yes, It's on stu—"

Alton dropped him immediately. Wombat's heavy body thudded to the floor.

"And you wonder why they don't trust you with any real action," Alton said as he began to charge his EVs.

The early morning 'loop car was as packed as the station had been when he had ducked in a few minutes earlier, looking over his shoulder to see if anyone was following. Commuters eyed his TALOS and augmentation warily, and he wondered if someone might alert security. But it didn't matter. He wouldn't let anything stop him at this point.

Last time he had come to Cosmost, with Bernardo, they had traveled overland, gliding along on the rich folks' freeway. Now, he was heading there underground, like a rat, to erect a civilization on a new world with the killer that had maimed his old friend. It would be his final betrayal.

But the Bernardo he had grown up with would understand, wouldn't he? The kid with whom he had suffered so much bullying in middle school, who had hated their peers, who had wanted to get so far away from his life that he had *literally become a new person*? Though, he had to admit that Christina probably wouldn't feel the same way. He shuddered. Wherever he saw her in his mind's eye, it was in her blood-covered dress.

He shook it off. Hadn't he never stopped dreaming about another flight, one that wouldn't *hurtle him back to Earth, dump him on the disappointing ground?* And hadn't he promised himself, God, the cosmos—whoever might exist or be listening—that if the opportunity ever came to escape for good, he would do whatever it took? For the first time, he realized that when he had pledged that nothing would stop him, he meant his better instincts as well.

They continued for a while, and Alton was surprised that more of the commuters didn't get off for work as they passed through the middle of downtown. But when they whooshed to a stop outside Cosmost, a big group disembarked, and Alton noticed for the first time that many of them carried lawn chairs and umbrellas and coolers.

He knew from watching news in camp that Cosmost had been erecting bleachers a few miles from the launch platform, expecting a big viewing turnout. If shit turned bad during the hijacking, he hoped none of these poor people got caught in the crossfire.

At the final stop, he went up through a hub mostly empty of people that led into the desert north of LA. As expected, he was near the Cosmost northeastern border. He accessed his eyeshade filters to dim the bright morning sunlight, then marveled at the ship and its boosters glimmering against the blue horizon of ocean and sky a few miles from where he stood.

Launch wasn't until evening, but he still didn't know where to find them, so he hurried down a gravel slope and began to hustle across the flat, cracked basin that stretched to the shore. He passed weathered signs that read *Private Property*, *Danger*, and *Keep Away* before reaching a twelve-foot electrified fence topped with razor wire. Just inside the fence, lay the enormous concrete mouth of the nearest Hydro-channel. Underground, it ran underneath the midlands, the Sierras, all the way back to the Trinities.

Shit, he thought. Even if he could cut through the fence without getting fried, it would probably trigger alarms. He looked around for anything that might give him an advantage, but there was nothing but scrubland and dirt hills. *I just need to find a hole*, he thought. *Somewhere I can slip through into the pipe.*

"Wait a minute," he said. "I don't need to find one. I can make one."

He went about twenty-five yards north of the fence and revved up his EVs until they blazed crimson and he could feel buzzing in his ears. He realized he should test them first, so he let loose two bolts into the hill behind him, then ducked, shielding himself from the dirt and rock that exploded everywhere. *Way too much*, he thought and dialed down the power.

He then took a half dozen steps back, then fired a careful, sustained burst into the ground where the pipe would be. He fired again, and then once more, until the soil and rock had blasted away and he could see the top of the aqueduct. He then tried to guide the beam so that it would cut rather than blast and was somewhat successful, sizzling a gash in the top.

He approached to discover that the piece he had lasered was still clinging to life. A swift kick sent it clunking to the bottom. He waited a moment for any residual heat to dissipate, then squatted down onto the lip of the hole and dangled his legs into the abyss, shining a light down to see how far it was.

It was at least twelve feet, too far to drop safely, but he would have to try, hoping he didn't crack an ankle and that his TALOS afforded him some protection from scrapes and bruises.

As he began to inch forward, he noticed three aircraft buzzing toward Cosmost from the southeast—roughly where Valeria should have been now. There was no way it could be her, he thought. He was just being paranoid. But if it was...

Please don't try to stop us, Val.

As he thought about her, it suddenly occurred to him why she had detested him so much, at least at first.

It wasn't because he hadn't embraced his culture or because he was some kind of impostor. It was because *he could choose the racial identity that people saw.*

While she would always be one thing in the eyes of others, he could pass for white when he wanted, assert his ethnic background when it was convenient, claim privilege with whichever group happened to be in power. He could even join a group of white supremacists.

He had always felt like a second-class citizen, having grown up poor around rich Latinos, having been disowned by his rich Mexican American father. It had never even occurred to him that he possessed this privilege.

But he would have plenty of time to think about that off-world. Now, it was time to go.

He took a deep breath and plunged into some kind of hot mesh. It wrapped him up as he fell, sparks lighting up the dark. He tried to break his fall but couldn't move his arms, and he thudded against the concrete floor of the pipe, yelping as his forearms smacked against the surface.

He could feel the electricity surging around and through him. Had he jumped into the electric fence somehow? Did it reach underground? He moaned and writhed until he felt something slide underneath him and roll him onto his back. A light blinded him, and he heard a voice he had thought—had hoped—would be lost to him forever.

"Prof?!" the voice exclaimed with its familiar note of sadistic glee.

Alton groaned. "You've got to be fucking kidding me."

CHAPTER 55

"DAMN! TALK ABOUT turning the tables," Lance snickered. He prodded Alton in the ribs with his boot.

"Stop it, goddamnit. We're on the same side now."

"Better wait and see if it's okay with my supreme leader," he said, jabbing him again. "You were the one who said I can't make decisions without him. Remember?"

"How the hell did you get here?" Alton asked.

"I told you in camp that nothing would keep us down," Lance said. "I was promised a spot on this boat, and I wasn't about to miss it."

"And how many more boys at Gypsum did you sacrifice to make that happen?"

Lance stuck his arm down into Alton's face. The EVs sizzled a terrifying black-violet, a hue Alton didn't know they came in.

"They sent me to check out the disturbance," Lance said. "I could fry you right here and say I thought you were one of *them*."

But before Alton could protest, another voice rang through the aqueduct, and Kiara was running toward them, her voice echoing down the tunnel.

"Cut him loose!"

"I'm afraid I need to hear that order from Big Daddy."

"*Now*," Alex commanded. In an instant, the web sizzled out and Kiara was helping Alton up as he rubbed his tender forearms.

"Cutting it *really* close," Alex said.

"You destroyed the ship I was using to get out of there," Alton said, "while I was on it!"

"I had no choice once they had you. Couldn't risk everything."

Kiara embraced him, and he felt the anger ebb.

"You're here now," she said. "That's all that matters."

"We gotta move," Alex said. "Still prep to do."

As they approached the mouth of the tunnel that opened out onto the grounds, the faces of Alex's disciples appeared like wraiths against the dark, curved walls of the pipe. Alton took a good look at their faces, mostly his age or younger, and they stared back. It felt surreal that these strangers would be his only friends and family for the foreseeable future. There were at least fifty of them—some with the forehead mark of the Nibelung, some not—and Alton wondered what would happen to the twenty-odd men and women who wouldn't make the journey.

"When did you get here?" Alton asked.

"Yesterday," Alex said. "It took longer than expected to get down from the mountains in those." He gestured to the four rocket-powered skiffs staged up the tunnel.

"Yeah, and it was fucking miserable too," Kiara said, rubbing her butt.

"So, what now?"

"Around 6:30, we'll jet across the basin toward the launchpad," Alex said. "It's about three miles from here. The skiffs move fast, and darkness will give us cover, but they *will* detect us before we get there."

"What sort of response do you expect?"

"They have a security team at the launch complex and another protecting the viewing area," Alex said. "We'll take out Team 1 when we get there, being careful, of course, not to blow up anything we shouldn't." He looked at Lance as he said this and the big man smirked.

Alex continued, "Their security will already have cleared the area around the platform of nonessential personnel, which will make things easier for us. By the time they figure out what's happening, Team 2 probably won't get to us in time."

"And if they do?"

"That's why we are blessed to have true believers with us." He turned and gestured toward the faithfully assembled. "Some have volunteered to handle any resistance while the rest of us board. And thank you again, my brothers and sisters."

He bowed toward them, and two dozen or so bowed back, lifting their arms in the Nibelung salute. *Ah, so that's it,* Alton thought. If they minded being used as human shields while the others made their escape, they didn't show it. Alton supposed he shouldn't be surprised, not after the thorough job of cult indoctrination he had witnessed at camp. Some of the Nibelungs there had never even met Alex and were still willing to die for him.

"And if they decide to blow us up when we're airborne?" Alton asked.

"As I told you before, we'll have three of the original crew with us," Alex said. "We'll be letting the world know those hostages are on board even before we take off. They're not going to slaughter their own astronauts, not in front of the whole world."

"What if that's countermanded by an executive order?"

"We won't have to worry about that."

"You said the same thing back in the mountains. What does that mean?"

"It means I made a deal with the devil a long time ago," Alex said.

"Not..."

"Guerrero?" Alex finished. "No, he thinks of himself as too pure. Anyway, he hates my guts ever since we almost took him out at the Torreses' house that day."

Alton flinched, hearing it spoken aloud, pictured Christina beneath the rubble, the hole blown in the back of the house, the steam and acrid smoke.

"But there are others close to him, both in the government and the military, who have been more than happy to keep this war going," Kiara said. "Without Hagen, there are no camps. There is no martial law. No West Coast White House. He's a necessary evil for what Guerrero's people want to achieve."

"I just had to keep escalating our methods until there was enough public support to make the camps politically viable for him," Alex said.

"The dirty bomb."

"Yes."

"Jesus Christ! You risked killing a million people!"

"No. The plan was always for the bomb to go off far from a population center, then pretend like we had made a mistake by detonating it prematurely."

"People still died!"

"Some. And a few more will die of cancer from the radiation," Alex said. "But overall, I achieved my aims with a minimum of bloodshed."

"Just those you deemed necessary to sacrifice."

"It's war, Alton."

"That's everybody's excuse! Just admit that you're a murderer."

Alex gave him a hard look, and he could feel the tension ripple through the group. "It's time to leave that kind of thinking behind now," he said. "Anyway, once the camps were in place, our high-placed contacts agreed to look the other way while pretending to search high and low for us."

"And how do you know they're going to continue to look the other way?"

"Because this is the best thing that could happen for them," Alex said. "Out there, we become the unknown threat. Once this war becomes interplanetary, it gives Guerrero and his people the ultimate excuse to consolidate power in a new and uncertain era."

"I told you this government was a monstrosity," Kiara said. "Now, you see why it's worth revolting against."

"This was never a revolution," Alton said. "Just an elaborate means to your ends."

"Of course it's a revolution!" Alex roared and his followers murmured their agreement. "This will be the greatest revolution anybody ever achieved! Once I changed our mission from fighting over this wasted world to ruling a new one, it wasn't hard to convince people to go from being pariahs to princes!"

The group beamed as he spoke.

"We can do a lot more up there to establish our way of life," Kiara added. "And imagine how inspired our followers on Earth will be to keep up the cause!"

"What about the Chinese?" Alton said. "I'm guessing they won't feel so inspired."

"Peaceful Martian coexistence is a possibility, at least at first. But it's inevitable that East and West will clash again." He smiled at the thought.

Alton squeezed his EVs lightly, emanating a faint crimson glow. Were the Chinese the reason they had outfitted him with these? Would he end up as one more weapon in some forever war?

As the group readied the skiffs and assembled the weapons and gear, Alton wondered if, despite all his risk and sacrifice, he shouldn't just bolt. Maybe it was obvious what he was contemplating, because Kiara came up and rested her hand on his shoulder.

"Did anything about what you just learned make you want to stay behind?" she asked him.

She had a point. If everything was shit, he might as well go where there was less of it, where any individual voice of change would have a better chance of resonating.

"Final walk-through," Alex said, and they gathered round as he powered up a hologram of the launch site that lit up the dark tunnel.

"Soon, the fueling and the oxygen purge will be complete. They'll transport the crew over and start loading them just before 7:00, at which time they'll begin the remaining system checks. We'll intercept them just as they arrive here, grab our three experts, and neutralize the rest with webs."

Alton was relieved to hear they didn't plan to kill the remaining crew.

The hologram fizzled out. "Now, get a little rest over the next few hours," Alex said. "And prepare yourself for destiny."

CHAPTER 56

WHEN DUSK HAD fallen and it was time to go, they piled into the skiffs with their gear. No one spoke, overwhelmed by the dread or the immensity of what they were about to do. Then Alex gave the signal, and they set off across the cooling desert. The breeze revitalized Alton, as did the blazing lights of the spaceport as they neared. He felt his stomach drop with excitement, and his misgivings were forgotten in an instant. The violet sky reminded him of the fateful night all those years ago at the festival, when he had met Kiara. He remembered seeing the ship departing Cosmost that night and how he dearly wished to be on it. Now a much more powerful rocket loomed right in front of them. Soon, instead of watching it disappear, he would be aboard, and it would be the Earth gradually fading from his view.

And then in an instant the reverie was shattered as the skiff in front of them took a battery of fire. It swerved left into the hard ground, bodies spilling out into the scrubland amid cries of pain and panic. The remaining craft stopped on a dime, and the others leapt out.

Alex barked commands over their internal comms. "Watch your fire!" he yelled. Then he was ordering a flanking position around their attackers and shots were fired back and forth, dropping bodies on both sides.

Alton took cover behind a skiff, looking for an opportunity to enter the fray with his EVs, but he was terrified that he would let loose an errant shot. Even slight damage to the ship's delicate, interconnected systems array would kill the launch. And if he hit one of the boosters, it would instantly vaporize the entire platform.

But it was a moot point, as the fierce firing wouldn't even let him get his head up. It seemed as though Alex had underestimated the size of the first security detail. Or maybe Team 2 had already arrived. Kiara came over the comms, voicing those same thoughts. "There's no way this is one squad," she said. "Somebody else is here!"

Then Alton knew . . . the ships he had seen earlier. "Everybody hold up a second," he said.

"Fuck that," Lance said, loosing a wicked bolt.

"I said hold up, goddamnit! I know who it is."

"Cease fire," Alex commanded, and the shooting stopped, the echoes bouncing off the platform before being enveloped by desert and sea.

Alton set his comms for universal reception, then said, "Val."

There was a beat, and then Valeria's voice was on their channel. "Made it back to your people, I see."

He couldn't deny it this time. Whether he was a white supremacist or not didn't matter if he had joined up with their cause.

"How'd you know we were here?" he asked.

"What you said when we were in the forest. Somebody kept tipping off Hagen. That's why they could never catch him. If it was Guerrero, or someone else high up, the White House obviously wouldn't be the target. The colony ship is the only other target in the region that makes sense."

"Oooh, she's good," Alex crackled over the comms. "Though it sounds like she didn't figure out the other part."

"What other part?"

"You want the honors?" Alex asked.

Alton hesitated, then said, "We're not destroying it. We're... taking it."

"For what?"

It was Kiara's turn to speak, and Alton could practically hear her scowl as she said, "What the hell do you think?"

There was another beat before Val's laughter rang over the channel. "What would you know about surviving up there? You'll die of exposure in the first week!"

"Maybe," Alton said. "But all that matters is I get there."

"That's not true." He was surprised to hear that she seemed genuinely disappointed in him. It gave him pause, but not enough.

"You're way outnumbered," he said. "Please just back off so that nobody else gets hurt."

"You know I can't do that," she said. "Mission first. Always."

"Then make it your mission to live for once," Alton said.

"No time for this," Alex said. "Light 'em up!"

The Nibelungs designated to stay behind had edged closer during the ceasefire. Their flanking positions in the dark lit up on both sides with savage firing. Some of them were going down as well but they were doing their jobs, giving the colony crew the cover they needed to escape.

Alton leapt out from behind the skiff, skirted the firing, and sprinted towards the platform. But then the shooting stopped almost as soon as it began. Whatever was left of their attackers had been quickly neutralized.

"Everybody that's coming get to the ship on the double," Alex said.

"Just one more cockroach to stomp," Lance said.

Alton pulled up short. "No!" he yelled. "She lives or I'm out."

"Then you're out," Lance said.

"Tell him, Alex!" Alton cried.

"Forget it Lance," Alex said. "Just get up here. Now"

"What's that, boss?" he snickered. "You're breaking up."

The desert was dark behind him, but Alton could make out Lance's position by his black/violet glow. He doubled back, racing to find Lance standing over Valeria, her TALOS burnt and shredded. It was just the three of them left amongst the fallen bodies. Their job done, the remaining Nieblings had fled the area.

"Back away," Alton said.

"I can't believe he chose you for this," Lance said. "You always were a cockroach lover."

Alton switched off his comms and raised his arm. Lance turned to see Alton's EVs dialed up and pointed at his chest. The smirk dissolved from the gorilla's face. "You got those on stun, right?"

"This is for Simon," Alton said, and fired, exploding Lance into a shower of blood and viscera so fine it was as though his body had been strained through mesh.

He knelt over Valeria, who looked up at him glassy-eyed but still conscious.

"You're going to be fine," he said, looking towards the lights in the eastern sky. "Help is on the way."

She tried to grasp his hand, but she was too weak, and he broke away.

As he neared the pad, he saw one of their people waiting for him by the open elevator. They dove into the lift and began whirring the five stories to the loading platform.

As they ascended, Alton looked down through the transparent glass of the elevator and was horrified to see Valeria crawling toward the launchpad. The moment the elevator let them out, he dashed to the platform rail.

"Go back!" he yelled down at her, knowing she couldn't hear him. "What are you doing?"

"We need to seal the hatch, Alton."

He turned to find Kiara standing just outside the capsule door, then looked down again to see Val, tiny and helpless, far below.

"We made it," Kiara said. "After waiting a lifetime. Don't fuck it up now."

"She'll be incinerated when we take off!"

"She'll be a martyr to history, then," Alex said, emerging from the capsule to stand next to Kiara. "The final obstacle we overcame on the road to a new human dawn. There are much worse things to be."

Alex was wearing a satin Cosmost command jacket like the one Alton had treasured so long before. It felt impossible to resist. It was almost as if the jacket was a tractor beam drawing him in.

He made himself look down once more. Valeria had no love for him. She would hand him over to Áquilar, return him to the camps, kill him, whatever duty dictated. She would probably be glad to do it.

But he couldn't rid himself of the image of Christina mangled in the smoking rubble, crimson on white, blood leaving her face. That thing that *he* allowed to happen. Because of his hurt. Because of his hatred for his father. Because of his hatred for himself.

"Alton."

Alex's voice was soft and honeyed like wood chimes on a breezy afternoon, and it drew him back into the moment.

"I have cancer," he said, just barely over the instruments and controls powering up behind him.

"From the dirty bomb. I was too close when it went off. That's why I look like this. The disease, the treatment..."

Alton looked up and down the once powerful body shorn of its youthful muscle and knew he wasn't lying.

"Now you know why we need you," Kiara said. "Why *I* need you. I told you to trust me."

"Why didn't you tell me earlier?"

"None of them know either." He thrust a thumb back toward the crew. "Who's going to follow me to another world if they know I'm dying?"

"Even if he does live for a while, he could be sterile," Kiara said. "And somebody has to usher in the new generation."

He looked at her, then back at Alex, comprehension hammering him like a bullet train. "But that's not the only reason, is it?"

"What do you mean?" Alex asked.

"First cousins don't make for the most reliable gene pool, especially not in a community as small as this one."

They both smiled, their ancient secret finally revealed.

One of the crew appeared behind them. "Incoming and closing fast. Looks like a whole division."

They looked to see dozens of lights clogging the eastern sky.

"We want to keep it in the family, Alton. Kiara trusts you."

"It will be everything you ever wanted," she said. "Space travel, life on another world... and me."

"But... I'm not white."

Alex looked back to see if anyone else was listening, then said, "We can work around that."

Alton almost laughed. "You never believed in your father's cause at all, did you?"

"You were right, Alton. It was a means to an end. And now that end has been achieved."

"You're a fucking psychopath."

He shrugged. "Most visionaries are."

Alton took Kiara's hands in his, smiled at her, then let them go and stepped back into the open lift, descending again before she or Alex could react. The last thing he saw of them was their stunned faces.

The door flung open at the bottom, and then he was grabbing Valeria and dragging her to one of the skiffs.

He punched it at top speed for maybe sixty seconds before the rocket engines thundered to life behind them, flooding the port with fire.

Shock waves rumbled underneath them, and they went tumbling from the skiff, rolling to a stop as the ship cleared its moorings and began its ascent.

He raised his arms and pointed his EVs at it. He charged them up to full power until he glowed like hell itself, the buzzing so loud in his ears he couldn't even hear the roar of the engines. Hostages be damned. He would take them all down.

When Valeria grabbed his hand and lowered it, he could feel the strength in it this time. And the purpose. And she was right. He wasn't a murderer.

He lay back. Tears flooded his eyes as he watched them fly away, the afterburn glowing in the deepening dusk. How many times had the three of them viewed launches from Cosmost and prayed for adventure? Now, his "friends" were embarking on that adventure, while he had been left behind. Again.

And yet he knew it wasn't the worst thing after all. He had tasted the stars once, briefly soared over the lawn of the labyrinth. It had been extraordinary, but he realized now that his place was on the ground.

He felt very lucky that his wings hadn't melted before he understood.

EPILOGUE

HE HAD DECIDED to look up his half brother and sister—on his request, Áquilar had discovered they were still in the Bay Area—and see if there might be a relationship to be had there. He was leaving that afternoon, but he had a visit to make before he departed.

It was a beautiful day in Los Angeles, the November light gentle on the citrus trees. He stepped through the French doors into Áquilar's courtyard, where they had gathered in what seemed like another lifetime. He found Val convalescing on a divan.

"No peace for the wicked," she said.

He sat down across from her. "You recovered fast."

"Not really. They just said I was too mean to the nurses. Kicked me out of the infirmary."

"Impossible to believe."

They laughed.

"Sorry you had to give up on your childhood dream," she said.

He thought about it. "Maybe it was time for me to let go of childhood."

She smiled. "Did the boss tell you she's running for president?"

"Yeah, she informed me of her grand plans upstairs."

"She's invited me to work on her campaign."

"I thought you had no use for politicians?"

"I don't," she said. "But I figured there has to be another way to change the world besides shooting people."

"I hope so."

"Why don't you come work on the campaign with us? Help us retire Guerrero. Get these camps closed once and for all."

"I think I'd be afraid that Áquilar would steal my other leg."

"So, what are your plans? A cabin by a lake, like she promised you?"

"I renegotiated my deal. Got her to give me something else instead."

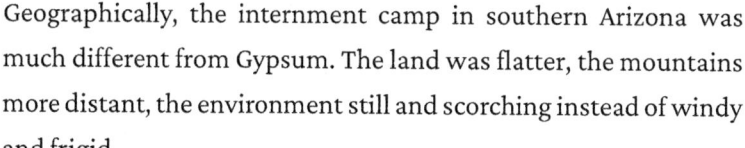

Geographically, the internment camp in southern Arizona was much different from Gypsum. The land was flatter, the mountains more distant, the environment still and scorching instead of windy and frigid.

The camp itself looked much the same, though—the barracks, chow hall, med shells, fences, command center. The only thing missing was the school.

But Áquilar had promised him resources to get one up here, and then at the next camp, and the next one, until a staffed school existed at every camp and was maintained and operated until the camps closed. He had selected fellow teachers to train, and they were there in the classroom, observing him on his first day back.

The prisoners entered, mostly Nibelungs, clutching their reading pads uncertainly. They took their seats and regarded him with curiosity but also recognition because he looked like them now, battled-damaged and scarred where his augmentation and EVs had been stripped out. A necessity to regain access to the camps, not that he had wanted to keep them anyway.

He had thought of them as sheep once, but now he saw that their eyes shone with the desire to learn, to engage with the world, perhaps even to try to be better. Or maybe they had always wanted to be better, and he was just now realizing it.

ABOUT THE AUTHOR

MICHAEL GREEN is a writer and professor of film studies and creative writing. He grew up in Tempe, Arizona, where he still lives despite the ever more oppressive heat. There, he earned his MFA in Creative Writing and his MA in Humanities at Arizona State University.

He was weaned on '80s sci-fi — *Star Wars* and *Star Trek*, *Blade Runner*, *The Terminator*, *Robocop*, and John Carpenter's *The Thing* — which still informs his vision and sensibilities to this day. Other jobs he has held include wildland firefighter, film critic, AI prompt engineer, and Domino's delivery driver.

Afterburn is his third book after his graduate thesis, *The Sepulchral City*, and *Escape from Aqualand*, starring a roster of DC heroes, which he wrote (and illustrated!) when he was seven. He is currently at work on his next novel, which will undoubtedly win him a Pulitzer Prize.

WWW.MICHAELBODHIGREENWRITER.COM

Printed in Dunstable, United Kingdom